# PIGGYBACKER
## VESSEL OF LOST SOULS
### BOOK ONE

## MIKKI NOBLE

Cover design by MoorBooks Design

ISBN: 978-1-9990151-0-7
E-BOOK ISBN: 978-1-9990151-1-4

First Edition: January 2019

# DEDICATION

To the loving memory of
Cory Alan Renaud.

*May you never be forgotten.*

# ONE

*Saturday, October 20ᵗʰ*

FORTY-TWO IS THE number of ceiling tiles I count before a nurse in red scrubs slaps the door and grunts, "McCartney, visitor."

I yawn, stretching my tired, achy bones on the thin cot and wonder what my life will be like if I ever get out of here and back home to Crater's Edge, where everyone knows your business and things never change.

I don't want any visitors; I don't want anyone to see me or even know I was here. I just want to be home in my own comfy bed. They should never have forced me in here.

It's been a week since I've had any freedom. Strange, magical things started happening yesterday. There are guards at every turn and I'm craving chocolate so bad my teeth ache. That's me, Marley McCartney, good girl turned suicidal troublemaker overnight. It's news to me since I'm quite certain there's not a violent bone in my body.

I sit up and swing my legs over the bed, careful not to

tear any stitches from my abdomen, and that's when I notice my copy of Pride & Prejudice floating in the air inches from my head, like a ghost is waving it at me. I groan, swatting it as if it's nothing out of the ordinary, even though it freaks me out. Its pages flutter in protest before landing in a broken heap in the corner. Maybe I do belong trapped in here. I'm seeing things and having nightmares. It's all Mom's fault. I won't forgive her for this—not as long as I'm trapped in here.

When my mother's face appears in the doorway, I look down at my unmanicured feet and wish they would at least let me have a nail file to tidy them up. Mom offers a smile I don't return. Her long red hair is tied back and instead of scrubs, she's wearing jeans and a t-shirt. "No work today?" I ask, not really caring about the answer.

"I'm off tonight."

"Right."

"Don't do this today, Marley."

I flop back on the cot, wishing she would leave and never come back. "I don't know how you expect me to act."

Mom sighs, shoving her hands in her pockets. "It's not my fault you're in here."

My body tenses. A flush rushes to my cheeks. I shoot to my feet and snap, "Not your fault? You're the one who sent me here."

"You stabbed yourself with a kitchen knife and you barely survived. What did you expect me to do? Wait around for you to try it again?"

"I expected you to believe me when I said I didn't do it."

"I want to. I really do." Mom pauses. I focus on the

chair in front of me; I just can't look at her right now. "Your brother misses you so much. He wants to come and see you."

"And you trust him to be around me?" I say the words, hoping to hurt her as much as she's hurt me.

Mom answers, anger burning in her tone, "Don't be ridiculous. I know you'd never hurt your brother."

"Of course not, but I don't want him to see this place, Mom. Then I'd have to explain why I'm here."

"He doesn't know you're here."

I stare at the ground, forcing myself not to look up at her. "Good. And you won't tell him, I know."

"Of course not, but he *does* want to see you."

I groan. "Just tell him I miss him very much and I hope to see him soon." Now I turn to her, silently demanding she not say anything to contradict me.

She holds up her hands in surrender. "Fine, fine."

I urge, "If you let me come home, he won't have to miss me anymore."

Mom shakes her head and sits in the cold, metal chair across from me, which is bolted down so I can't use it to harm myself—as if. "You and I both know why I can't do that."

"Maybe you could talk to the doctor. Be a character witness or something. They'll listen to you. You're a nurse." I don't know why I keep trying; she hasn't listened to a word I've said since the accident—yes, that's what I'm calling it until proven otherwise. I can't prove it went my way, but they can't prove it didn't.

"Well, I can't do it. I won't. I need to know you're safe."

"Mom, I need to get out of here before I become a *real*

mental patient." If it's not too late already. "This place...it's doing something to me."

"What do you mean?"

She wants to know what I have to say? "I—" Maybe I shouldn't say. What if I only tell her enough to get me out of here? What if she tells the doctor and I'm stuck here longer? Or she might find a way to get me out of here if I tell her the truth. "I started having these nightmares."

"Tell me about them."

"They're awful. Scary." I don't want to talk about them. I groan and shake my head. These nightmares leave me feeling weak, broken, helpless. "Why does everything have to change because of one accident?"

"Sometimes life works that way, kiddo. One choice can change your destiny."

I bunch the cheap sheets between my hands, anger flooding through me. She isn't going to help me. She thinks I belong here, maybe even *wants* me here. "If Dad were here, he'd believe me."

"That's not fair. And he would want to know you're safe, too," she insists.

"Just go." I stand and turn away from her, facing the small window that overlooks two Toledo buildings and a couple trees. I ignore the view to study my own reflection. "If you're not here to help me then leave."

"Marley—"

"Go," I demand, hoping she can't hear oncoming tears in my voice.

"I'll come back tomorrow," she tells me. I don't know how long I stare out the window. I only know I can't turn back until I know for sure she's gone.

My reflection is so unlike the girl I grew up knowing.

My pale skin once had a glow; now it's dull underneath the blinding fluorescent lights. My blue eyes are still big but there's none of the joy left; even my golden locks have lost their luster. I desperately need to escape this place. I don't know what I've become, and I wish I knew how to get back to who I was before.

Frustrated, I abandon my sad reflection and walk out of the room. It's nearly breakfast time and they'll be doling out pills for us crazy folks any minute. Not that I'm eager to take pills I *know* I don't need. Maybe if I just play the good little girl the doctor will let me go.

The youth center is pretty big but each section only fits about twelve people, or so I've been told. Its white walls and floors are meant to make us think of this place as sanitary, though I truly believe it's meant to make us feel helpless.

I never want to see white walls again. I miss my room, I miss my own things. They're full of color, joy and personality.

I hop behind one of the seven deadly sins—that's what I call the patients, out of sheer boredom—abandoning thoughts of home, for now. I call myself Gluttony. As in glutton for punishment. I must be one if I ended up in a place like this.

"Next," a clerk behind the glass informs the line-up of six. I don't see Wrath—everyone else just calls him Marcel. He must be confined to his room again. He gets into fights all the time.

The six of us wear the same stupid expression and the same ugly outfits. It clashes with my skin tone and tucks every curve away, as if they don't want us to remember we're human. My best friend Kimmy would be horrified if she saw me wearing this. She'd probably fashion a new line of hospital gowns just to save me the embarrassment.

I miss her.

"M&M, ready to be doped up?" Taylor Davis, a.k.a. Envy, bumps her shoulder with mine. She's my only real friend in this place. She is a sweet soul, but she has a serious problem with other people's stuff—as in, she thinks it's hers. She also knows everything about everyone here, so she's a good person to have on your side if you want to hold on to any secrets. Not so much if you have anything of value.

"Oh, as usual it's the best part of my day. How about you?"

Taylor bends her brunette head closer to mine to whisper, "Eager to add to my collection." She smirks.

"You're going to get in so much trouble, girl," I tell her, shaking my head.

This is the worst place for someone to be when they don't believe in pills, unless you're Taylor and you know exactly how to profit from said pills.

Taylor gives a hearty laugh and shrugs. "They'll have to catch me first."

Taylor is three weeks older than I am, turning eighteen last week. She arrived the day after I did, and we've been friends ever since. Her big brown eyes can either soften to golden flecks or harden like dragon scales; I've only seen the dragon scales once.

Taylor watches everyone around us, more guards than patients. I suspect that's how she keeps up to date on everyone. She says to me, lowering her voice, "There's a nurse here who says he'll buy my stash in exchange for a few extra cigarette breaks."

Taylor waves at a dark-haired man with dreamy brown eyes who nods back. "That was him," Taylor whispers.

As she ogles the hottie, my eye is drawn to the third-degree burns on her right bronze colored arm. She told me she got them when she was in fourth grade and refuses to give me any more detail. Says, "I don't even notice it anymore."

"How did you swing cigarette breaks in the first place?"

"I'm resourceful."

I shake my head, smiling. "That, I can believe."

"Help! I need your help. Please," a guy's gravelly voice calls out.

I turn to see who it is. Taylor is watching Nurse pill-pusher. I turn toward her; she's handing out pills to Taylor's friend Carla, whom I call Pride. She wears too much perfume and acts like no one is good enough to lick her boots, let alone look at her. Isn't anyone else worried about this boy? I silently urge the guards into action. Obviously, they don't budge.

I continue searching for him and it looks like no one else heard the boy. That means that I must be hearing things. I soak up that idea reluctantly. I'm just tired. I only *thought* I had heard someone scream.

I barely slept last night, due to the nightmares.

"Can you hear me?" There he is again, voice breaking. Maybe he's in trouble, whoever he is. Why isn't anyone helping him? What should I do?

"Did you hear that?" I ask Taylor.

She nods. "Yes, you're next in line. Get your fix, M&M."

I shake my head. "Not her. The guy screaming?"

She looks at me as if the joke is *not* funny. "No one was screaming. Except for maybe Crazy wigs Alana over there," she points to a string bean of a girl with knotted pink and yellow hair sitting at a table in the cafeteria section. Her roots are three inches long, though she's still riding the rainbow since they won't allow hair dye in here. I call her Sloth. I'm pretty sure she's the only real looney tune in this youth center. Unless I turn out to be one. Odds are not in my favor at the moment.

"It's not funny. I'm serious, Taylor."

"Me, too." She smirks, waving at Carla as she heads to the cafeteria.

Did she seriously not hear the boy screaming or is everyone playing some kind of weird trick on me? But what if this guy is in real trouble? Should I try and find him?

The clerk aims her angry tone at me. "Next."

"Go," Taylor says, nudging me to the counter.

"Name?" the clerk asks. I can't see the woman's face clearly because her hair is in her face and large sunglasses cover her eyes as if this were a beach resort instead of my worst nightmare.

"Um, McCartney, Marley E.," I mutter, knowing this clerk knows exactly who I am. First off, there are only seven of us and second, the woman has been forcing me to pill up for an entire week now. The least she can do is learn my name.

"Take these, Miss McCartney, and show me once you've swallowed." I take the container reluctantly and notice that my hand's shaking.

"Help me, please, Marley." His voice rings crystal

clear. He sounds as if he's standing right beside me, though Taylor is the only one close.

I drop both pills on the floor, inhaling hot air into my unsteady lungs. "Holy crap."

"Just hear me out. I need you."

*Who is this guy?* I wonder as his desperate pleas barrel in my ears as clear as glass and every bit as sharp, as if it's booming out of the PA system instead of inside my own head.

The truth claws its way in and bounces around my skull until it sinks in. It hits me like a sucker punch to my gut. There's a voice coming from inside my head. It's too late for freedom; I really *am* a mental patient.

No, I refuse to believe that. I must be dreaming again. Any minute now I will wake up with a sweaty neck and blood-soaked bandages.

Any minute now.

I close my eyes and try to calm my rapid heartbeat. My body falls against a solid wall. It's a good thing because my bones are shaking. I just need a moment of peace to calm my fears.

The wall speaks, "Take your pills." Not a wall; one of the guards, come to make sure I take my pills.

"Are you all right, M&M?" Taylor asks, squeezing my arm as the guard shoves the pills at me with a meaty paw.

"I'm all right. Just didn't sleep much, that's all."

I know she doesn't believe me though she doesn't press. She's good like that; always knows when to step back and let me process. We've only known each other six days and already, I'd trust her with my life.

If I take these pills, the voice will go away. It has to. That's why this... place gives us pills—to quiet the voices, to quiet the fear.

Once I take my pills and the guard is satisfied, I'm free to go about my day, pretending I'm not as looney as I feel. Us sins are free to pick up our breakfast, our horrible hospital food that no one ever wants to eat. Unless we're talking about Lust, known to his fellow patients as Joshua. He got his nickname for the obvious reasons and although he doesn't speak to me, I've heard he's had relations with all the nurses on the floor. The boy is over six feet, muscular, easy-on-the-eyes, and can eat anyone under the table. I'd like to know how he stays so skinny.

"Come sit with me," Taylor says. "Maybe some food will help."

I nod. "Maybe." Even though I disagree I don't say anything. I'm trying to be optimistic.

We grab breakfast: one slimy egg, a cold piece of toast, two small sausages, and an orange slice. My hands are still shaking but I force myself to hold the tray straight. No one can suspect I'm losing my mind, or I'll be here forever. "Why don't they serve anything healthy? I need to keep up my strength for training."

Taylor laughs and steals one of my sausages. "He-ey," I squeal.

"I don't think they let the cray-cray's become firefighters."

An icy sliver crackles up my spine. Does she suspect something? Play it cool, Marley. "I'm *not* crazy."

"I know. I know," she says, still munching on the sausage she stole from me. "What if I can get you a salad?"

My footsteps halt. I can already imagine the crunch of the lettuce, the sweet tartness of a tomato. My mouth waters. I want chocolate, but I need healthy food more.

"Don't play with me. My heart can't take it right now."

Taylor picks a table and sits. "I'll trade a pack of cigarettes. You'll have your salad at lunch."

"Oh, you're a lifesaver," I admit. Greed—Cassie to everyone else—says something to Taylor and I've lost her attention. Once she turns her head, I take one of her sausages. All's fair in food scraps and youth centres.

"What did you do?" Taylor questions me, noticing the missing piece from her plate.

I smirk, knowing that there's still sausage between my teeth. "Nothing."

"This means war." I know she's serious despite her gentle tone. We both know she doesn't care about the sausage anyway. She doesn't steal because she wants to; it's an instinct she's been trying to fight since childhood.

"You can have my toast." She takes it from my plate without a moment's hesitation. "Are we even now?"

"Not even close, white girl."

"Actually, I think I'm more of a peach."

We both laugh.

I finish my slimy egg. "It's almost nine. I need to go meet with Dr. Rydell. Find you later."

"All right, girl. Don't forget: salad for lunch. Don't be late."

The doctor's office is on the same floor at the end, near the stairs. It's a long, bright walk. Of course, there are two guards posted there at all times.

"When can I go home?" is the first thing I say to the doctor when I walk into his little 10 by 10 office. The pewter walls are bland, tokened with an award from Oxford, a degree, and a few certificates that I've never done more than glance at. Dr. Rydell drops his pen on the oval shaped desk. His furniture is expensive looking, but manly and plain. Roasted chestnut colored leather chairs are placed across from the desk that sits in front of a massive window overseeing a great view of the Maumee River.

I miss my lake. I miss Crater's Edge.

"Has that become our new greeting, Miss McCartney?" he wonders.

"Not if you say yes."

Dr. Rydell doesn't react, although I can tell from his smoky eyes that he enjoys our visits on some level. He throws his Harry Potter glasses on the desk and says, "Then I'm afraid 'When can I go home?' will be added to my repertoire of greetings."

I flop into one of his chairs and look him right in the eye, silently wishing for—no, demanding - he return me to my little town and simple life. "Come on, doc. I'm not suicidal. I didn't try to kill myself, I swear it."

"I know you believe that, Miss McCartney, and as much as I want to, I can't just take you at your word."

"Why not? I'm not a liar. I've never lied to you once."

"That's very noble, though not the point."

"Not the…" I shoot to my feet before I can stop myself and I snap, "It *is* the point!"

Dr. Rydell is shocked at my outburst but only for a second. And that was the only thing that could have stopped the outburst. I'm taking it out on him and he's only doing his job.

When I flop back into my chair, I take a deep breath and think my next words through very carefully. I growl, "Shouldn't you trust someone until they give you reason not to? Like, innocent until proven guilty."

"Lives are at stake. When lives are at stake, I can't take any chances." He doesn't reprimand me for getting angry. I may not have a violent bone in my body, but I've found a few angry ones since being shipped here.

"Tell me this, what reason would I have to stab myself? Seriously."

"That's what we're here to find out."

I sigh, look at the floor, and pick at the seam of the ugly leather chair beside me. "I can't tell you anything. I still don't remember." Not for lack of trying. Over the last week, I've had plenty of time to reflect on that day. Multiple chances for a flicker of memory to flutter to the surface.

"That's a shame. Why don't we talk about school?"

"What about it?"

"Your mother said your grades have been slipping."

I shake my head. "I broke up with my boyfriend and missed a couple tests. Is that a crime?"

It's his turn to shake his head. He gets to his feet, tucks his tie back into his dress shirt, and walks over to me, sitting in the chair I've been picking at. I force myself to stop. "Why did you break up with your boyfriend?"

"We grew apart."

"And?"

"I don't want to talk about this. My grades didn't slip *that* much. My friends are all wonderful. I babysit my six-year-old brother a lot, but he's cute as a button so I don't mind much. There is no reason to take my own life, doctor."

Dr. Rydell pauses, looking out his small window. Then he questions, "What about your dad?"

"He's gone."

"I know." I look over to find him watching me expectantly.

"He's gone. It's hard. It's always going to hurt. I know that." Of course, I do. After a year, the pain hasn't dulled in the slightest. "That's another good reason why I would never take my own life. My dad would be so pissed — I mean, angry. My dad was a firefighter. He liked to save lives and that's what I want to do."

If I can still be a firefighter when — or if — I get out of here. Taylor's warning about the cray-cray's nags at me, pulls on the logical part of my brain.

"That's very admirable."

We talk about my life for a while. I lose track of time until Dr. Rydell looks at his watch and stands.

"Doc, please let me go home," I ask.

"I'll tell you what, let's meet again in two more days. If you still feel this strongly and you don't get into any trouble until then, I'll consider it."

I throw my head back and try not to swear. Two days? That's like 500 in teenage years. I can't stay here two more days. "How about one?"

This time he does let out a laugh. It's a nice laugh, the kind that reaches your eyes and causes crow's feet to deepen. He seems like a really nice man, but I can't like a man who's holding me hostage. "I don't negotiate with teenagers."

"One and a half?"

"Your session's over." He walks back to his desk and looks at his calendar, not looking back up at me. "Now get out of my office, McCartney."

I hear him chuckling to himself as I walk out. I don't know what I have to do to get out of this place.

When I get back to my room, there's a boy waiting for me, standing in the middle of the room, with his hands at his sides and looking around the drab, barely furnished room. He's handsome in a Hollywood kind of way; unruly curly auburn hair, dark eyes, and ruler straight eyebrows.

He's cocking a grin at me and that only cements the Hollywood thought. He seems familiar. Where have I seen him? He's not a patient that I've met.

"I've been waiting forever," he tells me.

"Sorry," I say. "Uh, who are you?"

"I'm Gavin. Gavin Slater."

"Okay, what are you doing in my room, Gavin?"

"I'm looking for you."

This confuses me. Is this guy a patient that I've never seen? Maybe he's new. Maybe he's from another section. "Why?"

He opens his mouth to speak when Taylor peaks in. Her eyes narrow as she frowns. "Who are you talking to?"

"What do you mean?" I ask, looking from her to Gavin, confused. "I'm talking to Gavin."

She looks around the room, as if searching for something, until her eyes reach me again. "Babe, there's no one in the cell but you."

# TWO

BY THE TIME lunch rolls around, I don't have much of an appetite. Taylor, being true to her word, got me a salad for lunch. It only has four slices of lettuce, three cucumbers, and two tomatoes, but it's better than nothing so I shut my mouth and pick at it until I've finished it. Taylor doesn't even try to steal it. I suppose it's because she's worried about me. "This place is getting to you, girl," she'd said. "Get some rest."

Gavin's in my room when I head back after lunch. He's peering over at the book I'd tossed into the corner. I groan and toss my hands up in frustration. Then a sound slips from my lips that can only be described as a laugh cross hiccup. How does my mind fight itself? How do I stop myself from going crazy? I shout at the boy, "What do you want?"

"I need your help."

I nod and walk right past him to pick up the book. "Yeah, I get that. How am I supposed to help you, Gavin? I can't even help myself."

"What do you need? Maybe we can help each other?"

My mouth opens, and the words are swallowed before I can release them. Gavin disappears right in front of me.

For the second time today, my classic book flutters to the floor. I clamp my eyes shut. *I'm not crazy. I'm not crazy. Not. Crazy.*

*You're not losing your mind,* Gavin says inside my head. *I'll explain as soon as I can. I'm sorry I keep freaking you out.*

I have to get out of this room.

*If I can get you out of that place, will you consider helping me?* Gavin wants to know.

What? Get me out? How can a figment of my imagination break me out of prison? I don't know where I'm going, but I know I need to do something other than stand here and wait for my crazy side to take over.

*I'm real, Marley,* Gavin says. *I really need your help.*

*Why me?*

His voice seems like it's drifting further away when he answers. It's more of an echo now. *I'll explain everything when I can. Just trust me, please. I'm not a figment of your imagination. Will you help me?*

I stop in the common area, where three of the deadly sins are playing a game of poker. None of them even glance my way. *If you get me out of here, I'll do whatever you need me to do.*

*Deal.* The word echoes throughout my mind. Am I going to get out of this place? Go home? I can't even imagine.

Taylor walks through the double doors, talking to the hottie we'd seen earlier. When she sees me, she says something to the nurse and walks over. "Are you okay?"

"I'm not crazy," I say with no conviction, worried that

17

the statement is pure fiction.

"It's this place." Taylor puts her scarred arm on my shoulder, spins around, and heads toward my room. When I flop onto my bed, Taylor tells me, "It makes you feel crazy."

It's meant to comfort me. If I'm being honest with myself, it's having the opposite effect. I don't have the will to fight it anymore. Everyone keeps telling me there's something wrong with me. What if they're right? What will happen to my family if I die? Sammy. What kind of childhood will he have? Will Mom survive the loss? Or will she leave Sammy an orphan?

It's suddenly difficult to breathe. A wave of panic slams into me so hard I'd have fallen over if I weren't sitting down.

"Breathe, girl." She pats my back. "Get out of that damn head of yours."

When the waves calm, and I can breathe easily, Taylor says, "Come with me." She stands, pulling at my arm and leaving me no choice.

"Where are we going?"

She drags me out of my room, down a white hallway, dressed up with a large blue stripe that disappears into a set of double doors.

"I want to show you something."

I grumble, "Can it wait?"

"Nope. I'm not giving you the chance to doubt yourself. That's what they want." Taylor opens the doors. I haven't been on this side of the floor and I have no idea where we're going.

I chuckle softly as we turn the corner, now following a red stripe. "Conspiracy theorist."

"I'm not going to be here much longer. When I do go, I want to make sure that you're okay."

"Are you getting out?" I ask, trying not to sound jealous as hell.

Taylor scoffs. "Not if I screwed everyone in this place. What I meant was the doctor will figure out which floor I need to be on and they won't want me with the general population."

"Do they have a floor for klepto's?"

"I have no idea what you're talking about." She smirks, knowing *exactly* what I'm talking about.

We stop at a closed door. When Taylor opens it, I nearly laugh. There's loot everywhere, out in plain sight: jewelry, clothing, knick-knacks, and other trinkets. She's obviously brought me to her room. "What's all this?"

"I don't mean to take things; it just happens. Most of the time I don't know I'm even doing it. If there's something in here that belongs to you take it."

"I don't have anything to steal. Except for my food."

"Ha-ha."

"Is this what you wanted to show me?"

She shakes her head and digs something out from under her cot—the trinkets jingle as they roll toward the wall.

Taylor pulls something out and waves in the air for me to see. A pair of dog tags hang loosely from her hand. She reaches down to cup them. "This is the only thing that's mine. My grandfather's dog tags from the second World War," Taylor confesses. "I grabbed them during the fire."

"And that's how you got that scar?"

She turns to it and nods. "I was six. These tags are the

only thing I have left from that life. No pictures and barely any memory of them."

Maybe that's why she steals, I think to myself. She's never had much to begin with. "That's terrible. I'm sorry."

"The firefighter who saved me stayed with me all night at the hospital. He went above and beyond. I think it's because he had a child at home and he felt bad for me."

Dad used to tell me stories about the people he and his crew had saved. Mom hated it, but she allowed it as long as I didn't have nightmares. Hearing Taylor talk about her rescuer only cemented his teachings even further. I *am* going to be a firefighter, no matter what it takes. "I'm sorry you had to go through that."

Taylor waves her hand, as if it's nothing to worry about. "Just promise me you will be like that guy. Firefighting is more than putting out fires."

"I know. I'm glad you got such a good one when you needed him."

Taylor throws the dog tags back under her mattress. "Let's go for a walk."

"YOU'RE GOING HOME today, and you didn't tell me?" someone questions me, shaking my shoulder and pulling me from sleep.

"What time is it?" I brave the morning light by cracking open one eye and instantly regret the choice.

"Are you going home?"

It's Taylor's voice interrogating me, I realize.

"What are you going on about? Why are you in my

room?"

"Answer the question, peach girl."

I sit up in bed, since I am clearly not going back to sleep. "I don't know what you're talking about. No one told me I was going home, Taylor."

"I just heard one of the nurses say it."

I try not to get too excited. "Really?"

"That's what I heard." Taylor sounds disappointed.

I don't want to see her unhappy, though a trickle of excitement courses through me at just the mere prospect. "I don't want to leave you," I inform her.

Her tune changes quickly. "You can't stay here. I won't be too far behind. I'm eighteen now, not a minor. I'll play it up for the shrink that I was misguided and how I've changed my ways."

I nod. "Can I make a suggestion?"

"Let's hear it."

"Don't lift any more items while you're in here."

Taylor croaks out a laugh as she tosses my pillow at me. "You think that would really help?" She inhales sharply and catches the pillow as I throw it back.

She laughs so hard she cries. "Well, it's the only advice I've got, so I hope so."

"Let's go eat some slimy eggs. This could be your last meal here," she says, walking toward the door.

"Best news I've heard all day." I couldn't tell her how happy I was to go home. "You'd better keep in touch when you're on the ouside."

Taylor scoffs and starts walking away. "Friends for life, peach girl."

We pick up our trays of lumpy oatmeal and burnt toast and my stomach curdles. Dr. Rydell turns the corner then. He's wearing his usual white shirt but with a blue tie and khaki pants, I notice, as he waves me over. "Time to see if you were right," I tell Taylor, pointing at the doctor.

I walk over, wondering what I'll say if he's sending me home.

"Let's talk in your office," he jokes, walking toward my room. I don't laugh. "Have a seat," he says when we arrive. "I spoke with your mom today. You got your wish. You're going home."

"Really? Thanks, Doc." Trying not to embarrass myself by squealing or jumping. "What made you change your mind?"

He smiles, leaning against the door jam, and the hem of his white coat flutters. "Miss McCartney, you're about as crazy as my Aunt Phyllis." He explains, "If you knew her, you'd understand. That woman is a saint, though she is always getting herself into trouble."

His aunt has to be in her seventies or eighties. What kind of trouble can an old lady get into? "I've been trying to tell everyone that I couldn't have done something like that, but no one bothered to listen." Now someone has. My palms start to sweat as I realize the repercussions of going home. I desperately want to go, but I never stopped to think about what my home would be like in the aftermath of my accident—now that Mom doesn't trust me. I am finally getting what I want. I'm not sure how I should feel about it. I think I should feel amazed, eager, and delighted. Instead, doubt and nervousness weigh on me like a sumo wrestler.

"It might not seem like it, but I listened. However, I have a job to do. Not only do I have a job, I have a conscience and that conscience wouldn't let me release you until I was certain you wouldn't harm yourself."

I nod.

Dr. Rydell moves to the only chair I have in the room. When he sits, he offers, "That said, your mother doesn't seem convinced. Look, I was a teenager. A long, long time ago." I half snort, half laugh. "I understand the pressures that come with it. College is around the corner, your personality might be changing, boyfriends and friends are moving on a little, exams. I get it. Your mom just needs some time. She was afraid. She called three times a day, every day during your stay here."

"She did?"

He nods, clapping his hands on his thighs. "She did. She is very concerned. I know you're upset with her for bringing you here."

"A little." A lot.

Dr. Rydell chuckles. "We both know that's not the whole truth, but I'll let it slide. You're a good kid and you will get past this."

"Thank you, Doc."

"One more thing, Miss McCartney," he says as he makes his way to the door. "Your mother might want you to see someone on the outside."

"Like a psychiatrist?"

He shakes his head. "I don't think you need pills anymore. Maybe she'll send you to a therapist. Don't get too upset with her. She's doing the best she can, okay? It will take time to get her trust back, and there's no reason why you can't move on."

A headache starts to brew, so I rub my temples. Maybe it's because of the stiffness in my neck. Or maybe it's because this whole situation frustrates me to the point where I don't know what to do anymore. "How long?" I ask Dr. Rydell. "How long am I going to be accused of trying to kill myself?"

"I know you didn't. I don't know how, but I do. Your mother knows you better and if you didn't do it, she will realize that."

"Can't I just keep seeing you?"

He shakes his head and shoves his hands in his white coat's pockets. "I'm too far away and I can't see patients outside of this place. It's their policy."

My stomach plummets with the weight of my disappointment. "Okay, Doc. Thank you."

"Good luck."

It sucks that I have to break in a new therapist. Just as I have Dr. Rydell admitting that he knows I didn't do it. I'm definitely going to need that luck.

At least I can rely on the fact that the dreams and visions will stop when I'm out of this place.

# THREE

"MARLEY, I NEED you to go to the grocery store. I left a list of things for you to pick up. It's on the counter," Mom tells me as she stands impatiently in the living room doorway, keys in hand, while my brother and I watch some kiddy show I can only half pay attention to.

I groan. "But, Mom, I can't go. I'm grounded."

Sammy laughs at the show, though I suspect he's laughing at me. His blue eyes turn back to the TV when he catches me looking his way. He wipes his freckled cheeks on his long tan sleeve, hoping to hide his expression. He's only six but he knows what's going on in the house.

"Don't 'But, Mom' me. I have a really long shift ahead of me." She swaps her stern voice for a different approach. "Please do this for me."

"What's in it for me?"

Mom sighs—before the accident she would have laughed. I shouldn't joke with her right now, but I'm so happy to be home that I forgot to stay mad at her. "How about another two weeks without your phone?"

"Mom," I smile. "That is *not* the way to negotiate."

Mom doesn't smile, but I can see a light catch her eye. Normally, she would have come back with another snarky retort like, "*I don't negotiate with teenagers.*" But we haven't been normal in this house for a long, long time. I miss it. I hadn't realized how much until this moment.

She looks down at her watch and says, "I have to get to work. Sammy, Mikey's mom will be here any minute." To me, "If you go to the grocery store, we eat tonight. Simple as that." She walks out without another word.

'Mom one; Marley zip,' as Dad would say if he were here.

"I have to get to work now but you two keep tallying up the score. I want to know who won," he would say before he left for work.

I am partial to food, so I head into the kitchen after Sammy catches the bus, crumple the grocery list and cash into my pocket, and head out the back door. The grocery store is two blocks if I go through the path in the backyard—six if I walk around.

When I get there, the place is quiet—and very bright. The fluorescent lighting reminds me of the youth centre. I try to ignore that thought and listen to the beeping of the scanners instead. I don't get five feet in the door before Mr. Mullane walks out of his office to greet me.

"Marley McCartney. Where have they been hiding you?"

I freeze. They told him? Shame washes over me before frustration settles in. I know Mom used to work here when we were kids, but she shouldn't have told him. That's my personal business. Doesn't a girl have any right to privacy?

I don't know what to say to him now.

"I've seen your mom in here a few times. She said you were sick. You look good, kiddo. Feeling better?"

Oh. She didn't tell him. Thank God. "I *am* feeling better. Thank you, Mr. Mullane."

"If you need anything let me know. My door's always open. I always had a soft spot for your family. Your mom was one of my best workers." He bends to whisper the last line.

Mr. Mullane is an intelligent man, though he's constantly on the go and doesn't have much time for anything but work. I always liked him. Especially because he would always let me choose a piece of candy when I had to wait at the store for Mom.

Back then his hair was fluffy and brown—fluffy is the only way to describe it. It's receded at least six inches since.

Mr. Mullane offers a smile, showing his missing a front tooth. Mom said it happened during a robbery attempt. No one was hurt but it gave Mom the push she needed to become a nurse.

"Thank you, Mr. Mullane. Mom speaks highly of you, too."

He offers a smile as big as the moon and hugs me before skipping back to his office.

I grab a basket by the front door and head down the vegetable aisle, realizing that I forgot to check what we had at home. I sigh, thinking about how easy my life used to be. My breathing slows as I remember running up and down these aisles as Mom closed up the store. Dad would be at home waiting for us with a big hug. Tears sprinkle to the surface at the memory. That was before Sammy, when it was just the three of us.

*Help me, Marley. Please, a* familiar voice calls out.

Terror the size of a frog jumps into my throat and my heart skips into its own rock band tune. I spin around to see if he's behind me. Down the cereal aisle, across from me, there's an older gentleman in a suit and a gray beret reading the label on a box of Wheaties and a puffy-eyed mother with messy blonde hair pushing her little girl past all the sugary cereals. She half smiles at me as her child protests in a high-pitched squeal. It's as if she's apologizing. I nod so she knows there are no hard feelings. We've all been there. Mom used to have the same problem with Sammy.

If the scream I'd heard wasn't from anyone in this aisle, maybe it came from the next? I refuse to believe insanity followed me here from the youth centre. It's a big grocery store; the sound could have come from anywhere.

*Can you hear me?*

No, no. The crazy train has left the station. I can't be hearing voices.

I can't deal with this again. Nope. I don't want to. *Go away, go away, go away,* I chant, hoping my brain will ease up on the voices.

My heartbeat flutters in desperation, as I bounce the basket from one hand to the other. This cannot be happening again. What am I going to do?

*Help me, please, Marley. You promised.*

I can't take this right now. I've been out of that place for less than twenty-four hours. The mother of the crying baby gets one look at me and walks the other way. I might as well crawl into a hole and save myself from social suicide right now.

I need to leave—who cares about the groceries I was sent to pick up? I turn the corner, heading up the frozen aisle, looking around to make sure no one is staring at me for losing it at the chip rack. What I see freaks me out worse than anything I've ever experienced; I do a double take and then stop.

Inside the freezer door where my opaque reflection should be is Gavin's. I spin around to see if there's a guy standing behind me; there's no one.

The hairs on the back of my neck stick out, urging me to run. Ignoring the warning, I turn back, shift my basket, and open the freezer door. I need to see if this is just a trick. These visions need to stop—they can just go back to Toledo for all I care.

When I open the cooler, a wave of icy air drifts into my lungs, forcing a quick calm over me. All I find are strawberry, vanilla, and chocolate flavors of different ice cream brands. No teenage boy.

The cool air causes me to shiver, sending goosebumps down my arm. I let the handle go, momentarily content. It doesn't last. Gavin's face is still there when the door falls shut.

All those terrible feelings reappear. His curly hair whips around as he pounds on the glass. His big, maple brown eyes are wide, and his straight eyebrows shoot up as his forehead wrinkles. The terror in his eyes leaves me with head-to-toe goosebumps. Those eyes…

A terrible recognition knocks me over the head. Gavin wasn't only haunting me at the youth centre, he'd also been haunting my nightmares.

"I wish you'd leave me alone," I tell the figment of my imagination, the one currently pounding on the freezer door. The longer I watch the strange phenomenon, the more I feel my own panic grow. His suffering becomes mine, spreading through me like smoke and becoming worse with each moment until I think I might pass out from the anxiety. My eyes never stray. An invisible force field holds me there.

Then a loud bang relieves me of the phantom pain. I actually jump like there's a snake at my feet. I realize someone behind me has slammed one of the cooler doors, mercifully wrenching my focus away from the image of the frightened boy. I almost thank them. When I turn back, the horrible vision is gone, my pounding heartbeat the only sign it was ever even there.

The boy from my nightmares is now haunting me when I'm supposed to free of it. Why is this happening? What have I done to deserve this?

I've been trying to chalk up the nightmares as nothing more than a girl on pain meds carrying a suitcase full of emotional trauma, but as of this moment, that theory is trashed. At a loss for a rational explanation, I finally come to terms with the fact that it wasn't the youth centre causing the visions. I've gone bananas and may just have to tell my new therapist when my mom-mandated session eventually comes up.

*Marley, I got you out. Please help me,* the voice in my head calls out.

Before I realize what's happening, the basket has slipped from my hand, and I'm running—first out of the frozen food aisle, then past Mr. Mullane's office, where I note him watching me with a cell phone up to his ear, then out of the store, not knowing where I'm going or what I'm doing, as long as I get far, far away. Nothing can stop me.

Except the agonizing feeling in my gut—I feel the wound pop open and the sting forces a long hiss out of my throat. I forgot about my stitches. I curse at myself and slow my pace, not even a block from the grocery store, and in my haste, I've accidentally run the long way. The house is five blocks away.

Untucking my shirt from my pants, I release the wound from its bindings. It's bleeding so I apply pressure to the bandage and keep moving, slower now. A block later I check the wound again. I can't stop the bleeding.

It's coming out as if the wound is a fresh bleed and panic settles in.

No, I'm almost home. Everything will be all right, I tell myself.

# FOUR

FLOATING ABOVE A gathering of black-clad figures surrounding a rectangular hole in the ground, I'm hit with the realization, I must be dead.

You've gotta be kidding me. All the crap I survived lately, and I end up here anyway. What a cruel, cosmic joke.

"Still waiting for the funny part!" I call out to the universe, which I imagine as some grumpy old man with a tangled beard down to his arthritic ankles. He grips his wooden cane with his long, horror-movie fingernails and smiles evilly as I panic. "I can't be dead. Someone screwed up."

The whistling wind reminds me where I am: floating twenty feet above what is to be my final resting place, a neat black rectangle with only the shade of a wide evergreen and a massive oak for comfort. As my focus drifts back to where I hover, amid the oak tree leaves, my head snaps up. "People don't fly. People don't fly," I chant.

Even through my barely contained panic, I realize it is a paradoxically beautiful day for a funeral. I search the unfamiliar faces scattered throughout the tree-lined cemetery. I don't remember my death but since I'm here, obviously some kind of accident has happened. Maybe I was bored to death in Mr. Booth's math class and conked my head on the corner of my desk, dying of blunt-force trauma.

So, I'm dead. That's it then?

"No," I scream at the universe. "I don't want to be dead."

When nothing happens, I change tactics and plead, "Please."

Do dead people go through the five stages of grief? Which one am I on now? Maybe I can skip bargaining and get back to being a normal teenager—angry at the world for no apparent reason.

Looking down at the crowd and the open grave, I find it impossible to deny the truth. Cross off denial.

A gust of wind blows me out into the open, away from my treetop hiding place, and settles me smack-dab in the middle of the crowd. Ignoring my sudden wave of nausea, I call out, "Hello! Can anyone hear me? I'm right here."

No one hears or even sees me. I almost want to scream and call them names, but I hold back as it occurs to me that I will never know if I would have changed the world. Seeing these people standing over my grave and crying makes me think that I at least did something good in my mere seventeen years.

Then I'm struck with a piercing regret that I don't get to see myself one last time—at least to make sure that they didn't screw up my makeup and make me look like a circus clown, like they did to my great Aunt Petty, short for Petunia.

Suddenly a stranger's face appears in front of mine. I try to speak but her soft, kind eyes look right through me, causing my already aching stomach to plummet to my knees. I wave a hand in her face, but she doesn't see me. My hands fall to my sides as defeat sinks into my veins.

The woman looks to be in her forties, older than my own mother. Her green eyes are so bloodshot I can barely make out the color. A few stray curls of strawberry-blonde hair flicker in her face, refusing to be tamed inside her bright green butterfly clip. She doesn't seem to notice or care. A frown deepens her cleft chin as she dabs at a tear and walks right through me. *What a cliché,* I think as a shiver creeps down my spine, slow and icy.

Where's my family? My mom, my brother? I look more closely at the crowd. And where's my dad? He should be here to greet me. He would *never* miss my funeral.

I turn around. An older woman tucked in a flowery purple dress takes the strawberry-blonde woman's hand and says, "If you need anything, please call me. Anytime, Debra." Her words are hard to understand. When she smiles, I realize the lady has no teeth.

"I don't know any of you!" The words blurt out of my mouth. "Why are you at my funeral?"

Tears run down my cheeks as my last moments come back to me. It's not fair. It was an accident. I didn't mean to rip my stitches. It shouldn't have killed me.

The crowd begins to disperse, and it's only then that I see a framed picture of a young boy. He's my age. He has

34

dark eyes and a mischievous grin teases his cheeks. I recognize the sky-blue background as the same type we had for picture day last year. *He's cute, but who is he?* I don't think he went to my school. I would definitely notice a guy like him.

Before I realize what's happening, I'm whipped up, away from the daunting cemetery, past the trees, over the mausoleums, and into the sky. A rushing sound fills my ears as I'm thrashed through the air at jetliner speed. There's a pulsing from my chest that I can feel all the way up in my head.

*A heartbeat? Dead people don't have heartbeats.* Something is desperately wrong with this whole nightmare, reinforcing my earlier suspicion that someone made a terrible mistake.

Abruptly, I plummet through the air. Panic sets in and my already racing heart begins pumping like a steam engine about to explode as I slash through heavy fog and closer to the ground. *Dead people can't die,* I remind myself. *The fall cannot kill me.*

Knowing this, I still flinch as the ground closes in. I shudder to think about what's going to happen and close my eyes tight.

Splat.

A loud groan escapes my throat as I land on my derriere and then wake up in my own bed.

I rouse from the nightmare and search my body for broken bones. It takes a minute for my mind to sort reality from nightmare. Everything's intact. My heart continues to beat madly as I flop back on the pillow. A sigh slips out. Why do I keep having this dream?

Sweat tickles my neck as my bedroom comes back to

me in fuzzy pieces—mostly from memory because it's so dark, I can't make much out. Apparently, I closed the curtains before falling asleep, which I do not remember.

I know the room better than the back of my hand; it's mine, and it's comforting. Chocolate curtains cuddle soft pink walls, and there's a matching oval carpet at the foot of my bed where my cat, Ruby, used to sleep. A pencil-thin peak of sunlight slips through an open inch. My modern cappuccino colored furniture looks sleek—Mom doesn't agree with my taste, but that's okay because she's old and has her own era, with flowery couches and washed-out wood tables. Pictures and mementos are scattered about my room, baring witness to my emotional trauma. The rose and pearl sheets I got when I first started high school have fallen to my waist—along with the quilt Nana made for me back when my parents informed her that they were expecting a baby girl.

*It wasn't a nightmare.* I swear I hear the words as if someone else is in the room, but I'm alone.

That's when I hear footsteps in my room and panic.

It's my mom, I realize when she pulls back the curtains and illuminates the worry on her face. She looks at me and I can see the horrified expression in her bright blue eyes. She's still dressed for work in her purple scrubs, which means I couldn't have slept very long.

"Mom, what's wrong?" Tension slips into the room, as quiet as the sandman and just as quick.

"Mr. Mullane called me. Said you freaked out in the store." I barely notice the slight irritation in Mom's tone at first.

I tell her through cottonmouth, "I was just tired."

This is when she notices the blood-soaked bandages

on my nightstand. "I'm sorry. It was an accident," I let her know. Her expression seems to soften slightly, though it might be a trick of the light.

"I know, Marley. You've said it a million times. I should check your stitches and change your bandages, anyway."

I lift my *Vampire Diaries* nightshirt up slightly, which I don't remember changing into, so she can see the damage. The gauze I'd placed on top of the wound is visibly caked in blood. It had been healing nicely — at least I thought so, but I'm not a doctor.

Mom sighs. She's clearly upset with me. "You should be more careful."

She leaves the room and comes back with cleaning supplies, a damp cloth, cleaning solution the doctor prescribed, gauze, and tape. She sits beside me, placing the supplies at my hip. It stings when she pulls the tape from my skin. I only just manage to keep my mouth shut and not cry out.

Despite the fact that I've apologized and have tried to explain my side, Mom and I can't get back to the way things used to be: laughing and joking, hugs and kisses, happy. For the second time today, I'm feeling nostalgic.

Frustration becomes a knot in my belly. A thousand words swarm inside my mind, the least of all is the word *sorry*. How many more times can I use that one? Nope, I need something else.

"Mom, do you think I might be able to go to school this week?" I ask, realizing quickly that those weren't the words I'd planned to say. *Hopefully she is in a giving mood,* I think, silently wincing and preparing for another lecture.

She doesn't look up at me, but I can see her lips purse

as if I've forgotten to do the dishes or take out the trash. "Not now, Marley."

"I've already missed almost two weeks. I'm gonna fall so far behind that I can't catch up." She should be sympathetic to that sentence. After all, education is ranked at the top of my mother's good parenting list—if she had one, that is.

Am I fighting with her about school? It's come to this. Most kids love to stay home, but my house is feeling more and more like a prison sentence than the house I grew up in.

"I'm sending you to a new therapist. Once you meet with her, we will discuss it," Mom finally says. "I really need you to be more careful until this wound heals." The mom I know and love is seeping through a crack in the angry curtain she's hung up. It makes me feel a flicker of hope that she'll one-day stop being so disappointed in me. "You don't want to end up back in the hospital."

"Okay. I will try to be more careful."

With a practiced hand, she bandages the wound and then tries to leave without another word, as if nothing happened.

I can't leave it like this—not after that terrible nightmare. "Mom?"

"Yes, dear?"

I know she's still upset and she's trying to hide it. Of course, it doesn't work because she's my mom and I know her. "I love you."

Her demeanor relaxes a bit. Mom turns to me and says, "I love you, too, and I always will. I have to get back to work. If you need anything call the clinic."

She works at the Walk-in Clinic, the only one the town

has. Luckily, it's pretty close and her boss is very forgiving when it comes to Sammy and me. Mom tells me that he has three children of his own and five grandchildren. I've seen pictures of their modest clothing and frowning faces, though I've only met one of his daughters. And that's because she forgot her wallet and came in to pick it up while I was talking to Annie, the receptionist. Seeing her in real life left me with a much better impression of her.

No matter how angry Mom is now, she can't stay mad forever, I tell myself. I'm her only girl, and she loves me more than life itself — which she's told me several times throughout my years.

Even with the nightmare edging to the back of my mind, I still can't bring myself to go back to sleep, so I pull the curtains into the tie-back, securing them, and sit in the chair beside the window. I look out at the changing season. The browns, reds and yellows have begun to eat at the green. It's the combination of colors that make me feel most hopeful. It's that time of year when multiple colors mingle and create a wonderful piece of art that will be an entirely different design next year.

I wish Mom wouldn't be so upset with me. I know I didn't hurt myself. I just know it; but how do I prove it? Now, if only I could remember what happened to me. If only I could go back to school to escape these worries.

I yawn and look at the clock on my nightstand. It reads 11:30, which means I slept for almost two hours. These nightmares really need to stop, I demand of my subconscious mind as I lay back down and hide under the covers.

*It wasn't a dream,* I hear the voice tell me again. It's Gavin's voice. There's no time to dwell on it because the doorbell chimes. It's the only motivation I need to get out of bed. The prospect of a little human contact is what I really need, preferably with someone who is not mad at me.

# FIVE

THE NIGHTMARES FALL away as soon as I see the concern on my best friend's face. Her green eyes, the lids powdered her favorite light pink shading, go wide when she gets a good look at me. Her massive amount of curly brown hair flutters in the wind as she stands in the doorway trying to figure me out.

"Kimmy," I exclaim, throwing my arms around her. "How have you been? I feel like I haven't seen you in forever."

"It's been too long," she says, in her usual dramatic way. She doesn't talk much around others but with me I think she feels like I won't judge anything she says. "I haven't seen you since before they moved you to Toledo. I texted like a million times."

"My mom took my phone privileges away. I got back home yesterday."

Kimmy walks into the foyer and unbuttons her jacket before shrugging it off her shoulders. "I know. Your mom called mine and asked her if I could bring your homework by."

"Of course, she did."

"I cannot believe she still isn't listening to you. She knows you better than anyone."

I shake my head. "No, *you* know me better than anyone. She's just known me the longest." This thought doesn't make me feel any better. Mom's known me for my whole existence and she still has doubts.

I lead Kimmy to the back of the house and into the kitchen. After nearly tripping on a pair of my brother's sneakers in the hallway, I walk into the kitchen and shield my eyes from the sun shining through the patio doors. This is the biggest room in the house and the most open. "She still won't even look at me if she can help it."

"She has to get over it, eventually," Kimmy says. "Give her time. Whether you meant it or not, you scared her half to death. You scared us all half to death."

I scoff, even though she's right. "I know. I'm sorry. I just hope she forgives me soon."

"Is she talking to you yet?" Kimmy tosses her giant black, jewel-studded purse on the long island in the center of the kitchen before flopping into one of the bar stools. The purse sticking out like a red rose in a field of daffodils on the beige quartz countertop.

"Nope," I answer, not wanting to talk about how bad things have gotten at home since the accident. But Kimmy is my best friend. Who else can I talk to about these things? "She's been freezing me out since I got home from the youth centre. She wanted me to talk to her then, and now she wants nothing to do with me."

I notice the loaf of bread on the countertop and hunger takes over my thoughts. I go to the fridge for lunchmeat and mustard, piling it on as I always do. "You want one?"

Kimmy shakes her head, looking only slightly disgusted. I give her credit for trying to hide it. "Oh no. I ate at home." A few minutes of silence falls while I eat. Things have always been simple between us. Kimmy is like the sister I never had. She's got this innate ability to read people and get to the bottom of things. It's always been something I admire about her. I swear I can almost see the wheels spinning in her head, like an old water wheel, only faster. "Is something else going on?"

I knew she would suspect something.

"No," I say too quickly.

Kimmy's left eyebrow shoots up, as if she knows I'm lying. She puts her hand on her hip, assessing me. Then her eyes stray toward the floor and back to me. She leans forward and says, "Tell me about that place they sent you to. Was it totally awful? Were they good to you?"

"It was worse than I could imagine. The food was…" I can't even say it. Instead, I shiver and shake off the thought, knowing she'll understand what I mean. "My doctor was understanding. If it weren't for him, I think I'd still be there."

*That was me,* Gavin complains, and my cool calm is now a block of ice falling down my back.

Why won't the voice stop? I'm out of the youth centre—there's no excuse.

I shake it off and try to focus on my conversation with Kimmy. He'll go away eventually. I hope. "Mom's sending me to another doctor. I couldn't keep Rydell because he's too far away."

"That's awful."

"I met a cool girl there. She helped me a lot. Name's

Taylor. You'd like her."

Kimmy shifts in her seat. "What's she like?"

How to describe Taylor. I have to think a minute. "She's one of a kind. Bold, brave, says whatever comes to her mind. It's actually pretty funny sometimes."

"I'm glad you found a friend on the inside. But you're free now. And hopefully things will go back to normal soon. They will, you'll see."

I reach out, so does Kimmy. I throw my arms around her. It doesn't take long to realize we're both bent over the counter uncomfortably. Kimmy laughs. "This was a *terrible* plan."

We each return to our side of the counter, smiling. My stitches ache and I wonder if I've torn them open again. Mom will be *so* mad if I have.

"We missed you in karate class. It's not the same without you."

I flop the rest of my sandwich on the counter in front of me. "Can't do much with a gut threatening to break open every time I move."

Kimmy frowns. "Right. Sorry."

"It happened." I shrug.

"On the bright side, if you gain a few pounds you might be able to fit into my clothes."

I scoff, knowing that I'm nearly half a foot taller than her five-foot-nothing, and she has wide hips; mine are so narrow, they're almost boyish. I look down at my jeans and nightshirt, over to her cashmere sweater and black slacks. "You would love that, wouldn't you?" She's been trying to get me to dress more fashionably since we were six and she found ruffled mini dresses.

She smiles. Her teeth make an appearance and she

44

feigns indifference, but we both know the truth.

I finish my sandwich and then change the subject. "Mr. Cheng came by the hospital to see me."

"What'd he say?"

"He said that after teaching us for eight years he felt compelled to make sure I was okay. Can't believe we'll both have black belts next year."

"He doesn't like it when you call it a black belt," she reminds me, because it's traditionally called a *shodan*, meaning first degree black belt.

Mr. Cheng studied different types of martial arts from around the world. He's been all over Japan and China, learning their culture.

When he came back to the states and opened his own place, Kimmy and I were two of his first students.

"You're coming back to school soon, right?" Kimmy asks.

"She won't even discuss it with me," I answer. "How is school? What have I missed? Tell me everything."

I wipe my hands over the sink, removing all the breadcrumbs, grab a clean glass from the dishwasher and head to the fridge for some milk. Then I lean against the counter, thinking that if I clean the dishwasher Mom will take it easy on me for not getting anything at the grocery store. Then I let Kimmy's stories distract me from my thoughts. "April came out to her parents."

"She did?" A grin spreads across my face. "And how did they take it?"

Kimmy smiles too and scratches her ear. "They said they already knew."

"Seriously? Why didn't they say anything? She's been struggling with it for what? A year?"

I remember last year when she'd had a panic attack in the back of Kimmy's Mustang because she wanted to go to the Spring Formal with a girl from our class, but she couldn't because if her parents found out…

"At least. April said they suspected before *she* even knew," Kimmy offers.

I clap my hands together. "I'm so proud of her. That couldn't have been easy."

"No," Kimmy agrees. "Some people still don't understand it."

I open the dishwasher and begin to clear it—or as I'm silently calling it: Operation Make-Mom-like-me-again. "That's their problem." I grab a glass, open the cupboard, and place it on the shelf.

April is one of our best friends. Kimmy and I met her in sixth grade. She has always been more into sports and classic cars and less into fashion and boys than we were. Looking back, there were obvious signs, but we didn't see them until she admitted that she "might be gay" two years ago. No one had a problem with it. We just waited for her to become the woman she wanted to be and held her hand through the tough times.

Shawn was more forceful than any of us. "Tell them and if they don't like it that's their problem," he'd said. "Why should you hold onto this pain? They're your parents. They'll love you no matter what."

In the end Shawn was right.

I tell Kimmy, "We should have known it would happen that way. April's parents have always been cool."

"Yeah. They took her all the way to Hawaii for the weekend," she says, a little jealous, "to celebrate."

"Wow. I've never been more than one state over. Her

parents are awesome."

Kimmy gets up and walks around the counter. "Should you be doing that?"

"I'll just take my time. It should be okay. Tell me something else. How's Shawn?" Shawn is another one of our best friends, who also happens to be Kimmy's beau and the school's heartthrob.

"He's Shawn." My best friend says the words and I know exactly what she means. Her eyes light up when she talks about him. A grin the size of our state appears below her rosy cheeks. Kimmy never gets overly emotional or girly about it, but everyone at school knows that they are the real deal. Soul mates, if that's a thing. "Derek asked about you," Kimmy says, trying to be nonchalant.

I stop what I'm doing and sigh. I don't really want to know, though I am a little curious. "What did he say?"

"He just wanted to know if you were all right."

"What did you tell him?"

"That there was an accident and you will be back at school as soon as you're feeling better," she says, "and that's all he needed to know. Between you and me, I think he feels responsible."

"For what?"

"For you. I got the feeling from the way he was acting that he felt bad."

"No one's at fault and we both are, I guess. I don't know. I mean, I haven't spoken to him for at least a month. It's been almost two since we broke up."

"He seems upset about how things ended."

I groan. *How things ended? Really?* "It was a long time coming."

"You're both better off. He just hasn't figured that out

yet." She doesn't comment further as I finish unloading the dishwasher. "Well, I should go. I don't want to get you into trouble."

"Yeah," I respond. "It will be Mompocalypse if she sees you here. I'm surprised she hasn't hired a guard for the front door."

Kimmy looks like she's at a loss for words.

As if she heard me, Mom walks in the front door and calls out, "Marley, is that Kimmy's Mustang?"

Busted. "Uh, yeah," I say, somewhat unnecessarily as Mom enters the kitchen and sees us for herself.

"Marley needed her homework," Kimmy, not skipping a beat, explains and then points toward her purse. "And I brought notes."

Mom nods and smiles at Kimmy before turning to me. "Well, I hope you got all your homework because I have to head back to work in an hour and you're still grounded."

Another reason I need to get back to school. I need to see my friends, to be around people who don't judge me. It would be a nice change not to be under constant scrutiny. Mom squints her eyes and rubs her hand over her face before saying, "You two better talk about your homework if you expect to pass your classes."

"On Friday," Kimmy explains as my mother starts walking out of the room, "we talked about Greek gods and their offspring. I got notes. You missed a chemistry test. I am *pretty* sure I failed so don't ask me for help. Got more notes."

"Can't wait."

Kimmy straightens her shirt and ignores my comment. "You also missed a test in English. Mr. Couture gave me some assignments for you. I forgot them. I can swing them by tomorrow at lunch."

"That's all right. If you had brought them my mother would probably lock me in my room. I swear she wants to. She'd get away with it, too, because I don't have a phone to call anyone, and I can't climb out the window." I point to my gut. "Because of this stupid thing." I sigh and wish normal would hurry up and find me again. "What is everyone saying about me at school? They don't know, do they?"

Kimmy waves her hand in the air as if that would shoo the thought away. "They're gossip royalty. Don't worry about it. Someone will break up and they'll be gossiping about that."

"Right." I wish I could believe that. But they live to talk about me. Every move I make is another for the history books—one filled with permanent markered moustaches and scratched out faces.

Why do I even want to go back to school again? Butterflies awaken in my belly when I think of going back, but it's my life—mine. I can't stay cooped up in my house for the rest of my life. I can't stay wrapped up in my own head. The crazy will sink its teeth in so deep I won't be able to run from it.

Kimmy crinkles her eyes at me. "You think too much. No one knows the real story. Just the teachers." Her eyes stray to the window. She pauses before continuing, "No matter what we say, they'll gossip. Don't let those horrible people bother you."

"I've got other things to worry about." I debate telling her about Gavin, my hallucination. She's my best friend and has been for fifteen years. I don't understand what's happening, so how can I expect her to?

"Spill." Kimmy demands, practically reading my mind.

"Nothing. Just a lot going on."

"Marley." One eyebrow rises as Kimmy demands, in her best you-better-tell-me-because-I'll-find-out-sooner-or-later tone.

I turn my head away. I can't tell her. Can I? "You'll think I'm crazy."

"You've been through a lot. Whatever it is, it can't be as bad as you think."

"It is. It really is." I don't know what to say to my best friend, but I have to give her something now. The girl won't give up. She never gives up on anything.

*Tell her the truth,* Gavin's voice implores.

A groan tumbles from my throat before I can help myself. *Now, why would I do that? So, another person can think I'm crazy?*

Kimmy's eyes narrow, only silently questioning me this time.

The voice inside my head doesn't answer. Because imaginary people don't have to answer when they're spoken to. "Want something to drink?" I ask as I turn, plucking one of the clear glasses I'd just put in the cupboard.

"Sure," she says. I pour one for her and hand it over. "I'm worried, Lee. Tell me."

*So, you won't feel so alone,* Gavin finally offers, giving me a good excuse to tell Kimmy.

Then it occurs to me that maybe she'll have some advice—other than to not skip any of my therapist appointments.

Hesitantly, I admit to Kimmy, "I want to tell you the

truth, but I promise you won't believe me."

"You should know better," Kimmy says, aggravated. "We've been friends forever. We shared a bathtub together — granted, we were two, but still — that's a bond that cannot ever be broken." She sips her water.

"Fair enough," I whisper, before sucking in a deep breath of air and forcing the words out. "I've been having nightmares." Scary nightmares that have me nearly in a fever and crying big, fat, sloppy tears.

"Of course, you are. You've been through a traumatic experience. It's understandable."

"And I've been hearing voices — well, one annoying voice." The words rush out in one quick breath. *Please don't stop talking to me or tell my mother that I've lost my mind.*

"And?" Kimmy says without reacting.

"That's not enough?"

"I can tell there's more."

"I don't really know much more. The voice started yesterday while I was at the...you know. Then I saw him in my room, but no one else did. Then I saw his face today at the grocery store. It was reflected in the glass down the frozen aisle. He was banging and trying desperately to get my attention, but I didn't want to listen and ran away. It freaked me out; I think I might be crazy." I pause, take a swig of water and continue, "With the anniversary of my dad's death two weeks away and after the accident, it's not a far stretch. I didn't want to bring it up. You can't think I'm crazy, too. It's bad enough that *I* do."

I look at the ground because I can't look my best friend in the eye when she tells me I've gone psycho and I need help. I expect Kimmy to storm out the house or run in to the office and tell my mom. She doesn't.

"They brought back that show, didn't they? Are there hidden cameras filming this?" she jokes, smiling and looking around the kitchen.

I chuckle, unable to help it. "No. You know I'm not that funny — or cruel."

She does. Kimmy drops the smile from her face, clasps her hands together and leans back on the counter. "And are you going to tell your therapist about all this?"

Just as I'd feared. "Mom is forcing me to see someone new. I meet the new doctor tomorrow, but I really don't want to tell this new person. They could have me locked up and taken away from my family."

Kimmy shakes her head. "Your doctor won't want to take you away from your family. I know you have this fear of not being able to take care of your family since your dad, but you have to get over that and take care of you first."

A tightness forms in my belly at the mere mention of my father, as it always does. I toss the thought away before the tightness begins to form in my chest. If it gets in, it only grows throughout the day.

I nod at Kimmy. "You think I should tell her?"

Kimmy's voice is smooth and sympathetic when she answers, "I wish I could give you all the answers you need. You want things to go back to the way they were?"

"Of course. Yes."

"Then whatever you need to do to get there is probably the way you should go. Barring any illegal activities, of course," she jokes.

I offer up a smile because that's all I can do right now and say, "Okay. I'll think about it."

"As half of the Bathtub Cuties Club, I want to believe,

but this is just—"

"Nuts," I interrupt. "Believe me, I've spent the whole day contemplating a rubber room, coordinating outfits and everything. You'd be proud."

Kimmy's lips curve the slightest inch before she looks down at her shoes. She's ready to run. Only she's too kind to just run out on me. "I really have to go. This is a lot to process."

My stomach drops in disappointment, but I can't really blame her. She feels bad that her best friend has gone mental, and she doesn't know how to help. Who would?

I reach out to hug her and think better of it. "Of course. You know what, just forget I said anything. It's probably just the trauma catching up with me. I'm sure everything will go back to normal soon."

"I love you, you know," Kimmy tells me, offering me the hug she knows I need. I can tell by the way she squishes me close that she is more worried than she's showing. "We'll figure this out."

My stomach aches. I wish I never told her.

*You're not crazy.*

Oh yeah, that's a read comfort; the voice inside my head says I'm not crazy.

# SIX

MOM LEFT TO finish her choppy shift and with Kimmy gone, I decide to take the excuse to leave the house and head back to the grocery store.

This time I walk down the aisles with ease. Thank God because the store is much busier this time around. There are no voices, no hallucinations. I don't know what to call my outburst earlier, but I hope that it was a one-time thing and now I can move on. I pay for the groceries and realize I was practically holding my breath the whole time.

It's time to go and talk to my dad. I head west, to our favorite spot.

No weird voices or strange visions are allowed where I'm going—Fryer Lake. It's the place I usually end up when things get rough in my life. So many great memories are waiting to comfort me. We don't have much in the small town of Crater's Edge, but we love what we do have.

Most of the time I feel fortunate to live in a town where I can stroll a few blocks to enjoy the majesty of nature; it takes me only about fifteen minutes to reach the lake, even with stitches slowing me down. The scent of nature is the strongest here. The flow of the water slapping at the rocks on the shore is music to my ears, calming in a way that nothing else can be. Sunshine tickles the water, creating a diamond effect as the waves ripple closer, calling out to me, forcing a trickle of hope to bubble up inside me.

Removing my socks and sneakers and wedging them in the sand, along with our dinner groceries, I seek refuge at the peaceful shoreline and forget about the pain in my abdomen. Nearby, birds practice their lullabies and explore the skies surrounding me. I don't know what they're called, but they're small with red-tipped wings and dainty faded-yellow beaks.

"I wish you were here, Dad," I say, hoping that wherever he is he can hear me. "This year has been really tough without you. I wish I could hear your voice and get some advice."

The dreadful anniversary is a black spot on my otherwise perfect retreat. This could be a very big part of why my mind is slipping. It might even explain why I've been having nightmares and visions of this good-looking guy who is frightened, anxious, and—if my nightmares mean anything—dead as a doornail.

You've survived worse than this, I tell myself. No matter what happens, you won't go down without a fight. Dad would want it that way. 'Go out swinging,' as he always said.

The water beckons me, silently offering its healing services. Since my sneakers are already buried somewhere behind me, I give in to the call. Sitting on the nearest rock, I slip my first foot in the cool water, slosh around, and then dip in the second. The autumn weather is warmer than usual. I'm grateful just to be here at all right now.

Gavin's voice no longer sounds in my head. How about that? The lake is working its magic.

Happy memories wash over me as I splash my feet in the cool water, like when Dad and I used to camp out underneath one of the trees in a sleeping bag. I remember feeling safe and loved.

"I wish you'd never gone into that stupid store." A tear dribbles down my cheek. "Life isn't the same without you."

I was about five years old when my dad first taught me to fish. I can still see the bright smile on his cheeks as he showed me how to toss out the line. He stood in front of me, blocking the hot sun though he was off to the side — probably because he didn't want to get a hook in the butt when I threw my line out. He held his favorite fishing pole out to the river. Occasionally he would turn and smile down at me.

While he waited for a nibble, he was content, happy. "Why does this take so long? Where are the fish, Daddy?" I would ask.

He would laugh before he'd say, "Don't be so impatient, butterfly. It's okay to stop and enjoy yourself sometimes. Just let the fish come to you." He was always teaching me, always willing to listen. And he never judged.

I didn't understand what he meant then. It didn't hit me until he was gone.

That was the day I decided to take every moment, every memory I ever shared with him—happy or sad, good or bad—and hold them close as if they were tiny, precious baby birds.

Automatically, my fingers slip to the butterfly pendant that he gave me for my tenth birthday.

The emotions running through me soon become more than I can handle. I reluctantly leave my sanctuary and stray slowly toward my house. The hair on the back of my neck warns me of an invisible danger, and I can't seem to shake the feeling of being watched. "You think too much," Kimmy would have reminded me if she were here right now.

Because of the ominous feeling, I quicken my pace and groan aloud when I realize I forgot the stupid groceries in the sand. I turn around and see a man watching me. He's got dark red hair cropped closely to his head and tiny red ears, as if he's embarrassed about being caught watching me. The man nods, shoves his hands in his blue jacket, and walks right by me. I almost say something to him and I'm glad I don't because even after the man is gone, I still feel like I'm being watched.

The goosebumps on my neck follow close behind as I make my way home. I turn back and still see nothing out of the ordinary, which offers me a short respite from my paranoia. Despite it, my heartbeat screams a terrible warning. I can ignore the goosebumps, but I can't ignore my racing heart.

When I finally reach my front door, I unlock it, barrel in, and slam it shut, only breathing a sigh of relief when I turn the lock and the deadbolt shoots out.

The scent of lavender flowers calms my heated lungs. Mom always puts them in the foyer on the table. She says, "They're meant to chase your troubles back outside." I realize that despite her lingering anger, Mom is still looking out for me.

I crack an eye open and look around. The flowers are exactly where I thought they would be, on the thin pine table that lines the left side of the foyer. I toss my keys into the purple flower bowl and realize Mom's keys aren't there. Great. I have the house to myself for once. My eye drifts to the stairs and to the walls lined with a white and blue striped wallpaper my mother always regretted. It now reminds me of the youth center, so I don't like it either. My room is just up those stairs, but I don't want to go there just yet. If mom isn't home, I might be able to sneak in a few minutes on the TV.

I head into the kitchen, inhaling deeply, and I toss the groceries on the counter. While attempting to ignore the sweat dripping down my neck, I skirt past the island and straight to the fridge for a tall glass of milk. The coolness of it soothes my esophagus. Mid-sip, Gavin's voice calls out again, *Don't freak out. I just want to talk. Please.*

I nearly choke on the substance. "What do you want from me? I cannot be a crazy person right now." I shout louder, slamming the glass on the counter, silently daring the voice to tell me different.

My heart skips a beat when a milky hand emerges from the remaining white liquid in my glass. By instinct, my hand reaches out and knocks the glass over. It slips over the edge of the counter and shatters loudly onto the ceramic tile floor. I jump back, narrowly avoiding the glass.

*Please don't be scared.* His voice shouts desperately.

"Stop it! Stop it! Go away!" Great. Now I'm yelling at the voice in my head.

His voice, persistent, calls out again, *Why won't you*

58

*listen to me? Don't be afraid. You're not going crazy, Marley.*

"Of course, you would say that," I yell and dash up the stairs to my room. I reach into my drawer and pull out the one electronic item Mom didn't take from me, my old silver iPod. It's got a few dents and scratches, but it should still work. My hands shake as I rush to turn it on. If there's a way out of this, I'm going to find it. I shove the earbuds in and let the music drown out Gavin's hollering.

If Gavin answers I don't hear it; I don't want to.

*I know you think you're crazy,* his voice shouts over an old *Beastie Boys* tune, *and I'm sorry to do this to you, but I'm running out of time. Please just...* There's a short pause, giving me the impression that he's gone again. If I've not already gone off the deep end, I am at least swimming in dangerous waters. *Marley, look me up on the internet. Remember, Gavin Slater. You'll see,* he says.

I'm not listening anymore, I tell myself as I run down the stairs to clean up the broken glass of milk on the floor.

Halfway down, an envelope magically appears on the steps. I jump back and nearly fall on my butt.

What is going on? Why is all this happening to me? Something caused me to lose my mind. But what?

I don't believe in magic. But how else could I explain this?

*Open it,* Gavin implores.

Forget that. I toss the letter back on the floor and walk away. If he wants me to open it, I shouldn't.

Then the logical part of my brain offers its opinion: ignoring the strangeness is not working. Maybe if I embrace the crazy and help Gavin, these things will stop happening. Or maybe, my worst fears will come true and life as I know it will be completely over.

Then the words Mom said yesterday come back to me. "One choice can change your destiny." I don't know if I want to run toward this destiny or run away, but the latter isn't working.

I slowly head back to where the letter fell — the middle of my mother's rug in the foyer — and pick it up. There, in black, bold lettering is my name. There's no return address on either side of the envelope. I tear it open. Inside is a flyer for the Wacky Room, a gaming house for kids.

Questions flood my mind, more questions I can't answer. Where did this come from? Why did it just appear out of nowhere? What the heck is going on?

# SEVEN

IT'S AROUND SIX when Mom gets home from work, done for the day—just in time for me to finish cooking dinner and start implementing my plan. If she's going to send me back to school, she has to trust me again. If she's going to trust me again, I have to start acting like the normal, *sane* daughter she raised. Starting now.

She drops her purse on the table by the front door as I walk into the foyer. "I made dinner. Hope you're hungry."

"Oh. That's what that wonderful smell is. Great, I'm starving." She doesn't look at me.

Her movements are slow and for the first time, I notice the dark circles under her eyes and chastise myself for not realizing what she must be going through. "I did all my chores today," I say, as if that will make up for everything.

"That's good." She kicks off her heels, walks by me, and makes her way to the kitchen.

"How was your day?"

She sighs. "Long. So long. Did you get your homework done?"

"Yes. All of it."

She opens the oven to see what I've got in there, takes a big whiff of the cheesy aroma, and closes the oven again.

"Mom, I know you said you'd think about it but I'm going crazy in this house. Can I please, please go back to school? I promise not to do anything stupid. I promise to help more around the house and I won't give you a hard time."

"Marley." She stiffens. "I just got in. It's been a long day."

Jumping on her as soon as she walks in the door was probably not my best idea, but the words just slipped out. I'm going stir crazy and hope that going back will give me something else to think about aside from voices and recurring nightmares. "Mom, please. This is my senior year. I cannot flunk out."

"The school year just started. You're not going to flunk." She walks over to the fridge and grabs a bottle of wine, ignoring my presence completely while she opens it and pours the velvety liquid into a glass. This is when I get a good look at her. Her hair is dishevelled, she's leaning forward and holding onto a lot of stress, and she has a run in her stockings.

"Bad day at work?" I ask, leaning against the cool countertop on the island.

"No, just long. How's your brother?"

"Fine. He's in his room, playing with his Legos."

She grabs her glass and turns away—I wish she'd stop doing that. At the door, she turns her head and says, "When you see Dr. Crystal tomorrow, ask her what she thinks of you going back to school. If she is okay with it, then I am. I want to see a note or get a phone call."

A compromise I can live with. And the only one I'm going to get.

"Thank you, Mom."

"Now, let's eat this meal you've cooked for us. I'll go and get Sammy. No more talk of school tonight."

I smile as I set the table, thankful for the slight hope she's given me.

FOR THE FOURTH night in a row I float above a graveyard, thinking I'm dead. Only tonight, after I plunge to the ground, I don't wake up.

I'm in a dark school gym. A torrent of shiny streamers overlay in a crisscross pattern above a vast hardwood floor and a basketball net hangs on the wall in front of me. There are streamers hanging on either side of it. Behind the net is a school banner—its swirly font out of focus from this distance—and an abandoned punch bowl table is set up in the far corner. The room reeks of alcohol and too much perfume. I wince and breathe through my mouth.

A man appears in front of me, dark eyes and an unkempt beard. Shadows cling to his face, making it difficult to see his features. His lips purse with a mix of fear and anger, and they are all I can see. "Who are—" My words jam in my throat when I see his shaking hand and the tiny, metallic grim reaper aimed in my direction. He can't hurt me, right? A gun cannot kill me. So, why am I shaking then?

I'm frozen in fear. Could this be how I died? I wonder. Did this creep shoot me? The man grumbles something unintelligible and a deafening pop echoes throughout the empty gym. I smell something burning as lead tears through my skin, knocking me back, viciously shredding muscle and tissue until it reaches a wall it can't tear through, lodging into a rib. At first, it's so hot that it feels cold. Then all I feel is empty. My heartbeat slowly fades beneath my bloody fingers as I clutch at the hole in my chest.

My life doesn't flash before my eyes; it doesn't even flicker. This is it? After nearly eighteen years in this world all I get is pain? A tear slips from my right eye.

There is no more pain, no more suffering.

Death is slow, but when it finally comes, I nearly welcome it.

Another scene scoops me up. Gavin is looking into a mirror. There's worry in his eyes. I feel bad for him, even though he's been practically terrorizing me. I can't help it; it's his eyes. They get to me.

A soft, comforting female voice echoes in the background. She calmly assures the boy that everything will be all right. "We are going to fix this together," she tells him. "It will all work out. You'll see, my boy."

He nods at the mirror, hopeful. Then a pool of dark red liquid oozes from his chest. His white t-shirt sponges up each drop. Gavin's horrified, and I realize he's the one who died, not me. It's been his death I've been experiencing in my nightmares. That's why there were a bunch of strangers at the cemetery—his family, not mine. Why am I dreaming of Gavin's death repeatedly? I've never laid eyes on the guy. How did he manage to find me, a small-town girl with her own problems?

I wake up in my bed and swipe at the tears running

down my cheeks as I sit up. I cannot believe I've been dreaming about Gavin's death this whole time. I hope that these nightmares aren't real, that Gavin didn't have to go through those things, even though I know differently in my gut.

I head into the bathroom to brush my teeth, wincing at the bright light coming through the window before I catch sight of the fright that is my hair. A light laugh bubbles from my chest. That's right. Because what else can I do but laugh? Apparently, the small bit of hope that dream gave me has lifted my spirits a little, which is just what I need.

As I brush at the knots on my head it occurs to me that I still have to figure out what to do about Gavin.

That's when mom's light tone calls from the bottom of the stairs, "Marley, would you like pizza or Chinese for dinner tonight?"

Takeout? That means I'll be stuck babysitting again. "What time are you working till?" I call out, peeking through my bedroom door.

"Should only be until eight or nine. I'm sorry, sweetie."

I groan and head downstairs.

Can't go to school, but I can spend my senior year babysitting my little brother. Just because of one unexplainable incident. How can I work through my issues with my little brother around all the time? "I can't go to school, but you trust me to babysit Sammy all the time."

Oh no. Why did I say that?

Mom's eyes crinkle. Her lips purse. Great, now I've done it. She turns to make sure Sammy isn't in the room. Mom lowers her voice. "Marley, we've had this conversation. I know you would never. . ." she pauses, as if searching for the right words. "We'll talk later."

"But I was hoping to go out tonight. It's been forever since I've done something fun."

Seriously? Why are these words flying out of my mouth? Why? I must really love being grounded. That was stupid. Now I've just pissed her off more; I can tell by the frown on her lips and the crease in her thin brows. "What do you want me to do, Marley? Stay home from work so you can go out with your friends?" I assume the question is rhetorical and bite my tongue—smartest thing I've done today. "Besides, you're grounded," she says as she points at me. "And you will continue to be until you tell me the truth."

"Lucky for me, you can't ground me until the end of time."

"Look, I'm sorry you feel like you have to watch your brother all the time." She rubs her temple, annoyed. "I really appreciate your help this last year. Believe it or not, I'm sorry it's been so hard on you."

I cross my arms, trying not to pout. "Okay." I may not believe a word she is saying right now, but at least she's talking to me. What can I say to get out of it, anyway? She's grounded me, and my not-so-healed stitches prevent me from defying her.

Stupid stitches.

"Well, despite your disappointed tone, I really do appreciate your help," Mom tells me.

My only thoughts are on this big problem and how I can get away from it. Will Mom even believe me if I tell her about Gavin? Probably not, but I decide I should. "Mom?"

She half-turns toward me with her hands on her hips. This time I see the impatience in her eyes.

"Never mind."

I can't bring myself to say the words. I know exactly what she'll say: "It's the stress of losing your father and almost dying yourself. It's making you see things..." Blah, blah, blah. "Tell your shrink when you see her." I don't have the heart or the stomach to listen to another lecture. Besides, I can say the same things to myself. Unless she can offer me a solution, it's best that I keep my mouth glued.

"I'll leave you the money and you order what you want for supper," Mom tells me as she moves past my sullen form. She looks down at her watch and adds, "I have to finish getting ready and hurry into the clinic. I have a patient coming in for a check-up, but I'll be home after. I can do my paperwork from home."

"Dr. Casanova is okay with you coming home all the time?"

"I told you not to call him that." Mom huffs. "And yes, Dr. Cassava knows I need to be with my family right now."

"You don't have to watch me. I'll be fine."

She ignores me. "I've got a meeting tonight, so I'll grab something to eat at work," she says before picking up her bag, setting it down in front of the door, and heading back upstairs.

The conversation done, my mind turns to the most important item of the morning: coffee. Its potent aroma is wafting from the kitchen. A strong, bitter jolt to get me through the day.

"Mom says you're watching me after school," Sammy mumbles, while stuffing his face with cereal as I walk into

67

the kitchen.

I snatch a mug and pour. "Looks like."

His big blue eyes look up at me, hopeful. "So, it's up to you if we go to the Wacky Room for dinner?"

The Wacky Room? The pamphlet pops up into the front of my mind. "Oh no. Anywhere but the Wacky Room."

"Wacky Room," the kid demands.

"Come on, munchkin. There's got to be another place you want to go to." I hope.

"Nope. Wacky Room," Sammy says, adamantly.

"But I'm grounded." And I don't want to ever go there again since that stupid flyer magically appeared on my stairs.

"Can we go? Please?" he begs, putting both hands together as if in prayer as he bounces up and down in his seat.

How can I say no to that face? Mirroring his actions, I say, "If it's okay with Mom, I'll take you after school."

"I asked her. She said I can go. But *you have to come straight home after.*" he mimics our mother's tone, which nearly has hot coffee shooting out my nose.

"It's almost time for school, munchkin. I'm driving you today. We should get going."

I hear the front door close and know that my mother has finally left.

Sammy whoops, wipes his mouth with his sleeve, and runs out of the room laughing. I've always admired his energy. What I wouldn't give to be six years old again. Not a care in the world.

Grabbing my keys off the counter, I make my way to the front door, where I snatch my purse from its hook.

Mom left the money on the end table by the door. Shoving the bills in my purse, I head out to my clunker of a car. It's old and it smells like pineapples, but it's mine.

After Dad died, Mom made sure I got my license. Two drivers for one house makes things a lot easier; only now, she struggles with two car payments since someone stole and totaled my dad's car and insurance only covered a down payment on another one. Over the summer, she lets me work part time. During the school year, I'm not allowed. "For two reasons," she'd said. "It's easier for you to help me with your brother when I have to work and second, I don't want your grades suffering."

*Like that matters now.* It's nearly impossible to keep my grades up when she won't let me go to school. One day she'll have to trust me again.

I hope.

Sammy rushes out of the house just as I open the driver's side door and hop behind the wheel. My music kicks on as the car starts. As always, my brother reaches up from the backseat and cranks the volume all the way to the left. He doesn't like my taste in music. The only thing he will let me listen to is Canadian music—any artist with any type of music, but they *have* to be Canadian. From *George Canyon* to *McLachlan* to *Drake*.

"*Marianas Trench*." Sammy shouts, interrupting my thoughts.

"I know. CD 6. You might want to turn it back up. And then you need to buckle up."

*So, he only listens to Canadian artists and you listen to everything but?* Gavin's voice pops up, making my heart bounce.

*And you like to pop up out of nowhere just for kicks,* I think

69

to myself.

The voice responds, *Hey, I'm dead. I gotta entertain myself somehow.*

*Sure, you do.* I can't believe a whopping fifteen minutes had passed where I had forgotten my unwanted guest. Kissing that peaceful moment goodbye, I pull out of the driveway. At least he's honest, I think.

I pull up to Sammy's school minutes later. *And that's not true. I like some Canadian bands. I like Marianas Trench, and they're from Vancouver.* Oops. I probably shouldn't talk to the voice in my head—not on purpose. To Sammy, I say, "Meet me right here after school, okay?"

"Yep," he answers, jumping out of the backseat and barely acknowledging me.

"Enjoy your day," I call, amused because he's already stopped listening to me.

*Boys,* Gavin declares.

Turning the music down, I tell the empty car, "All right, Chuckles. How do I get rid of you?"

He responds, more soberly, *I need your help.*

"Uh, right." *I think I got that much, but how?* "How do I know any of this is real?"

No answer.

Is he gone?

# EIGHT

*Monday, October 22nd*

SITTING WITH MY shrink is the worst place for me to be with everything going on, I tell myself as I get off the elevator on the seventh floor. The walls are the color of dog poop, but other than that the beige carpet is clean. There's a tall plant outside a clear office door that names it the office of Dr. Hannah Crystal, Therapist.

I push the glass door and a receptionist puts up her pointy finger as she talks on the phone. "Yes, that's right. We can reschedule for next week at the earliest."

The wait leaves me time to peruse the doctor's office some more. The walls are a better color in here, a soft rusty shade. She has glass furniture and two couches along the wall for patients. Is she that busy?

There are magazines neatly piled in the corner, beside a matching plant to the one just outside the office.

"Marley McCartney?" I hear.

I turn and meet the secretary's gaze. She's got grey eyes behind square red glasses and her thin lips are curved into what I believe is her best 'welcome' smile.

"Yes."

"Dr. Crystal will be out in one minute. Please have a seat." She waves at the seating area, just in case it wasn't entirely obvious where I should go.

Dr. Crystal's door opens almost exactly a minute later. My first impression of her is a positive one, despite my overwhelming fear that she's going to pull me from my family. She's tall, especially in her three-inch heels. She is a perfectly coiffed woman, thin and with perfect posture that I'm almost jealous of. She makes me feel like a leper. There's a shadow behind her dark eyes; she hides it with a smile. "Marley, welcome. Please come in."

Her smile almost makes me feel at ease. I just need to go in there and pretend to be sane for one hour. Sixty minutes. This shouldn't be too difficult.

Her office is much like the outer part. Crisp, clean. There's a matching sofa in here. It's a really big office. I nearly say as much, but I'm dreadfully terrified of saying the wrong thing. So, I sit on the dark sofa, sitting nearly as straight as the doctor.

I resist the urge to fidget as she picks up a notepad and pen from beside her; she doesn't need ammunition to steal me from my family and lock me away. If she had a crazy radar gun, I have a sneaking suspicion I'd already be strapped in the back of a white van and on my way back to the youth centre, Looney Tunes for Teens—that's not the name but it sounds so much better than the real one.

For the first fifteen minutes of the session, I say nothing, only stare around the cold, dark office. I learn small things about the woman who is supposed to *fix me* as I search. Her furniture is walnut and antique, with carvings of flowers and leaves. She keeps each piece in pristine condition. There aren't any knickknacks or keepsakes of any kind. I suspect that they would attract too much dust for her taste. On the walls are a few diplomas and a degree from Stanford; they're nestled in plain, oak frames and I'm guessing they're perfectly level.

How is this woman supposed to fix me when she clearly has her own issues? Did my mother even meet with this woman before she sentenced me to hours upon hours with her?

I continue my survey of the room. It's not a stall tactic, I promise myself, knowing different. She has large blinds that are open only to let in a soft light. I see a soft sprinkle of dust combing the air as the sun shines in, the only evidence that this woman isn't perfect. The only newer piece in the room is her metallic, oval-shaped desk planted by the far window. I wonder what the story is behind it, but I don't ask. It's not important.

A hint of vanilla mists the air around me. I didn't notice she had a potpourri jar at first. This brought my eye to her bookshelves, which are also in perfect condition.

The impeccable room matches the doctor's flawless appearance: her knee-length black-and-white dress is elegant and perfectly pressed, hugging at her curves. Kimmy would probably love her taste. She has her light hair tied back, not a strand out of place. Even her teeth are bleached white and flawless. I don't need to be a psychiatrist to know that this woman needs to be in control.

Dr. Crystal watches me as I peruse her office, though she doesn't speak. I wonder what she's thinking. No matter what I do in here it feels like the wrong thing. If I don't talk, I can't step on a verbal landmine.

Regardless of what I think of this process and the fact that I'm forced to be here, I need Dr. Crystal on my side if I am ever going to be able to go back to school and see my friends. I only wish I knew what to say to make that happen.

"Tell me, Marley, how are you feeling today? You seem a bit…" She pauses, as if thinking of the right word. "Distracted."

"No, I'm okay. A little tired, I guess."

"Have you not been sleeping properly?"

I shake my head, desperately batting away any glimpses of my vicious nightmares. "I was hoping to go back to school, but my mother doesn't think I'm ready."

The cliched psychiatrist response follows, "Why do you think that is?"

My annoyed teenage response slips out before I can stop it, "Because I don't sleep. Because she's angry with me. Because she's afraid I'll hurt myself at school. It could be any one of those reasons. I don't know. All I know is that I'm falling behind in every subject and I don't want to be the only one of my friends who doesn't graduate."

"You *should* go back to school," she states, shocking me. My heart flutters. Wow, that was easy. I smile, feeling a little hope. "But I need to make sure that you won't harm yourself or anyone else." My excitement quickly flutters out of the room like a deflating balloon. "*If* you can convince me that you're not a danger, I can make sure that you get back to school."

"I'm not," I insist. "Sorry. That was loud." Yelling at her isn't going to get her to convince my mother to let me leave the house. I summon a polite smile, even though I want to shout in frustration. Now I'm a danger to others? "I didn't hurt myself and would never hurt anyone else."

"If that's the case, talk to me. If you can show me you are willing to work with me, I'll tell your mom it's safe for you to go back to school. When we spoke on the phone it sounded like she was just as anxious as you are. I'm here to make sure you don't get overwhelmed and do something terrible."

"Like, try to kill myself?" I regret the words even as they're slipping off my tongue, and I can't take them back.

Dr. Crystal informs me, "I want to help you, Marley. Don't you think it's time we talk about why you were sent to me?"

"There's nothing to tell, really."

She looks at me, disappointed. Dr. Crystal is wasting my time, and I am wasting hers. But only one of us is getting paid to be here. The thought slips into my mind, but I don't want to make any more mistakes, so I force it back out again.

I try some honesty and tell her, "I don't remember anything about that day." I need her to help me get back to school, but I won't lie to do it. "Look, I'm sure you are really good at your job, but what happened was an *accident*. It had to be!" I blurt out. "My mom doesn't believe me. No one believes me."

Dr. Crystal mistakes my bitterness for resentment. "And have you given her a reason to?"

"What do you mean?"

The doctor's face is deadly serious when she replies, "Since you got out of the hospital, you've been distant with your mother, haven't you?"

A snort sneaks up my throat and splinters through my

mouth. "No." I think it over, mentally double checking my answer. "I don't think I have. I mean, I try to talk to her. She shut me out." Now I hear the resentment in my voice.

"Perhaps, your mother feels like you're pushing her away," Dr. Crystal suggests.

There's an awkward silence between us. I wish I knew what my mother was thinking so I could tell Dr. Crystal, but I don't.

*I think you're just fine,* his voice cuts through the barrier I've been trying so desperately to hold up.

*Stop it. I need to get through this meeting,* I say silently. *If you leave me alone, I promise I will at least listen to what you have to say, okay?*

I'm bribing the voices in my head now? If this is all real, I will never be able to bribe him. Whatever he is.

Crazy people cannot bribe the voices to go away.

"Marley?" Dr. Crystal interrupts my thoughts. "Are you all right? You look a little flushed?"

"No, I'm fine. What were we talking about?"

"We were talking about your mom. I was just saying it sounds like she needs a little more time to process what happened."

"Okay."

Dr. Crystal leans in. "Are you sure you're all right?"

Shake it off, Marley. Ugh. I'm trying to show this woman I am not crazy and I'm doing a bang-up job so far. "I'm sorry. Yes, I was just thinking of stuff. We have been through a lot lately, me and my family."

Dr. Crystal's eyebrows contract, barely causing a wrinkle on her flawless ivory skin. "I can't help you if you don't tell me what's going on."

"That's what I'm here for."

Dr. Crystal begins writing in her notebook. "I heard that your father passed away this time last year."

I nod when her eyes lift back up. I definitely don't want to talk about that right now. Or ever.

"And that made you feel devastated, angry, lost?" she asks.

I nod. "Sure. All those things. My dad and I were really close."

"Maybe we should start there, then." I don't like it, but I don't want to argue. "What is the last thing you said to your father?"

"Why does that matter?"

"It might not. If I'm going to help you, I might have to ask you questions that make you uncomfortable. My job is not glamorous and at times you might dislike me, but I really think I can help you." She offers a simple smile and her thin lips barely move. "Do you remember the last thing you said to him?"

"I said, 'Dad, please grab me a… a pack… a pack of gum.'" Those were the stupid, final words I said to my dad." Tears bubble up and sit in my lids.

"I'm terribly sorry. You know his death wasn't your fault, Marley."

I nod. A blurry tissue appears in front of me. I blink the tears away, trying to suck them back in. "Thank you. But if I hadn't asked him for a stupid pack of gum he might not have stopped at that store."

"You don't know that. Maybe he was going in for something else. Do you know where he was heading when he left?"

"Yes," I answer, dabbing at the cool teardrops still lingering. "He was supposed to go to a baseball game and

I was stuck at home babysitting my little brother."

Dr. Crystal writes in her notebook without looking down at the page. This kind of weirds me out. Should I just continue to talk? Wait until she stops and looks up at me, as is polite? I don't want to be here anyway, but if I can't talk to her then I'll be stuck here forever.

That is *not* an option. I have to get my freedom back. Even if that means I have to practically talk to myself, I guess that's what I'm going to do. I continue to talk. "My mom had to work. Back then, she only worked part-time. I should have gone with my dad. I always went to games with him. But I had an exam to study for and Sammy isn't into sports."

"If you two had gone with your dad, you and Sammy might have been hurt, too. Your father would not have wanted that."

"No, he wouldn't."

"How are your grades in school?"

"Pretty good. I get decent grades," I answer, stuffing the wet tissue into my jacket.

"And what about your friends? Do you have a lot of them? Boyfriend?"

I shake my head. "No boyfriend, not anymore. We broke up weeks ago. I have a few close friends. We've all been friends for years."

"Would you have a hard time convincing them that you didn't harm yourself?"

"No," I answer instantly. "My friends would believe me because I don't lie to them. And they know me the best."

Dr. Crystal nods. "Before I make my decision about school, I have a couple more questions."

I stiffen, prepared to run out of this office if necessary. No, be cool, Marley. Stay calm. You're doing good. "I'm ready," I tell her. How much worse can they get?

"Is there anything you remember at all from the day of the accident? A small fragment, anything."

I shake my head.

Dr. Crystal shifts in her seat, lifting the left leg over the right. She nods. "You were alone? There was no evidence that someone had broken in?"

"I don't think so. If there was my mom wouldn't be so mad at me."

She doesn't acknowledge that I spoke. "Marley, I need you to give me a straight answer when I ask you this. I won't judge. This is a safe space," she pauses and leans back. "Did someone tell you to hurt yourself? Do you hear voices?"

"Voices?" My heart rate rises as I feign shock, though it's easy. I didn't think it was that obvious. It takes a moment for me to talk since my mouth has gone completely dry. "No. I don't remember a thing from that day though, so I can't answer for sure. I haven't heard anything since then." I cross my arms and unfold them again, so she can't accuse me of being angry.

I get the impression she's suspicious of my answer when she narrows her eyes. "Anything you say in here is protected by doctor-patient confidentiality. You can tell me anything and it stays between us. I need you to know that."

Yeah, right. And I'm dumb enough to believe that line. "I'm sorry," I answer. "There is absolutely nothing to tell you. I'm doing everything requested of me. I came here. I'm talking to you. But I will not lie." Even though I *am* lying. I'm lying to Dr. Crystal, my mom, and Sammy. I'm such a hypocrite. Even though I'm lying purely for my family, it feels selfish, wrong. Mom and Dad would be so disappointed in me.

"You think I'm the bad guy here and I'm only trying to help you, Marley."

Now I feel stupid. "I know, and I appreciate it. The only way my life is going to go back to normal is if I can convince my mom of my innocence and I don't know how to do that."

"I certainly think that your relationship with your mother is a big part of this and I'll help in any way I can." She closes her notebook, looks at the clock. I notice that I've still got fifteen minutes left. "I think we've covered a lot in your first day. Why don't you head out? I'll see you in a couple days."

I have to force myself not to run out of the office and over to the elevator. I'm replaying the session as I make my way to my car. How can I prove my innocence?

Once I'm in my car, I decide to use the extra fifteen minutes I'd gained when she let me go to drive through town and appreciate the fall foliage—a calming exercise. The fall colors, the last of the flowers blooming, the bright sun beaming on the hood of my car, the kites in the park, flying freely in the breeze.

The drive helps me forget how my life was turned upside down nearly a year ago *and* that it's happening all over again. Staring ahead, I press down on the gas pedal and block out everything. The sights and the scents are familiar to me, but the pull of the gas pedal underneath my foot is all I care about.

The frightening events of the past few weeks fly out

the window as the car rockets down the road. Maybe I should just run away to Mexico—or Canada. I envision losing myself in the woods or running wildly with a herd of caribou, but quickly shake the vision from my head. Running away from problems never works; plus, some of my problems are *literally* inside my head.

Besides, I left my passport at home.

When I pull up to the house, my mother is waiting at the front door. "Dr. Crystal called. I expected you fifteen minutes ago."

Apparently, the confidentiality thing starts after office hours. "Sorry. I had to take a drive. It's stuffy in that woman's office. Fifteen minutes isn't the end of the world, is it?"

"That's not the point, Marley. I need to trust you. That's never going to happen if you don't talk to your doctor and come home when you're told to."

"Fine, Mom."

It still surprises me to know that she doesn't trust me anymore. I've never had that problem before. Desperation kicks in. I have no idea where to start to mend our relationship, but I have to get my mother to trust me again.

"Dr. Crystal said you could go back to school," Mom says as she walks into the house and away from me.

Along with my skepticism comes a tightness in my chest and an increase in pulse. Did she just say I could go back to school and walk away like it was nothing?

When Mom's out of earshot a squeal flies up my windpipe. I'm going back to school? But didn't Dr. Crystal just say I couldn't? That she needed to know I wouldn't hurt anyone? I didn't think she would let me go back so quickly. Never mind the reason; I'm not asking questions.

Mom sighs as I walk into the house, jerking me back into the present. "I'm heading back to the clinic. I want you to stay home until you have to pick Sammy up. Is that clear?"

"Crystal."

"Have the leftover pasta for lunch if you want," she informs me on her way out the door.

I toss my keys in the flower bowl and decide I could eat. I head to the back of the house, into the kitchen, and toss the leftovers into the microwave. I listen to the faint beep of each button and let my mind wander.

The loud beep of the microwave shakes me from my thoughts, reminding me of my hunger. As I reach for a fork, I see Gavin again. The boy from my nightmares. Right in front of my face.

No visions, no voices. This time his face is plastered on the front page of the newspaper. His big brown eyes seem full of happiness—so unlike what I've seen in my dreams or visions. Gavin has a wide grin with a mischievous air and dimples to magnify his troublemaker expression. Once I see his name in print, it's hard to deny the truth—he's real.

Even worse, he's dead. A dead boy is talking to me. This is all real. I have to sit down. I can't believe this is all real.

But what am I supposed to do with this fact? It doesn't really change anything.

There's a split second where I think it's odd Mom got the newspaper since she reads it on her tablet and then I read the article about Gavin.

Confirming my suspicions, I read the headline twice: "TRAGEDY STRIKES LOCAL HIGH SCHOOL DANCE."

*Police were called to a disturbance at Billy Sans High School Friday night, where they found seventeen-year-old Gavin Slater bleeding from a gunshot wound to the chest. Slater died before paramedics could revive him, just before 9p.m.*

*Slater, known as ambitious, outgoing, and caring to his friends and family, was attending a high school dance when a deranged man broke into the school and held several students' hostage in the gym. Slater acted bravely and lost his life saving a fellow student.*

*Although the man is still on the loose, police are confident they will be able to find Slater's killer quickly.*

*If anyone has any information…*

I stop reading.

If all this is true, why is he talking to me from beyond the grave? Why did he pick me? Why is he driving me batty and not someone else? What makes me so special?

*In my defense, I tried to get you to look up my name before,* Gavin tells me. *But you're one stubborn girl.*

I don't laugh at his joke as I tuck the paper under my arm. I grab my steamy bowl, and rush to my room, closing the door quietly behind me before I huff, "Cut me some slack. It's not every day that someone hears a dead person in their head." I try to pause and think things through. I can't. My mind is frozen on the fact that this whole thing is real. "This is all true. I can't believe it."

Gavin's voice echoes in my mind, *the good news is, you're not crazy. Bad news is, this dead guy needs your help.*

"Why me?"

*It has to be you. You're the only one who can save me.*

"Save you? I don't even know you. Why me?" I repeat. "Wait. How can you hear me if you're dead?"

*It's hard to explain, but if we hurry and do this right, there's a chance I can have my life back.*

I stare down at Gavin's school picture. His blond hair is tousled, like he'd been outside playing football just before the picture had been taken. A broad smile brightens his large, puppy-dog brown eyes. The dimples on his cheeks paint a clear picture of a mischievous teenage boy. I smile. "You think I'm the only one who can save you? Again, why me?"

*You and I are linked.*

# NINE

THE DOOR SLAMS downstairs, making my pulse jump. "Marley, Kimmy's here. Make it quick."

I didn't even know my mother was home again. We need to have a revolving door installed. She's always coming and going, it seems.

I bookmark my philosophy textbook and close it. I can't believe Kimmy's here. I thought getting permission to go back to school was good, but this is so much better. After yesterday, I figured she wouldn't be talking to me anymore. She's only here to see if I'm still hearing voices, she must be. That thought makes me sad—despite the fact that I know that's not possible.

Maybe I should tell her what I found out. My best friend in the whole world believes I'm crazy. But how can I lie to her? I don't think I've *ever* lied to her.

My palms begin to sweat, and I wipe them on my jeans. I only wish that Gavin hadn't disappeared from my head before he explained further.

I won't lie to her, I can't. Let her believe what she wants—I'm not lying. After fifteen years, she knows me better than anyone in the whole world. She'll have to understand that I am not going crazy. And if she doesn't, I have the proof. Snatching up the newspaper from my desk, I leave my room.

I hurry to the stairs and don't slow my pace on the way down. I throw my arms around Kimmy. She hugs me back, though it feels different.

I pull away, put my index finger to my lips, signaling for her to keep quiet and I whisper, "Let's talk in my room."

"And no, she can't go into your room," Mom knowingly shouts from her little office off the living room.

Busted.

That's two for Mom, and I still have zip.

Kimmy's face is blank. Normally, I can read her nearly as good as she can read me. Today feels different and I don't like it.

The only other option for us is to talk out on the back porch. It's far enough away from the office that we won't be overheard. I wave for her to follow me, check that the paper is still under my arm, and head down to the kitchen and through the patio doors.

Kimmy swallows loudly and clears her throat. I can tell she's worried, which always leads to annoyance. She greets me with: "Your homework." She pulls a stack of papers from her massive purse with unknown logo on it and plops them on a patio chair.

"English and geography?" I ask, turning to face the kitchen window so I can see if my mom is coming.

She nods and whispers, eyes looking toward the house. "I've been worried. That's why I came during lunch. How are you doing today?"

"Better. I'm sorry I said anything yesterday."

"You can tell me anything. You know that," she tells me. "You tell your therapist?"

"No." I give a stern head shake. "I don't *want* to tell anyone about it." I didn't even want to tell Kimmy. Steeling myself, I continue. "I've got some good news, though. I found out the boy I've been seeing and hearing actually does exist—well... did. He was murdered on Friday night. Look."

Kimmy takes the paper I shove at her. She eyes me suspiciously for a moment, as if weighing my sincerity. Finally, she looks down, reads, and turns back to me. "This is the boy? From the grocery store?"

"Yes."

"Ooh, he's a hottie." She stutters, "I mean, this whole thing is tragic."

I bob my head, not knowing which statement I'm confirming. "It's okay if you don't believe me. As long as *I know* I'm not insane, I think I can live with it."

Kimmy looks at me. "I want to believe. It's just... hearing voices? A classic case of Nuts-R-US, isn't it?"

"I don't think I'm insane, if that's what you mean. I certainly did two hours ago. And especially yesterday." I tell her, referring to the talk we had without saying so.

Kimmy sighs, then squeals. The newspaper I'd handed her hits the patio floor. I look up, following her horrified gaze to inside the house. She points, eyes wide, mouth agape. I turn to see Gavin's face reflected on the fridge's steel surface.

*You're scaring her,* I tell him, hoping he can hear me.

*I seem to have that effect on women lately.* His voice sounds weak and far away.

"I'm sorry, Kimmy," I say. "He seems to think he's cute."

*Hey!* he shouts, offended, his form vanishing from the shiny fridge. *I'm adorable.*

I ignore him. "Are you all right, Kimmy?"

She doesn't budge. "I—I..." Kimmy stutters.

"I know. It's hard to believe." She stares dumbfounded at the fridge and I fear she's broken. I can't blame her. When he first appeared to me and Taylor didn't see him, I freaked. "It's a lot to deal with," I tell her, "like you said. Just know that I'm not going insane and neither are you. I promise."

"I—" Kimmy doesn't finish her thought. Instead, she bends down to retrieve the newspaper, staring at Gavin's picture. "Why?" She clears her throat. "Why is he talking to you? What does he want?"

"You believe me?" I shout, not hiding my excitement.

"How could I not?" She points at the steel fridge. "No way you'd pull off a prank like that."

"Are you two almost done out there?" Mom calls.

"Almost," I call back.

We sit in silence for a moment. I don't want her to leave.

"I only have fifteen minutes to get back to school before English anyway." Kimmy tells me, turning to leave.

"Kimmy, are you okay?"

She looks at the fridge and then back at me. "I might be in a minute. Maybe. Still processing." She tilts her head slightly and nods toward the fridge. Before I can ask her to stay a couple more minutes she asks, "Any memories come back?"

I shake my head. "Not yet but they will. I don't quite

know how yet, but they will."

"Have you thought about it?"

"All the time."

"No, I mean, retraced your steps?"

"I've tried. Haven't remembered anything important. Like why in the world I would do such a thing. It's not like me at all."

"It's not," she agrees.

"Since we know I'm not going crazy, we should celebrate. Will you come to dinner with us? Sammy wants to go to the Wacky Room. You can bring Shawn. Just don't tell my mom," I whisper, looking through the window to see if she's anywhere close.

"Yeah, we'd love to. What time?"

"Five?" She nods. "Meet us here?"

"Okay."

"I'm sure you've had enough time to talk about homework, girls. Time to go, Kimmy," my mother demands from the kitchen doorway. "I'm sorry. I have to get back to work."

"Can I borrow this?" Kimmy holds the paper out to me. I nod, and she offers me a hug. "Hang in there. We'll get you through it," she whispers and walks back through the house, leaving me alone with my mother.

"What was she talking about? Get you through what?"

I shove my assignments into the crook of my arm and decide I'd rather be doing anything but talking to her. "All of it, Mom." I walk through the kitchen and to my room, gripping tightly to the tiny sliver of hope that Kimmy gave me. I can't let my mom ruin this. It's all I have right now.

*Gavin, are you there?* No answer. Maybe it's a one-sided connection. Maybe he needs to open it from where he is before we can communicate.

I have a couple hours to kill before I need to get Sammy at school, so I head back upstairs. Anywhere my mom is not is okay with me right now.

When I get to my room, I find another surprise waiting for me. My laptop and cell are sitting on my bed. I nearly throw myself onto them in excitement. Civilization. I'm a part of civilization again.

Mom wrote a note and left it in between the phone and laptop, to make sure I'd see it.

> *You can have the laptop for school work, but*
> *you're still grounded.*

She's coming around. "Yes!" She must be starting to trust me again. I cannot wait to catch up on social media. I miss the real world so much.

*I'm sorry I keep disappearing on you,* I hear Gavin say, as I check my Insta. *I'm only just learning to control my magic.*

"Magic?" I ask out loud.

*Yes. There's magic here.*

"I wish that didn't make sense to me, but after everything I've seen and heard this week, it does."

*I wanted to explain why I need your help.*

I reluctantly toss the phone aside and walk to my window, looking out at the beautiful fall day. "Great."

*There's a ritual you can perform that will bring me back.*

"What?" I shout, certain I heard him wrong.

*It's a lot to take in. I really wish I didn't have to put you through this, but I don't want to be dead.*

I shiver at the thought, as I try to wrap my head

around this news. "Sure. No one wants to be dead, but I can really bring you back to life?"

*Yes.*

A shadow draws my attention back into my room. It's Gavin. He's in my mirror. He's much calmer than the first time I saw him reflected through glass. I turn to him. He's such a good-looking boy. It's a shame he died so young. Though, if I believe what he's saying I can change that fact. "What do I have to do?"

*Follow the signs,* he tells me. I see his lips move in the mirror, though I still hear his voice echo in my head.

Gavin's reflection disappears and somehow, I know he's gone. This magic thing is extremely annoying.

KIMMY AND SHAWN arrive together. Shawn offers me a quick "hi" and a smile that makes creases appear by his deep hazel eyes. He bends his head down to kiss Kimmy on the top of the head before he disappears into the living room — off to play with Sammy, as always.

Kimmy turns to me. "He loves that little guy."

"I know."

"How's our new friend, Lee?"

"Still dead. Still not happy about it."

"And?" she pushes.

"Long story. Basically, I'm going to do some kind of ritual to bring him back to life."

Kimmy's eyebrows shoot into her forehead. "Bring him... what?" She looks more shocked than I was. "Why didn't you tell me this sooner?"

"Because I just found out. Besides, it's a lot to handle and I knew you'd freak out. I know I did, at first."

She shakes her head. "Fine. You're right." She stares off into space a moment. Then suddenly, she thinks of something and asks, "He's been dead since Friday, right?"

I nod.

"How does the ritual work, exactly? If he's been gone that long, he will be… his body will be…" She doesn't say the words. I follow her train of thought, though.

"I don't know how that works. Maybe the ritual will fix any…decay?" I stumble on the word, too.

"I hope so."

"Check this out." I reach into my pocket, revealing the envelope that had appeared earlier.

She looks down as if she expects it to jump out of my hands. "What is this?"

"I have no idea," I admit. "It just appeared."

Kimmy's eyes go wide. "Appeared? Should I ask?"

"Appeared. It wasn't there, and then it was. I might not have believed it if I hadn't seen it with my own eyes."

She looks at the envelope skeptically and reluctantly asks, "What's it for?"

"I'm not entirely sure."

*It's a sign that will lead you to your first ingredient. For the ritual to bring me back,* Gavin answers.

"Oh, that explains it," I mutter aloud, still not entirely used to communicating telepathically. "Gavin says it's for an ingredient. This will apparently lead me to it."

Kimmy looks down at the paper and up again. "So, he just appears in your head?" Kimmy doesn't realize she's done it, but she points to my head.

"Yeah, it seems like. I haven't gotten used to it yet."

"This is too weird. I'm sorry. I'm trying to be a good friend, but…"

"What you're doing is great. At least I have someone to talk to about it."

She nods. "What's taking the boys so long?"

"They're probably talking about a video game. You know them."

We both stand in the hallway, patiently waiting.

"How does this work exactly?" Kimmy questions. "Can he hear what you're saying?"

"Gavin? I'm not sure how it works, but yes, sometimes he can. I don't think he can keep the connection open very long. So, he's not here all the time."

"How does he do it?"

"He never said." My dreams flutter to the forefront of my mind and something dawns on me. "I think it has something to do with mirrors."

Kimmy sighs and shifts away from me. "This is too weird."

"Tell me about it."

"We still going to the Wacky Room?"

I nod, trying not to think about the magical envelope. "That's the plan. My brother's looking forward to this. Oh, and I found a present in my room," I happily add. "My mother has decided I can have my electronics back."

"Yay! Lee's back on the grid." She does a funny dance, swaying her hips like Shakira and raising the roof at the same time.

I roll my eyes, although laughter bubbles up despite myself. "Your inner dork is showing again."

Kimmy dramatically pretends to shove said dork back into her pocket.

Sammy and Shawn stroll in. Sammy's face is lit up like its Christmas morning. "Let's go. Let's go."

I snatch my keys, and we all head out. Sammy and Shawn huddle in the back seat of my car so they can talk about the games they're going to play before supper. Sammy will play basketball and baseball with Shawn only, but his all-time favorite: the one where they smack at animals as they pop up.

Kimmy and I only roll our eyes and laugh.

The first thing that hits me when I arrive is the smell. The wonderful aroma of fast food sucks me in like a bar calls an alcoholic. Children run around, screaming and playing with their toys. They toss basketballs, shoot toy guns, click at pinball games, and some are eating with their families. The air is warm on my skin, so I remove my jacket. That magical envelope might have freaked me out, but I am really happy to just be out of the house.

Shawn and Sammy disappear into a sea of people. I've been expecting as much. They'll show up when they're hungry.

"Ski ball?" Kimmy asks.

"I've got money." I pull cash out of my pocket. "Let's get some tokens."

After nearly an hour, we each have a handful of tickets. Ski ball has always been a favorite of mine. I used to stand here and rack up tickets by the handful. Sammy had a lot of stuffed animals as a baby. Shawn and Sammy find us at a table shortly after. "I'm hungry," Sammy informs, slapping his wad of tickets in front of me.

"All right, munchkin. Here are your tickets," I say, placing my ticket bunch on top of his. "We can get you a prize after you eat."

His eyes light up when he sees the chain of tickets I won for him. Kimmy passes hers over to Shawn—who then passes them over to Sammy.

After we eat our dinner, Sammy wants to look at prizes while Kimmy and Shawn go off together to decide on a game to play. Sammy is picking out a silver toy gun and a sheriff's badge when Kimmy comes up, out of breath and says, "Look what I won."

I look at the sheet. It's got a gold vase with two handles that nearly gleam back at me and a list of names. The trophy begins to shine brightly, as if by magic.

"Look where I'm at," Kimmy tells me.

I read. "Second place. Wow."

She laughs. "And look where Shawn is at."

He comes up behind her and claps his hands on her shoulders. "Ha-ha, it's not that funny."

"It's hilarious," Kimmy exclaims. "He got fourth," she pretends to whisper back to me.

I smile, though I no longer hear what they're saying as I understand what I'm supposed to do now. I know why the pamphlet appeared at my house.

"Lee? You okay?" I hear Kimmy ask.

"So, no matter where you finish, they give you a trophy?"

Kimmy and Shawn both go wide-eyed. "Well, certificate, but yeah."

"This could work. I like it."

*You're onto something, love.*

Kimmy and Shawn look more confused than before. So, I tell Kimmy, "I have to do this. For you know who," I whisper.

Once we get there, Sammy stands underneath the sign

95

that asks if you are tall enough to go in.

"You're an inch short, little man," a girl in a black, turquoise uniform tells him.

"It's just one inch," I complain.

"Rules are rules. It's about safety, you know?" she says, "you know" like she doesn't give a damn about the rules, and it ticks me off.

Focus, Marley, I tell myself. "Maybe I can come back another time," I say to Kimmy.

"No. I'll sit with Sammy. You go."

"Are you sure?"

She nods. Without saying anything, I understand that she wants all the magic stuff to stop, too. If I do this, it might.

Kimmy hands the girl enough tokens for me and Shawn. "Show her how to play, would you?"

Shawn nods and offers Kimmy a kiss. My stomach is spinning with anxiety, even though I know I'm guaranteed a trophy for my efforts.

Gavin says, *You're doing great so far. Better than I could have hoped for. Some people don't believe in this stuff until it's too late.*

*Dreadful,* I answer. *Hopefully one day you can explain more about how this works, like how you keep popping into my head without me knowing you're there.*

*Love to. Soon,* he tells me. *Just try to have some fun and be careful. Don't go popping any stitches on my account.*

Laughter spills out. *I'll try not to.* Shawn looks at me sideways but doesn't say anything.

*And thanks for doing this,* Gavin says.

*I just hope there are no nasty surprises in my future,* I tell him, heading into the gunroom.

He responds, *Me too.*

Shawn and I pick the blue team. Five other people dress in blue and yellow vests.

"Any advice?" I ask.

He whispers before we begin, "If you see a target that's framed in yellow hit it as many times as you can. And," he adds, "don't get shot."

A buzzer goes off.

Shawn signals he is going to the left and that I should go to the right. I don't hesitate; finger on the trigger, I follow his directions. It's brighter than I'd first thought it would be and higher up. The "battlefield" is two floors. The ceilings have to be at least thirty feet high. Passing by a yellow target, I shoot. A video game buzzer blares repeatedly and very loudly. Once I am done, I decide to switch to offense. Every time someone with a yellow vest comes near me, I aim at them as I duck behind the first thing I can find, attempting to stop myself from being lasered.

The noise reminds me of the casino games I've seen on TV. I duck to the left and hammer to the right, searching for the enemy and enjoying every minute. A yellow vest tiptoes around the corner, and I shoot him before ducking quickly behind a short wall. He swears and takes cover behind a taller wall. My vest vibrates as the guy manages to get a shot in. I turn the corner, heading away from him.

I don't swear like he did. I just turn away from him before he can shoot me again.

Buzzing noises from the other guns ring throughout the maze. I keep turning corners, looking for yellow vests.

A blue vest appears above me, testing her luck on the second floor, and I nearly shoot her. Catching myself just in time, I give her a thumbs up and keep moving. I duck behind another wall as I realize Yellow Vest is following me. His footsteps are growing louder behind me. As he draws closer, I hide behind a brightly lit wall. When he gets close, I peer around the corner, weapon ready and shoot him a few times as I duck behind another wall. When my vest vibrates again, I run the other way, determined to lose the follower. His strategy seems to be to follow me and rack up his points on my vest.

No way will I let him. I lose him quickly by hiding behind a wall and heading in the opposite direction.

A few more minutes go by. I rack up a few more points. An announcement comes over the loudspeaker, "One-minute left."

With time left for only a few more shots, I find another yellow target. I aim my gun and hit the sign with a constant laser until it won't let me anymore. My gun makes jingle sounds, while I keep my eye open for the enemy.

This is the most excitement I've had in weeks. I'm breathing in big gulps, trying to slow my heartrate. *I'm so out of shape*, I think silently. The final buzzer sounds.

I hang the vest back in its place and tuck the gun on the rack as Yellow Vest comes into the room. He sees me and glares. What's his problem? I don't have time to ponder an explanation before Shawn comes around the corner. "Have fun?"

"I did actually."

He smiles and we make our way out of the maze. "Here is your trophy, Lee." Kimmy comes up beside me. She hands Shawn a piece of paper and shoves one into my hand.

"Thanks." I look down at the sheet and indeed, there's a trophy on it. Third place overall. Not too bad for an amateur. "It's perfect. Just what I needed."

This is easy. Maybe a little *too* easy.

*Your friend is right, you do think too much. I have faith in you,* Gavin tells me. *Just keep following the signs.*

*That makes one of us.*

*Oh,* he says, *you'll be fine. Just don't overthink it.*

"Everything okay?" Kimmy asks.

"Everything's fine. You three keep playing. I'm heading out for some air."

"What do you want to play next, buddy?" I hear Kimmy ask as I walk away, feeling like I've only just begun.

# TEN

THIS TIME WHEN I dream, it isn't of death or funerals. No sunny day. This time, the scene is much less disturbing and not at all painful. Thank God.

I am inside Gavin's head and seeing things the way he sees them. It's *his* death I've been seeing, his afterlife moments. Puzzle pieces seem like they're falling into place.

The dream begins with Gavin lying in bed, tossing a ball into the air, catch and repeat.

"Hey, you." A whisper catches Gavin's attention. "Over here." The small voice is from a young boy.

Gavin lifts his head from a fluffy pillow and searches the room for the intruder. At first, he doesn't see anyone, and I can tell because he does a second sweep of the room. Then I see him. Across the room, beside Gavin's tall black dresser there's a massive hole in the wall that hadn't been there before. At least, I don't think it was.

"Come with me. I want to show you something," the boy says, gesturing with his arm but not making his way out of the hole.

"Who are you?"

"I'm a friend. And I can help you if you let me." The boy waves him over again and lifts his small chin.

Sitting up in bed, Gavin hesitates to move. I would, too. I survey the boy's appearance as best as I can from this vantage point. A dark mop of hair explodes from the child's head, like fireworks falling from the sky, and he has an innocent smile, but that's all I can make out. Gavin moves closer and I can see the boy better. He has a thin nose between two large blue eyes and thin lips that are curved into a bright smile.

"Help me what?" Gavin demands, suspiciously.

The kid in the wall responds quietly, "Help you escape."

"Escape what?"

"You know."

I don't understand what's happening here. Who is this boy? Where did he come from? And why is he in the wall? "I don't know what you're talking about," Gavin admits.

Good. At least I'm not alone.

"I can help you get off this island. Escape *her!*"

"Circe, you mean?"

The boy nods.

"I don't need your help," Gavin insists. "Circe is helping me."

"But I can get you more power," the boy arrogantly informs him. "I can give you gold and riches."

"I don't need power or money. I just want to go home," Gavin insists.

A knock sounds on the door. Gavin looks toward the closed door for only a second. The boy is gone when he turns back. He'd disappeared just as fast as he had shown up, leaving no trace of his presence. Gavin touches the grey wall where the hole had just been. His hand touches solid drywall.

"Is everything all right?" A woman's muffled voice comes from the other side of the door.

Gavin calls out, "Everything's okay. Sorry if I woke you." His tone doesn't reveal the way he's feeling, at least I don't hear it. I can sense his confusion, but Gavin gives nothing away.

"May I come in a moment?"

Gavin looks from the white door to the wall and back. Rubbing his hands across his face, Gavin moves and reaches for the doorknob.

He opens the door. "Sure, come in." The woman's face is pale, but not sickly. She offers a tiny smile to Gavin as she clutches the doorknob. Her features are small. She wears no makeup and doesn't need any. Her blond locks have a hint of strawberry. They're long and flowy, which reminds me of Kimmy's hair. Her smile falters slightly, showing me how high her cheekbones are, as she looks Gavin over, crinkling her crescent brows at him.

She walks into the room. "Is something wrong?"

Gavin says, "No," right away. The woman gives him a moment to confess the truth, but he doesn't.

She offers a small smile and doesn't confront him. Her smile is warm. That's what I like most about her, I decide. In the very air around her, positivity and happiness thrive.

"Sweet boy, you couldn't wake me. We do not sleep here. The physical body needs rest but your spirit…" she pauses, looking around for a spot to rest.

"Your spirit," she repeats, sitting in one of the chairs across from the bed, "is always conscious. That is why people in the land of the living have dreams, because your subconscious mind is always awake."

Gavin sits back down on the bed, across from the woman. He doesn't say anything about the boy in the wall. I want to advise him he should tell her, though he can't hear my thoughts. I figure he has just arrived at... wherever he is and doesn't want her to think he is insane — something I can relate to. If she believes he is crazy, she might decide not to help him anymore. I don't know if this is what he is thinking. It feels like I'm projecting my current situation onto him. I make a mental note not to do that in the future.

"That explains my two nights of lying here in this bed with my eyes wide open and my mind racing." The woman nods in confirmation at Gavin's words. "What do you do for fun on this island of yours?"

"I have my hobbies. You will develop your own when we're not preparing."

"Preparing for what?"

"The journey I hope you will take," she answers, without actually telling him anything.

Gavin nods, patting his hand on his thigh, as if there's a song playing in his head. "Circe, you told me I could go back home. How does that work?"

"Call on your mate. She can reunite your spirit with your body."

She wants Gavin to call on his mate? What does that even mean? Is she talking about me? Is that why he's been talking to me?

No, that can't be. That sounds crazy.

"You will need to convince her quickly. There isn't much time," Circe warns, standing to her feet, straight as a board. She scans the room as Gavin gets to his feet, looking directly at the spot where the boy had appeared.

"Why? Is there some kind of—deadline?"

She nods and says solemnly, "Seven days is all you're given."

This much I already knew. Did he tell me when I had to complete the ritual? I don't think so, but that explains why he had been in such a panic to get my attention. "Holy…" Gavin looks away.

I wish I could see his face. I wish I knew what he was thinking about.

"Time is different here," Circe offers. "It will seem like much longer to you."

"So, I've been here for two days, how long has it been in my world?"

"Almost twelve hours."

"That's all?" he questions, relieved. "I've got lots of time then. Right?"

"I must express how important every minute is. Don't take it for granted, sweet boy." She clasps her hands in front of her. "I will show you how to contact your mate. Your fate lies in her hands, I'm afraid." She hesitates before adding, "And people can be…" She pauses, searching for the right word, "Unpredictable. You'll most likely have to convince her that she's not crazy, and that won't be easy. She won't want to listen to you. Logic will get in the way."

I'm predictable apparently.

Gavin nods, sighing. "How do I contact this mate of mine? Do you have a good long-distance plan?" he asks, smirking at his own joke. I catch the look from his reflection in a mirror on the wall.

Circe laughs. "I will teach you. Learning to use magic is not as difficult as you'd think. When you have the right teacher," she adds.

"Magic?" he asks. I can hear his skepticism. Gavin offers, "Okay, let's get started."

Circe smiles and claps her hands together. "I like your attitude. Follow me."

Gavin follows her down a long hallway, full of paintings and pictures of memories. I only get to see what he sees, which is unfortunate since I'm curious to see what hangs on the walls. Circe unlocks the third door on the right and steps back, tilting her head to silently give him permission to enter the dark room. He hesitates. "Bravery is feeling the fear and doing it anyway," Circe informs.

Silent, he steps into the room. The light blinks on. What I see catches me by surprise. It's a massive room full of mirrors—new and old; metal framed, wood framed, and plastic; square, rectangle, and oval shaped. Mirrors scattered everywhere, across the bare hardwood.

When Gavin steps in front of one, it reveals a young girl's reflection—one I recognize immediately. Because I've seen it a million times. It's mine, my face. I don't know why I'm shocked; they've been talking about me this whole time. Yet, surprise spreads through me anyway. Gavin searches my face. I can see him getting closer to the mirror; my face gets bigger. He's memorizing my features as if they are new—and they are—to him. I have no choice but to watch myself through the mirror. My long, naturally wavy blond hair, baby blues, and wide smile look different through his eyes. It's like watching myself on a video in front of me through a second camera. In the mirror, I'm feeding a baby Sammy at the breakfast table. As I watch my family and myself from Gavin's point of view, I try not to sob when my father enters the room.

"Is this her?" Gavin asks Circe, his eyes fixed on the reflection. "My mate?"

My jaw drops. My thoughts stop like someone has pumped the breaks in my brain.

Gavin is looking to Circe as if she has all the answers. He's got such an expectant look in his eyes and she's smiling back.

What did he say? His what? I couldn't have heard that right. I'm Gavin's mate? What are we, penguins or something? Then I remember why I can save him and no one else can. He'd said we were linked. That's what he meant about us being linked. This just keeps getting weirder.

Circe moves in closer and answers, "That's her, yes."

He turns to another mirror and sees a different scene with me in it. I'm sitting applying make-up at an old white vanity that my mother passed down to me when I was twelve. Gavin notices the light scar kissing the tip of my index finger from when a Koala bear scratched me at the zoo, edging near the knuckle, as I draw a maple shade on my eyes, comb black mascara on my lashes and dab pink lipstick on my full lips.

"This is… a lot to take in," Gavin says.

Gavin's gaze doesn't falter from the vision of me. I wonder to myself what he's so fascinated about. I'm not a beautiful girl. Cute, sure, but my hips are a little too thin, my thighs are too thick. While I'm being honest about my flaws, my nose is too long, and my butt is too flat.

"What's her name?" Gavin questions.

"I don't know that information. It's up to you to find

out. That's your first task. The faster you figure it out, the faster she can start helping you."

"No pressure," he jokes.

"No, none at all," Circe tells him, as if not getting his sarcastic comment.

"Can you give me a hint?" Gavin finally looks away from my image.

Circe is standing a foot away, looking into the mirror in front of her. She ponders a moment before she turns to him and offers, "It's easier than you might think."

That was his hint, I question to myself? Gavin nods and turns to admire the mirrors in front of him.

"I'll leave you alone for a while. When you get tired or when you find your answers, come find me." At the door, she adds, "Good luck. Also, I'm afraid I have to add that the faster you take to find her, the sooner you can go home."

Gavin turns back to the mirrors and watches me at different times in my life. There's no sound. Gavin says, "How do I find out your name? How can I get you to help me?" he asks the room.

The room remains silent.

He cocks his head. I only see visions of myself. I wish I could offer him some help. If this is a real scene, why am I seeing it? Why am I seeing Gavin watch me in the mirrors? When will all this start making sense to me?

Gavin seems to be asking his own questions silently because he huffs in frustration. "I don't know what to do here."

Gavin soaks in the scenes in front of him and concentrates on what he wants to do. Wanting to hear what I'm saying, he shouts across the room, "Turn up the volume."

Nothing happens.

Gavin searches the empty spaces on the walls for a volume button or an intercom.

He finds nothing.

It's easier than it seems, Circe had said. Gavin growls with frustration.

Gavin reaches up and touches my face in the mirror as if I might look up from my vanity and give him all the answers he desires. "What's your name, love?" Gavin asks.

Behind Gavin, I hear my mother's voice bellow, "Marley? Are you home?" Her voice filters through one of the mirrors; Gavin turns to it. This time, I'm sitting at a computer desk in my dad's old office.

I watch myself answer, "Yeah, I'm up here."

"Fascinating. What did I just do?" Gavin wonders. "Touching the mirror must activate it somehow." Gavin's wheels spin as he tries to figure it out. I can't hear his thoughts, but I can tell by how he stares at the floor and paces back and forth that he's contemplating his next move. Then he stops at a mirror and touches it. This time nothing happens.

"How did I do it the first time?"

He turns to another mirror and looks behind the frame for a speaker. There is nothing, again. "All I did was touch it, right?" He doesn't get an answer. I don't expect him to; he didn't really ask a question. Gavin grunts.

One more time, he touches the mirror.

Again, nothing.

That's when I figure it out. He touched the mirror the first time and then he asked a question about me. Ask the question, I try to tell him, as if he can hear me. The mirrors answer your questions. Ask another question.

Gavin pulls away. I hear his foot tapping on the floor. "It's easier than it seems," Gavin says, finally understanding. "They will answer my questions if I touch the glass. They answer my questions." He shouts in excitement. "This is perfect. All right. What do I want to know?"

He thinks a moment. "Where are you from, Marley?" Gavin reaches up and touches the cold surface a second time. The image ripples underneath his hand as if the glass has turned to water and another image appears.

I'm standing by the front door with my cell in my hand. "1457 Glenshaw Place and what's the total?" I listen for a moment before I ask, "Is delivery extra for Crater's Edge?" I must be ordering from dad's favorite Italian restaurant. They had just started delivering, but the restaurant is just outside of town. I wrap my fingers on the side table like it's a piano. "We'll pay the extra. Thanks. See you in a bit."

"This is so cool," he shouts. "Do you…" he thinks for a moment, "like horror flicks?"

I wish I could just tell him these things, but once again, the mirror gives him the answer. "Do you want to go and see the new *Fright Night* movie on Friday?" A familiar voice asks.

"I can't stand those types of movies," I hear myself say. "You know that!" Gavin doesn't catch the mirror that is playing the scene, but he gets his answer.

"I bet you're a comedy girl. You look like a comedy girl." There is no question in there, but the mirrors must think it warrants an answer because a mirror by Gavin fogs up as if a storm were rolling in, clears and reveals

Kimmy, Shawn, Mom, Sammy, and myself huddled together on our L-shaped couch, sharing a bowl of popcorn and laughing at the big screen.

Gavin drops his hand, happy.

I've always preferred to laugh. Especially after my dad died. Life is too precious, I've learned.

"How old are you?" Gavin asks, pulling me back out of my thoughts.

"It's your seventeenth. Let's go out and celebrate," Kimmy pleads, in front of a row of dark green lockers.

I remember that day. It was only a week after I'd lost my dad. I didn't want to celebrate anything. I was only at school because I didn't want to sit at home and think about him, about my broken heart.

I didn't hear my own response and Gavin seems to be enjoying this too much to quit. For fun, he tests the power of the mirrors. "Are you single, Marley?"

The mirror to the left does the usual and clears. I'm standing in front of the same green lockers, only this time, I am standing there with a tall, dark-haired boy of the same age. His hazel eyes bore into mine and I know instantly what scene it is since it was only a month and a half ago. My boyfriend—at the time—looks down at me, silently pleading and trying to look smooth while doing it.

Derek doesn't know what to say. I cringe at the memory. *Please wake up. Come on, Marley.*

No such luck.

Derek's hands are in his pockets, displaying obvious discomfort. His dark hair falls over his forehead as he looks down. I had just broken up with him in this moment, and I'm not in a hurry to relive the day when I broke his heart—not even in a dream. Especially not from someone else's point of view.

*Wake up. Come on. I don't want to see this anymore.*

It doesn't work.

The scene continues. The eyes of mirror-me drop. Tears threaten to fall. "Derek, we've just grown apart. I've changed." He nods. "I consider you one of my best friends, and I don't want to lose that."

"But we're over," Derek questions quietly.

"I think we've been over for a while. It's just taken me this long to catch up."

When the scene dissolves, my stomach twists. Gavin shakes his head and lets his hand drop. The experiment ends as quickly as it started, I realize, as he makes his way out the door, without turning back.

Thank God. Who knows what else he might want to know or what I might have to relive.

"How did it go?" Circe wants to know when Gavin finds her tending to the garden. Gavin must have made a face because Circe's lips press together, and she says, "That well?"

"Her name is Marley," he says. "And she's from my hometown."

She smiles up at him. "Fantastic. That's a beautiful name. Good job, sweet boy." Her smile melts, her features become serious. "Now the real work begins."

Then I'm carried into another scene by the grey clouds I've come to associate with these dreams. This time I'm racing through some kind of obstacle course, still watching through Gavin's eyes. It looks nearly impossible to me, but he's getting through it.

It consists of large pipes and a lot of rope. Water billows below him in a wide pool. Gavin crosses it shakily.

His concentration is tremendous. When he finally reaches the end, there's a gold-and-blue trophy ready for him.

Instead of picking it up and celebrating, Gavin stares at the gold object—clearly seeing something other than a pretty trophy, something I can't. I see what he's looking at just as Gavin swipes a blade through a tiny thread. I'd have never seen it if he hadn't been examining the area.

I find myself gasping in astonishment as the thin string whispers to the ground. I wouldn't have been able to get through that obstacle course. I know that instantly. I never would have noticed that string for one, and I'd probably have taken a nose dive into the water at some point.

"Amazing!" The comment whistles from the background. Gavin turns. Circe claps her hands together. Her mouth curves into a smile. "I get everyone with that one. Once in a while, a special boy or girl comes along and surprises me."

What is all this? Why is Gavin jumping through hoops like a dog? Is this a test of some kind?

"Out of curiosity," Gavin gives a lopsided grin. "What would have happened if I hadn't seen the wire? A bucket of paint would fall on me? Feathers? Water?"

"Curiosity killed the cat, they say."

"I'm a teenager. Don't they also say that teenagers know everything? Could it be *because* of our curiosity?" Gavin wipes his brow free of sweat, clutching his trophy.

Circe smiles. "You've shown great intelligence in your actions and in your stories. You passed. That means your mate will get the first ingredient soon, if she hasn't already."

A puzzle piece snaps into place. That's why I got the

message from *out of nowhere* about the trophy. Now it makes sense. Gavin passes a test, and the ingredient appears.

"One down, four to go," Gavin announces.

The dream is whipped away, sending me back to consciousness and back into my own mind.

I shiver as I sit up in my own bed. I feel like I'm stalking Gavin in my sleep, now. The dreams *must* have been real, I think to myself. Right?

Concentrating on other things, I realize that for the first time in three days, I'm feeling rested and refreshed. Even my stitches aren't bothering me.

A quick glance at my clock reveals that I've slept through the night. I barely open my eyes and sit up before my little brother comes barreling into the room at warp speed. A two-second warning is all I have to block my healing wound before he jumps into my lap.

"Umph," slips from my lips. "Ooh, you're getting heavy."

"No, I'm not," Sammy denies, his voice muffled.

When he lifts his head, I see purple and brown streak marks on his face and the transference to my pajamas. He smiles innocently. Who could be mad at that face? "Just tell me it's not something gross all over my clothes."

"Peanut butter and jelly. Sorry."

I smile and ruffle his chestnut colored mop of hair. "It's okay, munchkin. Now get lost so I can change, and you can get ready for school."

He is gone faster than he arrived.

*Your little brother is a terror, isn't he?* This time when Gavin speaks, I can hear laughter in his voice.

*He can be, yes, but he's harmless.*

I shuffle through shirts in my closet. A red camisole? Pass. Beige sweater? No. It's my first day back at school. I need the perfect outfit. A cute blue shirt with three-quarter-length sleeves catches my eye. It was a birthday present from Kimmy two years ago. It will go nicely with my brown-and-white checkered scarf, and a pair of skinny jeans. Even Kimmy might like the outfit.

*It's perfect,* Gavin offers his opinion. *Hey, I know a thing or two about terrors; maybe I can give you some pointers.*

*You have a little brother, too?*

*No, I don't. I have an older one,* he admits. *I was the terror in my house. Maybe I should give your brother pointers instead.*

*I'd rather you didn't, Gavin.* It hits me as I say the words to him that I'm already finding it too easy to talk to him, a dead guy I've never even met. For some reason it feels like I've known him forever.

*I know you're in a tough spot,* he says, reminding me of his presence and making me wish that these thoughts would quit popping up in my mind. *Sorry I dragged you into this. I wouldn't have if I had any other choice.*

I lift the brush from my vanity to untangle sleep knots. *I could live with it if these strange dreams went away. And the reading my thoughts part is just a tad creepy. I don't think I could ever get used to it.*

*Think of it this way, maybe one day it will come in handy.* There's a short pause before he continues. *Tell me about the dreams. I don't know about them. What kind of dreams?*

*Nightmares, actually. I've been dreaming about death —
yours, specifically. They're horrific. I'm sorry you had to go through that.*

*And I'm sorry you had to see it. I just hope they find the guy. I'll ask Circe about your nightmares.*

*Good. Maybe she'll know how to stop them. They're getting strange.*

He admits, *It can't be fun dreaming about death every day.*

*I didn't dream of your death this time.*

*What did you dream about?*

*I was dreaming of you, Gavin. You were talking to a little boy. He was hiding in the wall and,* I stumble on the words, not wanting to tell Gavin that I saw him spying on me, *you were looking for me in a room of mirrors.*

*Oh,* he exclaims. Sincerely, he tells me, *Sorry about that. I'm a curious guy.*

*I noticed,* I say, shaking it off. *I'm over it. I'm just happy to be going back to school.* A question circles my mind and I catch it. *Gavin, what did you mean when you said, "One day it will come in handy?" Are you always gonna be inside my head?*

No answer.

*Gavin?*

He admits, *Sorry, keeping this connection open is a little tiring. Did you end up getting the ingredient?*

*I did. Yes. A trophy on a piece of paper.*

*That's so great. Thank you.*

*One down. Four to go,* I say, repeating Gavin's earlier comment, while placing my scarf around my neck.

*Just one question: how am I supposed to feel bad for spying on you when you're spying on me in return?*

I hadn't thought about it that way. *I'm just as bad as you are. That's great.*

A rumble sounds in my ears as he chuckles. *I'm just kidding. It's all good.*

*I can't wait until this whole thing is over.*

*After you get the ingredients, you complete the ritual to put my soul back into my body. I'm guessing I have only three more days?* I look down at my cell, making certain I'm not late for my first day back.

*It's Tuesday morning.*

*And I died Friday night at 8:44, I was told. The ritual needs to be completed by then.*

Applying a dab of makeup to my eyes, I reply sarcastically, *Just over three days to get four ingredients. Shouldn't be a problem.*

*I hope not. Just be careful and be prepared for everything.*

*What does that mean?* I inquire as I pick up the mascara.

*I'm just worried about you. That's all.* I toss the tube on the vanity, turn to pick up my backpack, and head straight out the door. *I can't explain the dreams yet, and my killer is still out there somewhere. Please hurry – and be careful,* his voice is distant and then it's just gone. I feel his presence disappear. It's quickly becoming a habit to feel him with me.

His killer. Why hadn't I thought of that? But why would he come after me? It's not like he could possibly know I can speak to Gavin.

On my way downstairs, I set an alarm for Friday at 8:44 p.m. I have a feeling it will come in handy.

# ELEVEN

*Tuesday, October 23rd*

*EAT A BURGER for me. I miss real food*, Gavin tells me after the lunchtime bell goes off.

*Is something wrong?* I ask, shoving my books into my locker. I look around to see if my friends are waiting for me. Kimmy's across the hall standing beside Shawn's locker. She sees me and enthusiastically waves me over.

Gavin comes back with, *I just wanted to make sure you hadn't skipped the country on me.*

I roll my eyes. *That wouldn't actually work, would it?*

*Nope*, Gavin responds.

Kimmy and Shawn smile and fall in line with me.

"Hey, girl. How you holding up?" Shawn asks, elbowing my arm in a brotherly way.

"Fine." I am not getting into it in the middle of the hallway. The lockers have ears—nosey, bullying ears. Hopefully that one question is the end of it.

My morning's been uneventful so far. No one has paid any particular attention to me. Exactly what I want.

Gavin and the ritual I have to complete are the only things I can think about. After begging to come back to school, I should be able to concentrate.

Not even at lunch. My friends behave as if nothing has changed, which is a welcome escape from worry.

But everything *has* changed. School, fooling around, worrying about grades—they all pale in comparison to saving someone's life.

*They are important. You just have to remember who you were before.*

*I don't even remember who that was,* I explain. *I haven't seen her for so long.*

*I bet your friends can help remind you.*

He's not wrong, so I jump back into the conversation my friends are having about prom. I have to point out, "Prom is eight months away. What's the rush?"

"We don't want to miss out on the best dresses. The cheerleaders will snatch them," Kimmy reminds me, tossing her wide green eyes in my direction. Kimmy's father is Italian, so she has a dark complexion and beautiful curly brown hair, but her eyes, those, she gets from her Irish mother. "We only go to our senior prom once."

April speaks up, feigning annoyance, "That's our Kimmy. Always overprepared."

Shawn complains, "Yeah, she even made me—*her boyfriend*—ask her to the prom." He pauses and turns to Kimmy before he emphasizes, *"Before the school year even started."* He pretends to complain a lot, but we all know how much he adores Kimmy and how he will do anything she asks.

The thing I like most about the two of them being

together—besides how good he is to her—is the height difference. Shawn has over a foot on her. His lanky build and her curvy one together are adorable, a surprisingly perfect fit.

He wiggles his dark, bushy eyebrows at Kimmy and everyone laughs, knowing she is overprepared for everything in life, not just prom. Her purse consists of a wallet, mini first-aid kit, water, emergency manicure set, needle and thread, a phone charger, and a notepad. There's more, I'm certain, but I've always been afraid to ask.

A month ago, I might have been just as excited for prom. As of this moment—and for good reason—I'm not looking forward to it. It doesn't mean the same thing to me anymore.

Kimmy realizes that. "I'm so sorry, Lee. I forgot. No more talk of prom." She gestures with her thumb and index finger, swiping them across her lips and smiling. As if that silent promise will actually stop her from talking.

"No, I'm okay. It is what it is," I reply.

She nods—clearly not convinced. "You're doing better than I would be. If Shawn and I were to...you know, I'd be a soupy mess."

Shawn smiles, throwing his arm around her. He bends his head and kisses her temple. "Me, too."

I smile back at them. "Yeah, but that's because you two are meant for each other. Derek and I—well, not so much."

Speak of the devil. As if his ears are ringing, Derek chooses that moment to walk into the lunchroom. He turns his hazel eyes in our direction and is heading toward our table until someone calls out his name. He turns that way and disappears into the crowd. I manage to hold my sigh of relief in, trying to look strong for my friends, since my friends are his, too.

"Since when are they so chummy?" April comments when the crowd disperses, and she spots Derek sitting with Genie—a.k.a. Virginia Hill—my arch nemesis. At least, if this were a comic book she would be. When she flips her curly red hair at him flirtatiously, I want to vomit.

"I'm done eating. Geography is next, and I have a homework assignment to hand in," I admit, hoping no one will call me on it. It isn't a lie. Well, not a total lie. It *is* an excuse to leave, and they all know it.

I'm more than happy to escape the crowded lunchroom and glad no one follows me. I knew it would be difficult to be around Derek, but I didn't expect it to be this hard. He's already moved on, which only suggests to me that I made the right decision. Regretting it or second-guessing myself isn't helpful. So, why is it still so painful? Because we've dated since I was fourteen? We'd been friends long before that.

So, we broke up. Big deal. People grow apart all the time.

Maybe that's the reason I'm taking this so hard. Even though we were never good for each other, I still care about him.

Getting to my locker through welling tears is a sad routine I haven't done in weeks. It has to stop, and so do these depressing thoughts. Confirming to myself once more that I did the right thing, I tell myself that we can both do better for ourselves and he can do way, *way* better than *Virginia Hill.*

I anxiously spin my locker combo and try to forget

about my simple, unimportant fears.

"You think too much. I can see the wheels spinning," Kimmy appears and taunts, snatching my geography book out of my hand and shutting my locker, which bangs back open in protest. "Quit daydreaming, Lee. Come on."

I shut my locker properly, smiling.

GYM, WHICH HAS always been my least favorite, is after geography. It isn't about exercise. Being a firefighter requires me to be in the best shape possible. It's just that I enjoy workouts, karate, running, and dancing. Playing sports, not so much.

I'm not paying attention when Genie and her friends block my path. "Things weren't the same without you here, McCartney."

Here we go.

Genie's friends nod, scowling my way. Marissa and Reba Jones—both just as bad as Genie. "So, I hear you tried to off yourself." Genie lifts her chin.

"I don't care what you've heard." I try to act like it doesn't bother me that she's heard. How did she know? I think it over and come to realize she's probably making up a story to get me going.

Stay calm, Marley. Stay calm.

Genie is a bully and always has been. She'll probably remain that way for the rest of her life. "What makes a girl do something like that? Do you miss Derek that much? 'Cause that's not going to get him back, you know."

"Let me pass," I demand.

Genie laughs, and her pack of friends follow along. They used to bother me, but not anymore. Well, maybe a little. I can at least be honest with myself. It bothers me that she is one of the most popular girls in school. It bothers me that she is a dreadful human being, and yet my ex-boyfriend sees something in her. It bothers me that I can't walk down a hallway alone without being verbally attacked by the she-wolf and her friends.

My father's words echo from the far reaches of my mind, "Don't let it bother you, honey. Those girls will have to carry it with them for the rest of their lives, knowing they bullied their peers. Don't let their problems become yours. You might even pull one of them out of a fire one day."

He'd said that to me once, and I will never forget it. How can a few well-chosen words from a bunch of prissy, stuck-up snobs bother me after that?

"I don't want Derek back." I squirm past the girls and let out a sigh as I turn the corner. Is it just me or is she getting worse?

I don't know what Derek told her about our breakup, but for some reason she's worried about her relationship with him. I never would have figured *her* for self-conscious.

The hallways are crowded and loud, but Gavin's voice echoes in my mind clearly, *Your friend's right. You do think too much.*

*And you're back,* I say to Gavin.

As we talk telepathically, I make my way to the gym. Luckily, the accident gives me the excuse not to participate. One of my stitches could pop. Although they are mostly healed, I'm going to take the short reprieve the wound offers me. *How are you feeling — you know magic-wise?* I question Gavin. *Is this conversation going to wear you out?*

*Not as much, now. Since our connection has gotten stronger, I can do a little more. I still get drained if I use too much magic but talking is easy enough now.*

Genie and her friends saunter into the gym, not caring that they're late.

"Dodgeball day." The teacher shouts, not noticing the late-comers. I still haven't got her name down, Larrabylip, Larinsus, Loonertip — something like that. "Split up. Two teams of seven. Go."

*Dodgeball, eh? Maybe I could help.*

*No, Gavin. I'm not ready for dodgeball. Not even close. Thank God,* I tell him when I see Genie eyeing me like she can't wait to throw something at me. That girl has always been vicious. If my abdomen wasn't already scarred, she could do her own damage — but knowing her, she'd aim a bit higher, like, all the way higher. *Besides, we don't know what's going to happen. I may need you for something later.*

*Oh, yeah? Like what?*

*I'm not sure yet.* I walk to the far side of the gym, where my arch nemesis is *not.* I steer clear of her as much as possible when I'm healthy. Right now, I don't even want to be in the same room with her.

*Is that the one who stole your boyfriend?*

I scoff, thinking of the day Derek and I broke up. The poor guy didn't see it coming, but I knew I wasn't in the right place to be in a relationship. *Oh, she wishes! Derek and I broke up at the beginning of the school year. I had just outgrown our relationship, I think. Genie got my sloppy* seconds.

*Not very friendly of you,* Gavin tells me, teasing. *Tsk-tsk.*

*If you knew what she did to me growing up, you wouldn't be so judgy. She was awful. In third grade, she crawled under my desk in the middle of history and tied my shoes together.*

*Original,* Gavin deadpans.

*And very painful. I knocked my head on the corner of the desk and had a goose egg for a week. On the positive side, she did get detention.* My hand goes to the spot I'd hit my head. I don't even realize it until I'm rubbing it like it's a lamp and there's a magical genie inside.

*See? Karma works. Believe in the power. Believe.*

*Shut up,* I joke. I watch the game, knowing that if I don't, Genie will "accidentally" toss a ball at my head.

The teacher throws three balls into the middle of the room. They bounce and roll with the force. The whistle blows, and everyone scrambles to be first to start the play. *I always hated this game,* I tell Gavin, happy to be sitting on the sidelines. *Once that girl gets a ball, she would throw it at me, no matter where I was — even if she had to sacrifice one of her own.*

*Is she really that bad?* Gavin asks.

*That bad? She's actually worse.* I recall the last time we played this game.

*Oh, I see it,* Gavin tells me.

I stretch my hands out on the cool bench and lean back. *What does that mean?*

*I mean, the mirrors are showing you in gym class. From before, I mean. I can see that Genie girl eyeballing you.*

I remember, replaying the scene in my head. I was at the far end of the gym, looking out for flying balls when Genie whipped one right toward me. Another girl in my grade, Sara—who had the unfortunate luck of standing in front of me—got hit right in the face. I thought I heard something break and I was four feet behind her.

"Below the waist. You know the rules. Keep it clean." Mrs. L. screeched.

I ducked as a ball headed toward me and managed to catch another one, taking out one of Virginia's friends. Out of the corner of my eye, I saw the look she gave me and knew I was done for. Tuning out the screech of running shoes and bouncing balls, I concentrated on staying as far away from Genie as I could.

That trick didn't work.

I tossed the ball and nearly knocked out another one of Genie's friends. Before I knew it, all three balls were headed in my direction. Instinct forced me to run with my eyes closed, as if nothing bad could happen if I couldn't see, which obviously didn't work.

With my eyes closed, all three balls slammed into me as I knocked into one of my teammates. One bounced off my gut, one into the side of my head, and the last blasted into my ankle, the pain taking me down.

"Nice job, McCartney." Julie, the girl I'd run into, hustled out from underneath me. Rushing to her feet, she got back into the game and tossed me a glare if I got within ten feet of her for the rest of the game.

Suddenly, another ball smashed into my gut. If I wasn't crumpled on the floor, it would have knocked the wind out of me for longer than a few seconds. When I finally looked up, I saw Genie high five one of her friends; she looked my way and smiled wickedly.

That's when Gavin says, *Wow. That's dreadful.*

*And that is why I hate this game.* I tell Gavin.

*I wish I could have been there to help. That girl really is evil,* Gavin says.

*Hey, if you have to use your powers to keep me safe from really bad people, that's fine, but not here at school. I can take care of myself. Once in a while.*

*I know,* he says. *I just don't like bullies.*

*I get it, and that's very kind of you. She's not worth stressing over. Most of the time I can ignore her.*

*I can't believe that teacher let her get away with that.*

*Genie would always apologize and promise it was an accident. She'd toss an innocent smile at the teacher and no one would be able to prove she did it on purpose.*

Genie is very persuasive. Thinking about her smiling up at the teacher and showing her big, googly eyes makes me angry — maybe just a little jealous. I wish I could lie like that without a very loud conscience knocking on my door.

*One day we'll get back at her.*

I think on his words. *You like to fix things, don't you?*

*No comment,* Gavin jokes.

*The only thing I need to do, aside from help you, is figure out what happened to me during the accident. If you have any ideas on where to start, I'm all ears.*

*Actually, I do have one. I don't know if it will work, but I could always ask the mirrors. I know you don't want me invading your privacy —*

*Yes, yes,* I interrupt. *That's a brilliant idea. Please.*

*Consider it done. Circe says its time to start our next magic lesson. You should be getting another ingredient very soon, I hope.*

Genie stands, still eyeballing me like *I* was the reason she'd been thrown out of this game. *That's great. Can't wait. And Gavin? Thank you for keeping me company during gym.*

*Anytime, love.*

Maybe I shouldn't keep getting closer to him. What if I fail? No, Marley. Don't even think it.

*By the way, I asked about your dreams. Circe doesn't know why you're getting them, but she was curious.*

*Terrific,* I say silently, knowing that meant they weren't going to stop. *Thanks, anyway.*

*I'm sorry. Good luck.*

*You too, Gavin.*

Genie scowls at me from the bleachers on the other side of the gym. The only satisfaction I get is knowing that she is now sitting on the sidelines along with me.

"WELCOME BACK, MARLEY. How is everything today?" Dr. Crystal asks.

*Horrible. I'm sitting here with you again. This dark and dreary office is suffocating me.* The retort doesn't come out; all I say is, "Fine." This is a waste of time but I have no choice, no choice but to keep sitting in this uncomfortable chair while these ugly, rotten apple–colored walls close in on me.

"Look, Marley. I know you want to believe what happened was an accident and I know you want everyone else to believe that. However, *I* am the one who has to believe it. When that happens—and only then—will you be able to have your freedom back. So, you might as well talk to me."

I nod, fidgeting with my jacket. Then I realize her words aren't entirely true. If I can get through to my mom,

I won't have to come here ever again. "I don't know what to say about the accident. I've been trying to remember something, but there's nothing. Just a big black ball of nothing for that whole day."

Her lips lift in a small smile — not a friendly one. No, this one said, *All right, I'll play along for now.* "Okay, Marley. Close your eyes." She pauses for me to comply, which I reluctantly do, to get this over with. "Think back to the day. It's October 5th. It's a Wednesday, so you're getting ready for school. Maybe you go downstairs for breakfast. Think back. What did you have for breakfast that morning?"

"Pfft. Beats me. That was almost three weeks ago."

"Try," she insists. "Slowly breathe in and out. Think back. It was a Wednesday. You got up to get ready for school, went downstairs..."

Am I in therapy or am I being hypnotized? I sigh and slouch back in my chair, annoyed with the exercise but also, if I'm being honest, that it's not helping. I want to remember more than anyone else wants me to.

"Marley. Think," she repeats. "We're starting slow. Don't think about anything else. What did you have for breakfast that morning?"

"Um—" I wrack my brain, knowing she won't drop it. Coming up with nothing, I make something up. "Waffles, I think. My mom made them. Sammy had strawberry, and I had blueberry."

"Is that a memory or are you just guessing?"

"A little bit of both, I guess. Sammy always has strawberry on his waffles."

"Well, at least you tried. Let's come back to that." I reopen my eyes. "How's everything else going? How is your family?"

"I don't know. Things are okay in my life right now. Getting better anyway. I'm back to school now. My little brother is always entertaining. My mom and I aren't really talking, but even that's getting better."

"Have you spoken to her about the incident recently?"

*Not a chance!* "No, I don't like to bring it up. I don't think she likes to, either. She still doesn't believe me."

"And how does that make you feel?"

"Horrible. She's my mother. She should always believe me. It's not like I lie to her on a daily basis." Except for lately, because I don't feel comfortable admitting to her that a dead boy is haunting me. If I'm being honest, she wouldn't believe me, anyway. Mom doesn't believe in the impossible. "It's been hard since my father died, but we're getting through it. We *were* getting through it. Actually, life was starting to feel normal again. Then I had the accident. My father would have been disappointed if I had even thought about hurting myself—which is why I never would."

"Could your mother believe that maybe you love your father more than her?"

*Is she for real?* Gavin pops up in my head.

"I don't know. She won't talk to me."

*That's what I was thinking,* I tell him. *I have to be here, though. My mother is forcing me. She's just doing her job.* If it weren't for that reason, I'd probably tell Dr. Crystal off. "If that's what you really believe, then maybe my mother should be here instead. It's not possible to love either parent more than the other—not for me. Just like it would be impossible for a parent to choose a favorite child." I continue ranting, "One of my parents is here and the other is gone—for good."

"And that's what you believe?"

"It's not really about believing. He died. He didn't just leave us, he was murdered," I insist, letting annoyance slip into my words like viper venom.

"I meant about a parent not loving a child more than another, Marley." She eyes me suspiciously and I realize I've stepped into it.

"Oh."

"Look," she says after a short silence. "I know how you feel, Marley. I lost my fiancé in a car accident two years ago, and I never got over it. These things take time. Everyone deals with grief differently."

*That's very sad,* Gavin says.

*It is.* "That sucks. I'm sorry," I say. "Everything was fine until this accident, so my mom's attitude toward me has nothing to do with my father's death. I don't think I need a degree to understand that."

I couldn't stop my words even if I'd wanted to.

Dr. Crystal asks, "How can any of us know what others are thinking? It may be that she was hiding her true feelings from you and the accident brought them out."

"Again, maybe she should be here and not me."

"Marley, you are the one who tried to kill yourself, not your mom. The way she is dealing with her problems seems to be working for her. You, on the other hand, need a little nudge."

"I don't know how many times I have to repeat this, I did *not* try to kill myself. Somehow, I fell on that knife. I must have, because I would never do what I'm being accused of. Can *you* tell me why she doesn't understand that?"

"I think we should have a family visit next time. I'll give your mother a call and see when she's available."

"Either way, I have to be here."

Why won't this session end already? I feel like I'm beating my head against a brick wall. Dr. Crystal doesn't know my character. She can't tell when I'm lying or telling the truth. But my mother? She should know. She's been with me every day for the last seventeen years.

"I think a family session would help clear things up," Dr. Crystal says. "Before we finish up, I would like to ask if anything else is going on in your life. Anything at all that's troubling you, Marley."

I'm only going through the most important trial of my entire life. A boy's life hangs in the balance. If I screw it up...

"No, nothing that I can think of," I tell her instead.

"Last time you were here, you were acting a little strange. I told you then that you could tell me anything and it doesn't leave this room. I won't even tell your mother. Whatever you say stays between us. I just want to help."

"There is nothing else going on in my life right now. There's prom. But that's eight months away, so I'm not stressing about it. Even though some of my friends are. I'm a little stressed about my grades. Well, I'm still worried that I'll fall too far behind, but that's all."

"Marley, look, if I don't pry, you might not end up telling me what is really wrong. That's why I ask the questions I do."

I nod. "I just don't think I need therapy. This feels like a waste of my time. *And* yours."

"None of my patients are a waste of time. If you only

want to talk about your frustrations with home and school. That's fine. We'll start there."

"All right." *I'm glad you're with me,* I tell Gavin. *I don't think I could stand this interrogation without you.*

*Therapists,* he snickered.

It feels strange but I'm getting used to Gavin's presence in my head, so much so that it doesn't shock me as much when he appears.

"This was very fun as usual. See you again," I tell her as I check the time on my phone, so happy to have it back. It's time to pick Sammy up from school. I pick up my purse and walk out of the office. *Wish you could be at all of those with me, Gavin.*

*I'm here for you anytime you need. This bond goes both ways.*

*That's very sweet,* I tell him. And I decide maybe this telepathy thing isn't so bad after all.

# TWELVE

THE HAIRS ON the back of my neck jump as I leave the office and walk to the bank down the block. As the money pops out of the ATM, I notice that it isn't quite a match to our currency. It's a piece of paper that has a lion on it.

What the heck is this?

Then I realize. It's another ingredient. I nearly screech with glee.

When I look back down the message is gone, a twenty-dollar bill in its place. I shove the bills in my purse and head back to the car.

I grab Kimmy at the high school and pick Sammy up at his school. He tosses himself into the car and hugs my neck. "Marley, can I go to Mikey's for dinner?" he asks.

"Did you ask his Mom?"

"No." He offers an innocent smile.

"Is he still here?" I look around but see no sign of my brother's best friend or his mom. "We'll take you there now and if it's okay with Mikey's mom, you can stay. Kimmy, you don't mind, right?"

"Not at all," she says, handing Sammy a candy bar

from her purse.

It's quiet on the ride to Mikey's. I'm not entirely sure what to say in front of my little brother, since he's only a little boy. He won't understand what I'm going through and I am not going to burden him with my issues. I have more than ten years on him and I still don't understand what's happening. How many people out there know that dead people could actually come back to life, I wonder.

When I pass people on the street, am I going to wonder whether they were once dead? Will I recognize one if I see one? If they were officially dead, did that make them zombies? Will they eventually lose their minds? Will they want to eat human flesh? Human brains?

Gavin appears, laughing. *I love how your mind works.*

*Stop laughing. I'm trying to understand this entire messed up situation. I have so many questions.*

We pull into Mikey's driveway. "Pick me up late, okay?" Sammy requests.

"See if it's okay first, munchkin."

Sammy tosses the empty candy bar wrapper on the seat and rushes from the car, and up to the house.

Kimmy shares her thoughts, "Mikey's probably got a new video game."

"That sounds about right."

Sammy runs back to the car, shouting, "I can stay." I push the window button until it's halfway down.

"I'll pick you up by eight." Sammy tosses me his pouty face. My little brother is the cutest thing. "That's the best I can do, munchkin."

"O-kay," he grumbles, running into the house.

"He's such a cutie," Kimmy says, removing her sunglasses and popping them in her purse.

I smile and roll up my window, silently agreeing. "Where are we going to eat? I'm starving."

"I don't care. Anywhere."

"What do you feel like? Italian? Mexican? Chinese? Canadian?"

"Italian, I guess. Sounds good," Kimmy admits.

"Italian it is. I know a place." I begin driving my Honda over to the low-lit, quaint little Italian place my father used to take me to. We sit in comfortable silence on the way there.

When we arrive, a load of memories attached to my dad, as well as the familiar scent of bread from the fire powered stove, envelope me in a warm, unexpected embrace. Kimmy and I make our way to a table in the back, past a family of five, a family of three, a few sets of couples, and a couple empty tables.

I finally break our silence. "We need to talk. You're the only one I can talk to about this predicament—aside from Gavin."

She picks up her menu and reads it over. Folding it nicely, she says, "I still think this is strange, but I'm here for you. Whatever you need."

"I'm worried. I only have until Friday or he doesn't come back. Ever."

"Let's get this show on the road, then. Why haven't you brought him back yet?" Kimmy's shoulders roll as she laughs at her joke and tucks her napkin into her lap.

Her joke squeezes a chuckle out of me, along with a few untamed nerves. "I wish it was that easy." We pause to give our orders to the waitress. "I have to wait until the universe gives me the rest of the ingredients—I'm still not sure how *that* works. Then I have to perform a ritual to bring him back to life."

"Oh, is that all?" she questions sarcastically. "And you only have until Friday? That's just three days from now. I hope you don't have too many ingredients to get."

"Five."

"And you only have one so far?" she wonders.

I nod, frowning. Then I recall the latest clue. "But I think I'm close to a second."

"No wonder you're getting so anxious."

*I will explain what I can until the connection closes if it will help*, Gavin offers.

*Yes, please.*

*Have you heard of Limbo?* he asks me.

I answer, *It's for souls who haven't crossed over or are lost and don't know which way to go.*

*Yes. And Limbo is between our world and where we're supposed to go to next — whether it be heaven or hell or another place, I don't know. Have you ever heard of the name Circe from Greek mythology?*

*You've mentioned her name once or twice.* I shake my head as I respond and feel stupid when Kimmy looks at me funny. I tell her, "Gavin's giving me some info while he has the connection open." As he explains things to me, I explain them to Kimmy.

"I'll give you a minute to chat with him. I'm going to say hi to Shawn's parents. They're sitting over there," she points to the middle row of tables to an older couple, slurping on spaghetti. They're into their food and conversation and don't see us. "Just don't get caught talking to yourself," Kimmy says, smirking.

Gavin continues, *She was said to be a very powerful witch — a minor goddess even.*

*Oh. Yes, I do remember her now. She was the daughter of a sun god, I believe.*

*Right. Daughter of Helios and her mother was Perse, an Oceanid. Circe was extremely gifted with herbs and drugs, but not too powerful with magic. She was banished to the island Aeaea, condemning her to a life of solitude and misery. Destined to be alone and powerless for all eternity. That island, it's in Limbo.*

*Why was she banished?* I ask.

*She was banished because they said she killed her husband. But she didn't kill him. She was going to leave him for Odysseus. Someone used that information against her because they wanted to get rid of her.*

*Not cool,* I tell him.

*For eons, Circe was alone on this island, being driven mad with loneliness and utter boredom. Not even other gods and goddesses are allowed contact with her.*

I visibly cringe at the thought of being alone that long. How anyone could survive like that, I don't know. They would have to be one strong-willed being. I admire the sheer strength she has.

*The good news is that Helios took pity on her and didn't take away her abilities when he abandoned her on the island. He must have thought she couldn't get into any trouble with her gifts. One day she started experimenting with herbs and flowers and accidentally discovered a portal that connected her to our realm. Because she's also gifted in necromancy, she was able to guide spirits onto her island. But the spirits always disappeared, leaving her alone again.*

"Tragic." I accidentally say out loud. And Kimmy warned me not to.

*No matter what she did, they all eventually left her. So, she did the only thing she could do: she started experimenting again. One day she realized that all these people had one thing in common: they were all killed by a Limbonian – a spirit who escaped limbo without doing the ritual. She doesn't know why or how, but only these types of spirits stray to her island. Circe kept experimenting and eventually found another loophole. This one would give her the power to send these "gifted" or "magical" people, the ones killed by Limbonians, back through the portal into the land of the living with their soul mate's help.* My breath hitches at his words. They circle in my head like vultures would their next meal.

Gavin continues and I don't have time to dwell, *Circe calls the gifted people, like me, Piggybackers. Unfortunately, she's still alone, but she has people like me to talk to. I personally think they disappear because of the curse her father put on her: that she has to be alone for all eternity.*

*That's so sad. How could anyone do that to their own child?* I ask.

No answer.

*Gavin? Are you there?*

Again, no answer. He's gone.

Kimmy comes back to the table just as our food arrives, Kimmy's penne and my personal pizza. I tell her all that Gavin told me, about Circe and Piggybackers—minus the soul mate part that I'm still mentally chewing on—and how she's alone on the island. "He's on the island with a woman who killed her husband? Is he safe?" Before I can answer Kimmy continues, "Wait. We just learned about this the other day. She turns boys into animals or something."

"What?" I question, a little too loud. An older gentleman turns to see who's making all the commotion. I give him an apologetic smile and lower my voice. "Is that true?"

"It's mythology." She shrugs. "It could be."

Now I'm worried about him. "Gavin says she was set up for the murder. Maybe someone made up the turning boys into animals, too." I hope.

"That's Circe's side of the story," Kimmy says.

"Gavin has spent a lot of time with her. She seems like such a nice lady. She's been helping people for centuries."

Kimmy forks a bite of penne and then responds, "Gavin's spent like four days with her. That's not enough to know someone's character."

"No," I inform her. "But four days in Limbo is more like two weeks."

"That's still not enough time to get to know someone."

I think about her answer for a moment. "Under normal circumstances, I'd agree. But they've been on the island alone with nearly two weeks to get to know each other. And they don't sleep," I add.

"Well, let's give her the benefit of the doubt," Kimmy says, finally clueing in that I need her support right now. "For now. Someone may have muddled the story a bit in a couple millennia. Tell me more. Like, what's a Limbonian?"

Gavin explained this. "Someone who escapes from Limbo without the help of their soul mate," I say, putting the crust from my last slice down, and trying not to dwell on those words.

Kimmy shakes her head and squints, "That doesn't sound good. And what's a Piggybacker, exactly?"

"A person who has been killed by a Limbonian is able to live off the soul of their soul mate for one week. That's why they call them Piggybackers."

Kimmy's face contorts in confusion. "Soul mate?" she says, confused. "So, Gavin is sucking on your soul?"

I laugh. "No. It's more like he's existing on the same wavelength as me, I guess."

"What will happen if you can't bring him back?"

I don't want to think about it. "Let's just pray that doesn't happen."

Kimmy pushes her plate away. "I still don't understand how any of this is possible. And how come everyone doesn't come back from the dead if this is all true?"

"Only a person killed by a Limbonian makes it to Circe's island. Those are the only people she can help. Sometimes their soul mate isn't around, or their soul mate doesn't believe in what the Piggybacker is telling them. I didn't at first."

*There's more,* Gavin reminds me, appearing in my head again. *Tell her about the powers.*

"The people who come back are... changed," I tell Kimmy.

"What? Like mutants?" she questions me.

Gavin answers Kimmy's question and again, I relay the answer. "No. Piggybackers have powers. They have one magical power, one ability—whether it be fire, invisibility, telekinesis, speed, whatever. Circe teaches the Piggybackers how to hone our skills. She makes sure they're good people before she sends them back to the land of the living. She hopes that Piggybackers can one day get rid of all Limbonians.

"So, when Gavin comes back, he'll be what... enhanced? Like a superhero?" Kimmy wants to know.

"Gavin 2.0." Kimmy and I giggle at that.

*Superhero? I wish.* Gavin says. *Or, witch, I guess we'd call it. But I should warn you that not all the spirits get to go back to the land of the living. Occasionally, things go wrong. If they don't come back quickly enough or if the right herbs and ingredients aren't used in the ritual, Piggybackers can come back with amnesia or hallucinations.*

"Harsh."

*I know. That's why Circe shows the Piggybackers how to communicate with their soul mates. Fewer people fail when they have a little more guidance. Especially when it involves teenagers.*

Kimmy reminds me, "The hardest part of all of this is going to be getting around your mother. You're still grounded, aren't you?"

"Yeah, but I'll come up with something."

*I should probably warn you, the chant you have to say is in Greek. You may have to practice it a bit before the* big day, Gavin warns, emphasis on 'big day.'

*Joy.* Just another thing to look forward to. *You'll be able to help, right?*

*I hope so. It won't be that hard. You're pretty smart.*

After the waitress clears our plates, a white flower appears on our table. The wood opens up as if quicksand is spitting out its prey. *It's Moly. Believed to be the snowdrop flower used in ancient rituals to prevent brain damage. It's Circe's favorite flower.* Goosebumps rise on my arms and prick along my spine.

"Brain damage?" I say out loud. Kimmy's eyebrows shoot up and she looks around the busy restaurant to see if anyone else has seen the flower appear. I make a grab for it and explain, "Gavin says it's Circe's favorite flower; it prevents brain damage."

I can't pretend not to be scared at the sound of the words. This whole piggybacking-witch-goddess thing is getting more and more frustrating by the minute.

"He'll be fine, Lee."

I've gotten too close to Gavin. Even the thought of failure breaks my heart. I can't fail. Not now. There is no way I can have Gavin's death—or anyone's for that matter—on my hands.

We sit in silence while Kimmy stares at the table where the flower had appeared.

Our silence gives me the chance to dwell on those two words hovering in my head like a raincloud. Soul. Mate. Gavin is my soul mate; this is why I'm the only one who can bring him back to life. I remember Circe explaining it to him in the dream, but I'd pictured cute little baby penguins, not this. Will I die too if I can't complete the ritual? Where does he go if I can't bring him back? I have so many questions—too many questions.

Gavin *really* is my soul mate and that explains why I'd felt so close to him so quickly. But... I have a soul mate; the words sink in.

And that soul mate is dead.

*Breathe, Marley. I know.* Gavin appears. *Talking to a dead guy was hard enough. I didn't want to overwhelm you with that information.*

I excuse myself and escape to the bathroom. "Why didn't you tell me before?" I ask Gavin while I run cool water over my face.

*I didn't want to freak you out.*

*I wouldn't have freaked out.*

He points out, *What are you doing now?*

*I'm not freaking — okay, maybe a little. But Gavin, this is not usually how people meet their soul mate. At least I think it's not. They're supposed to meet in person, like each other, and then start dating. Not bring them back from the dead.*

*We can do all those things, love. We'll just do them a little out of order.*

*But… it's not fair,* I tell him. Looking into the mirror and spying my sad reflection, I sigh. It's not like I have much of a choice in the matter.

*Oh, and Marley?*

*Yes,* I ask.

*I have a strange question.*

*Go for it,* I say, hoping that my tone shows he can ask me anything.

Gavin slowly admits to me, *Tomorrow is Wednesday in the land of the living, right?*

*Yes.*

*That means my memorial is tomorrow. Do you think you could go, so I can see it?*

*Uh, I guess so.* I mean, it sounds like a weird request, but it's really not.

*Are you sure?* he asks. Before I can answer, my cell phone buzzes in my purse. It's Uncle Sam. Why is he calling me? I haven't spoken to him in so long. "Hello?"

"Hey, kiddo. I'm trying to reach your mom."

"She's probably at the clinic. Did you try her cell?"

"I did," he tells me. "Listen, there's been a break-in at your house. Can you come home? I'll keep trying your mom."

I rush back to the table and grab my coat. "I'll be right there. Thanks for calling." I hang up the phone. "You okay to come to my house?" I ask Kimmy as I toss money on the table.

"Why? What's going on?"

"Someone broke into my house."

Her eyes go wide. "Uh, yeah," she bellows. Of course, I'm going to your house. I'm not leaving you alone."

"Thanks," I tell her, heading for my car. "If you wanted to bail, I would understand." I can feel her eyes angrily boring into me. "What?" I question when I finally look over at her. "You know me better than that. I'm not gonna bail, not when you need me the most." We hop into the car. "Besides, I really want to be there when you bring Gavin back."

"Okay," is all I say.

"But when we're done, we are concentrating on prom and other normal teenager stuff, like boys and shopping and all that other superficial, non-magic, non-scary stuff. Deal?"

"Deal." I agree. Kimmy holds out her pinky finger. Reluctantly, I follow suit. I'm still anti-prom, though I can pretend for Kimmy's sake. I may feel different in a couple months.

Kimmy and I link our pinkies, just like we've done since we were kids. We smirk at each other, waving our free fingers in the air, like jazz hands.

"We should probably come up with a new handshake, too."

# THIRTEEN

I'VE ONLY JUST allowed myself to breathe a sigh of relief when we turn the corner and see the crime scene outside my house. Two cop cars are flashing their bright red and blue light on the neighborhood; one is blocking my driveway. Three cops huddle together beside their cars, two tall guys and a medium-built woman. A fourth, angry-looking officer, walks out of the house just as Kimmy and I get out of the car.

"Can I go in?" I ask the huddle of cops. "This is my house."

Two of them—a tall, dark and handsome guy with thick eyebrows and a curved grin and the lady cop, who has close-cropped boyish hair and pursed lips—go to join the man coming out of my house. The remaining man looks up from his notepad. Bright, trustworthy eyes stare back at me. His build is hard and muscular. His demeanor is comfortable, yet alert, and his bald head reminds me of Mr. Clean.

"Neighbors reported a break-in," he tells me. "Do you have proof that this is your residence?" I pull my driver's license out and show it to him. "Do you know where your parents are?"

"Marley," Uncle Sam calls out from behind me. "Let her through, guys."

I rush over to him, noting that he still looks the same even though I haven't seen him in a year. His black hair is a little longer than I'm used to and his cheeks are too chubby for his otherwise thin face. He pulls me in for a hug and turns me toward the house. Kimmy follows closely beside me and remains silent. "I have to warn you, there's a lot of damage in there so be careful when you go in."

"Did they catch the guy who did it?"

"I was about to canvas the neighborhood, but my Captain found out we're related so he assigned another detective to the case. Don't worry, she's great. One of the best."

"Uncle Sam, you remember my friend Kimmy."

He looks over, drops his hand from my shoulder and offers, "How could I forget? Hi, Kimmy. You two were thick as thieves growing up."

"Still are," I say as Kimmy waves back. I'm not surprised she doesn't speak; she isn't talkative when it comes to strangers.

"The television and the computer are in there. Although, I have to warn you, a lot of your things have been destroyed. The area's been cleared. Go on in and tell us if anything is missing. I'll be right behind you."

My heart is racing as we walk over the threshold. If Uncle Sam says it's bad, it's bad. I just hope they didn't break all our family photos. Fortunately, no one had been home.

"What about Sammy?" Kimmy reminds me.

I curse at myself, digging my cell out and noticing I'm nearly an hour late. I dial Sammy's friend and wait.

"Hello?" a woman answers.

"Hi, this is Marley, Sammy's sister. I'm on my way to come and get him now. Can you let him know?"

"Oh, Marley, your mom just picked him up."

"Perfect." I hold back a sigh of relief, not even worrying about how Mom knew he was there. "Thanks." When I hang up, I turn to Kimmy and explain. "My mom is coming home with Sammy, *right now*," I stress. "She is going to kill me!"

Kimmy sighs. "You're overreacting. I'm sorry, but your mom can't actually blame you for someone breaking into your house. Even if you two still aren't talking. There's no way."

I follow instructions and walk through the foyer toward the living room, searching the room. I try to figure out if anything's missing. The first thing I notice is that the table's been knocked over. Lavender flowers fell on top of my father's picture. I pick up the picture. Despite being dropped, his big brown eyes are still smiling up at me. Anger boils through me. The nerve they had. My father's picture? No respect for the dead; it doesn't make a bit of difference to me that they probably didn't know he's dead.

Uncle Sam tried to warn me, though I wasn't quite prepared for this. Our things are tossed and strewn about everywhere. Our computer has been destroyed. They even smashed our TV. And our dishes. Who does that? It's a total disaster. "Maybe I can tell her a tornado ran through here." Kimmy chuckles. "Knowing my luck lately, she'd probably blame me for that, too." Kimmy begins picking up anything that's not broken.

I'm not sure how I know, but I feel certain they were looking for something in particular and that it has to do with me. Someone knows what I am doing for Gavin and doesn't like it.

But why? Why are they after me and Gavin? How did they know about Piggybackers? They *must* know about them if they want me or him. It's the only thing that makes any sense.

I shake off my thoughts. My heartbeat is already drumming a mile a minute. One thought I can't shake: this all feels too big for me to handle alone.

Running up to my room, I take the stairs in twos. Just as I suspect, my computer is gone, and all my drawers have been turned inside out. My things are thrown on the floor and anything they could break, they broke.

Something else occurs to me then. "No, no, no. Please don't be gone. Please don't be gone." I plead with the trashed room, wading through piles of clothing, papers, books and various items to get to my bed. Lifting up the mattress and the bed skirt, I find nothing. My journal is gone.

Now I definitely know they're after me. But who? And why? And how am I a threat to them? They don't really think I will say anything about Gavin in writing, do they? Obviously, they don't think I'm the smartest toy in the sandbox. As much as I don't want them to read my personal stuff, maybe they'll leave me alone after they've read it and find nothing about Gavin.

"Marley. Marley. Where are you?" my mother screams, shuffling through the debris as I had. "Are you okay? What happened?" she demands when I appear at the top of the stairs.

"Someone broke in. They stole my laptop." I don't say anything about the journal. If she knew they were here because of me, she would be even more sour, and my mother has enough to be upset about when it comes to me lately.

"Have they taken anything else?"

"I'm not sure. I did a quick sweep and ran up here."

"Come help me clean this up, please. We'll check into a hotel for the night as soon as we give the police a list of missing items and let them do their job."

Obediently, I head downstairs. *Is everything okay?* Gavin asks.

*Yes, but it's a mess here. Someone broke into our house.*

*Was anyone hurt?*

I say, *Luckily, no one was home, but they took my laptop and my journal.*

*Anything else?*

*No, I don't think so. They smashed almost everything else.*

Gavin groans and then sighs. *You think they were there because of me?*

*I don't know. All I know is that weird stuff started happening when you appeared and the weird-o-meter skyrockets more and more every time I get out of bed.*

*I'm really sorry I got you into this. If you want to back out, I understand.*

I gave Kimmy that same choice not an hour ago. *Life is hard,* I tell him. *That doesn't mean you quit or give in. I am not a quitter, and I will do everything I can to bring you back.*

*I don't know what to say.*

*There is nothing to say. I just want to get this over with, so my life can go back to normal. But, Gavin, I'm not going to quit on you.*

*You might not say that after I tell you what Circe told me,* Gavin's voice trembles. *She believes someone is targeting you to get to me. After she hears about the break in I don't know what she'll say. But I think you came to the same conclusion. Has anyone been acting strangely around you?*

*No, I don't think so,* I answer, while searching the kitchen for missing items and trying not to fall on any knives — again — or trip over broken dishes. *Why are they after me, Gavin? Or why are they after you? Did Circe have any idea?*

*Uh, no. Nothing really.*

I know he's lying instantly. It's in his voice. *Gavin, whatever you're hiding from me, I can handle it.* I skirt by a pile of broken dishes.

*No —*

*Tell me what it is you're hiding,* I interrupt. *Don't keep me in the dark.*

*I don't want to scare you.*

*Gavin...* I warn.

*It's just a theory, but based on what Circe has told me, I think it's because of my powers.*

My stomach drops for the third time today and my already pounding heart speeds past double. My nerves have been going haywire all day. *So, they're trying to make it so you can't come back at all? Is that your theory? Does that mean they're going to kill me?*

*No. I don't think they will kill you. I swear I wouldn't let you do the ritual if I thought they wanted that.* He sighs. *I think they want my powers. I'm just trying to think of all the possibilities. I only hope, as my powers grow stronger, I'll be able to stay with you for longer increments. Then I can help if you need me.*

*I'm not as worried about myself. What about my family? And Kimmy? We already lost my dad. We can't lose anyone else,* I confess. I cannot lose anyone else, not Gavin, not Kimmy or Sammy or Mom—no one!

*I know.* Gavin disappears from my head. I turn to leave the kitchen and find Kimmy standing in the doorway. "Your mom's going to take me home when you're done. How's everything in here?"

"Just fine," I lie, knowing that she'll see through me instantly.

Predictably, Kimmy says, "Something's happened. Tell me."

A knock at the front door interrupts our conversation.

I hear the door open. Kimmy and I peak around the wall and see the back of my mom's head.

"Hi, Mel." Uncle Sam walks in. "In light of what happened, I'd like you guys to stay at my place for a few nights."

"I don't know if that's a good idea, Sam."

"Please. I miss you guys."

Just as he says that, Sammy comes running up to him and hugs his thigh. "Uncle Sam!"

Mom groans in defeat. "Fine. We'll stay at your place until I can clean this mess up. Thanks."

I'm glad that's settled.

"You're not off the hook, Lee. I want to know what he said," Kimmy warns.

We make our way slowly out of the kitchen. "How do you know he said anything?"

"I can read it all over your face."

"Fine. How about we talk about it later?"

"How are we going to do that? You're grounded. You had a hard enough time convincing her to let you out tonight. Your mom isn't going to let you out a second time."

"I'll think of something," I whisper.

Heading into the living room, I find Mom sitting on the couch. "The house is trashed," Mom points out, tears in her eyes, "but I couldn't see anything missing. Are you girls ready to go?"

"We are. It will be okay, Mom," I say, silently thinking about how to get out of my grounding just long enough to save Gavin.

She stands, wipes her sweaty palms on her thigh, and agrees, "It will be."

I ask, "Where's Sammy?"

"He's with your uncle. We're going to meet him at his place."

We drive for a few minutes in silence. Kimmy gives me this look of pity. The expression melts so quickly I feel like I imagined it.

As we pass the school, I see a light coming from our mascot, Terry the lion. It bounces off him like flashlights are aimed at his torso. It takes a minute for me to clue in. It's another ingredient.

I know what I have to do next. Well, at least I think I do. It's not like I can steal a whole statue. "Mom, do you know that boy who died last week? His family is having a memorial for him tomorrow, and I would really like to go."

"Not now. Can we discuss this later?" Her tone is irritated, and no one can blame her, but I don't have a choice.

"There's not much time later."

She sighs and turns down Kimmy's street. "Did you know him very well? Is that why you want to go so badly?"

"Not as well as I should have," I hedge. I can't tell her that I didn't know him at all when he was alive. She'd say no. I'm not lying, I tell myself, just fudging the truth a bit.

"I think it's a lovely idea that you go pay your respects, but it's a school day and you're still grounded."

"Please, Mom. I promise I'll go right to school after."

"You begged me to let you go back to school, and now you're asking to be let out? I don't understand you sometimes."

"It's just... well, he was my age, and two weeks ago I almost died. I feel like I *have* to go."

She thinks about it. "I suppose."

"It starts early. Is it okay if I stay at Kimmy's tonight?"

"Fine, fine." Her tone is angry. Clearly, she just wants the conversation over.

"Mom, are you going to be okay?"

She nods.

When she pulls up to Kimmy's red brick house, I smile and say, "Love you." I rush out of the car before Mom can change her mind.

As soon as Mom's Journey turns the corner, I turn to Kimmy. "Go get your keys. We have an ingredient to find." She nods and hurries inside the house.

I wait by Kimmy's sports car, thinking about Terry the lion. The universe isn't sending me a sign to try and steal a thousand-pound statue, I hope. Maybe I can take a scraping of it? *Do you think that would work, Gavin?* I ask, not expecting an answer.

Kimmy comes out a minute later. I reach for the door handle and suddenly I'm no longer standing in Kimmy's driveway; I'm standing in the room of mirrors with Gavin—in the room *with* him—looking right into his gorgeous brown eyes. "Uh, hi," I say nervously. "How did I get here?"

Gavin jumps and clutches his chest before turning to me, pulling a laugh from me. "You scared me."

"Sorry."

He inhales sharply and says, "You're not actually here, Marley. You can't be. You're not dead."

"I'm confused."

"Me too," he says.

Suddenly, the door opens behind Gavin and in walks a very beautiful blonde woman in a gorgeous white dress. She has high cheekbones, a small button nose, and extraordinarily long legs. Her eyes are the color of the ocean, and I know exactly who she is. I saw her face in a dream once. "Circe."

"Happy to meet Gavin's soul mate finally. Sorry it is under such miserable circumstances, but I am glad you're here."

"What happened? One minute I'm standing in a friend's driveway, and the next I'm standing in an alternate realm. Did I die?"

"No, you're not dead. Don't worry, sweet girl. This just means that your connection to Gavin is growing stronger." She brushes her hand over my hair in comfort. Her presence is very calming in my panicked state, although I have the feeling she isn't telling me something. "Were you speaking with Gavin telepathically when you appeared to us?"

154

"No, I—well, I had said something, hoping he could hear me, but I thought our communication was only one way."

"It is usually, but the link can grow—making it easier to communicate through the veil. That must be what's happening here."

"If I'm not dead, how am I here?"

"The part of you that is connected to Gavin is here. In your world—the land of the living—you are currently driving around in a car with your friend, and yes, I believe your mascot idea will do the trick."

How did she know about that, I wonder.

Circe continues, "But you must hurry. Every moment that Gavin is here in this realm makes it harder for him to get home. Gavin and I will do our part on this end if you keep doing yours. Get back to your friend and be careful."

Circe touches my butterfly pendant. "This is beautiful."

Then I'm back in the car with Kimmy, back in the land of the living. I don't even remember getting into the car. When we pull up to the school, the full realization hit me that I have technically been in two places at once. Awesome!

Although, it's amazing I can be in two places at once, I should *not* do that again. If only I knew how to control it.

Seriously though, what kind of science fiction fantasy drama have I gotten myself into here? No more calling out to Gavin, I warn myself. That must be how I did it.

"Are you okay, Lee? You've been acting strange since we got to my house. Actually, you've been acting strange for most of the night."

"I'll explain it all after we get this mascot—when

we're back in this car and I know we're safe."

Our mascot is a statue of a lion named Terry—I never figured out why. The football team rubs his mane for good luck before every game, so they'd notice if Terry went missing.

"We're taking Terry?" Kimmy asks, looking horrified, when I stop at the statue.

"No. I just need a piece of him."

"Oh, a piece. That's *so* much better," she tells me, sarcastically. "You're cutting up a piece of history, you know. Shawn would be so upset with you."

"I think that even the school's running back would understand I'm just doing it to save someone's life."

She moans. "It's for a good cause, you got me there. Let's take him down."

"You got a knife or something in that bag of yours?"

She rolls her eyes at me. "Really? You don't believe in the purse by now?"

I chuckle. "All right. Hand it over." Kimmy reaches into that magic bag of hers and reveals a Swiss army knife. "Perfect."

"What about a bag or a vile? I believe in the purse," I joke, looking up to the sky, as if I'm telling the universe of my belief.

Kimmy's already holding out a small bag when I look at her. "Thanks."

I take it and shave off a bit off the back of the lion's leg. Terry's up on his hind legs so no one should notice a couple shavings missing on the underside of his leg.

"They shouldn't notice it back there." She echoes my thoughts. No one knows how she does it, but she's always had the gift.

"Does Shawn get annoyed when you do that? Read his mind?"

"I can't read his mind as well as others. I think that's why I love him so much. He's mysterious." She says the word *mysterious* like Dracula would have said something — long and overdrawn.

"Isn't that one of the reasons Edward thought Bella was so fascinating?"

"Who and who?" Kimmy asks me.

"I really thought you'd get that one. Never mind." I shove the shavings in my jacket. "I think we should get out of here before someone sees us."

"And you can tell me what happened to you earlier."

# FOURTEEN

MY DREAM CONSISTS of two scenes. Both are in Gavin's point of view. The first is abrupt and to the point, and the second frightens me to bits.

I dream of a little boy with a large amount of dark hair and chubby cheeks. I place his voice immediately with the boy in the wall from a previous dream. "Have you thought about my offer?" the boy asks Gavin.

"Yes. Kind of," Gavin responds nonchalantly.

"If you come with me, I will get you power and riches. Who wouldn't want those things? We will pass through the Valley of Truth and the Pearl River. Over there is a portal into your world."

"What do you get out of it? If I go with you, I mean."

"I have everything I need," the boy responds quickly — almost too quickly. As if he was ready for that question.

"You're telling me that you know where to find the portal. No way, Circe would have told me, too."

The boy shrugs. "Maybe she's waiting for the right time. Maybe she does not wish to tell you at all. But I can send you back no matter what."

Gavin sits up in his bed, scratching his head, he admits, "I don't believe anything you're saying."

"She's the one lying to you, not me. She probably told you she was alone on the island. If that were true, I wouldn't be here."

"Good point. Right now, it's your word against hers. We could go ask her."

The boy sighs and starts playing with a golden yoyo he pulls out of the shadows.

"Are you going to sit here waiting for me to ask her?" Gavin asks, grabbing his computer chair and bringing it closer to the wall.

"No, because I don't think you will."

Gavin sits. I almost laugh, though annoyance suits my mood better. "You are making it really easy to trust you, kid," Gavin says, his voice saturated with sarcasm.

The boy throws his yoyo into the air and sticks out his tongue. "I know what sarcasm is, you know."

There's another short silence between them.

"I'll show you," the boy says, like it's a huge secret and he's just dying to share the burden. "I bet that's more than she's done."

"Sure. Let's go."

"That's not what I meant," the boy tells him. He raises his arms in the air and claps his hands together three times. Fireworks explode and crackle from the contact. Small sparklers hover to Gavin's left. They magically form a television screen in the air. I'm surprised at the boy's use of power. I believe Gavin is too, when I hear a small gasp escape his lips, though he doesn't say anything. He just watches the magical screen.

A gravel road appears. The picture begins moving as if someone walking the trail has a camera attached to their forehead. Their pace is quick. I'm not sure where they're going until the path clears and a deep valley appears in the distance. It's wide and spreads as far as I can see. A few trees are peppered throughout the property, but that's all for the view. Knowing it's the Valley of Truth that the boy had mentioned before, I gulp in thick air and wonder what Gavin's thinking.

"Why is it called the Valley of Truth?" Gavin questions.

So, we *are* on the same page.

"That would ruin the surprise," the boy tells him. The screen evaporates into oblivion, and the boy is gone—just like that, with no further explanation, just as before.

Frustrated, Gavin leaves the room, in search of the path he'd just seen.

Mountains feather the horizon. Trees dance along with the light breeze. Peace is part of the air in this place. People in the land of the living—including myself—forget to think about the simple things. Gavin wanders around forever before he sees the patch of oak trees from the magical television screen. I can tell because he stops to look them over. Up ahead, there's the gravel road that the kid said would lead to the valley. After a long trek up the path, I see the edge of the valley creep up ahead.

So, the boy *had* been telling the truth. What's Gavin going to do with this information? Maybe the boy is telling the truth about everything. After what Kimmy said about turning boys into animals, I'm not certain I trust Circe explicitly. We already know she lied. She told him she was alone on the island and we've seen the little boy. She seems so sweet and caring; not at all like the way people describe her.

*It's entirely possible she doesn't know about the boy*, I try to tell Gavin. He doesn't hear me.

"Hello, Gavin," Circe's soft voice floats up from behind him. "I see you've found the Valley of Truth."

Gavin stares at her. She wears a smile, as if she knows what he's up to. "Uh, yep. I was just out for a walk."

"A long one it would seem," she says, without a hint of accusation or annoyance.

"Just clearing my head."

She admits, "After all these years I still find myself wandering around, finding new places to explore."

Gavin nods and kicks a stone as a little brown rabbit hops by. His black eye turns toward Gavin, looking right at him, at me.

Circe claps with appreciative happiness and then turns back to Gavin. "What's bothering you?"

"I'm not ready to talk about it. I hope that's okay."

Circe touches her hands to her chest and surprise jumps from her lungs. "Why wouldn't that be all right?" Gavin doesn't answer, so she adds, "Whenever you're ready, just know you can talk to me about anything."

"Thanks, Circe."

She nods, touches his cheek, and leaves Gavin to his own thoughts. I'm grateful, but it would be nice to have some kind of reassurance. Doubt spoils the blood.

I don't like that he's having doubts; I wish there was something I could do to help.

Before long that scene melts away, and I'm in the room of mirrors—still watching through Gavin's eyes. He touches the mirror and asks, "What happened to Marley the day she was stabbed?"

Even as the clouds fog up in the mirror in front of him, I can't wait to find out the answer. My heart stops as the clouds finally roll away. I'm in my kitchen, sitting on the bar stool. I'm reading from a textbook — which one, it isn't clear and nothing seems out of the ordinary at first.

I'm alone in the kitchen, so when mirror me looks up I suddenly start to panic. My face is stoic, like I'm in some kind of a trance. Usually I have the radio on in the background. Today, for some reason, it isn't playing. Mirror me walks robotically over to the kitchen window and closes the curtains. But not before I notice a distinct shadow of someone standing off to the side. I can't see who it is.

Mirror me turns, circling around the island to the knife block beside the fridge. Slowly but surely, I take one knife out, examine it, then put it back. The second one is bigger — I have no idea what it's called, but I know what's going to happen. I still scream, "Don't do it," like it will make the slightest bit of difference.

Although watching it happen, even in a dream, is much more terrifying. Almost as bad as watching Gavin get shot.

The knife goes up in the air and whips down without hesitation and mirror me crumbles to the floor in a bloody heap.

Gavin swears, and I wake up in bed, heaving in a panic and clutching my stomach.

# FIFTEEN

*Wednesday, October 23rd*

WHAT AM I doing here? I didn't know Gavin before he died. What if someone realizes I'm a fraud?

No, don't think like that, Marley. Play it cool. No one will suspect a thing. People don't crash funerals. Do they? I shiver. That's a freaky thought.

I find the corner furthest from Gavin's family and lean against the wall, wiping my sweaty palms on navy blue dress that has small pompoms along the sleeves and a thin white belt, and I look out the front window. I wish I was out there.

Gavin's aunt has a really nice home, open-concept and large enough for a family of six. I got a quick peak at the dining room and noticed they had a conference-size table and two more large windows, facing the backyard.

Despite the fact that it's a beautiful home, I just want to get out of here.

"Marley, you look like you're stressed," Kimmy whispers.

"I don't like funerals."

"It's a memorial for the hundredth time, girl. Funerals usually have a body."

"Sorry. I don't like memorials," I correct. "That's all." It's a lie. I can't help but wonder why Gavin didn't tell me what he'd seen in the mirrors.

*I'm sorry, love. I should have told you,* he tells me, popping up in my head.

*Yes, you should have.*

Being here at Gavin's memorial is making me feel so guilty about it. He never wanted to die, and he did. I stabbed myself and survived. It's not fair.

*Quit giving yourself a hard time. I know you think you know what you saw, but there is another explanation. I'm trying to find it. That's why I didn't tell you right away. And don't stress about me, either.*

*Thanks,* I tell him. *But I can't help how I feel. That dream changed everything and it changed nothing. I thought I knew what I was capable of, but that dream told me otherwise. Being here today just makes everything so real.*

*We'll find out what happened. Don't worry, love.*

A tear slips from my eye and I swipe it from my cheek.

Kimmy takes my elbow and leads me closer to the front of the room, toward Gavin's picture. As far as I'm aware, they haven't released Gavin's body yet. My feet are stiff. Despite it, I manage to move slowly with Kimmy standing beside me. Luckily, no one notices because most of them are moving the same way. Grief is a limb toxin, and everyone here has caught the same disease.

*It's a little awkward, I know, but you'll get through it. I promise.*

*Stay with me?* I urge.

*You don't have to ask. How many people get to see their own funeral – or memorial?* He chuckles.

*Don't make jokes. Not now.*

*Marley, no one knows why you're there. Just pretend we went to school together. You'll be fine. Trust me,* he says.

*Fine. If you can be positive, I can be too.*

*That's more like it.* The woman beside me sobs. I pass her a tissue, trying not to start crying. *Don't let it happen again,* Gavin warns playfully.

Kimmy nudges my arm. That's when I notice a woman walking up to us. A redheaded woman with teary eyes and puffy cheeks. She's hugging herself as if she's caught a chill. My nerves heighten the closer she draws to us, but I manage to tamp them down. There is no way she can know why we're here or who I really am.

*Exactly. I'll tell you what to say if you get stumped,* Gavin helps. *Don't worry.*

"Thank you both for coming. Did you two go to school with my nephew?" the woman asks once she reaches us.

I'm preparing my answer when Kimmy nods and says, "We didn't know him all that well, though."

The sound of the woman's voice is broken with tears when she answers. "That's too bad. He was a really good kid."

"We're sorry for your loss," I feel compelled to say.

*That was the perfect thing to say,* Gavin says, obviously sensing my total discomfort. The woman attempts a smile. I have to give her credit for keeping it together so well. I'm sweating buckets and just hoping it doesn't show. *Don't worry, Marley. Their pain won't last,* Gavin reminds me.

*I hope so.*

"Please stay for some food. My sister has been receiving a lot of food from friends and neighbors. She couldn't possibly eat it all." Gavin's aunt smiles, then visibly reprimands herself for doing so. "Thanks for coming. Gavin would have been so pleased to see you here. He was such a people person." A young guy waves her over. The woman smiles weakly at us and a tear drips from her eye as she turns to walk away.

"Wow! That was intense," I whisper to Kimmy whose face mirrors what I'm feeling. A combination of emotions whip through me at dizzying speed; sadness, loss, anger. Kimmy's mourning a murdered teenage boy, but I'm mourning the loss of my soul mate. I didn't feel a gaping hole the moment he passed away, though I'm certainly feeling one now. And it grows the more I get to know him. "I've never been to a funeral like this one."

"Memorial," she corrects. "We'll get through this. Whatever you need. I'm here to help," Kimmy tells me, hugging me close for comfort. I want to feel comforted, but nothing can comfort me until this is all over.

*Gavin, are you still there?* I call.

*I'm not going anywhere, love. I'll keep the connection open as long as possible.*

I smile. *Do you have any idea when Circe is going to give you the last ingredients? I need this to be over.*

Kimmy and I walk around, offering condolences to as many people as we can. Well, Kimmy does—and considering how much she hates talking to strangers, I think she's doing an amazing job. I'm so lucky to have her. I smile and shake hands even though I'm not in the mood to exchange pleasantries.

*We* will *get through this. Look how far we've gotten already.*

He's right. I know he is. So why can't I shake the feeling of dread?

*Come on, Marley. You're doing more than you can understand. You know how important this is and that's why you're afraid, but you don't have to be. We'll get through this together. And if you don't have faith in me, have faith in your best friend, who's telling you the same thing.*

*You're right, Gavin,* I say, trying to shake my feelings. *Thanks for being with me. I know this must be weird for you, too.*

*A little. And any time. Now get out of there. I don't feel like making another speech. Makes me feel preppy.*

That comment squeezes a chuckle from my lips.

"What are you laughing at?" Kimmy asks.

"Gavin. He thinks he's funny."

*I know I am, you mean.*

At the same time Kimmy points out, "You laughed. You must think he is, too."

"Maybe. And extremely modest."

"At least he'll always be entertaining."

"Yes, there's that."

I have that being-watched feeling again. I look around to see who it is, but I can't see anyone. Kimmy's attention is on a couple who's talking about where they will eat for dinner tonight, as the husband stuffs a mini cupcake in his mouth. The wife, who is wearing a simple black dress, is playing with his tie. Then I notice the hem line on her skirt goes nearly up to her panty line and I turn to Kimmy. She raises an eyebrow at me. Without saying anything, I nod, knowing that she agrees the dress is entirely wrong for a funeral — memorial, I mean.

We walk out of the house and the air feels instantly cooler and lighter. I inhale sharply, so happy to be out of there.

"I FEEL BAD for his family," April tells us after we confess to missing the morning to attend Gavin's funeral — memorial. Sitting on the lawn in front of the school's sign has become a tradition among my friends. Today, I don't have much of an appetite, despite the good company and the sunny weather.

"Me too," Shawn agrees, stealing one of Kimmy's chocolate chip cookies.

"He's a good guy," I respond automatically.

"Did you know him, Marley?" Shawn asks, curious.

"Me? No." I say, "I read the article that said he saved someone's life. He had to be a good guy to take a bullet for someone."

April nips at a baby carrot before asking, "Did the police ever find the guy responsible?"

"No, I don't think so."

"Wow. This is so hard to believe. A kid is dead because he went to a dance."

"He died because of a bully with a gun," I correct forcefully.

An awkward silence arises. What can anyone say? Gavin is dead, but he did nothing wrong by going to that dance. It's a horrible fate that no one deserves.

*You're a feisty one, Marley McCartney.* Gavin pops up in

my mind, frightening me. I nearly spit out the water I'd just sipped.

I recover before anyone notices, except for Kimmy. She's been watching my reactions throughout our whole conversation.

*Gavin, why are you popping up out of nowhere in the middle of my lunch break?*

*Sorry, McFeisty. Please don't turn your wrath on me*, he jokes. *I just wanted to see how you're doing and to let you know I passed another test.*

*Perfect. When do I get my ingredient?*

*You should get a sign soon.*

I smile at Kimmy. Everything's good now, I try to tell her using the best friend force. I haven't yet told her about my dream. It doesn't seem like a big deal after going to a funeral.

*Memorial, remember?*

*Don't you start, too*, I tell Gavin, but there's a smile in my voice. Kimmy corrected me all morning. "Sorry, didn't mean to snap. I'm under a lot of stress lately—although, that's no excuse," I tell April. It's unlike me to get angry, and she knows it.

April nods and smiles. All's forgiven.

I can't wait to get the next ingredient. We aren't even halfway, and it's Wednesday already.

*Hold on. Don't be so hasty. It's not like you're going to leave school to go and get it. We have time to chat, don't we?*

Going back to eating my lunch I ask him, *Gavin, are you ever serious?*

*Only on weekends*, he informs me, his laughter echoing in my skull. *And the occasional holiday.*

In my mind, I roll my eyes, despite the fact that he's

amusing.

*All right. This is me attempting to be serious. I'm a little bored being dead. So, I figured I would talk to you and get to know my soul mate a little better.*

*I don't mind talking to you, but can we keep the soul mate thing on the DL for now? Maybe we can start by just being friends.*

After all, if I fail he'll disappear from my life forever and I'll have to live with the fact that I was technically responsible for my soul mate being dead.

*Whatever you feel comfortable with. Friends it is, love.*

I don't say anything about his term of endearment. I've gotten used to it. *Thanks,* I say. *What do you want to talk about?*

*How's your family holding up? Is everyone safe and okay?*

*Yes, I spoke to Mom this morning. They settled into my uncle's just fine.*

*Good. How's Terry the lion holding up since you married him?*

I look up at the statue twenty feet from our lunch spot. The lion is still standing on its hind legs with its two front paws in a fighting position, the same old Terry. *It's a statue,* I tell him. *It didn't feel a thing.*

*Hey, be serious for once in your life,* Gavin returns.

*I just don't think I can pull it off. I tried once.*

*Take it from me, life's too short not to laugh and have fun.* Gavin says.

*Does that mean you've changed since you died?*

*No, not really,* he admits. *If I'm being honest. I just have more appreciation for the bright and cheery now.*

*I think we would have been friends if we'd gone to the same school.*

*I believe you. I would have been drawn to you the minute I saw you.*

I smile, still pretending to be listening to my friends and their conversation. *You truly believe that, don't you?*

*I was,* he admits. *I mean, when I first saw you. Sorry, I shouldn't tell you that. I don't want to make you uncomfortable.*

I'm about to say something, but Gavin beats me to it. *You know, I was a baby when my dad left but as I grew up, I saw how hard it was on my mom. The only way I knew how to help was to make sure she laughed and had fun once in a while.*

*You like to fix things, Gavin. From what I know about you, I can say that she did a good job as a single parent. She's very lucky to have you.*

"Mr. Couture's test..." Shawn starts.

I question Gavin, *When did your dad leave?*

*I was two. They adopted me and he split three days later. Told my mom that if she couldn't have any more children, he would find someone else who could.*

*That's harsh. What a shame. Seems like he's missing out big time.*

Gavin sighs. *I'm not worried about myself because I never knew the man, but my brother was almost five and the creep was his biological father. It's harder for him to brush it off than it is for me.*

*Let me get this straight: the man left the family he already had because he said he wanted more?*

*Yeah.*

*If you ask me, he doesn't deserve anyone, and you guys got lucky.* I pack up my lunch.

*I think so, too. But I'd never tell my family that. Hey, why don't we practice the chant for the ritual?*

*Sure. That will take my mind off things for a while,* I say to

Gavin. "I'm heading in," I inform my friends. "See you guys later."

WHEN I WALK into the hall between classes, Kimmy's standing there, waiting. Genie's on the other side of the hallway giggling and pointing at me with her friends. My best friend doesn't notice the giggling fools. Though, she rarely pays attention to them. "Hey, girl. How was gym?"

"Peachy," I answer. "How was math?"

"Oh, you know," she answers. "Walk you to your locker?"

"Sure. What's up?"

"Nothing. I just wanted to see how you were holding up after this morning," she tells me, turning down the hall to the left.

"Kimmy, are you okay?" I ask, grabbing her elbow.

"Yeah, why?"

"Because my locker is that way." I point behind us.

"Oh." She lightly smacks her head with her palm. "I wasn't watching where I was going, that's all."

"You sure you're all right?"

"Of course! So, tell me about Gavin." She sees my expression and notices my worry. "I'm sorry. How are you holding up? That's what I meant."

"I'm fine. It was a funeral of a young boy. It was difficult to be there, that's all."

"I'm talking about at lunch. You seemed to be a little

distracted. Was he talking to you?"

The bell rings, giving me an excuse to escape this conversation. Why it's bothering me, I don't know. "I'm late. We'll finish this up later. Bye." I run down the hall, wondering what's up with Kimmy.

# SIXTEEN

A RED LIGHT forces me to stop the car. Before I can answer whatever question Kimmy just asked, the light turns; however, instead of a green light, there's a green arrow pointing to the right. That's odd. Why is the arrow pointing to the right? This light normally points to the left.

Instinctively I turn my head and see a black, rectangular construction sign that states in vivid yellow lettering:

*Face your fears, Marley McCartney.*

A construction sign with my name on it. Maybe the universe is giving me another ingredient. I will never get used to the universe sending me messages, but Gavin warned me one was coming.

Someone honks their horn, knocking me out of the vision.

"Lee?"

"What?" I go back to paying attention to our conversation.

"Your face just paled. What's wrong?"

"That sign said, 'Face your fears, Marley McCartney.'"

Kimmy looks in the direction I've been staring. "No, it's a construction sign, Lee. It says Blueberry Crescent is closed until next week and where to detour."

"What?" I look back, ignoring the angry honking behind me. She's right. "Wow."

"Yeah. Are you sure you saw what you saw?"

"Yes, I'm sure."

That honking is driving me mad, so I give the guy what he wants and turn the corner. "So. What *are* you afraid of?" Kimmy asks me, as we drive along the riverfront.

"Right now? Failing Gavin. Other than that, I never thought about it before. I guess I'm afraid of what most people are afraid of, you know. Losing my family, failing a class, getting my heart broken—not getting into a good college."

I was never afraid of the dark like most children. Everyone's afraid of losing a family member. After living through it once, I'm certain I can't go through it again. It's not a fear I would choose to face.

A funny noise escapes Kimmy's throat. "A broken heart, really? That's what you're afraid of?" she exclaims, like it's a shock to her. "In all seriousness, you did the right thing, you know."

"What do you mean?"

"I like Derek. He's my friend, too. But he doesn't treat you as well as you should be treated. It was cute when we were younger, to see you two together. You were extremely happy at first. Recently, your relationship just seemed to... fizzle out," Kimmy confesses. "And I think you should be happy."

I never told her how worried I am for my friends. How the breakup made them feel. With Kimmy, I don't have to say these things out loud.

Normal, that's what I want. If everything can just go back to the way things were before Derek and I took that step, I'll be happy. "Thanks, Kimmy. You're right. Derek and I aren't good for each other."

So, I'll just focus on something I can fix—like Gavin's problem, or my own, I think. Someone had been outside the window when I stabbed myself. I need to have a conversation with Gavin about that dream. And I'm not telling anyone about it until I do. Is it possible to slip into crazy and not know you went there? I mean, clearly, I did stab myself, but I don't remember it. What would make me do something like that? Maybe I went crazy for a terribly brief moment and tried to take my own life. I'm not having those urges now. That must mean something. And I'm pretty sure Gavin is the only one who can help me.

"Ooh," Kimmy squeals as if she sees something interesting. "Are you crushing on Gavin?"

"Give me a break, Kimmy." I half laugh. "How can I crush on a boy I've never even met?"

"You've been inside each other's heads for what? Four days, now? Maybe more? You probably know him better than you think you do." We get out of the car and head for the coffee shop. Thankfully there's only a short line.

"It's not like that," I swear.

"Oh-kay," she says sarcastically.

"There's nothing I can do to convince you, so I need to figure out what else I am afraid of."

We order our lattes and sit at a small table in the far

corner. "All we need to do is have you face your fear and then what?"

"That's it, I guess. It takes courage to face your fears," I answer. "So, I face it and get a souvenir of the event."

"Oh. Hello, Marley," a cheery, familiar voice speaks.

Looking up from my drink, I see a pristine woman. Hair perfectly placed, clothing straight from the ironing board, shining a flawless set of pearly whites at us. "Dr. Crystal. Hi."

"How are you?" she asks, innocently.

"Doing fine, thanks."

"And who's your friend?" Dr. Crystal inquires, looking at Kimmy.

Kimmy waves her hand, going back to the shy girl I know her to be around strangers.

"Nice to meet you," Dr. Crystal says. "Any friend of Marley's..." she never finishes her sentence. "Oh, what a lovely purse. I have one just like it. It looks like the same designer, too," Dr. Crystal points at the gold, metallic label that has a weird 'P' symbol on it.

"You do?" Kimmy asks, dropping her shyness for her love of fashion. "I've had this thing forever and I can't find the maker to save my life."

"Oh, probably because they went out of business and didn't sell many."

Kimmy smiles and says, "Right. That must be it."

Dr. Crystal leans back on her heels. "Well, I should get back in line. Need my caffeine fix. You girls get back to your conversation. Have a good day."

"Bye," Kimmy says, as Dr. Crystal's heels tap across the floor. Waiting until she is out of earshot, Kimmy whispers to me, "Did you see her outfit?"

"I knew it!"

Kimmy's eyebrows rise in curiosity. "What?"

"I knew you'd like her style."

She flicks at her coffee cup lid and whispers, "So, about these fears—"

"Yeah, we should get going," I interrupt. "We have work to do." I leave my latte on the table and walk out, without another word.

"Where are we going?" Kimmy asks as I start the ignition and pull out of the parking lot.

"I need to face my fears, I think."

"Sounds like fun."

"I beg to differ," I tell her. Then I think about this afternoon and how strange Kimmy had been acting. "When I saw you outside the gym after lunch, you seemed off. Is everything all right now?" I ask. "Has something happened?"

"No," she responds. "Wait. When you saw me outside the gym? Today?"

I nod.

"I wasn't outside the gym today."

"What are you talking about? I saw you. We talked. You walked me to my locker."

"No, I didn't. Shawn and I went right from math straight to history. I never saw you after lunch, Lee. Not until after school." I stare, waiting for her to admit she's playing a prank on me. "I swear I was with Shawn. You can ask him yourself."

"Kimmy, this isn't funny."

"I am not playing a trick on you. I swear on the Bathtub Cuties Club that I was with Shawn all afternoon and didn't see you after lunch."

I think about it. Kimmy would have come clean by now. If she'd been joking, she wouldn't be able to hold back her laughter this long. I turn to look at her and find her watching me with a wary look.

Then it hits me. Outside the gym, Kimmy hadn't corrected me when I said "funeral." She'd been correcting me all morning, without fail. She'd constantly reminded me that it was a memorial and not a funeral. There is no way she would have missed that when we spoke outside the gym. It makes me sick to think of anyone masquerading as my best friend.

It's about time I get some answers instead of more questions. And my friends are not going to get hurt because of me. "I must be thinking about a different day, then. Sorry," I tell Kimmy, hoping she'll drop the subject.

We drive for who knows how long. I'm not thinking about fears; I'm trying to figure out my other problems, like who would have the power to transform into my best friend when Kimmy shouts excitedly, "Lee, pull over."

"Why?"

"I just thought of something."

I can't see what she's looking at until I park in front of a little bistro and bright red hair catches my attention. "Kimmy, what are we doing?"

"Genie's tortured you for years."

"That's true, but I'm not afraid of her."

Kimmy opens her door slightly. "Let's just have a chat with her."

That's when Derek steps out of the restaurant and takes the seat across from Genie. "Oh. Maybe this is a bad idea."

"Yes, but Derek is our friend," I say. "We should be

179

happy for him."

Kimmy nods, watching the scene before us in awe. "I don't think I can ever get used to it."

"Me either."

"We can try to figure out something different, if you'd like."

Pulling the keys out of the ignition, I make up my mind to give it a try. If not for my friends or myself, then at least I can do this for Gavin. Despite everything else on my mind, I'm afraid of losing someone again.

"Hey," I say quietly, as I reach their table. Derek and Genie turn to stare at me. *Remain calm,* I chant. *Remain calm.* She can smell fear. "How's it going?"

"Um, okay," Derek answers, sipping on his water. Genie continues to glare at me — as if I should be ashamed of myself for being anywhere near her without express permission.

"We were just driving by and thought we'd say hi."

"Well, you did. So now we can get back to our date," Genie grumbles.

Derek gives her the stink eye before turning back to us. "What are you two up to?" he asks.

"Just out for a walk," Kimmy lies.

Genie mutters "Walking the dog" under her breath.

I really want to let that comment slip into oblivion, but I'm about to lose the battle when Gavin's voice rings in my ears, *Face your fear.* He's right. The years we'd spent arguing is ridiculous.

Then I realize what my real fear is.

"Well, we should get going," I tell them. "Before we go, Genie, we're going to check out dresses for prom this weekend. We'd love it if you came."

She shoots me a pained expression. "I'd rather scoop my eyes out with a spoon." Her tone is sweet and laced with poison.

"Your choice," I respond. "Bye, Derek," I say and notice a halo of light around him, as if he's got a body halo. I know I've done the right thing. "Enjoy your meal."

"I know what you're doing," Genie screams as we start to walk away. "And it's not going to work."

"And what is that?"

"You noticed that Derek was moving on and thought you could get him back. Well, it's too late."

A slap in the face I don't even see coming, though I should have. I guess I can understand the mix-up. It's the way she thinks. "Derek and I were friends long before you two started dating. It can't be that far of a stretch to believe that I'd want our friendship back."

Genie scoffs, turns and sits back in her seat as if we were never there.

"What the hell was that?" Kimmy squeaks, when we're out of earshot.

My phone beeps. I dig it from my pocket and read it. Smiling, I show it to Kimmy. "That's why."

The text read:

> Sorry about that. I'll talk to her. I still want to be friends, too.

We get in the car and buckle in. "So? You got a text message. What does that mean?"

"I realized I was afraid of losing Derek as a friend. We don't work together as a couple, but we were always good friends. Is it so wrong to want that back?"

Kimmy sighs. "No. I miss him, too."

"I needed to show Derek that we could still be friends, even if we all loathe his new girlfriend."

"Maybe he sees something in her that we don't."

We turn to each other—secretly hoping that's an option, despite the fact that we both know it isn't possible. We break out into laughter at the same time.

"I hope so, for his sake," I finally say, before starting the car.

I GO DIRECTLY to the kitchen when I get to Uncle Sam's house. His house is a lot smaller than ours, darker and manlier. Its walls are plain beige and pictureless. The kitchen is my favorite room. He decorated it with a gray marble countertop, white cupboards, and a stone backsplash that awards us the only dash of color in the room: a salmon pink glass, along with black and grey ones checkered along the three walls.

Uncle Sam is proud of the room, and it's my mother's favorite as well. I find her sitting at one of the bar stools. Her hair is disheveled, thrown loosely over her shoulders. Her palm is wrapped around a glass of wine, which means she had a rough day. Tension walks right in behind me. She barely glances up from her tablet to look at me. It's been like this for way too long, I think.

"Mom, can we talk?"

"It's been a long day, Marley. Can it wait?"

She's always asking me that. How long does she want to wait? Until it's too late, like it is with Dad? "No, it can't wait."

"Is everything all right?"

Is everything all right, Mom? No, it's not. My whole world is upside down, everything I ever believed is backward. But I can't tell *her* that. I can't tell my own mother that I've been going through the trial of my life. "No," I manage to say. "Things are not okay. I want things to go back to normal."

She closes her paper. "I just don't see how that's going to happen, dear. Not any time soon."

"I know you see my accident as some kind of betrayal, but I promise, *promise*," I emphasize again. "I would never, ever do what you think I did." That dream only proves it to me. That girl was *not* me. That much I'm certain of. I know myself, and no one can tell me any different. "I'm even in therapy. As if I were guilty. That should prove I'm trying my best to get our relationship back."

"That just shows that you feel guilt, Marley."

"That's not it. It's what *you* wanted. I thought if I did what you asked of me, you would stop being angry and listen."

"You don't have anything to say that I can believe."

A strong sense of disbelief overwhelms me. Did she just take away any small hope I had with just a few words? How do I get her to listen to me? "You know me, Mom." I demand.

She sighs and takes a sip of her wine. "I find it hard to believe — even for someone as accident prone as you are — could fall on a knife and nearly destroy your liver."

"Me, too, and I can't blame you for being upset. You

know me, Mom. I'm your daughter. I have a lot to live for. It's not like I'm depressed all the time. Once in a while, maybe, if we're being honest. But who isn't?"

"I can't have this conversation right now, Marley."

"When, Mom? My graduation? My wedding day? On my deathbed? I can't live like this anymore."

"Marley." She raises her voice, anger and annoyance slips into her tone.

"Mom, please. Can you please try to understand what I'm going through? I don't remember what happened to me. I feel alone in this, and you were always there for me. I don't know what to do without you for support." My eyes water against my will. I don't want to cry about this anymore. She's my mother—the woman I look to for guidance. There is no way I'm letting that go without a fight. "Can't you be mad at me without freezing me out?"

She remains quiet. I can see her thinking as she sips from her wine glass. The wheels spin quickly. Then her expression softens slightly as she says, "Okay, Marley. Come sit. We'll talk." She attempts to suppress the anger in her tone. I appreciate the effort. Her anger isn't going to disappear overnight—I get that—but I desperately want my mother back. She doesn't know anything about what's happening in my life and I can't tell her everything, but I can't fight with her anymore. The only thing I won't do is lie.

I take a seat in front of her. For a few minutes, we remain quiet. "If you don't remember what happened, how can I believe that it didn't happen on purpose?"

"I don't have any answers, Mom. I wish I did, and that's what kills me." I wince; bad choice of words. "Every angry look you give me, every time someone looks at me

184

funny at school, every time I go see the shrink, I am reminded of the fact that I almost died and really don't know how it happened. Even Dr. Crystal should tell you that I don't fit the profile of someone ready to take their own life. And it has nothing to do with Derek. If I could survive Dad's death, why would a little breakup, well, break me?"

"How are things between you and Derek, now?" she asks.

We're actually talking. I don't want to get too excited, but I allow myself to get comfortable and settle in for a conversation long overdue. "Yesterday I probably would have said not well. Today, he gave me a little hope that we'll get our friendship back."

"Some things you can't get back, Marley. I hope you know that. Although I'm rooting for you both."

"I know it, but why should my other friends suffer because Derek and I didn't work together? I have to at least try."

"I know you do."

"He's dating Genie, now."

"What?" she asks, her eyes widen in astonishment. "You're joking."

"No." I laugh. "I'm serious."

"Do you think he's trying to get back at you?"

I shake my head. "I think he actually likes her. Weird, huh?"

"I'm having a hard time wrapping my head around it."

I snatch my mom's nearly empty wine glass off the counter and fill it, giving us enough time to think of topics to talk about. The one thing I really want to share with her is off-limits. "How are you? Did something happen at work today?" I finally come up with.

"I'm doing okay, sweetie. Really quiet at work, usually. Today, not so much."

"Any bites?" I always ask her that when she's having a bad day, and it always gets a chuckle. She used to get bit by kids almost daily.

Today, she only smiles. Baby steps. I'm anxious to get over this hurdle, so I take the win. "I didn't see any children today, believe it or not."

"That's good."

"Thanks. How did that boy's memorial go? That was this morning, wasn't it?"

"It was awful, Mom. Someone so young just gone one day." When Mom found me lying on the kitchen floor, she was probably thinking something similar in her haste to get me help. I can't even imagine. "The ceremony was beautiful, and there were so many people."

"It was very nice of you to go. I'm sure his family appreciated you being there." I fidget with my chipping manicure. "I spoke to your therapist today. I told her that I wouldn't be coming in for a family session."

"Really? Why not?"

"Well, I don't think you need to go anymore—after tomorrow. Today only proves that you're getting better. I don't know if it was seeing someone so young who passed away, but you seem—different these past few days. I hope you know how important you are to me, Sammy, and your uncle."

My stomach jumps, and a smile hits my lips. I nod, unable to hide my joy, despite the fact that my mother still believes I tried to take myself out. Dr. Crystal doesn't seem like a bad person, though she might be a little too prim and proper. It's thrilling to know I won't have to see her again after tomorrow. I don't want to see her at all. If Mom is in a generous mood, I am not arguing. It's a fair compromise. "Where is Uncle Sam?"

"Already left for work."

"He's on afternoons? That sucks. I was hoping to see him."

"Yes, it does," she agrees, looking down at her paper again.

My mother-daughter time is coming to a close but I never want it to end. "Mom, I love you. No matter what."

"I know, sweetie."

I get up and start to leave, not expecting the pit in my stomach to be bigger than it had been before we spoke. I was wrong.

Mom and I used to have conversations like this every other day and I hadn't really realized how much I missed them before this moment.

"Marley?" Mom calls.

"Mom?"

"I love you, too. We'll get through this, just like we've gotten through every other tragedy in our lives. I'm really, really happy you're okay."

"Thanks, Mom. Being strong women sucks sometimes," I confess.

Mom smiles back at me. "It's exhausting."

# SEVENTEEN

GAVIN HUDDLES WITH his friends in the crowded and noisy gym. He seems to be having a good time. "The girls are looking good tonight," his friend with the long, skinny nose screams over some Fall Out Boy song I don't recognize.

Gavin agrees with a whooping noise.

"You should talk to one of them. Dance with them. Sheila moved away a year ago. It's about time you get another girl."

"As soon as one catches my eye, Charles. Don't worry. I haven't quit on women."

"Who's that?" Charles asks loudly, changing the subject. He turns toward the exit, where his friend is staring.

"Who?" Gavin asks.

Then the "he" comes into view. The man is cloaked in a dark trench coat and hunching over. He walks as though he were drunk. His features are hidden by a combination of low lighting and a hood.

This cannot be good.

As the man walks closer, I notice that the doors have been chained. A deep pit appears in my gut. I have a bad feeling about this. That's when all hell breaks loose, set on terrorizing Gavin and his friends.

The man whips out a gun and blows a giant hole in one of the speakers. The music dies. The man aims the gun at the dance floor. "All of you sit down. No one leaves and no one moves." His voice cracks, unsure.

I don't want to see this again, to relive the day my soulmate was taken from this world, but I haven't figured out how to end these dreams.

When everyone sits in the corner, huddling close, the man asks, "Which one of you is Gavin Slater?"

The man went there for Gavin? He meant to kill Gavin the whole time? My temperature rises just as my anger does. I want to run at him, to claw his eyes out for what he's done.

No one responds. Gavin looks around the room; everyone is avoiding his gaze. What I notice is the old man doesn't ask for jewelry or phones, which makes the pit in my stomach grow deeper. What does he want with Gavin?

Clearing his throat, Gavin asks in a calm voice, trying to act brave for his friends, "Please, sir, don't hurt anyone. I'm Gavin. Whatever you want, please just take it and go. No one will call the cops. You have my word."

"Sh—shut up! I don't want your junk," the man shouts. "I want what you stole from me."

"Do I know you, sir?"

Something changes in the man's eyes, they lighten and widen. It's as if he's realized something. "I'm going to pay you back for everything you've done to me. You *will* suffer. Now shut up! No more talking." The old man's eyes warn him to keep quiet—not to push his luck or get anyone hurt.

What could a teenager have done to the old guy anyway? How could anything be so bad that the old man would risk jail time and people's lives by taking hostages and waving a gun around? Gavin wouldn't have stolen from this man, that much I'm sure of.

"Excuse me," a young boy asks. "I need to go to the bathroom. I'm sorry, but I can't hold it much longer."

"Too bad. Hold it."

Gavin implores, "The bathroom is just down the hall. You can see him from the door right there. It's me you want anyway. Why not just let everyone else go?"

"No one leaves!" the bad guy shouts, waving the gun in the air.

The teen boy huddles closer to his friends and Gavin turns back to the old man. "What is it that I stole from you?"

"Everything. I had it all until you came along, you… you filthy little mutt. You took everything that mattered to me."

The gunman stops speaking for a while, only paces back and forth, frustrated and paranoid. Every once in a while, he would sputter mindless words to himself. I pray someone will come to the rescue, but I know they aren't coming.

I can't just sit here and watch this happen, again. What can I do? I pinch my own arm, but that does nothing. I'm not an angry person but this scene really draws it out of me. I can't help but wonder why this terrible person would want to harm a helpless child.

"Excuse me?" someone says. Gavin looks up, eyes landing on a skinny blonde, chest heaving.

"No. Whatever it is you want, I don't care." the bad guy screeches horribly.

The girl squeals and crouches down in her position like a puppy caught misbehaving. "Look," Gavin says. "We're just trying to get through this in one piece. There's no need to scream. Just let us know what you want." When the man whips his gun in Gavin's direction; he sucks in a gulp of air and holds it. My temperature spikes as I look on in horror. Gavin stares down the barrel of the gun, never backing down, even though he's a ball of nerves on the inside.

"Don't be a smartass, kid. I've got nothing to lose here."

Suddenly, the blonde girl drops face first into the floor. The gunman automatically points the pistol toward the unconscious girl.

I don't know what Gavin's thinking, but he reacts quickly, driving himself forward and blocking the gun's path to the girl. That's when it happens. Gavin's world is turned upside down and there's nothing I can do to stop it.

A sharp blast of pain blindsides him and takes him from his high school gym. The cold heat of the bullet tears through his chest as fear blasts through his entire body. Gavin burrows into himself and still manages to choke out the words, "Don't hurt them."

Darkness explodes behind his eyes. Gavin gasps through shallow breath and understands that he's dying. I know this because I can feel it, too: the excruciating agony that pulses through him pulses through me. Tears spill down my cheeks as I realize Gavin doesn't want to leave this world.

But the pain won't let him stay.

Within minutes, he's no longer in the realm he's spent an extremely short seventeen years in.

I watch the scene vanish through Gavin's eyes, feel the pain he felt. We shoot into a blinding darkness before we're back in Gavin's room—the room that Circe has given him during his visit on the island.

Gavin happens to be looking at the wall as the large black hole appears. The little boy materializes. Gavin attempts to grab him and yank the little boy out. Instead of hitting palpable flesh, his hands smash into a rock-solid wall. Gavin hisses and the boy howls in fits of mocking laughter. Endlessly.

Gavin nearly leaves the room, holding his hands close to his chest. If he could strangle the boy, he just might have. Maybe.

"I'm... I'm sorry," the boy admits through choppy breath. "I'm sorry. I just came to see if you thought about my offer. I'm guessing by your reaction that you still need time." The boy shuffles and begins to leave.

Gavin panics and calls out, "Wait!"

The boy hesitates and then rushes back with a victorious smile on his tiny features. "Yes..." the boy says.

"Tell me more about your way. Why'd you say you could get me more power? How? And will I still be able to go home?" Gavin asks, sitting in a chair in front of the gaping hole in the wall.

Who is this boy, I want to know? Large features scatter along his tiny face. Big green eyes are sculpted underneath long black lashes. A wide grin soars above the boy's cleft chin. He looks trustworthy, but I get a bad feeling from him.

From what I can tell in this dream and others before it, Gavin has the same feeling. I want to tell him how I'm feeling while I watch the scene unfold, but it's only a dream and I can't communicate with Gavin in my dreams.

I can only watch. Every horrifying scene I live through breaks my heart all over again.

"Yes, you can still go back to the land of the living," the little boy answers Gavin. "But I can send you back with more power because I know where to find it."

"Where?"

"Not telling." The boy shakes his head vigorously and begins picking his nose. Gross, kid. My brother's six, and he doesn't do that anymore. And this kid is at least a year older.

"Then why are you here?"

While the boy digs for gold, he whispers, "To see if you will come with me."

"And where would we go?"

The boy doesn't budge. He looks Gavin in the eye, with his fingertip hidden in his nose, and he admits, "I can't say, but I want you on my side. I want to give you more power, and maybe there is something I might ask of you in the future."

"Like what?" Gavin prods.

"I don't know, yet. Maybe I will want to visit the land of the living. Everyone always wants to go there so badly."

"It's easy to understand when you realize that that life is all we know. There's family and loved ones we leave behind."

"Maybe I might want one of these family things."

Gavin runs a hand through his hair and paces along

193

the length of his bed and back. "Then why don't you talk to Circe? She could be your family."

"I don't think so. I don't like her. She is mean when no one is looking," the boy tells Gavin. "She turns boys into animals, you know?"

Gavin grinds out the words, "I doubt that."

"You would choose her side!" the boy whines.

"Don't get testy, kid. I'm talking to you, aren't I?"

"I don't get to talk much. To people."

Gavin stops pacing and turns his head toward the hole in the wall. "Why don't you come out of the wall and sit with me. We can continue our chat."

The little boy shakes his head.

There's a short silence. I presume both boys are thinking of topics to talk about. "Fine. We can talk like this. Where are your parents?"

"Never had any."

"Where did you come from, then?"

The boy visibly thinks about the question by rolling his eyes to the ceiling and leaves them there a moment and then answers, "I don't know."

"Where do you go when you're not here? Do you have a hut or a cave? Maybe you have a house you stay at on the island?"

The boy shrugs.

"All right," Gavin says, smacking his hands on his thighs, desperately trying to keep his tone frustration free, but I can hear it. "Can you tell me your name?"

The boy starts shaking his head before his eyes land on something in Gavin's room and he responds happily, "Cola."

"Cola? No one gave you a name, did they?" Gavin

asks after his own eyes land on the soda can at his bedside table.

"Yeah. It's Cola, duh." his tone defensive. That's when he decides to dig for gold again.

Gavin holds his hands up defensively. "Cola, fine. It's nice to meet you. I'm Gavin." The boy nods, and there is another long silence. "What if I went with you, Cola? What should I say to Circe?"

"Who cares? Just come with me." This time when he screeches, his tone is angry and childish.

"I have to tell her something," Gavin tries to speak calmly, hoping not to scare the kid off.

"I guess you're not ready. I'll come back." The boy eats whatever is on his finger and then disappears. I cringe, roll my eyes, and wish I never had to witness that. The hole vanishes as if it were never there. Gavin stands there for a moment and then he leaves his small room.

Instead of the changing scenes, my subconscious mind stays with Gavin, following him as he paces down the hall and out the back door. When he finds Circe, she's sitting on the deck of her old cabin, underneath a wide umbrella, looking out at the trees and the flowers. Beside her, a paintbrush magically depicts the beautiful scene in front of us onto a white canvas.

"Hey, do you have a minute?" Gavin wants to know.

"Anything for you, sweet boy. Come, have a seat beside me, and we will talk." A chair magically appears beside her. She pats it, beckoning him over. "Would you like something to drink?"

"I'm a spirit. I don't need to eat or drink."

She nods, smiling back. "We talked about this. It's nice to taste life through a simple glass of liquid occasionally. A lot of my..." she pauses to find the right word, "guests enjoy soaking their pallet. It reminds them that there's hope. And besides, no calories." She chuckles, waving the easel away.

"That's why there was a soda can in my room," Gavin says, realizing the reason why. Gavin happily accepts the drink when it appears in her hand. "I've been having these visits, and I thought I should tell you about them. It's happened a couple times, now. He's a little boy who calls himself Cola. He shows up and promises me more power if I go with him. I thought there was no one else on the island."

"What else did the boy say?"

"That's just it. Nothing else. He doesn't tell me how or why. He told me about the Valley of Truth and the river of..." Gavin thinks for a moment. "I don't remember. That's why you found me standing there the other day. I was — curious."

"The Pearl River," she confirms. "The portal *is* actually there. I know that's what the boy told you. I never lied to you."

But what about Cola, I think.

Circe continues, "I'll understand if that's what you're thinking right now."

"I'm confused. He just kept asking me if I want more power."

"And do you?"

Gavin looks her in the eye and says, "I just want to go home. I don't care about power. I don't even need magic."

"But you could help a lot of people. You have to know that."

He nods, accepting the fact. "That would be nice. But

there are so many people in my realm who help others without any magical help. Why am I so special?"

"You're being modest. Everyone is special. It's just some people are more special than others because of what they choose to do with their gifts. You are a very talented, intelligent, and caring young man who will do great things. You should be proud of yourself and all you have accomplished — even in your short number of years."

"I can promise to try to help others if I have magical powers when I get back but what do I do about this boy who keeps haunting me?"

"What do you want to do?"

"I came out here to get your advice."

"I can't tell you what to do. You have to make the choice."

Gavin pauses only a short moment. My guess is to consider his options. "I want to stick with you because you care about what happens to me when I get on the other side. You care about what happens to others and you don't seem to give empty promises. Even if I went back with no powers, I would be happy just to go back."

Circe squeals with excitement. "Well done, sweet boy. You've passed another test."

"What do you mean? I haven't done anything."

"Oh, but you have done more than you think, Gavin. You had an opportunity to take another path, to be greedy, and because of who you are you chose to stick with me, even though you were offered more power. You were loyal, even though I'm sure the boy tried to create doubt in your mind about my sincerity. You are selfless and honest. Qualities one needs to return to the land of the living."

"That's great. What happens now? Will the boy stop

pestering me?"

"He comes and goes, but he is just an illusion," Circe tells Gavin.

Oh, that explains it, I think to myself.

She continues to explain, "He's a part of this island — a devil to trick you into betraying yourself. I could not warn you of him because very horrible things happen when I warn my Piggybackers of the tests. He's not real. I have never laid eyes on him myself, but many visitors have told me of him." She pauses for a moment before turning to Gavin. Putting a hand on his cheek, she says, "I hope you know that I did not lie when I told you I was alone on the island. He might have told you that to confuse you."

I want to believe her; she seems so convincing. But then again, she's had centuries to perfect the craft of lying.

Gavin nods and sips his drink. The cool liquid explodes like tiny firecrackers on Gavin's tongue and down his dry throat. It feels and tastes like he's actually drinking. I feel what he's feeling, though sometimes I wish I could hear his thoughts. "That explains why I couldn't nab him from the wall. He is not very convincing, if that makes you feel better."

"It does. Truly. Thank you. Some souls have fallen for it, I'm afraid. They go through that portal and become the very thing I'm trying to prevent."

"Limbonians?"

"Yes," she says sadly.

"I wish you could save them all."

She nods and rocks in her chair. "I wish that, too."

Gavin looks at the liquid in his glass, mesmerized by the liquid puddle. "Do you know that my mom's chili is famous?"

"I don't believe you've told me this."

"She calls it "fire-ant chili" because every bite feels like a thousand fire ants nipping at your tongue, or so she tells people. I love it and so does my older brother. This chef from Paris bought the rights from her just so he could make it at his restaurant. In French, it's something like *fourmi de feu piment.*"

"Fascinating. You must be proud of her."

"I am."

Gavin pauses to take a sip of his drink, looking out at the horizon.

"What are you thinking about, Gavin?" Circe's words slide right into his happy memory. "You have a blissful expression in your eyes."

"Just my mom and all the fun times we've had. The three of us were so happy."

Circe touches his shoulder reassuringly, "And you will have that again. Your mate will be given another ingredient, which will make four."

After the dream ends, I get out of bed in total darkness and stumble into the bathroom to stick my head in the toilet. After witnessing Gavin's death, I don't want to see food ever again. I hope they caught the creep who shot him and stuff him behind bars for good.

Sweat drips down the back of my neck as I sit there, trying to will my stomach to settle. After a while I'm finally able to stand on shaky legs. These nightmares need to go away, right now.

Flicking on the light, I search underneath the sink for something scented, since the smell is making my eyes water.

I snatch a can from under the counter, shake it and

spray vehemently. When I put the can back underneath the counter and stand up, I notice all the spray fogging up the glass. Geez, Marley.

So, I get some window cleaner from under the sink. Out of the corner of my eye, I see it. Looking back at my foggy reflection, a single word reads:

*Kyle*

Apparently when Circe told Gavin that his soul mate would get the next ingredient, she meant it. But what does it mean? Surely, I can't use a human for a ritual. Can I?

# EIGHTEEN

*Thursday, October 25th*

*MARLEY, DID YOU get the next ingredient?*

*Yes, I got the ingredient. I'm not happy about it though*, I admit as I wipe the message from the bathroom mirror.

*Why? What is it?*

*Apparently, I need Kyle. Who's Kyle?*

*Oh no*, he says. *Kyle's my brother.*

I wash my hands and brush toothpaste onto the toothbrush Uncle Sam left out for me. *How am I going to use a human being for a ritual?*

*Maybe you need his blood or something. Don't spells usually call for that kind of stuff?*

*Ew!* That sounds disgusting. *I hope not.*

*My brother's quite the character. He's easy to talk to. And… I have a feeling you two will get along just fine.*

"Fantastic!" I tell the clean mirror. It sounds so easy. *Yeah, I can just say, "Hey, how's it going? I'm doing this to save your brother," and poke him with a needle or something. Doesn't sound difficult at all.*

*Maybe you'll think of something else,* Gavin tries to comfort. I snort in an unladylike way while walking down the dimly lit hallway and back to the room Uncle Sam made up for me. I try to come up with a plan while in search of my bed. *I'm sorry if I woke you, love.*

*I wasn't sleeping,* I tell him, yawning into the night time air. *I woke up after having another bad dream.*

*About me?*

*Yes.*

Gavin admits, *Sorry. Wish they would stop. I got so excited that I passed another test, and I wanted to tell you right away.*

*That's why I need Kyle.*

*I know. I find it strange, too.*

*Sounds needlessly fun. So, tell me about your brother. Is he anything like you?* I want to know, meaning it as a compliment—well, most of the time. The sound of my voice, even in my own head sounds less awake now. Rest calls out to me. I only have two more days to get two more ingredients, so a little rest may be a good idea.

*Kyle? In some ways he is. I mean, he's not as funny as I am, but he's a good guy,* Gavin tells me. *Luckily, he's home from college for — well, you know. I'm not sure how long he is going to be here. He goes out of state, so it has to be done fast.*

*Leave it up to me. I'm on it.*

*You mean, you have a plan?*

I roll into bed and under the blankets. "I wish."

AFTER SCHOOL, I head toward Gavin's house, using

the address he gave me. I'm not entirely sure this will work. Then again, I don't have much of a choice. It's the only plan I currently have, and time is not on my side. With Gavin's deadline fast approaching, I refuse to even admit the word failure into my vocabulary. In fact, if I fail it will be the worst thing I've ever done.

A strong-jawed jock steps out the front door as I pull up in front of the house. Even underneath a heavy jacket I can tell the guy is buff. He looks nothing like Gavin — in fact, they look like total opposites — but I remember Kyle from the funeral — memorial. We hadn't spoken though I saw him waving his aunt over; she never left his side after that.

The memorial.

A shiver rockets up my spine. I don't even want to think about it. If you can get through this next hurdle, Marley, you'll be that much closer to your goal, I remind myself.

I follow Kyle all afternoon, waiting for an opportunity to present itself. We stop at the post office and then the grocery store; finally, he goes into a coffee shop. When he opens his laptop and gets comfortable, I know this is my chance. Pulling myself out of the car and smoothing my clothes, I take a deep breath and mentally prepare myself for what I'm about to do.

I've never been the flirty type. In fact, I've always been the quiet one, the easygoing one. The girl who sits near the window and daydreams while the teacher drones on and on about this or that. I get good grades, but I am far from a genius. I am not into vampires or werewolves or any of that stuff, like the other girls my age. I'm more into reading, karate, hanging out with my friends, and training.

If I think about it, I have to admit that my life has become way more entertaining in the last few days. Before Gavin came along it seemed like all I did was babysit my little brother or hide from my mother. Now, I'm out in the world again, trying to make the adjustment rapidly for Gavin's sake.

Get it together, Marley. You're only going in to talk to a boy. This should be simple. You're not exactly a duckling. Get in there and get some DNA so the boy can have his brother back. DNA? That's a lovely thought. If that's true, I can just get a lock of hair. I got this. That's so much easier.

*Yeah. What she said.* Gavin sarcastically trills in my mind. *And you look lovely, by the way.*

*Thanks. What do you suggest?* I ask him.

Gavin laughs, *Just walk by and yank his hair out, then run away.*

*I should have known.*

*You really should have,* Gavin confirms. *What about the cup?*

*What cup?*

*If he's at a coffee house, then he's probably going to have a cup, which will have his DNA on it, too. Get the cup when he's done with it.*

I walk into the coffee shop and realize it's so busy there's nowhere to sit. Then a plan strikes me. Sliding a few coins from my pocket, I purchase a drink, then sidle over to Kyle's table. The cup on the table is glowing. I realize that this will work. I ask, "I'm sorry, but would you mind if I sat with you? There isn't anywhere else to sit."

Kyle glances up from his computer. One quick glance

and then his eyes are back on the screen. He gestures toward the empty seat but doesn't speak.

I instantly regret my decision to come over here. This is a bad idea. He barely even looked at me. I really shouldn't have done this.

That's when Kyle clears his throat and says, "Sorry, I was reading an important email. I didn't mean to be rude, Miss..."

"Oh. Marley," I say, after realizing what he's fishing for. "And that's okay... I understand. I didn't mean to interrupt. Just needed my caffeine."

"I'm Kyle by the way. Have we met before, Marley?"

*Oh shoot. He recognizes me from Gavin's funeral.* I pick at my coffee cup, trying to think of something to say. Words won't come to me.

*Memorial,* Gavin corrects. *Don't worry. Just act dumb. It will work. Trust me.*

I do trust him, so I play dumb and say, "I don't think so. I don't really get out much."

"I see. My mistake." Kyle sips his coffee quietly for a moment, looks at his computer, and then closes it. "Well, Marley, it was really nice meeting you, but I need to get to an appointment. Take care of yourself, now."

"Same to you, Kyle. Thanks for the table."

"Any time."

*Wow. I'm surprised. He's usually more of a flirt than that,* Gavin informs me.

*Maybe I'm just not his type then.*

*Oh, no. You're exactly his type,* Gavin declares. *Beautiful, funny, smart, and* female!

*Thanks, I think.* I watch Kyle get into his car and realize then that he has his coffee cup in his hand. *See what happens when you distract me, you trouble maker?*

*Sorry,* is the last thing he says, a bite of laughter in his tone. At least someone finds this amusing.

I follow Kyle for another two hours, watching and waiting for a sign of the coffee cup, before he finally goes home. I don't see the coffee cup in his hands when he trots up the stairs. Luckily, sunset began ten minutes ago so the sun's beginning to hover at the edge of the landscape. Pretty soon it will be dark out and then I can get the cup. I have to. I can't get this far and fail.

*Marley. You can't do it,* Gavin protests. *You could get into serious trouble.*

*I don't have a choice,* I tell him, watching his house for any sign of where his family is and what they're doing.

*I know that. I just don't like the way this day is going. You shouldn't be endangering yourself this way,* he shouts in my head. I can hear the frustration in his words, but there is no other way to get that DNA.

"If you have another plan, please enlighten me."

Gavin sighs. It sounds like he's about to give in. *I wish I could help, but long-distance magic really drains me. If I help, I may be gone for a while.*

*You can be my backup plan,* I tell him.

*Just be careful. All right?*

*Of course.*

I wait another few minutes, drumming my fingers on the steering wheel of my clunker of a car. When I'm certain that no one is near the windows and doors, I make my way to Kyle's car. Instead of creeping in, I try to make it look like I'm getting into my own vehicle and pray no one thinks any different. When the door clicks open for me, I send a silent thanks to the heavens and reach in for the coffee cup.

"Who are you and what are you doing in my son's car?"

The voice scares me so much that I jump and hit my head off the roof. Panic slithers quickly up my spine and straight into my blood stream, poisoning my brain cells so I can't even muster up a bad excuse. Oh, crap. I'm going to jail. I'm never going to finish high school, and my mother will never speak to me again. Or worse. She could make me talk to the shrink until I graduate. What am I going to do? There is no plausible excuse for being here and I have no idea how to get out of this predicament.

Think, Marley. Come on, I tell my brain. What excuse do you have for being in someone else's car?

"I'm calling the cops," Gavin's mom says. I back out of the car, holding my injured head in my hands, moving slowly so I can hopefully drum up even a bad excuse. "You," the strawberry blonde wearing a housecoat and slippers points right at me. "Come with me. I'm keeping my eye on you until they get here," she threatens.

"Wait. I can explain. Please." My mind is still racing. What excuse is not illegal or supernatural related?

The woman turns, her fury matched only by the fiery hue of her hair. Her arms are crossed and a trickle of anger furrows between her eyebrows while she waits for me to speak. I still have no words or explanation to offer her, but I am thinking.

That's when Kyle comes out. Nope, this cannot get any worse. What am I going to say to these people? My breathing intensifies and my hands shake.

Gavin's laugh echoes in my mind. Of all the things for him to do at any given time, that is the absolute worst. *This is so not funny,* I reprimand. *I should just let you rot there. Wherever you are.*

*You're right. It's not funny.* His words in my head are breathy from his laughter. I'd roll my eyes if Gavin's family wasn't standing there staring at me like I'm a car thief.

*Help me, Gavin. Or get out of my head.* I'm so panicked, my heart throbs a mile a minute and my brain is still not conjuring up an excuse. I can tell them I'm homeless and was looking for money. No, I don't look homeless. I can tell them I thought it was my car. No, they look nothing alike.

Dang it, I'm going to jail.

*I'm sorry, Marley. It's just… they're my family, and I know they're not usually like this.*

*What? Protective?*

*They're always that but my mother, she's unusual. She cares about people. Normally, she'd probably ask you what you're looking for and why you need it so badly and then hand it over to you.*

*She just lost her son,* I say. *She doesn't feel anything but grief. I remember that feeling. When I lost my father, grief stuck with me for months — constantly hovering over me like one of those dark, depressing cartoon rain clouds.*

Kyle speaks up, "Uh, Marley, right? Did you follow me here?"

"No, I didn't. I, um—" Something metal magically appears in my free hand.

*It was his father's. Tell him he left it at the café,* Gavin tells me.

*Thanks.* I can finally breathe. "I'm sorry. I was just going to put this in your car. I didn't want to bother you at home this late. You left this at the café. It looks expensive, so I wanted to get it right back to you." I hold my hand out. "I was actually trying to avoid this awkward moment. Looking back, it was kind of silly to go into your car. I'm sorry, ma'am, if I scared you."

Kyle makes his way closer to me, while his mom just stares, looking very skeptical. When Kyle gets closer his eyes light up. "I—thank you, Marley. It—yeah, it's important. It was my dad's. You know, I don't even remember putting it on this morning."

I offer an innocent smile, knowing his mother is still watching me skeptically. I concentrate on Kyle's welcoming smile instead of the surly one that is at the edge of my vision. "It happens sometimes," I say.

"Thank you, again. Really." Kyle examines his watch, like he's trying to remember putting it on that morning. I feel bad about lying to him. He tilts his head and asks, "Hey, how did you find me?"

"Oh, long story," I elude. "I'm just happy I did."

"Me, too. Do you want to stay for a cup of coffee?"

I turn to look at Kyle's mom. Her expression is the only answer I need. "I shouldn't."

"Are you sure? It's the least I can do after you went to so much trouble."

"That's very kind of you, Kyle, but I really should get home to my family. My mother is probably getting worried." No one will suspect that I'm lying, since it's nearly dinnertime.

"All right. Some other time, then."

"Sounds good. Bye. Sorry again," I offer to Mom, but she doesn't budge an inch on the angry scale. What's with all the moms not liking me lately?

The wooden texture of the paper cup in my hands is my only comfort. It's another ingredient I can cross off my list. Gavin's mother could have called the cops at any time and I would have been done—Gavin would have been done. Or she could have called my mom and I would've been squirming in a straitjacket before nightfall. Or, I could be sent back to… nope, not going there.

I cannot wait to finish this ritual and go back to my normal life.

*I'm sorry about all of this.*

*Me too,* I say as I get into my car. *Now your mom hates me.*

*That part sucks, but I'm happy it worked out, Marley. I don't think I have the power to break you out of jail,* Gavin jokes.

"You're always joking. This is serious, Gavin. I never would have been able to explain why I was stealing Kyle's cup." Seriously? Did I really just say those words? It's a freaking cup, for crying out loud. They wouldn't lock me up for stealing a cup—maybe slap a stalker label on me.

*What would Kimmy say right now?* he asks.

I roll my eyes.

Gavin confesses, *I know I'm always joking. If you can't laugh at times like these, fear and sadness creep in and it's harder to get rid of them. That's what my mom always told me. That's probably why we were always laughing in my house.*

I breathe a heavy sigh of relief and shove the key into the ignition. My hands shake as I turn it and listen for the sound of freedom. Once the engine revs up, I floor the gas pedal. Fogging up my window, I inhale and exhale several times as I put distance between myself and Gavin's place.

*Marley, I have to go for a little while. Only one more*

*ingredient to get and this will all be over. Don't get yourself into any trouble while I'm gone,* he requests. *I won't be there to rescue you.* Gavin's laughter echoes off the walls in my head.

*I will try,* I tell him. *But I'm not promising anything. See you soon.*

No response, as I expect. I try to remain optimistic, knowing that the deadline's coming up quickly. With only one more ingredient to collect, there is reason to feel hopeful.

Looking down at my watch it occurs to me that I'm nearly late for my appointment with the shrink. Not that I really care, but since speaking to Mom, I don't want to do anything to upset her. Otherwise, she may change her mind and make me continue seeing Dr. Crystal.

No thanks.

Her office is only fifteen minutes away. It's 5:30, so I have half an hour to make it there. More than enough time. Pondering the silly notion that I'm afraid to be late to an appointment I don't even want to go to, I don't notice the old white van pull up beside me until it's too late. It veers up ahead and turns at a forty-five-degree angle—thanks geometry. Knowing that really came in handy, I think sarcastically. The van screeches to a stop right in front of me. Before I have time to react, my car is slamming into the van, but only with enough force to rattle my bones and dent my front end—luckily.

I check—nothing broken, although my engine hisses in annoyance.

Before I know it, two men are ripping me out of my car. I try to yell, "I'm okay."

Neither will listen. They don't seem to care. My

stitches tear and this time I'm certain of it. The snap of the scab opening feels crystal clear. A sharp pain slithers into my gut. My pulse spikes with both anger and fear.

When I realize what's happening, it's too late. "Let me go!" Screaming and jerking around, I hope they drop me and run away. "Why are you doing this? Where are you taking me?" I shout, desperate to get an answer.

They don't give me one.

The street's quiet, but someone *must* have seen the accident. Surely, they won't get away with this.

The two goons head toward the van and toss me into it. My knees scrape along rusty metal as I slide across the cold, metal floor. The goons pile in right after me.

One captor comes at me as the other shuts the doors, locking the three of us in the back. The echo of the creaking doors sounds like prison gates. I'm not getting out of here, I think, when I see one of the goons holding something gray that peaks out of the guy's gloved hand.

What is it? I can't tell. Is it a knife?

"What the hell is going on here? What are you doing?" I demand answers with a fake bravado, as warm blood drips down my belly and soaks into my shirt. I have definitely broken a stitch in the struggle. Adrenaline whistles through my veins, luckily delaying the sting of pain for a blessed moment.

Neither says a word. I can't see their faces because they are covered by dark hoodies and they're wearing gloves. There are no memorable things about either one of these men—aside from the fact that they're both men. There's nothing I will be able to give the police if I happen to survive.

And Gavin won't be able to help me with this one.

How am I going to get myself out of this mess? "Please don't kill me," I say, deciding to change tactics.

One of them moves closer. I crouch in the corner of the van. "No. Please."

The man grabs both my hands. I try to struggle, and still he manages to tape my hands together. It was tape, not a knife. That should be a comfort, but it's not. The other man holds my feet together as I try to kick free. The first guy kneels at my feet and tapes them, leaving my mind to dredge up the horrible possibilities of what's about to happen. What do they want from me? Why aren't they talking? Neither man says a word. It all happened so fast, I hadn't even thought to look at the license plate.

How am I going to get out of this? "I don't have any money," I warn them. "So, if that's what you're angling for, you've got the wrong girl."

"We just want to ask you a few questions. That's all." The man's voice comes out nasally.

"Why would you have to kidnap me for a few questions? And why would you need to tie me up?"

"Precautions," the other one says. His voice is deep, but nothing extraordinary to note about him, except for the fact that when he was tying my ankles together, I noticed a slight bend in his pinky finger. Maybe he broke it at some point—or maybe it was because of his glove, Marley. It isn't enough to go on, and I'm no Sherlock Holmes—but at least it's something.

The first guy catches my attention. "You are Marley McCartney. Yes?"

"What? You kidnapped me and you don't know who I am?"

"Tell us your name."

"Why should I tell you anything?"

The second guy—still holding my feet—squeezes angrily. "Answer our questions and maybe we'll let you go."

I don't believe that, but my options are limited. "Yes. I'm Marley. Now tell me what you want from me."

"Do you know a boy named Gavin Slater?"

Oh, good gracious. How many people know about that poor boy? "Gavin Slater? That's the boy from the papers, right? I never got the chance to meet him before he died."

"Don't lie to us." Deep Voice shouts. "If you want to see the outside of this van again."

I squint my eyes at the guy holding my feet, hoping they can't tell how afraid I am. "Look, I don't know why this is so important to you, but I never met the guy." I stress. "We went to different schools. Hung out in different crowds. Trust me, I did *not* know him."

Which is not a lie.

Deep Voice reaches into his pocket then. He pulls something out. I can't see what it is, although it's very small. He scoots closer to me, and that's when I see the mole on the back of his wrist. I make a mental note while attempting to scurry backward, finding out I'm already sitting as far back as I can get. He has something in his hand, and he's coming at me menacingly. There are too many possibilities running through my mind for me not to feel fear rush to the surface of my palms, in the form of sticky sweat, adrenaline fading. It could be a knife, or poison.

It's a vial, I realize when he opens it. The guy puts it to my lips. It's a liquid of some kind, dark brown and thick. I squirm back and forth. Whatever it is, I know I don't want it in my mouth. These creeps aren't to be trusted, especially if they're here for Gavin. Somebody had it out for him, and I'm not going to make it easy for them. Although I don't recognize his voice, Gavin's killer may very well be inches away. I've seen his face in my dreams. The angry expression is ingrained in my brain for all time. It's most likely the same for Gavin.

I try everything I can to keep the foreign liquid from touching my lips. Fighting my bondage, squirming, and squeezing my lips closely together. I kick at the guy by my feet kangaroo style; it's no use. He's able to get most of the liquid into my mouth, dribbling some down my chin and across my cheek. It tastes worse than Mom's breakfast shakes when she went on a health kick a couple years back.

The other hooded man holds his hand over my mouth, forcing me to swallow the horrible liquid.

"There. Was that so hard?" That's from the man who holds an empty vial.

If I wasn't tied up...

I shout, with a bad taste in my mouth. "What the hell was that?"

"Truth serum."

I roll my eyes, involuntarily. Seriously? These guys were *really* wacked. "You don't really believe in that stuff, do you?"

"Let's see," he says. "Do you know Gavin Slater?"

"Yes." The answer slips off my tongue and out into the air before I even know the words are escaping my throat. Can it be true? Does truth serum really work?

"How do you know Gavin Slater?"

"Through the newspaper and his family." Okay, that isn't so bad. Luckily, it is the truth, otherwise...

The other man speaks up then, "Can you speak to him right now?"

"No." I answer. Thank God Gavin had helped me with his brother and is *literally* incapable of speaking with me for the next little while.

The kidnappers seem to think harder about their questions. Unfortunately, they smarten up real fast. "Have you been communicating with Gavin since he died?"

I plant a "you're crazy" look on my face while I chant, *Lie, lie, lie,* in my head. "Yes," the word slips from my lips as the back door of the van bursts open with a whistle and a loud bang as metal hits metal.

Please be the police. *Please!*

"Let her go, dirt bags!"

That voice, it's so familiar. I can't see who she is through my captors.

One of the men holds up his hands and angles himself toward the back door. That's when I see Taylor aiming a gun at the bad guys. I can't believe my eyes. Is this a trick? What's she doing here? I've never been so grateful to see anyone in my entire life. "Taylor, what are you doing here? You shouldn't be here."

"I could leave." She offers me a smile. "If you enjoy being tied up, I can't stop you." The girl shakes her head, not letting her gaze leave the men.

"Seriously?"

"That's what I thought. I'm not leaving without you."

Damn. If she gets hurt because of me, I will never forgive myself.

"You should listen to your friend," one of the goons

tells Taylor. Suddenly, the gun's whipped out of Taylor's hand. It tumbles to the ground with a loud metal clank. I panic and kick the goon on the left with my bound feet again while the other one pursues Taylor.

She dives for the gun like they do in the movies, dropping out of sight. Under different circumstances, I would have been proud. Right now, I just want to see us both get out of here alive.

I hop onto my feet and am able to wrap my arms around the fallen man's neck, trying to hold him back. Once Taylor gets to the gun, we could get away from the two goons.

It doesn't get that far, unfortunately.

The man between my arms bounces his head on my skull. I'd have fallen back if my arms weren't taped together. Pain rushes in as a large welt begins forming on my forehead and the two of us go down. My vision blurs as the agony settles inside my head and squeezes.

The man lifts my arms from his neck and knocks me down. Then he walks away.

Suddenly, I can't move. Somehow, I'm stuck to the floor of the van. How?

"Taylor, look out!" I call as the man disappears in the direction Taylor had just gone.

A gunshot roars through my eardrums and panic instantly shoots up and settles into my belly. It's louder than I realized gunfire would be. Fear instantly envelopes my body. "Taylor!" I call out, through rocks in my throat.

"I'm all right," I hear her say. "Let's get out of here. Come on. Hurry."

"Can't." I attempt to wiggle, no movement. "I'm stuck."

She reaches down and tries to help me up, but I'm glued to the floor. "I can't tell how you're stuck."

"I shouldn't be. The guy knocked me over, then pushed me. Then he just walked out of the van."

"That's because we're not done with her, yet," goon number one admits, hopping back into the van. "We still have more questions."

Taylor turns to the guy holding his arm and corrects, "I don't think so. We're leaving. Might I add that you should be ashamed of yourself, kidnapping a teenage girl."

"I told her we just had a few questions. No one was supposed to get hurt. I think it's a little late for that, now." The man looks down at his arm. I can't see what he's looking at, but I realize he must have been shot while Taylor was trying to help me.

"I didn't mean to shoot you," she says, pointing toward the arm he's holding. That's when I see the gun is still in her hand. "Besides, it's only a graze. Don't be such a baby." Taylor demands, "Just let her go and we can forget this all happened."

That's when the second man jumps in the driver's seat and the engine turns over. "It's too late for that. You two are coming with us now. And you," he nods toward me, "are going to answer our questions."

"Why is a dead boy so important to you?" I ask.

The man looks down at me and takes a step forward as the van picks up speed. Taylor takes advantage of the situation and clubs the man with the gun she still has in her hand. He grunts and goes down with a loud thud.

Before I know what's happening, Taylor pulls the gun up to the half-conscious man and tells the driver, "Let us go or your friend here gets it."

"You think you're tough, don't you?"

"I know I am. Stop this van and let... us... go." Taylor enunciates each word clearly and angrily.

"You are out of your league, little girl."

"You should listen to her," I say. "She *will* shoot your friend. And it will be self-defense." The pull on my body is lifted then. I take the chance they've given me and knock Taylor out of the van before we get too far away from our cars. We fall onto the pavement—which is way cooler in the movies, I realize. My chest rattles as we hit the pavement and roll. My head knocks into Taylor's at one point, taking its second hit of the day, and the gravel takes a few chunks of skin as a souvenir. Taylor's gun clanks to the pavement.

Neither of us have a chance to dwell on the scrapes and bruises. Taylor runs for the gun as I tear at the tape on my ankles. I scramble to my feet and we run as fast as we can. Hopefully the goons got what they needed and will be off my trail long enough for me to save Gavin.

Once on my feet and running, I chance the risk to see if the van is gone. It isn't. The driver has stopped and is glaring back at us. I think that he might do something bad, but he eventually backs off. Taylor and I run to our vehicles. I hop into the car with Flash-like speed, turn the key and reverse the car, then floor the gas pedal. I adjust my shirt and am able to pull some extra gauze out of the glove compartment. A little puss and some blood slip out of the wound. Luckily for me, it has mostly healed over, which leaves only a little wound for blood to escape from.

The man standing by the van watches my every move with angry daggers in his eyes, while holding his phone up to his ear. Though, in my rear-view, it's only Taylor on my tail. Once we drive for a few minutes and I know we are out of harm's way, I pull the sputtering car over.

"What were you thinking? You could have died." I yell as soon as she gets out of her car.

"You could have died too, peach girl."

I grunt, knowing she's right. "How did you find me?"

"GPS on your phone," she answers, like it's no big deal.

"And how did you know that I needed your help?"

She answers, "I got a text saying that you were in danger and that I should get to you right away. At first, I didn't believe it, but the sender was... persistent."

"That's so weird. Someone just randomly texted you? And you don't know who it was from?"

"No, it was a number I didn't recognize."

"How did you know it was real?"

"It came with a pic of you being tossed into a van by those two goons."

"Someone was there? Someone just sat back and watched me get kidnapped? That is so creepy."

"I guess so," Taylor agrees. "I'm just happy I got there before anything *really* terrible happened."

"I don't think they wanted to hurt me physically. At least not until they got the information they wanted."

Someone's been following me around lately. I knew it, even though I'd been trying to chalk it up to nerves or paranoia. It was probably those goons. Why would anyone have Taylor rescue me if they wanted to hurt me? It doesn't make sense. My world is unraveling around me. And it all seems to come back to one person: Gavin.

"Hey, Taylor? Where'd you get the gun?"

"Don't ask," is her simple answer. We both know she

stole it from someone. "Did you see it fly out of my hand? It was like magic."

"Weird. When did you get out? And how did you find me?"

Taylor shrugs. "You know me. I'm resourceful."

"Seriously."

"Well, I got out three days ago and decided to come here. I figured it was a small town. You wouldn't be that hard to find. Why so suspicious?"

"I was just kidnapped. I'm trying not to freak out about it."

Taylor leans against the side of her car. "What did they want from you, anyway?"

"To ask me questions about a boy who died last week." Apparently, the serum hasn't rubbed off.

"Do you think those guys were Limbonians?"

"It would explain how I was magically strapped to the floor of the van one minute and not the next." Just remembering it makes me mad. I never did anything to those people. Wait, how do you know about Limbonians?"

"It's a long story."

"Tell me."

"I'm supposed to protect you," she says, nonchalantly.

"Protect me? From those guys? Why? Who asked you to protect me?"

Taylor laughs. "You've got a lot of questions. How about I just tell you that it's someone who cares about you and we figure out what we're going to do about your car. I know a guy. Owes me a favor."

I'm dumbfounded. She managed to answer my question and skirt the truth at the same time. I have a feeling there's so much I still don't know. It's about time I get some answers. It's just then that my throbbing head decides it needs a break. I feel myself fading quickly.

# NINETEEN

"I LOVE HER. Is that even possible?" Gavin admits to Circe after their magic training session. Gavin's sweaty and breathing heavy, I realize, as he wipes his forehead with a towel. Who does this guy love and why am I suddenly jealous?

"And you've been inside her head every day for nearly a week. You must know things about her that appeal to you."

Gavin nods. "Well, yeah, but we've never even met. I mean, I've seen her hopes and fears through the Hall of Mirrors. I've seen her laugh and fight. She climbs the impossible mountains put in front of her, and she puts up with me popping up in her mind at all hours of the day. She's caring, brave, loyal. Not to mention bull-headed, straightforward, and worries a lot. She doesn't pay enough attention to label herself. She just does what she does in her own quiet way."

"And that's appealing to you?"

"Who knew? But, yeah, I guess it is."

"And have you told her this?"

"No. No, I couldn't." He shrugs and flops into the nearest swing, kicking his feet. He's talking about me. "Because you're worried she wouldn't feel the same way?"

"No, I'm worried that she would think I was crazy."

"I think you know her better than that. Besides, love makes you crazy."

Both good points. Normally, a week isn't a long time to get to know someone — unless you've been inside their head. He *is* definitely talking about me. He loves me? He *loves* me. I don't know how I feel about that.

"Okay," he decides, "I'll tell her as soon as I get home."

"You are getting a second chance. Do not throw it away — especially not love."

"I understand, Circe. I know I'm not out of the woods, yet, but I promise you that if all of us are successful, I *will* live my life to the fullest."

"Believe it or not, I think you have done a wonderful job so far."

"That means a lot. Thank you."

Gavin and Circe sit there, comfortably silent. I wish I hadn't heard any of this. It's such an invasion of privacy. If that's how he feels, I want to hear it from him.

Not in a stupid dream.

"There is only one ingredient left before you get to go home," Circe notes.

"I know it," Gavin responds, chugging a glass of peach juice that he makes magically appear, blissfully soothing his fired-up nerves with the cool, mollifying taste of pure heaven. "Can't wait. I wish I could take you with me."

"That's very thoughtful. I have to admit, this is the

first time that I am truly happy to send someone back to the land of the living."

"Oh?"

"For two reasons. I think you can do so much good that it would be selfish of me to keep you. And second, I have been worried about your soul mate."

Gavin nearly chokes on his juice—I'd have had the same reaction if I were in his shoes. As it is, I'm freaking out. "Marley? Why?" Gavin asks.

"I didn't want to scare her, so I didn't say anything. Gavin, I have never had a soul mate visit the island before. I didn't want to lie; it just felt necessary not to frighten your girl away."

"Nothing could scare her away. I'm certain of it."

Suddenly, I'm worried that Kimmy may have been right about Circe. She lied to me. She'd said she wasn't worried about my traveling there. She said it straight to my face. And she's supposed to be the good guy? How could I possibly trust her after this?

I had my doubts when Kimmy said she turns boys into animals, but I really did think she was a good person. Maybe I should start listening to the mythology and be more careful.

Circe says to Gavin, "I do not know this sweet girl as well as you. However, I should have known differently. Someone who could capture your heart must be an absolutely wonderful woman." Circe turns to admire the mountainous landscape. She sighs loudly before saying, "That was your last test. Your soul mate should receive the last clue for the last ingredient soon." She pauses. "For having faith in a love that doesn't make sense, a love that defies all logic. One that makes you feel weak and vulnerable and all-powerful at the same time."

Gavin laughs. "It seems like you're saying that because I'm feeling miserable, I get the last ingredient?"

Oh, Gavin. You're such a romantic. I laugh out loud.

Circe smiles back, "It seems like that, doesn't it?"

*MARLEY. WAKE UP. Can you hear me?*

I'm dreaming of Gavin, again. He sounds afraid, insistent. I'm in between consciousness and dreamland when I hear him. Something I'm almost getting used to. His exact words are too far away for me to hear. It sounds like he is saying "make up." *Make up what?* I question.

No answer.

I yawn, shaking off the remnants of sleep. It almost feels like something has strong-armed me back into consciousness and away from my dream of Gavin and Circe talking, probably the fact that there's a throbbing in my skull.

Then I remember the dream, where Gavin said he loved me. I make up my mind not to bring it up. No, if that's how he feels, I want him to tell me himself.

"Gavin? Are you there?"

*I'm here. I was calling you, but I don't think you could hear me. I passed the last test. That means you should get the last ingredient soon, and we're almost out of time.*

*What time is it?*

*It's late, but we've got to hurry. I've got a bad feeling.*

I shoot straight up in my bed, wide awake, feeling a bag of frozen peas fall from my head. *Please don't say that.*

The second the words echo in my head, I know he's right. A sinking feeling settles into my stomach. *We still have a whole day. Don't panic just yet.*

Wait a second. I'm in my bed at Uncle Sam's house. How did I get here? The last thing I remember is passing out in front of Taylor. And where had she come from? I want to go over the details, but I have to concentrate on getting Gavin back right now.

*I'm working on it,* Gavin tells me.

My phone beeps, signaling a new text message.

From anonymous. It reads:

> *This is something he holds dear. You must find it, or he will remain here.*

*I got a text message about the last ingredient. It seems like a riddle. I need something you hold dear.*

*All my stuff is at my house.*

*Your house?* I question. *As in, where your mom lives?*

Gavin laughs at that. He laughs hard and I roll my eyes at him. *That means you'll have to bust in there and find something to use in the ritual.*

I scoff. *You've got to be kidding!* I'm busy getting dressed and stop in the middle of putting on a pair of pants. So glad he can't see me right now. *What do you mean I have to break into your house?*

*It's not as bad as you think. I know where the spare key is. And you look beautiful, by the way.*

I blush and let it go, knowing he's only yanking my chain the way he usually does. "And if your mom finds me again? I can't go to jail."

*I think I can put a sleeping spell on my mom, so she doesn't*

227

*wake up and my brother sleeps like the dead.* He chuckles. *Which is actually a funny saying because the dead don't sleep.*

Shaking my head, I muse, *I hope it's something that's easy to find.*

*Circe said it should be something important to me.*

*I'll go get it, but Gavin?*

*Yeah?*

*I need to get dressed. Don't look.*

He laughs loudly in my ears. *I can't see you, love. I was just telling you that you look beautiful because I know you do.*

I finish dressing and run out of the room. When looking at the time on my phone, I realize it's only 11:30 p.m. Next, I dial Kimmy's cell. Luckily, she's still awake. "I'm glad I caught you before you went to bed."

"Oh, no. What's wrong?"

"Nothing. I just got the last ingredient, and I wanted to tell you. I found out I have to break into Gavin's house to find a personal item."

"What? Really?" Fear ricochets off every word Kimmy speaks, but I try to get past it, ignore it.

"Unfortunately, I got a message that said I need something that he holds dear and all of his things are at his home. I have to hurry. Gavin's getting antsy and I'm not going to ask you to come with me because if I get caught, this is a felony. I just wanted you to know that this is almost over."

"No, I should come with you," she protests. "What if you need backup?"

I exhale sharply, thinking that's a good point, but the words I say are, "I don't want you to get into trouble."

"I don't want you to get into trouble, either."

"I won't be alone. Gavin will be with me," I admit.

"I'll text you when it's done."

After a short pause, Kimmy answers, "Don't forget. I'll wait up. Good luck, Lee. Be safe."

"Night."

*That's a good one. Getting antsy,* Gavin says with laughter in his voice when I end the call.

*I thought you'd like that. I didn't want to tell her about the bad feeling you had.* I answer while running for my shoes and jacket. *I don't want to worry her any more than she is already,* I tell him as I slide brown flats on my feet and throw my grey jacket over my shoulders, buckling its small belt.

*I know. Whatever you decide, I'll back you up. We'll get through this, Marley. We're almost there. And then you will be off the hook.*

*What if I don't want to be off the hook?* The thought slips into my head before I could hide it. Oh crap. It's too late to take it back. *Forget you heard that.*

*Can't. Can't do it. And it's too late to take it back.* After a few short seconds of silence, Gavin continues, *Marley, I –*

The dream comes flooding back to me, then. It feels as if Gavin and I are remembering it together. *I think I know what you're going to say, and it's okay. I heard it all in a dream.*

*That is so* not *how I wanted you to hear it.*

*Which part?*

*What exactly did you hear?*

*You were talking to Circe about... your feelings, and she confessed that she was worried about me and then she said you had passed a test. That's when I heard you speaking to me. Boy, this is weird.*

*Tell me about it,* he says. *I wanted to tell you how I felt in person. Not in a stupid dream.*

*Are you taking it back?* I ask as I hop into my car, hoping he doesn't say yes and praying the roar of the engine doesn't wake my mother, who's probably very eager to lecture me on missing my appointment with Dr. Crystal tonight. I don't know how I'm going to explain that.

*Never.*

*Then we can have this conversation tomorrow. Face to face.*

GAVIN'S HOUSE SEEMS smaller at night. Ensconced by two tall trees, its brick blends into the shadow of nightfall and makes it nearly impossible to find. No lights are on inside or out, giving it a creepy vibe. I wonder if that is my personal feeling because I know I'm about to break into it or because it actually has a creep factor at night.

The house key is where Gavin said it would be, in the mouth of the blue glass frog. I'm quiet as a mouse as I slide the key into the slot and turn the handle—careful not to make a peep. A squealing, crying sound fills my ears. I jump a foot in the air and panic. I freeze, backing out without closing the door, trying to make myself as invisible as possible.

I search through the crack in the door, but I can't see much. *Gavin, what was that?* Before he answers, I realize it's his mother lying on the couch, crying. My heart breaks for her. That poor woman.

Gavin replies, his voice cracking. *I really hate knowing*

*that she's suffering so much.*

*I know. She misses you.* I pause, trying to decide what I should do here. *Can you give her some rest? I don't want you to hurt yourself, but she needs to sleep. Maybe you can help her and help me get out of here without cops getting involved. If she catches me again, I'll be wearing an orange jumpsuit for sure.*

*You don't even have to ask.* Blue smoke travels up through the floorboards and into the living room. It stops at the couch and disappears beyond my sight. I hear a sigh and the sobbing ends abruptly.

*Are you all right?* I ask.

*It was a simple spell,* he explains.

*This time,* I tell him. *How are you going to explain it when you come waltzing through the front door?*

Gavin sighs. *I haven't figured that out, yet, but I was thinking about using magic.* He laughs. *Lots and lots of magic.*

I slowly slide into the house and quietly shut the door behind me, pausing to listen for sounds. Nothing.

My eyes adjust to the shadows. When I think it's safe, I slip further into the dark room. Knowing there is no turning back, I ask silently, *Where do I go?*

*My room is up the stairs, first door on your left.*

After a few steps, I can see the landing.

I keep a close eye on his mother's sleeping form, just in case, as I tiptoe to the stairs. First door on the left, he'd said. *What is this item I'm looking for?*

*I don't know,* Gavin answers. *Something I hold dear, you said? I can't think of anything.*

I quicken my pace up the stairs, turning the flashlight on from my smartphone. When I pull open the door Gavin guides me to, I find nothing. The room is practically empty. *Gavin, there's nothing here,* I tell him.

*What do you mean?*

*The room is empty.* Who would do this and why? *What are we going to do?* I silently wonder.

*No need to panic, love. We'll find it.*

I look around to see if anything sticks out at me. Nothing shines, though there's barely anything here. A double bed is sandwiched between two black end tables on the other side of the room. Beside a modest dresser is a desk. The walls have been recently emptied. Dust lines are visible even in the small amount of phone light. There aren't any personal belongings in the room.

*Gavin, there isn't anything here. Parents don't get rid of things this soon. They like to preserve their child's memory – for more than a week anyway. What is going on here?* Seeing his room emptied out makes this even more depressing.

His voice is shaking when he responds, *I don't know. She wouldn't do something like that unless someone didn't give her a choice.*

*You think someone forced her to get rid of your stuff?* I demand silently.

*That's the only explanation.*

I plead, *So, what do we do now?*

A creak in the floorboards draws my attention away from the empty drawer. I suck in a big gulp of air and hold onto it, turn off the flashlight, and freeze to the spot. *Gavin. Who's out there? Can it be your mom?*

*No,* he answers instantly. *She's in a deep sleep. It's gotta be Kyle. Hide.*

*Kyle? Sleeps-like-the-dead Kyle? You have got to be kidding me,* I silently scream. *If I get out of this, you are in big trouble.* My feet spring to life. That corner looks nice and dark, I tell myself.

Gavin only laughs. *Don't be so worried. He probably just has to pee.*

*I wish I could be as positive as you are,* I tell him.

The footsteps grow louder as they get closer, and my heart jumps into my throat. I pray Kyle hasn't seen the light from my phone coming out from the cracks in the door. Then his footsteps stop outside Gavin's room, and I know I'm busted.

Gavin chuckles at my thoughts.

I nearly reprimand him. When Gavin's door creaks open, I can't even bring myself to speak even in my mind for fear that Kyle will hear it.

*Just don't turn on the light,* I pray.

Kyle stands in the doorway and peers inside. His hair is lazily mussed from sleep. He wears white boxers and a glazed expression—which I can barely make out in the dark—as he catalogs the nearly empty room in the middle of the night. I wait for his eyes to brush over my end of the room, and when they do, my heart stops for a moment.

Then the strangest thing happens. He sighs and glances at the floor for a long moment before shutting the door behind him.

I nearly sigh in relief, counting my lucky stars and finally allowing myself to breathe quietly.

*Holy crap! I almost got caught.* Gavin laughs as if I said something funny. *If you were standing here, I'd probably smack you right now.*

*I'd deserve it.* Slight pause, then I hear, *Whenever you're ready, I need you to look around the house for me if you're still up to it. Maybe Mom hid my stuff somewhere. Like you said, they usually keep their dead children's things for more than a week. But if she were being forced to take my stuff away, I'm betting she kept it somewhere in the house.*

*You know your mom,* I state. *I'll look if you can keep your family asleep. Just don't use too much magic.*

*Start in the basement. She hides everything there,* Gavin tells me. *I'll make sure Kyle gets right back to sleep.*

"Point me in the right direction."

*Go back the way you came and make a left.*

*By the living room?* I ask, knowing his mother is still sleeping there.

Gavin snickers, but doesn't respond. I wait fifteen minutes—hopefully giving Kyle enough time to fall back to sleep—then quietly make my way downstairs, weaving through the dark. A streetlight provides enough light for me to know where I'm going, but not enough to see very well. After two close calls, I can't risk turning on the light.

The basement door squeals in protest. I panic again, pausing to listen for sounds of movement. When I hear nothing, I know it's safe to proceed. Closing the door behind me, I turn on the smartphone's light and direct the beam toward the stairs. It's a finished basement, I soon realize. The stairs are concrete. It's not like any basement I've ever seen. There's even a living space set up on one side with an old gray sofa-bed, a flat-screen, a broken recliner, and a coffee table. Our basement ceiling is a lot lower than theirs. My dad used to have to hunch down. This ceiling is nearly two feet taller.

On the other side are boxes labeled "Gavin." *She did put your stuff down here.*

*Someone must have made her do it,* he says. *Maybe a relative.*

*I agree. I only met her for five minutes, but you could see the grief in her eyes.* I remember that look. It's the same look

I saw in the mirror after my dad was gone; it's the same look I saw in my family's eyes.

I slink over to the boxes. The first one is full of clothing. Searching through it, I find a ratty old T-shirt. It's gray, a young boy's size, and the Green Day decal has broken off into smaller pieces. I move all the rest of the clothing and find nothing but the bottom of the box.

*Open the next one.*

I do as he requests and find nothing of interest. I do the same for the next seven boxes. And that's when I see a faint light coming from Gavin's guitar case. I flick upon the locks and lift the lid. I lift the guitar and find an old guitar pick, shining as brightly as a bulb. *I've got the last ingredient, Gavin. When do we start?*

*As soon as you get my body.*

"Your *what?*" I scream, forgetting I'm supposed to be quiet and still trapped in the basement of Gavin's house. Not really looking forward to touching a dead body, either.

*How else did you think you could do it?*

I don't respond because I hadn't thought that far ahead. It makes sense, but it means another breaking and entering to potentially put on my record.

Getting up the stairs is slightly easier than going down, although my heart thumps at the possibility of being caught. A light blue cloud hangs over the couch. It's Gavin's magic. Its warmth spreads all the way to where I'm standing. Soon she will have her son back, I vow.

Freedom is only inches away now. I'm almost out the door when clumsy me kicks a stand by the door. It doesn't make a loud noise, but it seems that way in the dark, quiet house. I silently curse myself for being a bad criminal. My plan to open the door and rush out speedily is clearly a bad idea—and because of said plan, I'm paying close enough attention. Surely the noise woke both members of the household.

*You should be fine, love.*

*That was stupid of me,* I tell him. Opening the door let in a string of light, which illuminates the table I kicked. *Too bad I didn't have that a second ago.* That's when I see it—a simple cream-colored business card with the name *Dr. Crystal* scrawled in artless text. The therapist? She must be the one who convinced Gavin's mother to take his stuff away.

Once down the block, I pull over and text Kimmy:

> *Got the ingredients. Just have to go and get Gavin. Wish me luck. Xo*

# TWENTY

KIMMY INSISTS ON coming with me. "I really don't think this is a good idea, Kimmy. This is too dangerous."

"Because you're so immune," she offers sarcastically.

Crickets chirp around us as we approach the funeral home where they were keeping Gavin. Its lawn is wide and inviting as we walk across it through cover of darkness. The newer building holds a beige hue, simple and appealing. Kimmy and I shuffle toward the back of the building where no one will see us.

"I've never done something like this before. Well... before tonight anyway," I confess.

"And now you're about to do it for the second time."

I sigh, looking at the dirty window. "Have I mentioned this whole thing sucks?"

"Once or twice. Just think about it this way, you've been stabbed, have a dead boy talking to you, and some secret villain gunning for you. Could it get any worse?"

I snort at that comment. Not to mention, kidnapped and rescued by the one friend I made at the youth center, I think to myself. "Yes, way worse," I answer, dreading the thought and silently daring myself not to go there.

Kimmy pulls a crowbar from her purse and hands it to me, to pry open the window. "I should have worn different shoes for this," Kimmy notes. "I'm never going to get these stains out."

"You've got over a hundred pairs."

"That's true," she tilts her head in acquiescence. "But each one is special."

"I know and I'm sorry about your pretty shoes."

Gavin promised to take care of the alarm. *After that I'll need to recharge for a bit,* he'd said. He's been using quite a lot of magic already. I didn't want to ask him to use more, but we are so close now I can almost taste it. It's too late to turn back. "What is not in that purse of yours would be a very short list," I say to Kimmy, as I heft the crowbar into the window seam.

"Don't even try to guess," she whispers, patting her trusty purse.

I pull at the window, cracking it wide open. Kimmy holds it open, and I climb inside. Luckily, we chose a window with a flat cart underneath it. Although it slips slightly when my foot lands on it, I make it into the morgue without any trouble. The last place on earth anyone would ever want to be: a dark, musty old basement that smells like cleaning products, very strong, nostril-burning cleaning products. I almost gag. Better than the alternative scent in a place like this, I guess.

We are almost at the finish line. Not even the putrid scent of rotting corpses could stop me now.

Kimmy's foot dangles in through the window and then the other foot touches down. I hold the cart, so she can hop down. "Smells like roses in here," she whispers sarcastically, pulling a flashlight from her purse. "I may have to burn these clothes."

A shiver tingles up my spine. "Let's find him and get out of here as soon as possible."

"I second that," she responds. Kimmy starts at one end of the cooler doors while I start at the other. Using my phone's light, I search white labels for Gavin's name. Surprisingly, there are a lot of people here.

"Not here," Kimmy informs me, as we meet in the middle.

"He's not here, anywhere."

Dread explodes throughout my veins, and my stomach twists into painful knots. Every rock we uncover reveals another disaster. Whoever is behind all this is very smart and desperately riding my nerves.

*Gavin, I need an idea. We need a plan,* I say, despite knowing he won't hear me.

Suddenly, I am back in Gavin's realm with him. He's in his bedroom, playing a rock tune on his guitar.

"Gavin?"

"Marley?" he exclaims, getting to his feet. "What are you doing here?"

"We have a problem. A big one. I don't know what to do, and we're so close."

"Tell me." He places the guitar against the wall. It looks just like the one I saw in his case—of course, it does. Everything about this room is meant to make him feel comfortable.

"Your body is missing. Kimmy and I are there—at the morgue—right now. Your body is definitely *not* in that room."

"Let's go see Circe," Gavin suggests. "But we have to

hurry. You can't stay here. Circe will start to worry."

"I'm not very happy that she lied to me."

Gavin moves closer to me and brushes a strand of hair from my forehead. He looks down at my lips and tells me, "I know how you feel about liars, but she wasn't trying to hurt you. I swear."

"Okay," I say, my mouth suddenly dry as I look into his gorgeous eyes.

"Let's go," Gavin says, breaking the spell.

I'm still anxious about going to see her, but it seems like the only option I have. Please, let this work out, I beg the universe.

We find her outside on the grass, doing a yoga ritual in the cheery sun. "Circe, we have a problem," Gavin says.

Circe takes one look at me and nods. "I see. Tell me what's wrong."

"Marley is at the morgue right now, and my body's missing. Is there anything we can do to help?"

"Well..." Circe says. "You can call on your body and lead her to it. Marley, you get back home and wait to hear from Gavin. Thank you for coming, dear."

"Will he be strong enough?" I ask, concerned. "He's been helping me magically all night."

"Not to worry, sweet girl. You're too close. I will help him with this one."

I'm shocked and I don't try to hide it. "You can do that."

"Yes, sometimes. But only for my favorites."

"Thank you," I say, looking back to Gavin. "Be careful." I wrap my arms around him and I'm not surprised when I feel butterflies scatter in my belly. It feels so strange to touch him and yet so comforting. "You'll be back to life in no time."

"Thank you for everything you've done, Marley. Just don't get hurt."

"Best be going now, sweet girl," Circe advises.

I still don't know how I'm able to do it, but it gets easier each time I visit the island. I think about going back to my body, and then I'm there. Back in my own realm. And, unfortunately, back in the morgue. "Let's get out of here."

Kimmy helps me outside, and I lift her up. When we are finally out, she questions, "What the heck just happened to you? Did you do that out of body thing again?"

"Kind of, yes. It's complicated. Yell at me later. Gavin has a plan," I tell her. "We just have to wait until he tells us what to do."

So, we wait, hearts on edge as the seconds tick by. I can only imagine what the bad guy is doing with Gavin's body. The first things that come to mind creep me out, the next piss me off, and the rest—I don't even want to think about.

Then I feel Gavin reach back into my head.

*Are you ready? I'm going to connect with my body through you. Wait for the sign.*

*Gavin, is all this magic going to hurt you?*

*It's all right. I'm able to recharge faster now. Even when I use magic in your realm,* he verifies. *Besides, Circe said she'd take on the brunt of it. Don't worry.*

Don't worry? Circe lied to me. How am I supposed to trust she'll do her part?

Seconds later, a ribbon of blue, smoky light merging with a bright silver hue drifts from the morgue out into the open, and floats across the dark alley. I watch its trail until I can't follow it anymore and then yell, "Follow the light."

"What light?" Kimmy asks.

"You can't see that?"

Kimmy looks around and then shakes her head.

"It's Gavin. He and Circe are using magic to lead us to where they took his body. Let's go."

We run to where Kimmy's Mustang is parked. "Hurry." The bright light is already beginning to fade. Kimmy floors it. We follow the silvery blue strings out of the alley. It leads us by a park, down a few blocks, around a couple corners, and up the road. Exactly six minutes later, we're standing in front of a beaten-down brick building with vines creeping up its side and boarded up windows. The strings evaporate when I walk up to the door, its red paint cracking and blistering from years of neglect and weather stripping.

"His body is in *there?*" Kimmy grumbles.

The icy chill in my veins decides to stay for the night. This place should be condemned. Why would anyone ever go inside?

"We should scope out the place and come up with a plan," I tell Kimmy. Scoping out the old building is not my idea of excitement. It looks like an ancient, broken-down, roach-infested horror show.

Kimmy looks how I feel. The expression on her face — which I can see underneath the faint light from the moon — tells me she agrees with my conclusion.

"You go that way and I'll go this way. Be careful."

Even though I'm upset with her for hiding something *and* just dumping me at Uncle Sam's like a piece of roadkill, I wish Taylor were here to help. For some reason,

I think she'd be handy in a fight.

And I have zero ways to get a hold of her. I mean, drop a note on my pillow or something.

"You be careful, too," Kimmy offers.

My first step around the building nearly stops me cold. An overwhelming rush of panic sweeps over me, as if I've been dunked in a pail of ice water. I want to leave but this pretty, glowing, pink butterfly flutters past my face. So beautiful. It lands on my arm. It must be a comforting touch from Gavin—although the magic feels different, like it's someone else's. I don't know who else has magic, but I can feel comforting arms wrap around me, blocking me from invasive shadows.

I head back to the front and wait for Kimmy, who sneaks behind the bushes just after I do. "That was weird. I was ready to turn back, and I felt this… I don't know, calming presence."

"Me too. I think it's Gavin. He's trying to help," I inform her. "Get ready for a fight. I don't think they're just going to hand him over."

"I don't think we should be here. Maybe we should call the cops or something?"

"And say what?" I ask her. "We went to steal this boy's body, and someone beat us to it? Can you please get it back, so we can perform a ritual on him to bring him back to life?"

She stares back at me for a few seconds. "I wouldn't phrase it like that exactly," she manages to say with a straight face. "But… yeah."

"Let's just see what we're up against," I suggest, as I head for the door, not giving her a chance to deny me.

Kimmy reluctantly follows.

I reach out to grasp the metal handle and I can't. "What the…" I try again. Nothing.

"What's wrong? Is it locked?" Kimmy asks from behind me.

"I can't even get to the door. There's a… some kind of force field or something."

Kimmy chokes back a laugh. "What do you mean?"

"What do you mean, 'What do I mean'? Try it yourself."

As Kimmy checks the door, I talk to Gavin, *Are you there?*

*I am.*

*Good. I was worried about you.*

*I know, love. I just need a little bit of time to recharge. It won't seem like much to you, at all.*

*Okay. Rest up,* I tell him, feeling him fade from my head.

Kimmy swears, trying multiple times to touch the door handle.

I laugh, and then someone yanks me back. Before I can get a look at them, they cover my head with something that smells like potatoes, and Kimmy grunts. I pray she's gotten away — or at least got some kind of shot in.

"Let me go," I demand, trying to elbow the person.

It's more than one someone, I realize when I count the hands holding me back. At least two people have hands on me.

Kimmy grunts again. There goes the hope she'd escaped. "Kimmy, are you okay?"

More grunts.

"Kimmy can't come to the phone right now," one of the captors behind me says. "She's a little… tied up." He says it in a creepy tone that sends shivers through me—like he has nasty, unmentionable plans for her, and I know I won't let that happen.

I shout, while writhing against my captors, "Let us go. Right now."

"Slow down, honey. We're just getting started."

"Knock it off," a new voice says. "Get them inside."

They drag us in, not caring if we trip on the steps multiple times. It smells like gasoline is my first thought. It's a weird first thought to have when someone drags you through an abandoned building with a mask on, but that's what I thought.

I quickly came to my senses. "Let my friend go. It's me you want."

"Shut up." It was the voice of the second kidnapper.

"Besides," the creepy one said. "You're the one who brought her here."

When we get to the end of what seems to be a long hallway, one of the goons stops me and tears the sack from my head. We're in the doorway of a large room. It's darker than I expected. The room has no lights on, just two old gas lamps at either end of the room. They give off enough glow that I can see the walls are cracking and the floors are half-rotten.

Then I see Gavin's body on an old cot by the far wall. They haven't destroyed his body as I'd first thought they would. Thank God. That leaves me wondering what they're waiting for. If someone doesn't want Gavin to return, the simplest way to ensure that would be to burn his body. No matter how I spin the tale in my mind, I can't figure it out. Unless we have the kidnappers' motive wrong.

He's only a few feet from me. Just a few feet.

Then I notice them. There are two men guarding him. I barely see them in the lamplight. The first guard is short and balding; the second one, who's much taller, has a beefy fist wrapped around what looks like the butt of a gun that's tucked into his belt.

"What do you want from me?" I ask, looking around the rest of the room, hoping to locate Kimmy. I need to make sure she's okay. I don't see her. "And what have you done with my friend?"

"Relax," the mean one says. "If you behave, she won't be harmed."

"Fine. Just answer my question."

The guy turns his evil eyes at me. They're almost black and sunken, with puffy undereye. He looks like he hasn't slept since King Tut days. His face alone, would draw chills from me, but the expression makes me pause.

It doesn't seem like he's going to answer, but then he says, "Our orders are to make sure you fail. Now, stop asking questions or I'll tape your lips together, like I did your friend's."

The guy turns away and I am more than grateful. "How long do you plan to hold us hostage here?"

He whips back around—his eyes bursting with pure rage. I gulp and feel my heart speed up. "You don't listen very well, do you?" I definitely have that problem. "No. More. Questions!"

Then he leaves the room.

The captors holding me drag me away from Gavin and into the room across the hall. They flop me into a seat next to Kimmy. She still has the tape over her mouth, and she's shivering, though only slightly. Her face contradicts her body language; her expression is completely calm—no doubt planning a strategy for kicking every single one of these people in the butt.

"Are you okay?" I whisper.

She nods and then shakes her head so slightly I almost miss it.

"I should never have gotten you into this."

She turns her head toward me and I swear I can hear her say, "You think too much."

I nearly laugh. It takes all I have to hold it back. It could be nerves, it could be fear or anxiety, but we're here and it's all my fault.

I take inventory of the goons and try to drum up even a chance of escaping with Gavin's body. Two captors stand behind us. One is on the far right, by the entrance of the room. He's got a gun tucked into the front of his pants—or he's just really happy to be here.

There's an old, marble fireplace to my left. It's cracked and weathered from years of neglect—even the mantel is missing half its wood, like someone karate chopped it and lost the middle section. There are no chairs, aside from ours, an old desk that's seen better days, and the one window is boarded up. I wonder how badly it would hurt if we jumped through it.

"Does her mouth really need to be taped?" I say to the captors. "You have us surrounded. What are we going to do, talk you to death?"

"Probably," the mean one answers, coming back into the room with duct tape.

No. Not again.

Gavin, I could really use your help, wherever you are. The mean one comes at me, looking particularly happy with himself. Before he can tape my mouth, there's a loud bang at the front of the building.

# TWENTY-ONE

EVERYTHING HAPPENS SO quickly. Two of the captors run to check out the noise, including the mean one. Kimmy bursts from her chair and kicks the nearest captor right in the throat. He crumples to the floor, gagging. Then she uses whatever's in her hand to untie me.

Two more captors run at us. Kimmy gets into a fist fight with one, while I kick my guy. I land a couple good kicks and one elbow to his rib, before he nearly takes me down with a punch to my stomach. It's almost like he knew where to aim.

"Marley, you… okay?" Kimmy asks, while she kicks her guy's back leg and sends him down.

"Yeah," I say, not sure if I mean it. My captor comes at me with a fist to the face. I swing to the left, he misses, and I use my new vantage point to headbutt him in the stomach. Not my best idea, as he falls on top of me, struggling for breath.

I squirm out from beneath him, just as I hear, "Marley?"

That voice belongs to... "Uncle Sam? What are you doing here?"

He grabs the guy I knocked down, handcuffs him and helps Kimmy out. "Your mother called me. Said you'd missed your appointment with your shrink and you snuck out of the house in the middle of the night."

Not my best idea. Obviously.

"How did you find me? Some super sleuthing skills you detectives have?"

"Yeah," he says, pinning the second captor to the floor. With his knee in the bad guy's back, he looks up at me and answers, "Find my iPhone."

I laugh, despite being nervous about my mother's reaction. I turn to check on Gavin, who's still there. Thank God. How am I going to explain this to Uncle Sam?

"I didn't miss it on purpose. Just... there's a lot going on."

"Yeah, like being kidnapped?"

"That, too," I answer, still worrying about Gavin. "Kimmy are you okay?"

She's standing there, chest heaving, leaning against the old fireplace.

"Marley, look out?" Both Kimmy and Uncle Sam shout.

I turn and see a gun pointed at my head. It's the mean guy. He's got hatred in those dead eyes of his and he's aiming that my way, too. Now I understand the fear that Gavin felt in this position. I want to slink back into the corner and shrink to the size of a mouse, but I don't show him my fear.

Seriously, why do these people hate me so much? "You don't have to do this." I tell him, hoping my outright terror doesn't show in my voice.

"Drop the gun or I'll shoot," Uncle Sam warns.

The mean one turns the gun at Uncle Sam and they both shoot at the same time. A pit invades my stomach and my heart comes to a grinding halt. I see the bad guy go down, a dark, bloody hole in his chest.

I screech in terror and rush to my uncle. Tears that had wanted out, finally slip down my cheeks as I search for the gunshot wound. I find it. The wound is in his shoulder.

Uncle Sam questions, "Is he dead?"

Kimmy runs to check. "He's not breathing. There's a lot of blood."

Uncle Sam groans before telling us, "I'm okay. It's a shoulder wound." He pulls his radio out and says, "Officer down." He gives them the address and a staticky voice says some code.

I will never forget the scent of gunpowder as long as I live. It feels like it's burned into my nose for all eternity.

"You should get out of here. I don't want you involved when my backup gets here," Uncle Sam groans.

"I can't leave you here."

"Go," he says. "Your mother's worried about you. Go straight home and don't cry. I'll be fine. I promise. This is not my first gunshot."

"Are you sure you're going to be all right?"

"I'll be fine. Love you, kiddo."

"Love you, too. Thanks for coming to our rescue."

"Any time."

Then there's a groan from behind us. The mean one is sitting up, and aiming those dagger eyes at me. If he was angry before, that was nothing compared to the look he's giving me now—like, killing me wouldn't be good enough.

Kimmy and I get up, ready for a fight. When the guy hears the sirens, he looks at us both, growls wickedly and jumps through the back window that had been boarded up.

"What the hell was that?" Kimmy questions.

"I don't know, but I hope it hurt.

"Get out. Hurry!" Uncle Sam reminds us.

"Okay," I tell him. "Come on, Kimmy. Let's go find your purse."

When we leave the room, I remember Gavin. I'm not leaving him behind. There would be too many questions and the cops would never let us have him back in time for the ritual.

"We have to get Gavin," I tell Kimmy, hoping Uncle Sam doesn't notice us.

She doesn't fight me. We both run into the room as the sirens get louder.

"What are you girls doing?" Uncle Sam asks from the doorway.

I should have known a gunshot wouldn't keep him down. He's a McCartney, after all. "I…" I hesitate to lie to him. "He's my friend."

"He's dead. You have to leave him here," he demands in his best detective tone.

"Please, Uncle Sam." I look him straight in the eye and I hope he's got his best detective hat on when I tell him, "Gavin needs my help. I can't explain it right now, but Gavin needs my help. Please don't stop us."

He watches me with a careful eye. It takes him about thirty seconds to decide. Instead of speaking, he moves out of the doorway, to let us by.

Kimmy grabs Gavin's head and I grab his feet. He's much heavier than he looks, I think to myself. I wish he could help us with this. The police will be here any minute.

We both grunt and start making our way to the door. I spot Kimmy's purse, fallen to the floor, like an abandoned teddy bear.

Kimmy looks perturbed when she sees it lying there. We put Gavin down while she runs to get it.

"Hurry." Uncle Sam warns. "They can't see you here."

Kimmy rushes back, purse over her shoulder. We both stumble down the stairs, hefting Gavin's body to where we parked the car, grunting and sweating.

Screams of rage echo from the abandoned building. Suddenly, more gunshots blast through the quiet night air.

"Uncle Sam!"

"The police are almost here. We have to respect his wishes," she tells me, fear at the forefront of her voice. She's worried about him, too, but she's right.

Dang it, she's right.

"We have to hurry," she warns me again. "This boy's heavier than he looks."

*All muscle,* Gavin says, finally making an appearance.

*That's what all the boys say. Besides, she's holding the side with your big head.*

Gavin's outright laugh echoes in my head and suddenly some of the weight lifts off us. *That should help a little.*

*Gavin, something terrible has happened,* I tell him.

*Tell me.*

*My uncle showed up at the abandoned building and he got shot. Will the mirrors tell you if he's okay?*

*I'm so sorry. I can only see what involves you, love.*

I ask, *Is there anything you can do?*

*I'll try. Be careful.*

*Thank you,* I say, as we make it to the car. We heft Gavin's body into the small backseat. I stay with him, placing his head on my thigh, I shiver at the thought of having a dead person's head in my lap. The thought escapes, just as quickly as it appeared. This is Gavin, *my* Gavin.

The mean one comes rushing from the side of the building, screaming and attempting to fend off a light blue force field. At first, it looks like a shield, but then I realize that the guard doesn't have magical powers. Gavin is holding the man back, though the man is giving it all he has to get through it. A shadow appears beside the mean one. Crap! It's another bad guy — one of the guys that was guarding Gavin's body.

"Kimmy, floor it," I yell, signaling for her to gun the engine and get us as far away as she can. In a surprisingly lucky twist, we're in Kimmy's sports car instead of my tiny clunker. Hers will be faster, but the back seat is overcrowded, since Gavin is six feet tall. I bend his long legs on the seat, so he doesn't come back to his body with any surprises — like broken toes, for instance. Holding on to him for dear life, I turn to see if the bad guys are following. "Head toward the school."

"What? Why?"

"That's where we need to perform the ritual."

"At our school?"

"No. Billy Sans. Gavin's school. It's across town. And Kimmy?"

"What?" she asks, giving me the eye through the rear-view mirror.

"Hurry. Gavin's deadline is tomorrow." Today, technically, since it's after midnight.

Kimmy passes our school and keeps driving. It's dark, but there are a few stray vehicles in the parking lot and a few lights left on in random classrooms. I wonder which teachers have the misfortune of being stuck in there, but it doesn't matter. I can only worry about Gavin.

Looking down into his face, I finally see him for the man he is. Or rather, the man he is yet to become because his life's been cut short. He's a good man and deserves to live a full and happy life. That, I know without a doubt. I didn't know him before, but I trust that he thought of everyone but himself, putting their needs ahead of his own. That's the kind of person I aspire to be. Even now, all Gavin is worried about is his family.

*And you,* he tells me.

*I stand corrected.*

*I'm no hero, love. I didn't take that bullet for her on purpose. It's not like I actually thought he was going to shoot me.*

I correct him, *But you still moved in front of a gun with the risk of getting shot. You're my hero. And you are that girl's hero, too. She's alive because of what you did. That's just something you need to get used to.*

*Thank you. I have to go now. Good luck out there.*

With Gavin no longer in my head, my thoughts jump back into the present. I hope the bad guys have ceased their pursuit, and we're in the clear. But even as I think it, the terrible clichéd white van skids around a corner behind us. I should have known it wouldn't be that easy. It's the same van that I was held captive in, I realize. That means all those guys were probably Limbonian. "Who are these people and who do they work for?" I angrily shout, not expecting an answer.

I'm getting tired of being chased and followed all the time.

"I don't know," Kimmy tells me. "But he's gaining ground quickly."

"What do we do?" As I ask, the passenger of the white van—whom I can't see—is holding a gun out the window, aimed in our direction. "Gun!" I shout. "Lose him, Kimmy. Lose him."

It's too late.

I realize this when a loud pop nearly takes out my eardrums; then shards of glass from the back window fly all around us, falling like popcorn in a popping machine. This is what my life has become. Dodging bullets, kidnapping, talking to the dead, and car chases. I would almost laugh if it wasn't so awful.

"Are you all right?" I scream, ducking.

"All in one piece. You?"

"Same. Sorry I dragged you into this."

"What else would I be doing on a Thursday night?"

After the first bullet hits the car, I'm too afraid to lift my head. "Kimmy, be careful," I shout just over Gavin's head, trying to duck and keep him in my lap at the same time.

It's almost over, I try to tell myself. In a few hours, Gavin will be back in our world and that will be the end of the danger to me, my friends, and my family.

Or so I hope.

"What should we do?" I ask Kimmy.

Her answer is to reach for her purse in the passenger's

seat and shove it into the backseat. "Here's my purse. There should be something in there that will help."

Not understanding what she means, I open it and find a gun. "Where did you get a gun? You don't like guns."

"I never argue with the purse. Do you know how to shoot?"

I laugh, despite myself. "Of course not." I figure I can aim, since I did so well in laser tag. Of course, that wasn't in a moving vehicle with something that can actually kill.

"Hand it to me." She reaches back, swerving the car slightly. A click resonates throughout the vehicle before I feel cold metal touch my hand again. "Safety's off. Just point and shoot. Be careful. It has a kick to it—or so I've heard. Good luck, Lee."

"Don't worry about anything. Just drive."

I never figured I'd have to shoot a gun. I never even thought I'd have to use my martial arts. Mr. Cheng would be so upset that we'd fought offensively, instead of defensively, though I think he might forgive us this once. And now, I'm holding a man-made killing machine and aiming it at another human being, who'd been shot already and survived.

The first shot rings from my hands, hitting their front bumper. The van swerves, as if the shot caught the driver off guard.

Good. How do you like it?

"This is harder than it looks on TV."

"It is. Try using both hands."

Kimmy turns the corner, and the van slips out of view. "It's even harder to shoot with a dead boy's head in your lap," I say. Just as the van turns the corner, I take my chances and shoot again.

This time I take out a side mirror. Getting closer, I think as he gets a couple shots in—missing, just as I had. The next shot hits the windshield and the next one misses altogether. "How many shots are in this thing?"

"Ten, I think."

I'm not sure how many shots I've fired, but I know it isn't ten. So, I shoot again and again and again as Kimmy ducks from their shots. One of my shots manages to take out the passenger's gun. I whoop loudly, entirely certain I just got lucky.

We are safe for the moment. For about three seconds. Then the road begins opening up on us. The car's whining wheels tear through chunks of cement, dipping, diving, and climbing over sharp rocks. We aren't going to make it. Any second now, the earth is going to swallow us whole. Someone on their team must have magic. So far, the mean one hasn't shown any sign of having powers, except freaking me out with those evil eyes. However, roads don't just open up on their own—at least under normal circumstances. Maybe it's the passenger. Someone knocked that gun out of Taylor's hands the other day. It must have been him.

The thing that happens next, I'll never forget.

Our vehicle lifts into the air as if we are inside the *Grease* movie. The ride is so bumpy, I think I might get whiplash from all the jostling and jiggling. One of the bad guys definitely has powers. But why would they levitate the vehicle?

*Don't worry, love. We won't let anything happen to you.* Before I lose my lunch, the ride settles and becomes smoother. Up and up we go, like an airplane. I've never flown, but I imagine this is how it feels. The ball of nerves finally settles in my stomach. The car leans forward suddenly and dives ahead, causing the ball of nerves to expand. Bravely, I decide to look at the ground through the side window. The first thing I notice are the silver and blue swirls of light hovering underneath the 'Stang. Beyond that, the old white van and its terrible passengers are nowhere to be found. For now, we are all right.

Until I hear him. He sounds so far away and broken that it makes me shiver. *I have to go away for a while. It's going to be a little longer this time, I'm sorry. I had to make sure you were okay.*

"Kimmy, I think Gavin's in trouble." *Put us back down this instant, Gavin,* I screech in fear. *We're so close to the end and I can't have you burning yourself out before you return to your body.*

The car obeys, and we land with a loud thump on the city sidewalk. We are far enough away from the goons that they won't be a problem, though I worry about Gavin. *Don't pull any stunts like that again. I know you're trying to help, but you have to think of yourself, too.*

"I can't believe this is happening. They destroyed my car!" Kimmy shouts.

"Did your mother get Limbonian insurance?"

Kimmy laughs. "I think that boy's sense of humor is rubbing off on you."

I smile, righting Gavin's body again. "We have to get to that school quickly."

While flooring the gas pedal, Kimmy whips around a corner. The car protests; the ride is extremely bumpy since we're riding on the rims. "I don't understand any of this. Why would they steal Gavin from the morgue? It doesn't make much sense. Unless..." she pauses.

"They wanted me to fail. The mean one told me so. But why didn't they get rid of Gavin's body? If they want me to fail, isn't that the first thing they would do?"

"When you do the ritual, doesn't his body heal? That would mean he'd probably heal from other damage, too. Right?"

"Good point. So, maybe they were hiding his body until it was too late for me to do the ritual."

"What I don't understand is why do they care about one teenager?"

Yeah, what did Gavin do to the man who'd shot him? If anything. "There's got to be something we're missing. I don't know how, but someone has these Limbonian creatures wrapped around their finger."

"I didn't even think that was possible."

"I don't know if it is, but it would explain a few things," I say. "Kimmy, we have to get to that school, like yesterday." Panic slithers out, along with my words. I'm trying to hold it in. A deep pit in my gut is trying to warn me of something, if only I knew what it was.

Kimmy nods, offering no comment on my shaky voice. She makes a sharp turn at the corner and watches her mirrors constantly.

"I need to check on Gavin. Will you be okay for a minute?"

"Hopefully."

# TWENTY-TWO

*Early Friday morning, around 2:00 a.m.*

I CLOSE MY eyes and picture being with Gavin. I have no idea how I always end up in limbo when I think of contacting him, but I have a feeling it has something to do with willpower. So, I will myself onto the island in front of Gavin.

When I open my eyes, I find him lying on his bed. He's awake, though really pale. "This is what happens when you use power across realms?"

He sits up, not shocked that I'm here. "Yeah," he admits reluctantly.

"I wish you wouldn't do it, Gavin."

"I had to. Don't you get that?" He stands on shaky legs and looks me in the eye. "I don't know how any of this works, but I—" He pauses. "I can't watch you get hurt over me. I shouldn't have gotten you involved in this."

Anger nips at me, but it's more than that. I can see how much he cares—at least this time I'm not dreaming. "It's too late, now. I am involved, and we're going to get this ritual done." Gavin only looks down at the floor. "Don't you think I feel the same way about you, Gavin? I don't want to see you get hurt, either."

"The difference being I am already dead. I can't see you that way, too."

"And what happens to you if you use too much power?"

"Don't worry. I've got it covered."

"That's such a manly thing to say," I offer, not amused.

"Marley," Gavin says, standing and making his way over to me. He lifts a hand to my face. "You and I are meant to be together. I can't lose you before our life actually starts. You don't have to like my methods, but I am going to be with you. You're just going to have to find a way to live with that."

How can I argue with a confession like that? Seriously. Why would I want to?

Gavin looks into my eyes and moves closer still. He is going to kiss me. Butterflies tickle my belly in anticipation. Our lips are almost touching. I can feel the heat from his skin, as if our physical bodies were really about to touch.

And then I am back in the car. "Oh, thank God." Kimmy says. "I thought you weren't coming back this time. The van found us."

I look. She's right, although I notice we're almost at the school. Kimmy turns the corner. We're nearly there. The van turns the corner, gaining on us, which is much easier when you have four tires.

"Do you have to do the ritual at the school? Can't we just do it here in the car?" she asks.

"No. Unfortunately, we have to be in the place where

Gavin died. That's where his spirit will end up when he walks through the portal."

The van rams into us, the impact tossing my head forward, nearly knocking me into Kimmy's seat. The gun I've forgotten about clanks to the floor, and I barely manage to save myself from a broken nose while holding onto Gavin's body. Using my feet to keep me in the seat, I go for the gun again, but it's out of reach.

I sleep underneath Gavin, which leaves me a longer reach and I feel the gun. I grab for it and miss twice. The crashing and clanging of the vehicles sounds like missiles whistling past my ears. I finally get a grip on the barrel end of the gun—which is still warm—and I slide back onto the seat, maneuvering Gavin's head into my lap again. Gavin's school is just a few blocks up the road, but we don't have a shot of making it if I don't do something right now.

*We're going to make it, Gavin. Don't do anything stupid,* I tell Gavin, aiming the gun at the van. The mean one, in the driver's seat, sees the gun and doesn't seem phased. He probably doesn't think I will shoot him, so I fire my last few shots.

The passenger looks surprised before he gets really pissed off and swears at me.

The van's engine sputters and smoke billows from the sides. I knew I could hit the target from my vantage point.

Kimmy whoops as the van finally dies.

I turn back and by some miracle, I see the towering high school as we round the corner and nearly breathe a deep sigh of relief—only able to hold it back out of fear.

Kimmy's sports car is able to pry us away from the van. I thank my lucky stars we are even moving on slashed tires.

When we pull up to the front door of the high school, I turn to see the Limbonians running after us. Oh, what a sight to see.

We rush to the double doors and find them locked. I jostle them, hoping for another miracle. But I'm all out; the lock doesn't budge.

"Let's go. I have an idea," Kimmy shouts as we run back to the car. "We're getting in there one way or another."

Kimmy nabs her purse and pulls a pair of bolt cutters out. I can't help it; nervous laughter slips from my lips. The sound is guttural. It doesn't matter that we can die at any moment. It doesn't matter that we can fail. It only matters that Kimmy is a genius and her purse is a miracle that may have just saved the entire mission.

I snatch my backpack from the beat-up trunk—which is nearly impossible because of all the damage from the van—while Kimmy snaps the chain off the door, making it look easy. "It's harder than it looks. Trust me," she tells me, seeming to read my mind like she always does. When she rushes back to the car, there is a glistening of sweat on her brow, so I believe her. We carry Gavin's body up the stairs.

The Limbonians continue closing in on our location. If we hurry, we might just make it.

Once we make it inside the school, I suggest, "Put him down for a minute." Then I run and snatch a chair from the closest classroom. "What are you going to do with that?" Kimmy asks.

"Jam it against the doors—to hold them closed."

Success. The plan works. I pray it will hold them off

long enough for me to complete the ritual.

I turn, coming up with a wide view of a vast hallway and no idea which way to go. *Gavin, what way is the gym?* I ask, hoping he has healed enough to answer. *We're at the back doors.*

A few seconds later, he says, *Down the hall, to the right and down the hall again. It's through the double doors at the end.*

I respond while picking up Gavin's legs for the third time today, *We'll see you soon, Gavin.*

Once we reach the double doors, we hear the rattle of the back doors and realize the bad guys have finally caught up. Kimmy pulls a doorstopper from her trusty purse, props the door open, and we carry Gavin through. Where do we do the ritual? Thinking back to my nightmare of his death, I remember them being huddled in the far corner, across from the bleachers.

"Help me get this started, please." I ask Kimmy, while pulling the backpack off my shoulders.

"Hello, dear. Glad you could finally make it."

I stop dead in my tracks. Turning toward the voice I instantly recognize, I can barely make out the shape of her since she's hidden in the shadows. Realizing whose voice I just heard, I shout, "Seriously?"

That's when Dr. Crystal steps into the light. She looks the same as always. Her clothing is perfectly pressed, her hair utterly flawless and pulled tight behind her head. She wears a horribly victorious-looking grin on her lips that leaves me feeling violent. "It's you? Are you even a doctor?"

Crystal smirks. "Of course, I am."

"Who are you really and what do you want from us?"

I want to know.

"I think you know."

"You want Gavin's power for yourself."

She answers, "One can never have too much power."

"That's why you kept asking me if I was hearing voices. But how did you know about Gavin?"

"Who do you think set this whole thing up?"

"Set what up?" I demand. The answer comes to me, then. "You had him killed, didn't you?"

Dr. Crystal nods. "It was all too easy, actually. And kind of fun."

Instinct drives me to run at her, as if I can take her. I don't get very far. Kimmy holds me back. "She's not worth it," she whispers. "We have to get him," she nods toward Gavin, "out of here."

"You are not getting him," I shout, hurling my anger at Dr. Crystal as if it's a deadly weapon. "You are not taking his power, either."

"Oh, it's not him I want."

I turn to Kimmy. She tosses me a silent look that says, "I have no idea what she's talking about."

"That's right. It's you, my dear. I had to make sure you were the one before I made my move."

"The one for what? What are you talking about?"

"You'll see."

I hate mind games. People should say what they mean to say and get it over with. "If you expect me to go anywhere with you, you're crazy."

"Not without a fight. But I came prepared." Dr. Crystal waves her arm in the air. Kimmy and I both wonder what she's just done, until the doors open behind us. The two bad guys walk right in. She unlocked the door.

I curse. Then a plan hits me. I don't think about my actions. Out of desperation and a deep-seeded anger, I sneak into Kimmy's purse and wrap my hand around the slick, cold metal tube. I don't even remember tossing it back in. At the back of my mind, I realize that what I need is the first item I find when I reach in and I'm grateful. Whipping out the pistol, I point it at Crystal, determined not to fail after everything we've been through. "I'm not going anywhere with you. I'm bringing him back."

The woman in front of me smirks wickedly and waves her hand. The gun flies across the room and lands with repeated metal clanks. That's when I realize, "You were there when those two men kidnapped me, weren't you? The one who made the gun fly out of Taylor's hand."

She smirks, looking proud of herself.

"Why are you doing this? What do you want with me?"

"It's not time for the punchline yet, dear. You will find out soon enough. Let's just say I'm getting what I was promised."

"And what were you promised? Who promised you?"

"Oh, no, no. That's a surprise for another day."

Another puzzle piece comes to me, so I confront her on it. "What really happened the night I got stabbed? You know, don't you? Is that why you kept asking me if I'd remembered anything yet?"

The satisfaction on her face only grows. Am I mistaken or is that pride on her expression? "That was me. It was unavoidable. I needed to keep you close. I cannot believe you still don't remember. I thought you would have, even a little snippet by now. I guess I'm getting better at this magic thing."

"Why?" I want to know. Crystal was the shadow outside my kitchen window. I *knew* I couldn't have done something like that. I knew it! "Why would you do that to me?"

"Why?" She snickers. "Why should I tell you anything?"

I turn to Kimmy, who's as dumbfounded as I am. She shakes her head. I ask Crystal, "Don't you think you at least owe me that much?"

Crystal thinks about it for a moment. "Fair enough. Short version: I needed to make sure that you would end up in therapy, so I could find out if you were in fact Gavin's soul mate. I wasn't sure for the longest time. You are extremely good at hiding your feelings. Even when I magically appeared to you as your friend here, you still wouldn't reveal anything." Kimmy turns to me, looking horrified and disgusted. "Despite the way you look," Crystal eyes me like I'm a bum who hasn't showered for a year, "you are a clever girl; I'll give you that. It wasn't until the coffee shop that I began to really suspect that I was right. I heard you two rambling on about facing your fears." Crystal pauses to look at Gavin's lifeless body. "Then you admitted it to my friend here. That's when the fun really began."

Anger floods my body. I don't enjoy hating someone this much, but if anyone deserves it, it's her.

Now, I know what really happened to me, and I also know the truth about that day at school. Kimmy told me she had been with Shawn in between classes, and I believed her. It never occurred to me that Dr. Crystal would do such a thing—let alone, have the capability. "You should have done a little homework before impersonating someone I've known my whole life," I tell the witch. She only grins wickedly. "When that plan failed, you decided to have me kidnapped, hoping that I would tell you something, then."

Crystal nods. "I did only what I had to."

"What happened to you? I mean, no one could be this horrible and not have had something really bad happen to them." Kimmy scoffs.

Crystal's eyes darken. She reaches up to smooth her perfect hair. "That's none of your business."

"You had a boy killed! You tortured Marley, stabbed her, and had her kidnapped! I think you made it her business."

"I've already given you enough information. You can't hold these things over me forever."

I laugh. "Are you serious? What about the goons that *just* chased us down and tried to put bullets in us?"

"And destroyed my car!" Kimmy shouts angrily.

Crystal's stone demeanor flickers. She actually looks saddened for a short moment before she turns her eyes to the goons and back to us. Her face now emotionless. I don't think she's going to reveal her motives until she sighs. "A few years ago, I was killed. Circe saw something in me. The same thing she sees in Gavin, I imagine."

*I highly doubt it.*

"We went through the trials," Crystal continues. "And my soul mate—my fiancé—got the ingredients needed for the ritual. We had two blissful nights together. And then..." The distinct sound of tears invades her windpipe. "He was killed. Unfortunately, he was murdered by a human being, so he is gone for good."

There's nothing she could have said that would have

shocked me more. I remember her telling me she'd lost her fiancé. I just thought she was trying to connect with me — meanwhile, she was telling me her motives. I knew when I first met her that there was a darkness in her eyes and now, I understand why. "I'm so sorry." Crystal has done some terrible things, but I still feel bad for her. Losing someone is hard.

"I believe you. But I can't let anyone else go through what I went through. So, I'm actually doing you a favor if you think about it," Crystal informs us. "If you come with me now, Gavin won't come back, and you'll stay safe from harm."

"It's not like that, and you know it. You can't avoid pain completely. It's part of being human. And I *have* to bring Gavin back. I *need* to."

Crystal doesn't like my response. Showing her disdain, she sweeps her arm through the air; Kimmy and I go flying. Pain blasts up my spine as I hit metal. Blood oozes from a new wound in my head, and I can feel the sting of warm blood dribble down my belly. I pass out from the agony tearing through me.

The next time my lids crawl up and over my pupils, Gavin's gorgeous face invades my vision. I can see him perfectly now. I love his eyes so much. Why is he frowning at me? Then everything comes flooding back: the school, the gym, Crystal. Kimmy. Emptiness creeps into my heart.

*That's it, love. Open your eyes.*

Gavin's lips don't move. His voice is inside of my head, which means that this whole nightmare is true *and* it still isn't over. I haven't even done the chant, and he's here in this realm.

Wait... in this realm? He's back? "You're back?" I

excitedly hope.

"No, I'm not. You're on the island again," he says, while helping me up. I notice that we're standing at the edge of a field I've seen in one of my dreams.

"How did I get here?"

"I'm not sure, but you have to go back and save us both."

"I don't know if I can beat her, Gavin. She's very powerful."

He gives me his sexy grin. "You can, and you will."

"I hope you're right."

"You have to go. I'll be with you the whole time, love. Don't lose faith."

"Never," I tell him.

Circe walks up behind Gavin. She's staring at me with such love and admiration I think I might explode with it. She doesn't look angry or upset that I'm here and her smile is reassuring. Her head dips in a slight nod. Before anyone speaks, my body is being pushed through a portal. It isn't painful, although it's a tremendously awkward squeeze. As if my body is bending and contorting to fit into a hole meant for a small animal. This feels different than the other times.

I can still feel the warmth of Gavin's arms around me and I feel like I can do anything. After the wrenching pull subsides, I find myself back in the darkened gym of Gavin's school.

"You killed her!" I hear Kimmy's tearful voice. She's hovering over me and holding my hand.

"She's not dead."

"Lee, wake up. Marley!"

A loud crash and a grunt sounds behind Kimmy. I

open my eyes, wondering what's happening.

"Oh, thank God. I thought I'd lost you for a second there," Kimmy tells me.

"What happened?" My voice comes out groggy and hoarse and I touch the spot on my head that hurts the most. It's been patched up, I realize.

Kimmy's nearly shaking, but she's able to help me sit up. That's when the pain hits me, like a ton of bricks inside a truck full of anvils.

Kimmy and I are interrupted by another grunt and a screech, then another loud bang. We both turn to see what the commotion is. A woman is thrown into the shadows. Her tall frame is shadowed in darkness, even as she steps out of the shadows.

Taylor? Her eyes? They're a strange shade of blue — almost purple. I've never seen anything like it. Oh no. She's not working for Crystal, is she?

Crystal seems as shocked as I am to see her. "I won't let you do this," Taylor hollers.

Is she fighting Crystal? Why? Did Crystal hurt her, too? Lots of questions and no answers. I fear for Taylor, nervous about what I have to accomplish, though my head hurts too badly to concentrate on anything for too long.

"You're too late," Crystal shouts, waving her hand in the air. The basketball net comes crashing down. Taylor stands there, holding her hands out as if that will save her. Purple smoke materializes on her palms and then the net explodes as if a bomb went off. Pieces of debris form into metal and glass bugs. Taylor keeps her hands up to block as they fly at her. The girl waves her hands once more and the nonliving creatures go after Crystal.

That explains why Taylor knew about Limbonians.

She smirks. "That's the best you can do?" Crystal waves them off with a sweep of her hand; everything melts into the ground. "You can't defeat me. I'm too powerful for you."

"I don't have to defeat you. I just have to make sure Marley gets out of here alive," Taylor says. "And she's taking her boyfriend."

My what? She knows about Gavin?

Crystal laughs evilly, saying, "You work for me. I don't take orders from you."

"You've torn this family apart again and again. All for your selfish gain. So, in case you haven't figured it out, I quit!"

As the two debate, I try to get to my feet, though both my legs are jelly. I want to help. Kimmy helps me slink back into the shadows—more like drags me. Gavin's body is lying in front of the bleachers—unharmed from what I can tell, and I want him to stay that way.

My mind runs through many possibilities: how we are going to get through this, how I am going to complete the ritual, how we are going to defeat Crystal. Memories, fears, and grief all come flooding in with the storm of emotions I can't swim my way through. I don't need a head injury to have a hard time wrapping my head around everything that's been going on. Not only has Dr. Crystal tried to kill me multiple times, but she manipulated me and had Gavin killed.

Taylor throws Crystal across the room. She grunts in pain as she hits the ground. Taylor also has to fend off the two who tried to kidnap me. They seem like easy targets, I think, when Taylor lifts the gym's floorboards with a flick of her wrists and wraps them around the two goons. One of them is able to climb out from underneath the flooring. Taylor waves her hand and another floorboard knocks the bad guy down. "Stay down," Taylor yells.

Taylor turns in our general direction. Kimmy and I gear up for a fight. "It's all right, butterfly. I'm not going to hurt you."

"It..." I stutter, trying to form a thought, any thought. How did she know about that nickname? "My father is the only one who calls me that." Tears fill my eyes.

"I know. Who do you think sent me to protect you?"

# TWENTY-THREE

"MY DAD?"

Taylor nods, the edges of her lips lift slightly, as if this is great news. I can tell she's uncomfortable. Well, so am I.

My mind still holds on to the possibility that this might be a dream or a test. At the very least, a very cruel joke. It isn't possible. He died. "How? When?" I ask out loud while Kimmy helps me stand up.

"Lee, what's going on?" Kimmy asks, squeezing my hand.

"I—"

Before I can form an answer in my fuzzy mind, Crystal shouts, "No. None of you are getting out of here." Once again, she spreads her arms out and then lifts them in the air. The entire school begins to rattle.

It's no earthquake, I realize quickly. Thousands of rocks quickly pile up, blocking the exits. Dust kicks up in the air and when it finally settles, the entire exit is blocked.

This is definitely real. I couldn't make this stuff up if I wanted to. "What are we going to do?" I whisper to Taylor and Kimmy.

Taylor shouts, "This way. You two follow me. Hurry!"
She blasts a few of the rocks at the nearest exit. They turn
into a pile of ash.

"I can't. Not without Gavin." I shout, rushing to my
feet and hurrying to grab hold of his arm.

Crystal laughs and hits me with a blast of cool air. It's
strong enough to hold me back. I push the invisible barrier
as hard as I can. It doesn't budge. All I can do is watch
when the horrible woman takes hold of Gavin's body and
flames suddenly ignite, spreading from his arm to his
torso. "No," I screech, squirming and squealing against the
threat, desperate for a loophole, an escape of any kind.
Tears form in my eyes as I try everything I can to escape. I
can't lose him.

A strange feeling washes over me then. I can't
describe it; it's almost as if I'm being electrocuted. A
buzzing power surge soars from my feet all the way up to
my arms and spreads throughout my whole body and the
invisible barrier flies off me. I run quickly to Gavin and
throw my jacket around him, blotting out the horrible
flames before they do too much damage.

"No! How is that possible?" Crystal shouts.

I ignore her. A few stray tears streak down my cheek.
How could I not see this before? I know I'm in love with
him and I know I don't want to live without him, but now
I realize that I *need* him more than I ever knew.

*You have to be okay. I can't lose you, Gavin.*

He doesn't respond.

I look up through blurry eyes, just in time to see
Taylor raise her arms and throw purple cords at the rocks
blocking the exit. They jump and jiggle and then stop.
Taylor sends more threads and the rocks melt into sand

puddles. "Come on, girls. You have to go."

Taylor fends Crystal off, while Kimmy and I drag Gavin's body over the huge sand pile and safely out of the gym.

We've just reached the hallway when I realize Taylor isn't behind us; she's still in the gym. I turn to see her fighting with Crystal. "Taylor. Come on. We have to get out of here. Hurry."

"Go. I'm right behind you, I promise."

But she isn't.

Crystal aims her palm at the door. We watch them close behind us. My stomach sinks.

"We should go. She can take care of herself, Lee. You saw her in there."

I can't argue. I don't want to leave her, but it looks like I don't have a choice. Kimmy and I keep moving—dragging Gavin along—although every instinct tells me to turn around and face that lying witch with everything I have.

Maybe there's a way to bring my father back. It seems impossible that he can be alive after all this time, but the more I think about it, the more I believe it. For the past week I've been talking to a dead teenage boy. Why can't my father come back to life too?

The logical part of me argues that Piggybackers have only seven days to come back, so how can he possibly be alive after a year? I tell that part of me to stuff it. If my father is alive, we are going to save him. I'm not giving up on either man.

When we reach the front doors, we find two more goons, ready for a fight. Extremely eager and willing. Practically chomping at the bit.

Their expressions turn angry when they see us burst through the doors as fast as we can, dragging a body around and all. Their warrior stance makes me want to run in the other direction. Survival instinct tells me that if I don't fight now, I'll never fight again.

"We can take 'em," Kimmy says, reading my thoughts.

I nod, determined. *Gavin, are you there?*

No answer again. Where is he? Crystal better not have ruined his chance to come back.

"Fight or die," I say out loud.

"You know which one I choose," she says. "You know, I never thought karate would come in handy. Guess I was wrong."

"First time for everything."

We share a laugh, both putting Gavin's body down slowly.

*I'm here,* Gavin buzzes in my ear. *My powers aren't that strong right now, unfortunately, but I'll help. I think your friend is coming out soon.*

*I'm so glad you're all right. I was worried. You just rest up.* I breathe a sigh of relief, knowing he's okay, as I pose in my karate stance. "Let's get these guys, Kimmy."

Kimmy jumps the one on the left and I attack the guy on the right. He's a lot bigger than I am and so I'm expecting the first blow to my jaw to hurt. I taste blood in my mouth but I don't let it slow me down and kick him between his thighs. He grunts and bends over, hands down. He's distracted for only a moment and I kick him in the face. He falls backward, no longer grunting in pain. I think I've had my first k-o.

I look up just in time to see Kimmy punch her guy in

the eye and he drops. I'm so proud of us.

It doesn't take long for the men to start moving again. Fighting Limbonians is seriously a pain in the butt. Kimmy and I shrug at each other and pose for the next round. So much for my knockout.

Taylor comes running between Kimmy and I, wipes her brow, and waves her arm. Two tree limbs liquify and bend down. Each of them knocks a Limbonian back a few feet. One of the bad guy's slams into someone's car, while the other goes into the bushes where we can't see him. "Luckily, the greedy witch drains them of their powers. Otherwise...well, good job, girls."

Crystal shouts behind us before Taylor can finish that sentence, letting us know that once again, the villain has escaped injury. I just hope that if her head got chopped off or if she got hit by a car that that would be the end of it. This is feeling like a really bad horror flick, and that's why I never liked them. "Let's get out of here, fast."

All three of us bend down to pick up Gavin's body. "Can you magically put him in the car, Taylor?" Kimmy asks.

She thinks a short moment. "Yeah." Taylor waves her hand a pile of leaves on the ground and they melt before us, forming a solid looking brown puddle. The puddle lifts Gavin up and carries him to the car. "Get going. I'll meet up with you, later."

"Wait, where are you going? Come with us." I try to plead.

She shakes her head and turns back toward Dr. Crystal. "They're not going away. I have to fight."

"You can't. Not on your own." I shout fearfully. "We can help!"

She shakes her head toward the three people coming at us. Crystal waves her arm in the air and the earth parts at Taylor's feet, trapping her in the ground. "Run," she shouts, as her body begins sinking. "Go. You have to—" Her words are cut off by a tree branch that comes down and wraps around her throat.

"Taylor." I swear as I pull at the branches. I can't get her free.

"Lee, your friend is right," Kimmy urges. "We have to go. Now."

*You have to be safe.* Gavin chimes, *Go, please.*

I want to scream in frustration, though I don't have the energy. My head is still pounding a loud rhythm. Tears are now rushing from my eyes. I can barely see a hand in front of me. It's been hard enough for me to wrap my head around the fact that Gavin is talking to me from beyond the grave; then I find out that I can bring him back from the dead—which I think I've taken rather well. Now I have another friend in danger and my father might still be alive—after nearly a year of believing he was dead. This is too much for any *one* person to handle.

None of this is fair, I think, as Gavin magically reaches the car. "I'm not leaving Taylor." I screech, "Get out of here."

Kimmy starts to protest, then thinks better of it and nods, helping Gavin onto the back seat. She looks around and says, "Be safe," before climbing into the driver's seat.

Taylor frees herself, with little or no help from me. Without a word, she rushes at the three Limbonians.

That's when Crystal tosses some magic around, helping out her goons and I realize Taylor was right: she can't defeat Crystal. The woman has more power than

Taylor. But if I can take out the goons, she can concentrate on getting us away from Crystal.

Taylor's still stuck in the cement, but she's now beating the two men with the tree limb that had been wrapped around her neck. My father always said, "Go out swinging, kiddo." Not sure this is what he meant.

Crystal's standing at the front doors and watching, unaware of my presence. Change of plans. She is mere feet in front of me. I am so angry with her for everything she's done that I probably could have strangled her. I guess I do have at least one violent bone in my body.

Since I have no powers, surprise is the only thing on my side. I duck behind a tree and quietly make my way closer to her position. Taylor grunts when the taller man punches her in the jaw. The noise draws my attention away from Crystal for only a second.

My first mistake.

She's on me before I know what's happening. Using her own hands, she has me pinned. "Give up, Taylor. It's over," she shouts. "I've got her. You've lost."

"No!"

"Yes." Crystal laughs. The sound is cut off, and she grunts, releasing me suddenly. She thumps to the ground just as Gavin's transparent form appears, blue smoke still on his palm.

I can't believe my eyes. "What did you do?" Getting up I ask, "What happened? How'd you get here?"

"I knocked her out, but it won't last long. My spirit is still on the island, but you're seeing me because I'm energized," he answers.

"Gavin? You're a—a ghost."

He looks down at his silken, translucent hands and

says, "Hmm, how about that?" Then shrugs and looks up at Taylor just as she elbows one of the goons and then punches him in the face, knocking him out.

"How?"

"I don't know how." One of the goon's grunts. "But we should talk about it later."

"We should get back in there and complete the ritual," I tell him.

"I'm all for that, but we really need to take care of Crystal first. Make sure she doesn't interrupt us again." He looks down at her slumped form.

I look down at her and say, "Or hurt anyone else."

"That, too," he admits.

"What did you do to her?"

"Oh, I just knocked her out. She'll be fine," he tells me, raising his transparent arm. A tree limb bends over and weaves its branches around Crystal's unconscious form.

"Let her go or I light this thing up like the fourth of July!" One of Crystal's lackey's screeches. I turn just in time to see him wave my backpack in the air with a lighter underneath it. How did he get it? I must have left it in the gym. How could I be so stupid? Everything I need for Gavin's ritual is in that bag, and the guy knows it.

"Gavin, do what he says."

*Not until he gives us the bag,* he tells me telepathically.

"You throw us the bag at the same time," I demand.

The bad guy agrees with a nod. Gavin does as he's asked, releasing Crystal, and the bad man surprisingly holds up his end of the bargain, tossing my bag so it lands in a dirt pile near my feet.

The goon takes Crystal's limp form away, and the other bad guy follows close behind. *Why are they leaving?*

Gavin asks.

I expected a fight, but I can't worry about it right now. "Probably because Crystal is the one with the powers. Who cares? We have to complete this ritual like, right now!"

We need to finish Gavin's ritual and get him back to his body before anyone else tries to stop us. That's all I can worry about. One problem at a time.

Taylor looks a little winded and Kimmy is safe in her car, guarding Gavin's body. I call her to come back so we can finish the ritual.

"Taylor," I yell, running over to her, then. "Are you all right?"

"Thanks, M&M." She magically spreads the soupy gravel away from her and walks away. Then she turns back to solidify the concrete again. That's a cool power. "I'm good, now. Are you?"

"Yes. Gavin's here. Taylor, you have to tell me more about my dad."

"We can get to that another time. For now, we should finish your boyfriend's ritual and bring him back."

"He's not my—" I start to correct her, but then decide that I don't know what Gavin is to me. We haven't actually discussed it. Besides, she's right. If I can bring Gavin back it will be one less problem on my plate.

Kimmy drives up then. Her car's so totaled I'm surprised it's moving at all. I can finally see all the damage that was done. One of the headlights has been broken, frayed rubber kicks out of the rims, and there's a large crack in the windshield. No wonder she's angry.

I rush to the car to grab Gavin and tell Kimmy, "We're heading back in. The bad guys are gone."

"I see that. What happened?"

Gavin's spirit waltzes up behind me. Kimmy doesn't even glance at him. "Gavin," is all I say.

"Oh, cool. He's definitely handy. I'll give him that."

*You wouldn't be in this situation if it weren't for me, so everything I do seems like it's not enough.* Gavin's voice resonates in my head.

"You have no idea," I tell her. *Not true. And you deserve this*, I say to Gavin telepathically.

The three of us walk into the school. Kimmy walks beside me with Taylor close behind, carrying Gavin over her shoulders.

The gym feels different this time. Tragedy has already touched the building with a swift hand; now it's gripping the walls, suffocating the space. The damage that has been done will cost the school a lot of money.

I force my lead feet forward, as if I'm walking through a marsh. My heart races. Despite the fact that we are nearly done, I can't help but feel like something else might go wrong.

Probably because we let the culprit go.

*Marley, don't worry. We're almost done*, Gavin comforts.

Kimmy squeezes my arm as she practically drags me across the floor, which is when I realize I've stopped moving. Taylor walks in behind us. Her grunts and heavy footsteps remind me that she's carrying Gavin's body. I throw my backpack on the floor beside where she lays Gavin down.

I bend to my knees and pull out the first item while trying to remember Gavin's instructions for the ritual. That's also the first time I realize someone has covered the wound on my head. "Did you patch me up?" I ask Kimmy.

"I did what I could."

"Thank you." I smile. That purse.

"Lay the ingredients in a perfect circle over my chest," Gavin instructs. "Each item goes clockwise and put the moly on my forehead."

I place the first ingredient that I was given. Now that I'm finally doing the ritual to bring Gavin back, I'm nervous but determined. The first is my trophy from the Wacky Room, the second is the—what is it? I look in the bag. Oh right, the lion shavings—which I know Kimmy will give me grief about for the rest of my life.

Next is my phone. I reach into my bag, but there is no phone. *No, no, no,* I chant. *It has to be here.* Double checking my pockets, I try to hold panic at bay. The phone has the text message I need. From when I faced my fear of losing Derek as a friend. Where could it be?

"What's wrong?" Kimmy asks.

"My phone. It's gone. Can you call it? Maybe it got thrown across the room with me." I hope, but I'm sure I put it in the backpack.

Kimmy pulls out her bedazzled pink iPhone, while I pray to hear the sound of my ringtone. Suddenly, Kimmy's face pales, and she waves me over. She puts it on speaker. It's a woman talking, her voice way too familiar, worse than grating nails on a chalkboard. "I figured you would call eventually."

"Crystal?"

"Yes, dear. You didn't think it would be that easy, did you?" She laughs wickedly. "You and your friend are no match for me. Oh, and I've gone ahead and called the police to tell them about a break-in at the school, so you might want to get out of there."

Click. She's gone.

"She's bluffing, right?" Kimmy asks us.

I want nothing more than to say yes, but I can't put anything past Crystal. She's a devious, disgusting person with no morals. "Yeah, she probably did call the police," I tell Kimmy. "Let's get out of here."

"What about Gavin?"

"We'll figure something out," Taylor answers while gathering up my things and tossing the backpack at me. She picks up Gavin's body and leads the way.

# TWENTY-FOUR

WHEN WE FINALLY get back to my place, I want nothing more than to shower and sleep. Instead, I reach for the phone and I call Uncle Sam's cell. I need to make sure he's all right. Something has to go right tonight.

Just one thing.

He picks up on the third ring. "Hey, kiddo."

"Oh, thank God." I screech. "I was so worried."

Uncle Sam laughs and then groans. "Uncle Sam?"

"I'm okay. It just hurts when I laugh. Seriously, don't worry about me, kiddo. It wasn't that bad. They're actually sending me home."

They send people home an hour after they've been shot? That doesn't make sense to me. "Uncle Sam, you wouldn't lie to me, would you?"

"Never."

"Okay, good. Did you call Mom?"

"I called her and told her you were hanging out with Kimmy and got distracted. And that you would accept whatever punishment she deemed necessary—without complaint."

"You didn't."

"I did."

"Aww, man. You're no longer my favorite."

"Ouch. I just got shot. Take it easy on me."

I laugh, and walk over some debris to the sofa. I wipe it clean of papers and remnants of whatever else the robbers broke or ripped, and sit down. "Okay, since you helped so much tonight and covered for us."

"Not to mention, got shot!"

"You said that already."

He doesn't respond for a moment. There's a rustling on the other line before I hear him say, "Stupid shirt." Then he comes back to the phone. "Sorry, kiddo. Trying to get dressed. How is everything with you? How's that Gavin kid?"

"I'm having a rough day. Another long story that I'll have to tell you about some other time. Uncle Sam?"

"Hmm?"

"I'm really glad you came back into our lives. Whatever made you stop coming by in the first place?"

"I'm afraid you'll have to ask your mother that. I promised not to say anything."

I groan. Mom isn't going to tell me anything. I'd asked her before, and so had Sammy. She always dodged the question. "Promise me you'll stay this time?"

"I promise, kiddo. Anyway, will I see you when I get home?"

"I've got to take care of some more stuff at home. Can you cover for me again, please?"

"I don't know. You're gonna owe me big time after this."

"I already owe you big. I got you shot, remember?"

He laughs, this time not caring about his stitches. "Just be careful, you hear? And call me if you need anything. Anything," he stresses.

"I will."

"Oh, and Marley? I will expect you to explain everything to me. Got it?"

I hang up the phone and climb over the mess, walking into the kitchen where I turn to Taylor, Kimmy, and Gavin's ghost before shouting, "Does anyone want to explain what just happened? Any of it? The magical powers? Dr. Crystal? Circe? Why Crystal wants *me*? Because this past week is all a blur. I feel like I've been living some fantasy slash nightmare." Out of the corner of my eye, I see Taylor slink toward the front door. It could have cause me to break into a laugh any other time.

"Never mind. Tell me later. Why did you say my father wanted you to protect me?" I ask Taylor.

"I—" she stutters. "Just a minute." She leaves the room, not offering any more information.

I look at Kimmy, who lifts her shoulders, as if to say, "I don't know."

Taylor walks back into the room, with an older man in a trench coat. His eyes are droopy. Dark circles form a ring around his eyes. He doesn't smile, though his eyes seem familiar. Then I notice his tiny red ears.

Oh. I saw him at the lake the other day, I realize. "Who are you?"

"Hi, butterfly." He lifts a hand, offering an awkward wave.

My eyes stray around the room, as if my friends can confirm what's happening. I can't believe this. I can't. Can

I?

Everyone is staring at my... "Dad?"

"It's me."

"But... how's this possible?"

"It's a very long story, kiddo."

Gavin warns, "Marley, that's not your father."

"What are you talking about?" I demand. Kimmy stares at me as if I've gone crazy and I know that she can't see his ghost like I can. "Sorry, I'm talking to Gavin. He's here—as a spirit. I know," I answer her silent question. "Sounds crazy to me, too."

I search Gavin's features to figure out whether he is joking and then I turn to my father. "Gavin's right. I'm not the same man I was."

Confusion wraps itself around my stomach. "What— well, I can see that. Why do you look different?"

"It's a long story."

"Come on. I need some answers. There are way too many questions jumbling around in my head. Wait, you can see him?" I ask my dad, pointing toward Gavin.

He nods. "It's a dead thing, I think. The dead can see the dead."

"Why can I see him, then? I'm not dead."

"I don't know."

"So, explain why you're not the same man—aside from the obvious," I say, waving a hand at my father's appearance. A thought begins forming in the back of my mind; I can't quite reach it.

"He jumped back through limbo on his own. He's a Limbonian, love. I'm sorry. He's dying," Gavin says. "His soul is dying."

"No." That is *not* happening. "You're wrong!" I yell.

"We can fix this. We have to."

Kimmy steps forward then. I nearly forgot about her. "Listen to him, Lee. Your dad knows more than we do, obviously."

"I can't. Gavin says my dad is dying. Again." Tears threaten to fall, and I refuse to let them. That would mean I'm giving up and that will never happen.

Kimmy looks sympathetic. She'll always be there for me, no matter how crazy things get, though I can tell she doesn't know what to do or say in this situation. How could she? Taylor doesn't speak at all, just leans against the kitchen counter.

"I didn't want to do it," my father begins. "When your mom refused to help me, I had to find another way back here. I was warned that I could not come back if my soul mate didn't perform the ritual. I didn't listen, and this is the result," he says waving both hands at his foreign body.

I'm more confused than ever. "Mom wouldn't help you?" That nagging thought is scrambling to get to the surface. "Why not?"

My father shakes his head. "At first, I was angry and then I was just determined. Circe tried to help me as best she could, but it was too late. Before my spirit disappeared off the island, I made my way to the portal. She doesn't tell anyone where it is—for good reason, obviously—but I figured it out with a little help. I came back as a spirit."

I finally figure it out. What's been nagging at me. And it is so obvious, I almost want to kick myself. "You're possessing someone, aren't you?"

"It kind of just happened. I—I screwed up, butterfly. Crystal found me and told me she would help me get back into my own body, but I knew I couldn't trust her after she went after you. I never, ever meant for you to get hurt."

"I knew I was being followed. That was *you*." I make the words a statement. I'm secretly thankful it isn't a psycho stalker.

My father confirms, nodding.

"All of those goons at the gym were spirits possessing people, too?"

He nods again.

"Dad, I hate to ask, but… you didn't kill Gavin, did you?"

"No," he answers instantly. "No, that was Crystal. I don't know how she knew who Gavin was, but she pulled all the strings."

"Can she actually put you back in your own body, Mr. McCartney?" Kimmy wants to know.

Dad turns to her. "I still want you to call me Len, and she tried. Unfortunately… well, she wasn't strong enough."

"You have powers?" Kimmy asks.

"Sort of. Yes."

She wants to know, "How come you can't just get back into your body?"

My father sighs at the question, looking down at the floor, he rubs his forehead. "Apparently, when you come back from the island without your soul mate's help, your power turns sour. They become defective. That's why I wasn't at the gym. That's also why the road opened up in front of you tonight. My powers aren't working properly."

I wonder about both. Despite the fact that Kimmy's tires have been torn to shreds, nothing tragic happened.

"And that's why Taylor's helping you," I say. "But how do you two know each other? Did you both work for

Crystal?"

"Yes," my dad says. "But we met twelve years ago."

Something clicks into place. "My father was the firefighter who saved you," I say to Taylor.

"He was. He's been there for me ever since."

What she's saying is my father died, *Sammy and I* lost him, but a virtual stranger got to keep him and then pretended to be my friend. How is that supposed to make me feel? "So, were we ever really friends or were you just doing what my father asked you to do?" Why does everyone keep lying to me lately?

"I can't believe you even think that." She looks hurt, but I feel hurt, too, and I don't know if I can trust anyone right now. "Of course, we're friends, M&M."

I turn away. I don't know what to think right now. "Gavin, can you help my father?" I ask. Plead.

He hesitates. "I wish I could, but I'm only telekinetic. I don't have the power to heal."

Tears burn my eyelids, as I stand there helpless to save the man who gave me life.

My father openly sighs. "There's only one thing left to do. I can't go on like this anymore, butterfly. Living in someone else's body, unable to come home to my family, is torture." He turns to Gavin, saying, "You know what you have to do."

Gavin nods. Then slowly turns back to me, looking for confirmation. This is *so* not happening. I just need to wake up from this nightmare! Is my father really asking Gavin to kill him? My heart drops into my stomach. It isn't something I can handle in theory, let alone right here and now. Right in front of my face. "Marley, you should say goodbye to your father. He doesn't need to suffer any more."

That is Gavin's voice. His words sound so far away. I try to process all this information. It is all too much. Being stabbed and nearly dying, I can handle. Hearing a dead guy speaking to me, sure why not? Getting kidnapped wasn't a picnic, but I can even live with that.

What I can't live with is losing my father again. "N-no! This is not happening." I demand. "There has to be another way."

"I wish there was, love."

My father speaks up, then. "Butterfly, I'm tired. All I've been doing for the past year is trying to get my old life back. It's exhausting. You have to understand that."

"I can't," I answer, softly.

"It's not fair to you," he admits. "I get it, and I'm sorry. I really am, but you have to see my side. I can't go on like this."

"We can find a way to fix you," I plead with everything I have. "There has to be something we can do to get you back into your own body."

"You can't get your hopes up, Marley," Gavin warns.

"My father's alive, and he is standing right here in front of me. I can't just let that go. You guys don't know what that's like."

Kimmy is watching the whole scene in horror, as I am—despite the fact that she can't hear Gavin's part of the conversation.

Why are they fighting me on this? Don't they know what I went through after my dad died? What my little brother went through when he found out that he would never see his daddy again, or what my mother went through, knowing that her husband would never hold her again, never walk his little girl down the aisle, never see his children graduate? Can't they understand the pain we suffered? How can they even ask me to do this?

I physically can't stomach the thought.

"Do it, Gavin." Dad shouts. "I love you, butterfly. More than anything." He lifts his arms in the air and prepares to die.

Again.

# TWENTY-FIVE

MY HEART STOPS.

Before I can stop him, Gavin lifts his hands in the air, and I shut my eyes.

I hear myself yelling, "Stop!" I scream so loudly, I almost lose my balance. When I open my eyes, everyone's staring at me. My two friends, my father, and my soul mate, all with wide open eyes. "Wh—You stopped. Thank you," I say, utterly relieved.

"Dang, girl—"

"Lee, that was awesome," Kimmy shouts. "How did you do that?"

I stare back at all of them, trying to figure out how to answer that question. If this were a movie, the camera would be doing a panorama around the room, catching all of our faces. Kimmy's staring at me in admiration and amazement. Gavin's face is laden with shock. Taylor is both stunned and amazed. And my father... well, I can't really tell. "Do what, Kimmy? What did I do?"

"Magic," she and Gavin answer at the same time.

"What are you talking about?"

"Just now. You stopped me. I don't know how, but that was definitely magic."

"If this is some kind of joke—"

"Marley, I was about to…" He doesn't finish his sentence. "And you blocked me. With magic."

"You had pink smoke coming out of your palms," Kimmy says.

Instinctively, I look down at my palms. No magic coming out of them now.

That's right, universe. Keep piling it on. I can take it, I think sarcastically.

This whole week has been something out of a terrible movie. It's about making everyone around me happy and now I am standing here miserable and they're telling me things I just can't manage to wrap my head around. I'm pretty sure that hearing that my dad is alive was some kind of straw and that was the last one I could handle. Now I have magic? This is definitely my breaking point. It has to be.

I have to sit down. With no energy to move, I nearly fall down into the nearest stool and lean my elbows onto the counter. I question quietly, "I used magic?"

Gavin smirks. "Yeah, you did, love."

"Is it normal for the soulmate to gain magical powers, too?"

He shakes his head. I can see fear in his chocolate eyes. He's afraid of me.

*I'm sorry. I didn't mean to scare you*, I tell him.

He watches my face for a moment, as if it holds the answers he's searching for. I'm desperately trying to hold on to my sanity as he stares. *I'm not afraid of you, love. I'm worried. That's all.*

*I'm sure it's nothing,* I tell him. Gavin has powers, so why should I be afraid if I have them? No one has gotten hurt. I can learn to control my powers. I wonder how long I've had them. Is that how I've been sending myself to the island?

*Why aren't you freaking out?* Gavin turns his gaze on me with big eyes. He lifts his hand as if he is going to touch me and decides better of it, as if he were afraid I might break. I can sense his fear. A brush of anger and a stroke of love also touches his features.

I don't know what to say. If I stand here thinking about it, I might have a chance to become afraid, and that will only hold me back. I am going to bring Gavin back, then find a way to save my father. That is all I can focus on right now. Of course, every time I think that, something equally as grating pops up. I should probably not let that thought sink into my brain ever again.

*I'm sorry. It's just that no one I know of has powers, other than Piggybackers. And Limbonians,* he corrects.

A chill skips up my spine. *Well, maybe I died back in the gym. I was on the island with you; maybe I died for a few minutes and came back.*

Gavin continues to stare but doesn't say anything. Kimmy and my father also look worried, though they don't speak. Taylor, who is still leaning against the counter with her arms crossed over her chest, is the only one who seems happy about this new development.

"Maybe this is a good thing," I try to tell them. "If we both have powers, maybe we can save my dad. Crystal wasn't powerful enough, but we might be. Together."

*I don't know.*

*What's the harm in trying?* I ask, silently pleading.

298

*We don't know how you got these powers. What if they have dangerous side effects? I don't want to see you get hurt.* Gavin shouts in my head.

Before I can respond, I hear Kimmy question, "Don't you just hate it when it feels like the story is going on without you?" When I turn, she is standing next to my dad. Kimmy's holding his arm. He looks extremely weak. Unfortunately, even with a little magic in my system, I don't know how to help him.

*We'll find another way,* Gavin confirms.

*And if we don't?*

*Don't even think about it. If your father is willing, we will try to find another way.*

*But Circe —*

Gavin interrupts. *She would probably say the same thing if she could talk to us. We need to know where you got these powers from before you can use them.*

*Or,* I say to him. *We can use them to help us defeat Crystal.*

*You don't even know how to control them.*

*You could teach me.*

"Uh, guys. Don't just sit there. Tell us what's happening," Kimmy demands.

"Right. Sorry," I apologize for being rude.

Kimmy says, "We can save him, right? And don't tell me that he's gonna need brains or something because I do *not* need to have that image in my head for future nightmares." I had feared the same thing.

"I can't go back to my old life, and I can't go back into hiding. I won't," my father informs us, while looking right at me. "There's nothing left for me, butterfly."

"Mr. McCartney — I mean, Len, you should have some

faith in your daughter. She has done some pretty amazing things since you've been—away," she stumbles on the last word. "I was surprised at how strong and brave she was. When she told me about hearing Gavin speak to her from the beyond the grave, I thought she'd just broken. And then she did all this," Kimmy waves her arm in the air. "She stood up to a bully—twice. First Genie, then Dr. Crystal. She faced her fears. Not to mention trying to bring a boy back to life and saving you with magic she didn't even know she had. She even survived being stabbed by that insane creature that this one," she points at Taylor, "worked for."

Kimmy pauses and walks over to me. Looping her arm around mine, she says, "Boy, what a week."

We laugh. Sharing that laugh with her feels like ice cream on a hot summer day. Soothing, perfect. Just what I need. A non-stressful moment with my best friend in the whole world.

"You never said how you are able to do magic," my father reminds us, busting through the happy friendship barrier that Kimmy just built around me.

"We don't really know," I tell him. It's true, though I have my theories. "But I have a feeling that we might be able to figure everything out together. I see no reason we can't find a way to save you, Dad, if we stick together. We just haven't found the way, yet."

"I'll give you the chance, butterfly." Dad looks me right in the eye. "But I need to know that when the time comes...*if* the time comes that we can't bring me back you will do the right thing and let me go. Promise me."

"I—" What am I going to say?

"Marley!" My father pleads.

*You're getting your chance, love. Don't blow it*, Gavin warns.

Against my will, I say the words he needs to hear. "If—and that's a big if—I promise." In denial, I feel safe. There is no way I'm going to lose my dad again. No way. Not while he's standing right here in front of me and alive. Well, sort of.

Even in his condition, I won't give up on him. I am not letting him go without a fight. And that, I can promise.

"Dad, you should stay here, for now. I'll set up the basement for you. At least you will have somewhere nice to stay until we fix this...situation. For now, why don't you just get some rest?" I slide over to the cupboard for sleeping supplies: a blanket, some sheets and a pillow. "Get some sleep, Dad."

"Do me a favor?" he asks. I nod. "Don't tell your mother I'm here."

"We've been staying at Uncle Sam's because of this," I say, waving my hand to point out the messy house. "I'll get her to stay there a little longer."

"You can tell me about this later." Then he leaves and heads downstairs to where we have an extra couch set up.

I turn to Kimmy and Gavin and say, "How are we going to get back into that gym is what I want to know. Crystal's probably got trigger-happy guards lining the property by now."

Kimmy shrugs.

Taylor, finally speaking up, says, "We have to find the phone first."

Kimmy asks, "Can't you just face another fear?"

# TWENTY-SIX

"DO YOU THINK that would work, Gavin?" I ask him.

He shrugs. "I can't say for sure."

"Can you—" Gavin disappears before I can finish my sentence.

"What just happened?" Taylor questions, nervous.

"I don't know." *Gavin? Are you there? What happened?*

He doesn't respond. Nerves trickle into my blood stream. "I have to check on him."

I close my eyes and imagine Gavin's room. I imagine him lying on his bed, recharging, or whatever. I open my eyes to find I'm in his room, but he isn't. "Gavin? I call out. No answer.

So, I run out of the room. The first door I try is empty. As I rush down the hall, periodically calling out for Gavin, I remember one of my dreams, where we walked down this hallway.

I wanted to stop and look at the pictures. But they're not photographs, as I'd first thought. They're paintings. Circe's paintings?

When I look down the long hall, I realize the walls are full of paintings, dozens and dozens of them. A deep pit forms in my stomach. How could Circe's father abandon her here like this?

I leave the hallway and run to the door I know is housing the room I want.

The Hall of Mirrors.

I open the door and run in. Now, I'm staring at a shocked Circe. Her blond hair is perfect, and she is clad in beautiful white pants and a fluffy gray sweater. She sits cross-legged and seamlessly straight in front of the mirrors. "That's getting easier." I say, proud of myself.

"At such a desperate time, I will say I am really glad to see you." Circe stands, wiping her white pants off.

I was hoping to see Gavin here. I'm still not sure I can trust Circe. I guess I have no choice right now, but to hope for the best. "Why didn't you tell me about my father?" I ask before I even knew the thought was in my head.

"I should have. I'm sorry."

"Please don't hold back such important information. I'm tired of being blindsided," I admit.

"You're absolutely right. I was only thinking of you. You've already had so much piled on your shoulders, I didn't want to add any more weight. Although, I should to give you more credit, sweet girl."

"Thank you," I say, hoping she'll keep her word. "This was the only way I knew to help Gavin—and hopefully my father."

In walks Gavin, right on time. "Sorry, my powers kind of quit on me. Had to come back."

I run up and hug him. I let relief flood me, making me feel weightless. Gavin puts one hand in my hair and hugs me tightly. "I was worried."

"Don't be, love. I'm not leaving you."

I reluctantly leave his arms and turn back to Circe. "I wish I could give you good news about your father, but the truth is that no Limbonian has ever been saved. With that said, you and Gavin are very strong and extremely stubborn. I can easily see why you are meant to be together. If anyone can save Len, it will be the two of you."

Gavin throws his arm around my hip, pulling me closer to him. "See that, love? We rock."

Circe cuts into our conversation. "There is still hope for Gavin. But you will have to get your phone back."

"So, facing another fear won't work?"

She shakes her head, her reddish-blonde hair bobs. "I'm sorry, sweet girl. I wish I had better news to give you."

So do I. "Any help you can give me is appreciated. We're so low on time."

"I believe I know where you can find Crystal. But I need to warn you, she's not the one you're looking for."

"What do you mean?"

"She's a good woman. At least, she was when she was here. I don't know what turned her heart so cold, but I have a feeling it's more than the loss of her fiancé. I fear someone may be controlling her."

Catching on quickly, I inhale sharply. "You think she's been possessed by a Limbonian?"

She nods. "I do, yes. It's the only thing that makes sense to me."

Well, that's definitely important information to have. "How can I tell whether she's being possessed?"

"The pendant around your neck." My hand moves to

the cool metal and fingers the butterfly, as I've always done. "It's an ancient talisman created by one of my Piggybackers who had the power to manipulate metal. I don't know how your father came to possess it, although I am glad he did. The way it works is simple..." She explains it to me. I only need to touch Crystal while I'm wearing the pendant.

"One more question, if you don't mind."

"Of course not."

"Can Crystal actually bring my father back? Is it possible?"

"Like I said before, I've never seen it happen. Lately, it seems as if the rules are changing. You are proof of that. So, there's reason for hope." She smiles. "But if I am correct, you will most likely not get the help you desire from Crystal."

"Thank you," I tell her, but I'm already back in my own realm.

"Circe told me I can't face another fear," I tell Kimmy, who's watching me with concern.

"You spoke to her?" she asks.

"Yeah, that's why I've been zoning out. Apparently, I have the ability to travel between worlds."

"I thought you could only do that because Gavin was there."

"Yes. Gavin is still there. No one knows why I have this power, but it does come in handy sometimes." Kimmy actually looks impressed. "She told me where to find Crystal. We have to get that cell phone."

Kimmy swears. "Let's go."

"Wait, where's Taylor?"

"She went downstairs to check on Len."

"Let's go tell them what's going on."

We make our way downstairs. A cool breeze hits my skin as we get closer to the bottom. The basement is usually cool, but well insulated. That's weird. And then I realize what happened.

The basement window is flapping gently in the breeze. "They're gone," I say.

"Where did they go?"

The answer is so obvious, I should have seen this coming. Although the fear, anger, and worry that pop up, they are unexpected. The both of them can probably take care of themselves. "They must have gone to confront Crystal."

Kimmy groans. "What should we do?"

"We can't waltz in there without a plan."

Someone's cell phone chimes. It's Kimmy's. She checks it and says, "Oh, no. It's your mom. Should I answer it?"

I wince. "Yes. She's probably worried because she can't get a hold of me."

Kimmy touches the answer button and hands the phone to me. I mouth the word "chicken" and place the phone to my ear. "Hi, Mom. Glad you called. I have something to tell you."

"I have something to tell you, too, Marley."

My heart drops into my stomach and pulsates with the strength of a freight train. That isn't my mother's voice. "What do you want? And where is my mother? If you hurt her, I swear I'll never stop hunting you."

"Relax, dear," she says, patronizingly. "She's fine. And she'll stay that way, if you deliver your father to me."

"Now you want my father? Why?" My heart stops.

Where could he be? That means that Crystal doesn't have him.

I have one second to ponder where he might be when Crystal informs me, "I wanted you, but I guess I'll have to settle for dear old Dad. It's time to make another choice, Marley. It's your father or your mother."

How does she expect me to choose between my parents? "You rotten little —"

"Get angry all you want," she interrupts. "That won't save your parents."

*Marley? What's wrong?* Gavin asks.

*Crystal has my mother,* I tell him. "Fine," I lie to Crystal. "You can have what you really want, but my father stays here *and* I'm completing the ritual first." I try not to give my plan away.

"So, I can have Piggybacker boy on my tail? No deal."

"What if he promises not to come after you?"

Silence on the line. "Fine," she agrees.

"Where do I meet you?" I ask as Gavin's spirit appears in the kitchen, staring at me with concern and confusion.

"Where it all started. Be there in one hour or she dies, and I take you and your father anyway."

Click.

My stomach drops to the floor and a pit full of fear and anger replaces it. Mom must be so terrified. We let our guard down, leaving Crystal enough room to swoop in and take my mother. How could I let this happen? I should have seen it coming. We already know Crystal is capable of it.

"What happened? Crystal took your mother?" Kimmy questions.

"Yes, and we're going to get her back."

Gavin's ghostly form says, "Yes, we will, love. I promise."

"At the expense of my father's only chance," I confess. I don't tell them what is actually going on. They'll just worry about me or try to talk me out of it. I've already made up my mind. I can save three lives tonight if I do what Crystal wants.

"No," Gavin says. "We'll figure out something. Just like we always do."

"What's going on? I don't understand," Kimmy says, simultaneously walking right through Gavin's translucent figure, as she comes over to comfort me. I stifle a laugh when Gavin appears beside her with an annoyed expression on his face.

"It was Crystal. She's got my mom." Tears fall. I hadn't even noticed I was crying. I'm more angry and determined than sad. "She wants a trade. Mom for Dad."

That's my story and I'm sticking to it.

"What?" Kimmy shouts.

"I'll go," Dad says, appearing behind Kimmy.

"Where were you?"

"Getting back-up. There's a team outside. We are going to take down that woman if it's the last thing I do."

"Dad—"

"That woman has gone after my family for the last time. Don't try to talk me out of it, butterfly." He holds up a finger to stop me from talking. "And before you say anything else, let me just say that she wouldn't have been involved if I didn't come into the picture. And besides, I'm already dead. Your mom still has a chance."

I don't know what to say to him, and I don't have a better plan. He sighs and looks down at the floor. The stress on his expression is clear. He rubs the bridge of his nose. I turn to say something to Gavin, but he's gone. "Looks like you've made up your mind. What's the plan?"

"We are going to bring your boyfriend back and then make the trade."

"He's not my boyfriend."

Gavin laughs in my head. *Not yet,* he tells me. *Don't worry, love. You'll figure this out. Haven't you realized you're stronger than you think you are?*

I hadn't thought about it. I'm just trying to keep my family safe.

Kimmy says, "We'll get your mom back and then figure out how to help your dad, too."

"Yeah, we will," my father states. "Because I'm going in there to get her back."

Taylor chooses that time to walk in. "We should come up with a plan. The Limbonians are getting restless."

"Let's get out of here." Kimmy suggests.

"No, Kimmy. You could get hurt. You're the only one here without any power."

"There's no way I'm letting you walk into danger and not help. I don't need powers. I got these," she says, flexing her tiny muscular arms.

This is so messed up. What can I say to stop her? She's just as bullheaded as I am when she makes up her mind, maybe more. That's why we make such good friends. I'm terrified to have her there but if I know she's in there, I'll be able to protect her better. "Just promise you'll be careful."

"I will." Kimmy promises and stomps out of the room. I hear the front door slam behind her.

I look at the clock on the microwave. It's getting

desperately late. "We know where she's going to be. We still have time to get the phone and complete the ritual."

*We're cutting it close, love.*

*I know,* I tell him. "Let's go." I tell Dad and Taylor. Before heading out, I toss my backpack over my shoulder and send a silent prayer that everything goes according to plan. They will never forgive me for what I am about to do, but I don't care.

I am not about to sit back and watch people I love die.

It's not until we get close that I realize there's a blue Civic behind my car and it's filled with people. I nod at them and hop into my car. Taylor gets in behind me and asks, "Where are we going?"

"The gym."

# TWENTY-SEVEN

THE SUN IS going down, giving the cerulean sky a hint of orange hue. We're running out of time. No, Marley, I tell myself. Don't think about it. This will work.

When we arrive at the school, Dad says, "Taylor, help me with Gavin. Girls, be careful in there."

The second car pulls in behind mine. Four young guys pile out. "Let's take this witch down," one of the Limbonians yells as he hops out of the Civic. He looks eighteen, with jet-black hair and bright pink chewing gum circling his teeth as he talks.

Eighteen? Too young to die. A thought I've had a thousand times this week. Next week better be full of roses and rainbows.

When we finally make it to the gym—which is still torn up, just cleaner—Mom is surrounded by men and tied to a chair. Despite the remnants of tears on her face, her eyes propel anger into each and every man standing guard in front of her. If looks could kill.

Crystal stands a few feet away, acting as if this whole

situation isn't appalling. I want to smack her. I want to go after her smug face and dig my claws in, but Gavin stops me. *Let's be smart about this.*

*After everything she's done, you should be angrier with her.*

*I am angry,* is all he says.

"You brought what I asked for. Len, come stand by me and my pets will let your wife go," Crystal reassures, in an annoyingly calm tone. There are seven Limbonians standing on her side.

"Let her go first," my father demands.

Crystal laughs. "That is *not* how this works. I have the leverage. You do what I say. Come over here now and she lives."

"Dad, no," I whisper. *We can take them. Can't we?* I silently question Gavin. *We have eight here, plus you.*

He says, *She has eight, too. If they're all Limbonian, we don't stand a chance. And who knows how much more power Crystal has now.*

"We had a deal, Miss McCartney," Crystal says to me. "I expect you to hold up your end of the bargain."

"I want the phone first," I tell her.

She reaches into her pocket and pulls out my black-cased phone. "Your phone is here."

*Marley. Whatever you're thinking, don't.* Gavin warns.

"Don't do it, butterfly," Dad repeats.

Before I can say anything, Crystal speaks up in her annoyed tone. "Very well, then." She flicks her hand in the air. Mom's scream is muffled underneath the duct tape on her mouth. We all hear the crack.

"Stop," I scream, while Dad shouts, "No!"

Mom's pinky finger is twisted and is now facing the ceiling. Her muffled whimpers echo throughout the gym with the strength of a tornado.

I don't think. Neither Dad nor Kimmy is able to stop me. I rush at the witch, trying to save my mom.

It all happens so fast. One second, I'm running at her; the next I'm in the air. A sharp pain resonates through me as if I've been electrocuted. Luckily, Gavin is there, using his powers to cushion my fall. Instead of slamming into the wall and falling brokenly to the floor, I crush into a malleable substance. It feels cool to the touch, almost like snow, and I'm slowly lowered to the floor.

I hear my father scream and realize he also attacked Crystal. Since he has powers, he's able to get a shot or two into the mix before she reaches out with her hand and snaps his neck. My father falls to the floor with a crushing thump. My heart stops.

"No," I scream. I cannot believe my eyes. I've lost him, again? I will kill that woman if I ever get my hands on her. I try to get up but I'm trapped in the blanket of snow. I can't move an inch. *I'm sorry*, Gavin whispers in my head. That's when I realize he not only saved me; he's also trapped me to the spot. *For your own good.*

*I want to fight. I want to break her.* I've never been so angry in all my life.

*I know*, Gavin tells me. *She'll get what she deserves, I promise you.*

My father moves then. He gasps and chokes before rolling over to his side. I watch from my prison as he reaches up and twists his neck back to its rightful place with a loud, sickening crack. Relief is instant. Confusion follows closely behind, very closely.

Dad gets so angry the floorboards shake. Some of them wobble as if they're dancing to a good tune. My father growls and attacks Crystal—who has to fend off both my father and Taylor, now.

Mom's still tied in her chair and I can only watch and pray from my prison. She's wrestling with her bonds and shivering with anger, tears streaking her face. Two Limbonians stand stone still at each side of her. The other three have gone to help Crystal with her fight. They aren't a match for my dad and Taylor, however. Crystal has clearly taken most of the Limbonians' magic away. A plus for the good guys.

Two of my mother's guards join the fight as Kimmy comes over to help me up.

"Are you okay?" she asks.

"No. Gavin trapped me here."

With both of us trying to move me, my body budges a bit. Unfortunately, Gavin's magic is too strong, and I don't know how to control mine. *Gavin,* I shout in my head. *You have to let me up. There are only two guards standing in front of mom. I can sneak by and cut her loose.*

*No,* he screeches in my mind. *I don't want you to do anything stupid.*

*Let me go. You're wasting magic on me, when you could be using it on Crystal. Let me go, now. I can fight. I've nearly got my black belt. Trust me, I can take these guys.*

Against his will, Gavin finally lets up on the reins, giving me the break that I need to escape entirely. He doesn't like it, but I have to save my mom—she would not be stuck in this mess if it weren't for me.

Rushing to my feet, I tuck behind the battle and run the long way around the gym, hoping to come up behind the bad guys. Kimmy follows closely behind. When Mom notices me, I think I am done for. If *she* noticed me, it's likely the bad guys also noticed my pursuit. Freezing to the spot, I hide in the shadows and watch while the big battle ensues. The occasional grunt and screech reverberate off the walls. Flying debris shoots all around the room; their powers destroying what's left of the gym.

I finally make it to where my mom is tied up after quietly tiptoeing over to her chair and praying that no one can see or hear me. I wish I had more control over this magic thing—if in fact I can do what they all think I can do, magic would come in handy right now. The Limbonians have yet to turn around and see us standing there. Ducking behind Mom's chair, I desperately pull at the knotted rope.

"I'm sorry about this, Mom," I whisper for her ears only. "I wish that you'd never been involved in this madness."

Mom shakes her head. I'm only able to loosen the ropes. With each pull, frustration builds up inside me. I nearly scream. I'm failing. No. Come on, Marley. Think. There has to be a way.

But I don't have a clue. So, I do all I can do. I grip the porous strings and tear. They won't budge. Maybe Crystal tied them magically. Maybe they won't come loose unless Crystal takes them off.

I tear again, desperately flicking my nails in between the creases of each strand, hoping for a tiny budge. Suddenly sparkly pink dust flies off my skin, like fairy dust. I stare in awe. They were right. I do have magic. I wonder why I'd never seen the pink strings before.

The pink dust weaves through the strands of the rope, tackling the knots in front of me. I smirk. Slowly, the knots loosen, then pull free. Gravity takes care of the rope and if falls with a small thunk as it hits the floor.

Mom doesn't even bother with the tape on her lips. She jumps up and runs for one of the Limbonians in front of her. Instantly, I follow her lead, hoping to help. Kimmy takes on the second one.

I barrel into my guy, knocking his head on the floor. I'm on my feet fast and kicking him before he realizes what hit him. Mom does the same thing before she steps back, exhausted. I kick the Limbonian in the groin, extra hard for good measure, and he gasps, the air knocked out of him. Luckily, Crystal is in the middle of her own battle and can't save him. I dive for the rope that just fell on the floor and tie it around the Limbonian's wrists.

Mom tears the tape from her lips. She's out of breath when she says, "Whatever... the score is, you win. Thanks... for saving me."

Laughter slips out. I'm happy to see Mom acting more like she did before my hospital trip. "How do you know I'm keeping score?"

She gives a breathy laugh. "I know my daughter."

"I'm sorry I missed my last session with Dr. Crystal."

She waves me off. "I'm glad you did. That woman is psychotic. Now, go help Kimmy."

"Are you going to be okay?"

"Yes."

It's a good thing Mom warned me to help her. Kimmy does need some help, so I throw myself in front of a punch and get the wind knocked out of me. A rock-hard fist lands in my gut. Pain explodes like fireworks expanding from my belly up to my lungs. Down I go. A deep fire burns in my belly. I gasp loudly then groan in agony.

Mom screams, "Marley," and rushes over to me.

"I'm..." I inhale sharply, "okay."

Maybe not. I think my stomach is in my throat.

Kimmy manages to duck and swings around to kick the man in the face. She's always been small, but the girl has heart and a high range. I'm too busy choking on bile to say anything about it. Mom tries to comfort me.

From where I lay on the cold wooden floor, I can see the magical fight clearly. Crystal throws her magic at Taylor. Her color is an off red and not very bright. The energy is so dark, it's nearly black. It swirls in a tornado pattern around Taylor.

My father retaliates by turning the floorboards to mush at her feet. Crystal jumps in the air and magically throws him into the hole while Taylor frees herself from Crystal's magical clutches. Crystal frees the other two Limbonians, so they can help fight Taylor off. My father begins sinking immediately.

"Dad," I yell—or at least I think I do. My voice comes out as a whisper, due to the recent blow. Kimmy tries to help me up, but I still can't move. The bad guy got me in exactly the wrong spot.

I have to help Taylor and my father. This is not part of my plan, which is unravelling before my eyes. I need to get it back on track. But how?

Rescuing Taylor and Dad for starters. I want to take Crystal out for making us all suffer, each and every one of us in this gym, I'd bet. All because she wants more power. It isn't a good enough reason to torture people.

The angrier I get, the more pink fairy dust explodes from me. It's magic secreting from my pores. Then it hits me that I actually can help them if I concentrate hard enough. "Kimmy, get out of here," I whisper, as she watches the carnage. "Take my mom with you."

"I can't leave you!"

"No, it's okay. I've got magic, now. See?" I show her my glowing hands. "Take my mother to the car outside."

"Marley—" Mom protests.

"Please go and be safe."

I rush to my feet, ignoring the sharp pain. A pink rope weaves itself into the air and lands directly in front of my father. He grabs the rope, holding on for dear life, and then I'm able to pull him out of the pit. He grunts and lands on the floor with a loud thump. I don't breathe a sigh of relief until I hear the doors close behind Mom and Kimmy. My father stands up.

The three of us fight Crystal now while the Limbonians fight each other—the ones that are left standing. Even with the three of us, we struggle against Crystal's power. I toss pink clouds at her, hoping to hold her at bay.

Gavin was right. She might be too powerful even for three of us. *Gavin, what else should I do? I think I can help.*

*Go with Kimmy,* he says.

*She already left. I have to fight, Gavin,* I impatiently answer, as Taylor picks up the half-broken basketball net from the floor and whips it at Crystal. My father keeps her occupied by magically wrapping the hardwood floorboards around her, though they don't hold her for long. That must be his magic turning sour.

Just as the net is about to wipe her out, she manages to escape by weaving clouds of puffy smoke through the floorboards and burning them to ash. Crystal is able to jump out of the way in the nick of time. Taylor anticipates her move and waves her arm in the air. Crystal slams into the bleachers, smacking her head with a loud crack.

I know instantly. She's gone. Would she come back to life as my father had? I wait, dumbfounded and unsure. My father takes the tall Limbonian out easily, while Taylor fights the other one. I run to find the phone in Crystal's pocket and remember to touch her hand.

My necklace gets warm and turns black, which means that she is definitely possessed by a Limbonian.

Then my phone goes off. It's the alarm ringing. "No, no, no." It can't be. "No."

I'd set the alarm to go off when Gavin's time ran out. Tears fill my eyes as I follow the sound of the ringtone and scramble through her pockets. I can't fail now. This isn't possible. We're so close.

*It's all right, love. As long as you're safe. I know what you were planning to do. Now you can be with your family.*

"No!" I shoot up, holding onto the ringing phone. "We have to try. We didn't come this far to fail." My voice breaks as I say the words, but I'm more determined than ever. Maybe they got the time of his death wrong. They could have missed it by a few minutes. If we hurry, it has to be possible. "Taylor, where's Gavin?" I ask, while looking for my backpack.

"Over here. I got him. Where do you want him?" She bends down, picking him up like he's a bag of marshmallows.

*Don't worry about me, love. I'll be all right.*

"Well, I won't," I admit. "I just found you."

Taylor puts Gavin down as I find my backpack by the double doors and get the ingredients out. My phone reads 8:47 p.m. Only three minutes past the deadline. This has to work. I can't lose him.

"I have to try," I tell Taylor, when she turns her head to me.

"Get your man, M&M," she says without judgment.

Following Circe's instructions, I place the trophy on his chest, then the lion shavings. My phone goes on his heart, then Kyle's cup and Gavin's guitar pick.

The moly goes on his forehead. I put extra because of the time difference, hoping that will appease the gods. It's worth a shot.

I chant the words three times in Greek:

> *I call upon the goddess of light and love*
> *Weave your magic through my soul mate*
> *Release him from the grip of death*
> *Return him to the life that was.*

Nothing happens.

Arms come around my shoulders. It's my father. "You tried, butterfly. It wasn't your fault."

I look up through a face full of tears to see Gavin's spirit looking down at me. He gives me his mischievous grin before fading from view and my heart stops.

The tears come harder. After everything we've been through together, Gavin still died. How is that fair? What else could I have possibly done? Three minutes. Just *three* minutes too late.

I let myself sob into my dad's shoulder—even though it isn't really his shoulder I'm crying into. I'm so entirely exhausted and sick of feeling helpless.

Dad gasps. "Look, sweetheart."

I look up. The paper with the trophy is hovering in the air. Suddenly it disappears in a puff of white clouds, making a popping sound as it goes. The shavings do the same, along with the other items on Gavin's chest.

"What's happening, Dad?"

"I don't know, kiddo."

Finally, the moly rises a foot in the air and pops in cloudy white smoke and is gone.

Gavin's body glows a strong, beautiful blue. I think he might disappear, too. My heart skips a beat and my stomach sinks. But he doesn't disappear.

Right before my eyes, Gavin gasps and breathes heavily for a few moments. Color returns to his cheeks and the rest of his body comes to life. It worked?

"It worked." I shout, happily. After everything that's happened, I still cannot believe we brought a dead boy back to life.

*Believe it, love.* "You did a great job," Gavin says out loud. I stand up, in complete shock. I stand there and just look at him. This is real. *This is real.* He's standing here in front of me. Is it terrible that I'm kind of proud of myself? I know I couldn't have done it alone. A bubbling laughter spills out of me. I almost can't believe this is finally happening. When I reach out to touch his cheek, I'm surprised to find it warm.

Gavin tosses me that sexy grin and before I know what's happening, Gavin's lips are on mine. The instant our lips touch I know that everything will be all right.

And boy, do I kiss him back.

It's like nothing I've ever felt before. It's powerful and weakening at the same time. It's euphoric and grounding. It's the simplest feeling that binds me to Earth, making me feel whole.

A lot of books and movies will tell you that the earth

moves when you kiss the love of your life. And they would be right. I can confirm it. His lips are soft against mine, pressing hard as he holds me in his strong arms. I'm grateful, as I'd have crashed to the Earth if he weren't holding me up. This is suddenly my new favorite place to be.

He pulls away too soon and places an arm around my shoulder to drag me in for a strong hug. When he pulls away, he opens his hand and reveals a flower petal of some kind. He says, "A gift from Circe."

"Uh," I respond, looking down at the flower and wondering why she wanted me to have it. "She shouldn't have."

Gavin chuckles. "Eat it."

"I'm not eating that." I still don't know if I trust Circe all that much. I mean, she helped bring Gavin back, but she lied.

"Do it for me, love. I promise I wouldn't offer it to you if I thought it would hurt you."

"Eat the flower petal? You come back to life and one of the first things you want to say is, 'Eat it?'" He smirks knowingly, then nods.

*Eat the flower, love,* he says in my head.

*You're still in my head?* I roll my eyes and groan, feigning contention. "I should have known." I may not trust Circe, but I do trust Gavin. "All right. Here goes."

It doesn't taste nearly as bad as I think it will—actually, it's better than I thought it would be. It has a sweetness to it. My stomach tingles where the pain had once been, along with my head injury from the kidnapping and being thrown in the gym yesterday. They buzz for seconds. I panic, thinking I'd been tricked.

But then I look down and lift my shirt. All my insides are back in place and all the wounds have disappeared. Not even a scar.

I pull away from Gavin, half shocked and totally amazed. What? He doesn't have the power to heal. "How—"

Gavin interrupts, "I knew we could trust her." He looks around the destroyed gym. "Where did Kimmy go? Is your mom okay?"

"Yes, they're safe. I sent them out a few minutes ago."

"We have to go. Now." Dad pulls on my arm to get my attention, before running toward the door. I forgot he was standing there.

I follow, asking, "Why? What's wrong?"

"The two men you took out, they're gone. Look."

Both bodies are gone, including the Limbonian I tied up.

"They were going after Mom and Kimmy," I realize, picking up the pace, wanting desperately to save my family. If only I'd noticed the Limbonians leave. "We have to find her," I shout while the pit in my stomach grows.

"We will. I'll check this way," my father says and off he goes without another word.

"He's right. You're sticking with me," Gavin informs me.

"Fine. Let's go." We run along the corridor, listening for any sounds, or movement. Nothing. Searching for signs of which way they've gone.

Nothing catches our attention, until I see a swipe of blood on the side of the wall. It's Kimmy's. I can't say how or why I know that, but somehow, I understand what happened just from the single smudge of blood. She left us a trail to follow—probably nicking herself on purpose or using a previous wound to her advantage, knowing I'd see it.

"This way," I tell Gavin. We head toward the back door. Before we head out, I catch another smudge of blood on the wall. *She went through this door,* I tell Gavin.

*Let's go.* He doesn't hesitate.

When the door creaks open it reveals a long set of stairs. Someone had turned the lights on; I'm guessing it was the men who were looking for Mom and Kimmy.

"You're not going anywhere," a man's voice echoes from the basement.

"No, we've got you now, and your friends aren't here to save you." The second man's voice is nasally and creepy. I might have felt bad for him—almost. If he hadn't just kidnapped my family.

*Go slowly. We need to see what we're up against,* Gavin whispers in my mind.

I grab hold of his hand and then I'm not in my body anymore. I'm floating in the air—like in my nightmares—looking down on Gavin and my empty body. I'm flying. Seriously, this is cool, but what the heck is going on here? Who's doing this? Am I doing this? I'm flying down the stairs, toward the voices and I realize this *must* be my power, or maybe its residual power left over from the flower I ate.

Kimmy isn't visible, neither is Mom. I don't see anyone. Not right away. There are only shelves of books and office supplies. The place is mega dusty, though it seems like it's been used recently.

Then I see them. The first guy is standing between a couple shelves. The second guy is standing behind Kimmy and holding her hands behind her back. They've cornered her and caught her like she's a cat and they're two vicious, rabid dogs.

She looks so scared, I want to take them both out. Like everything else I can't explain, I know I need to be in my body for that. Just as quickly as I left, I'm back inside my body.

*That was weird*, Gavin exclaims, telepathically. *You... weren't here.*

*I know. I had an out of body experience. At least that's what I think it was.* We continue to speak telepathically since neither one of us knows what they'd do to Kimmy if they knew we were so close.

As we make our way down the stairs at a snail's pace, my heart pulses nervously. I wish this was over already. There are so many ways this can go wrong. What if I can't figure out how to use my powers at will? What if something happens to Kimmy? Where's Mom? If anything were to happen to either of them I'd never forgive myself. *She's on the right, behind the fifth bookshelf. One man is standing behind her. The other one is on this side. They've cornered her. Are you ready?*

He answers quickly and confidently. *Definitely.*

I go one way and Gavin goes the other. We creep slowly up to the right shelves. One of the men is speaking, although I can't make out the words over the pulse echoing in my head. He speaks in a rushed tone, his words threatening.

As I pass a supply shelf, I nab the closest and heaviest item I can. Gavin and I reach our targets at the same time. He takes the first guy out by hitting him on the head with what looks like an eighty-pound book as I sneak up behind my bad guy and conk him on the head with a jar of paint from the supplies, but I'm too late. Kimmy falls to a heap on the floor and blood, a lot of it, pools quickly from her neck.

# TWENTY-EIGHT

"NO-OO-O!" I SCREECH. Did he just hurt my best friend? Anger explodes inside me as if a bomb just went off. I feel it from the tips of my toes to the top of my head. So much so that it burst from the seems. Burst right out of me.

I shove so much magic at the bad guy, a black orb wrapped around a lightning bolt of gold about the size of a basketball floats out of his chest. The Limbonian crumples to the floor just as Kimmy had. The strange phenomenon hovers in the air. I don't care what it is; all I care about is Kimmy.

Unfortunately, I'm a few crucial seconds too late. My throat closes tight and tears swamp my eyelids as the reality crashes into me. She isn't breathing, and there is too much blood. I hit the floor hard, weeping. I attempt to reach out for her, but Gavin rushes me into his arms and attempts to carry me away.

"No. No. Take me back, Gavin. Take me back!"

"She's gone, love. There's no reason for you to see that. I will take care of everything. You just go find your father."

"You can heal her, right? Do you have another flower petal? Please, Gavin. Ple-ease," I cry, pleading.

"I can't. That was a one-time deal," he whispers softly. "I'm so sorry, love. She's gone."

"Maybe I can go to the island and ask Circe for another one." I close my eyes and picture the Hall of mirrors, as vividly as I can muster. I try to picture Circe's face like I did the last time.

This has to work. Please. I plead to the universe. Please, let me get there. It's never been more important for me to get to the island. I crack an eye open, but I know I'm still in Gavin's arms.

"I don't think you have the strength to use magic right now. I'm sorry."

"No. I'm not leaving her," I shout, punching him so he will put me down. "It might not be too late. Maybe I can help her. I have to try. Put me down." I cry. The knot in my throat makes my voice sound hoarse. Gavin does as I ask.

The black orb is following us, I realize, when I turn back. When I attempt to duck around it, the orb slams into me and explodes into an ocean of dust.

Coughing out black dust, I run back to Kimmy and pull her into my arms. Hoping and praying with every fiber of my soul for a miracle. If I was given magic for any reason, this has to be it.

I weave every bit of magic I can pull from this world and the next, the entire universe. Wherever I can pull it from, I do. We are surrounded by a tornado of pink clouds. I can't lose her. I refuse. "You're my best friend. Kimmy, don't go into the light. Please. You're the sister I never had. Please."

She doesn't move. Her eyes are glazed over. No, she can't be gone.

"Oh, no." I hear someone say softly from behind me. "Butterfly, she's gone. You have to let her go. I'm so sorry, sweetheart."

I weep more. Harder. Just hearing the words are a strain on any control I have left. "No," I cry tearfully. This can't be happening. Not Kimmy. God, you can't take my best friend.

"What do we do, now?" Grief causes my brain to fog and Gavin's words seem a mile away.

My father whispers in response, "Call the cops. Tell them there was a break-in at the school. They'll probably figure that Kimmy was kidnapped and in trying to get away, she was killed."

"Okay, I'll make the call and you can stay with Marley."

A loud crash and a growl resonate behind me. Slowly I turn to look. Through blurry eyes, I can see the shape of a woman. At first, I think it might be my mother, then I see my father is holding her in his arms, so it's definitely not Mom.

When Gavin goes flying and my dad goes down, I realize it's Crystal.

She's alive?

Her red magic swirls in fuzzy lights around the room. I try desperately to get up and help. Though I eventually get up, Crystal's magic knocks me right back down.

She's still alive and my best friend—one of the best people I've ever met—is lying dead on the floor of a dirty old basement of a dreary old high school? Hell, no! I break;

something snaps.

"This is all your fault!" I fight back. She doesn't know what hit her. Hatred, loss, and disgust flood me like sludge in a sewer bank. Pink magic weaves through Crystal's ugly red. The hue of my pink magic has darkened with anger.

Crystal is alive, Kimmy isn't; that only enrages me more. I can't see anything but black — blind abhorrence riddles in the hazy clouds of bereavement and disbelief. The more I think about it, the more willing I am to take the perfect, little bimbo out.

Dark pink swirls of light slam into her over and over again. Books begin flying past me, whipping in her direction. Thinking about everything the woman did, thinking about everyone she hurt and all the people she's killed is only more fuel for the fire inside me. It consumes me. It wasn't enough to take out her goon. All I can think about is giving this horrible witch everything that she's dished out.

Wind picks up around me. Shelves rocket back and forth with the power I wield. I can't stop myself. She tries to fight back. Tiny strings of reddish-brown explode in small spurts behind my large and powerful pink blasts.

Crystal tries to fight me, though it's no use. I can see that my magic is getting to her. It's not enough though. It will never be enough, I realize.

Nothing is stronger than my anger. It threads itself into every muscle, bone and tissue in my body. I can't stop until the woman is gone, a pile of angry, vicious and selfish ash on the ground. Avenging the man I love, my father who had been tortured, and the best friend I just lost is my only outlet.

*Marley. Stop. This isn't you.* Gavin's words barely

register. He's so far away.

"Butterfly, no. You're better than her." There is my dad.

*Marley. Please!*

The magic won't stop. I just keep hurling it at Crystal, oceans and oceans of it. She is still standing, and I can't have that. Anger spreads like an infectious disease. Like news in a gossip magazine, anger stretches through everything, anchoring itself into my very soul. Whatever it is, it's taking over.

*Kimmy wouldn't want you to do this.* Gavin's words melt into my head.

Instantly, everything stops. My magic ceases. My mind turns off. The wind dies down while books plummet to the floor—numerous loud, sharp bangs echo throughout the room as they land.

I drop my guard for a moment and see Gavin staring at me as if I've grown another head. Crystal takes the opportunity. She ties red magic around me, Gavin, and my unconscious mother—strapping us tightly together.

I swear under my breath and struggle against the bonds. Before we can escape, Crystal grasps my father in her web and drags him out of the room. "No," I scream. He tries to fight but isn't able to break out of her web.

I catch one of Crystal's Limbonians throwing my father over his shoulder. I don't recognize him. This one is new.

*That's the guy who shot me,* Gavin shouts. *We have to get him.*

The man from my nightmares. How could I forget?

"Why can't we get out of this thing?" I question, squirming against the bond.

"I don't know how you did it, but you probably drained your magic with that outburst. I didn't even know you had that much power."

"Can you get us out of here?"

"I'm trying. Stop moving."

I do as he requests. Gavin opens his mouth and blue smoke comes out—tangling and knotting itself around the red bond; it busts the trap with a snap like a pair of magical bolt cutters. Gavin catches my mother before she falls to the floor.

"The cops are on the way. We have to get out of here before they arrive."

I turn toward Kimmy. Books and paper debris are scattered around her, though her body is unscathed—aside from the knife wound in her neck, the wound that took her from us. There's no way I can leave her behind.

"I know, love, but we don't have the answers the cops will need. They can't know we were here. We can't explain any of it."

Gavin whispers reassurances in my mind. Reluctantly, I follow Crystal's trail.

This is never going to be over. Not until I get my father back. There is no time to grieve for a lost friend. No more time to cry. No time to break down. There is never enough time.

Gavin and I rush out the front doors just as the sirens start getting louder. My father and Crystal are nowhere to be found.

My Mom—who looks completely uncomfortable draped over Gavin's back—starts to wake up. Gavin slowly lowers her to the ground. She sways, as if drunk on tequila, and grabs her forehead. "Oh. What happened?"

Her voice is groggy and pained.

"Len found you." Gavin answers. "I don't know where he found you."

I suddenly realize we're missing a lot of our party. "Does anyone know where Taylor is?"

"Aww, did you miss me, M&M?" Taylor questions from behind me.

I turn to see her and three of the Limbonians we started with. The only one missing is the one who'd been so eager to take Crystal out. "Where's..."

Taylor answers, "He'll be back. They're nearly impossible to kill, didn't anyone tell you?"

The guys laugh at the joke. I'm not in the mood.

Taylor looks around. "Where's Len?"

My throat closes up when I try to speak again. "She got him," Gavin says.

Taylor swears. Then she looks right at me and realizes something. "And your friend?"

My only response is to burst into tears. Having to say it out loud is too much to handle. "She's—"

"It's all right, love. I'll explain it to everyone later," Gavin says, holding me against his warm, muscular chest. I feel broken. I've lived through my worst fear twice now. I lost another family member. Kimmy was and always will be my family. "We can't stay here. I'll take us back to your place," he tells my mother.

"Len?" Mom wants to know. "Who's Len?"

I can't answer her. I don't have the strength to explain that Dad is alive. I don't have the heart to tell her we lost him. Again. "Crystal. We have to find her." I swear under my breath. I'd lost my father and my best friend because of her. *She will pay*, I vow to myself. *If it's the last thing I ever do.*

"We will, love. I'm sorry, Marley, but we have to get out of here, now."

"I will make it my life's mission to find her. When I do, I'll hold her down while you punch," Taylor tells me.

MOM RUSHES INTO the house, forgetting it's been trashed. She stubs her toe on the broken coffee table. "I'll get it, Mom. Sit down on the sofa."

I head into the kitchen as if I'm walking through water, my legs filled with lead and my heart singing the blues. This is not how I thought this night would end.

Gavin comes into the kitchen as I lean into the freezer to find an ice pack. "Are you going to be all right, love? Can I get you anything?"

"There's nothing you can do." Tears begin to flow again. "Thanks."

I don't have any words to explain the brokenness that spreads through my veins. It's like ice and concrete bled together and created an entirely new world of suffering.

I walk by Gavin and bring my mother her pills and the ice. "What happened tonight?" she asks. "I'm so confused. I can't believe it's all real."

"Crystal kidnapped you to get to me, Mom. I'm sorry." *I'm sorry for everything.*

Gavin walks into the room and starts cleaning up the debris.

Mom smacks the ice to her forehead. "I just can't

believe it was real. I could have saved him. I could have saved him."

"Mom? What are you saying?"

"Last year, after your father died, I thought I heard him speaking to me. I thought it was my way of grieving. I thought... I don't know."

"You thought you were losing your mind, Mom. You feared for us, I bet." She moans and then her shoulders shake. She's crying. "He wasn't mad at you, Mom. Dad knew you. He understood you don't believe in that kind of stuff."

"I still..." She breaks off in a sob. "Should... have tried. I miss him *so* much."

I try to hug her, throwing one arm around her back. It's weird to see Mom cry. She's always a rock, even when she's angry and afraid for me, I never see her cry. She leans her head onto my shoulder. "You've been going through a lot this week, Marley. Is that because you brought this boy back?"

I nod, but she's not looking at me. "Yes."

"You're so much braver than I am."

I pull away from her, hoping she'll look up at me. When she does, I see that her eyes are impossibly red and puffy. "You are brave, too. You kept going. That's brave. You go into work every day to put food on the table for Sammy and me. That's brave."

Gavin, with a handful of torn magazines, leaves the room. "Oh, Marley. I'm sorry. I'm so so sorry," Mom cries.

"Stop apologizing. No one's upset with you." If I'm being honest, I am, but I get it. I didn't want to believe all of this at first either.

"Where's Kimmy? I want to thank her for helping you

through this week. Well, couple weeks, actually."

And that does it. She's broken the dam. It bursts so quickly, I could fill the Grand Canyon with my tears. "She's... gone."

Suddenly Gavin's carrying me to my room. He promises to explain everything to my mother. I think she knows, although I can't think clearly through my grief. I've lost a part of me and that would have been hard enough without everything else piled on top of it. I was numb after losing my dad last year, but the paralyzing feeling that touches the edges of every thought and feeling I have has me totally raw and open.

Gavin lays me down on the bed and sits beside me. "Can I get you anything, love?"

Tears fall down my cheeks. I have to run out of tears eventually. As Gavin lies down beside me, I curl into his chest and let the tears flow. He sits still and just holds me, waiting out the storm. I think of Kimmy, my perfect sister. She was always there for me. How can I go on without her? What kind of life is there without her? I can't even imagine how it will go on.

I drift in and out of a restless sleep and each time I wake, Gavin's there. He's there until I remember what happened and the tears flow again.

When I wake for the third time, Gavin hands me a couple tissues. My mind is still incredibly foggy, but one thing is clear: Gavin is here, he's tangible, alive. "So, what happens, now? With you, I mean." I croak through tears.

He thinks about it, taking my hand in his. "I don't know. I wish I never magically encouraged your mother to leave that newspaper on the counter. I hate seeing you hurt like this."

"Don't you say that to me," I warn. "I lost a lot today. I wouldn't have made it through without you."

"If you hadn't gotten involved..."

"Gavin?" Another tear drips down my cheek. He wipes it away with his thumb. "Please don't do this. Not right now. I don't blame you and you shouldn't blame yourself."

Gavin brushes my hair back. I sit up and pull him in for a hug. I know he will be my rock. "You're a very special woman, and I don't deserve you."

"Yes, you do. You're perfect."

The sobs I had beaten back claw their way to the surface again. It's true, I don't blame him for the way things ended. I blame Crystal. She's the reason for all of my suffering—not Gavin. She is the reason for a *lot* of suffering.

I try to think of something else. Trying to stay strong. "I wonder if Piggybackers only get one power so they don't let it get to their heads like Crystal did."

"Makes sense," he tells me, weaving a hand through my hair.

"I just wish I knew why *I* have powers."

"Don't worry about anything tonight, love. Try and get some rest."

"I wish I could, Gavin. I don't *want* to do anything or think about anything at all, but there's so much to do. I should call Kimmy's parents. And Shawn. He's going to be devastated. And we have to find my dad. And we have to kill that witch Crystal, and we have to—"

"None of those things have to happen tonight." He brushes a band of sodden hair from my cheek.

"Gavin—"

"I'm serious," he interrupts again.

He's right. I can take one night. A silence falls between us. I sit with him hugging me close. I let his strength hold me up and keep from breaking down again. "I'm worried about you," the words slip out before I know the thought has formed in my head.

"Why?"

I slip out of bed, feeling like I need to do something. My room needs to be cleaned up. "Gavin, can you tell me one thing?" I ask, picking up a torn picture from my dresser.

"I hope so."

"Are you indestructible now?"

Gavin laughs and shakes his head. "I wish. If you don't mind me saying, I'm glad you have powers, too. It's kind of cool, isn't it?" I don't have an answer to that. They aren't worth the price I had to pay to get them, and we don't know how I got them. "I think you got powers because Circe said my soul mate was strong-willed, intelligent, and compassionate and had a healthy sense of humor," Gavin answers my silent question. "Those qualities reminded her a lot of who she used to be before she was banished to the island. All the qualities she's looking for in Piggybackers. Maybe the higher ups — whoever that may be — also saw something in you."

When I reach down to pick up the pieces of another torn picture, things start moving around me. Pieces of the magazine flutter in the air for about five seconds before Gavin claps his hands and everything is cleaned and put back where it belongs.

"Gavin, I need to do something," I say, accusing him of taking away my task.

"You need to rest."

I growl in frustration.

"You're welcome," Gavin tells me. "Now come lie down."

"Thank you," I say, looking down at the piece of torn picture. It's of Dad and Sammy when Sammy was in baseball last year. My heart clenches.

Gavin sighs. "Sorry, I can't fix the broken items."

I search the room for anything out of place and am pleasantly surprised. His trick is handy for sure. "It's cool." I toss the picture on my vanity. "Circe said all that? About me?"

"You're the only soul mate I've got, love. That I know about." He winks, and I roll my eyes to the ceiling. "She said all those things, and also said you were a very good woman to put up with me. I don't really know what she meant by that, but she made me promise to tell you. Made me promise to recite it word for word."

"I have no idea what she was talking about, either. She must have been talking about someone else's soul mate." If he notices my sarcasm, he doesn't say anything. He sits up in bed, pulls me in, and hugs my hips.

"Are you going to tell us about the tests you had to go through?"

"Not allowed." He shakes his head and looks up at me. I'm holding onto his shoulders, but I can't stop myself from threading my fingers through his hair. "I can tell you that she's very particular about who she sends back. There are seven of them and you need to pass at least five to come back, that's why you needed five ingredients. And that's all I can tell you."

"I think I saw a couple in my dreams."

"I'm sure that's okay," he says.

"What are we going to do about Crystal?" I try to ask again.

Gavin releases me from his grip and stands. "We're going to have to figure out something, but not tonight."

"How are you planning on telling everyone you're not dead?"

Gavin kisses my nose. "I'll tell you tomorrow."

"Does it involve magic?"

"Yeah, why? Want to help?"

I nod, thinking I need to hone my skills. Especially if I am going to take on Crystal and her crew.

*Yes, you should.* "And we'll start in the morning." He picks me up in his arms and lays me on the bed.

"We have a lot of things we need to figure out," I tell him. "And some important things to talk about."

"After a good night's sleep, we might think more clearly." He leans over and begins taking my shoes off.

"Gavin?"

"Yes, love."

"Thank you for helping me get through this."

"Thank you for bringing me back. I don't know where I'd be if it weren't for you."

I smile, but throw him a stern warning, "Just don't do it again."

"Anything you need. Anything at all. You call. I'll be right downstairs."

WHEN I OPEN my eyes in the morning, the night's

events come rushing back and I don't want to get out of bed. I could sleep for a hundred days if my mother would let me. The only thing that helps get me up is the thought of saving my dad. And the sweet tang of revenge.

Unfortunately, there are things to do, and they may or may not get done without me. Making my way downstairs, I find my little brother, Mom, and Gavin gathered in the dining room eating platefuls of breakfast. "Thanks for letting me sleep. What have I missed?" I question the full room.

Sammy rushes at me as fast as his six-year-old legs can carry him. He hops up and I hug him close. "I'm sorry about Kimmy."

The sudden onslaught of horror comes so fast, I can't stop it. I have to bite my lips to hold back the tears, bidding them an "I'll see you later." Instead, I kiss my brother and say, "Thanks, little bro."

"You're my best sister. But she's the second."

"I know, munchkin. I know."

"I told him to let you sleep because you had a rough night," Mom tells me.

"Thanks, Mom." It's so good to hold him in my arms. He's getting a little heavy to hold all the time, but just seeing his face makes me feel better. "She loved you, little buddy. You know that, right?" He nods into my shoulder. I can't help it when I squeeze him close. "All right. I'm gonna put you down now. Gavin and I have some work to do."

"On a Saturday?" he asks, like it is the most absurd thing he's ever heard.

"I know. It's awful. Don't ever grow up, kiddo."

"I'll stop *right now*." He says the words, as if he's challenging growth to fight him on it.

It's nice to see Gavin sitting with my family, getting along with my little brother, like he's already part of the family.

Gavin turns to me and says, "Go ahead and get dressed. We'll talk on the way. Thanks for breakfast, Mrs. McCartney."

"Gavin, please call me Melissa."

He nods before I run up the stairs.

We drive to Gavin's house. He tells me the plan on the way. "I don't like it."

Gavin laughs. "I know."

"Are you okay lying to your mom?"

His face sours. *I didn't think of it that way*, he thinks. My jittery nerves worsen as we pass each block. I sit in the driver's seat and prepare myself. Quietly, I keep running over what I want to say when we get there.

*Don't overthink it, love. This will be easy. Just be convincing.*

In the two times I've been here, I never really paid attention to his house. Its brick is warm and inviting. Large windows welcome in lots of light. He has a large lawn with beautiful flowers checkered wonderfully across it. I can imagine the younger Slater boys playing out here. Tossing a football or wrestling or running through the sprinklers.

"Are you ready?" Gavin asks me.

"Yes," I say.

"Good." Gavin reaches up to the front seat and places a hand on my shoulder. A tingling sensation rushes through my blood. My skin glows for a short moment. As a comfort, I hold the weight that's added to my pocket as if it can protect me.

"Are you sure this is going to work?" I ask.

"Look in your mirror."

I smile, pulling down the visor. My subtle features have slipped away. I look into deep blue eyes, strong cheekbones, and plain, pouty lips.

Gavin waits in the car while I go to speak to his mother. When the doorbell sounds, this all becomes very real to me. There is no turning back. Sweat trickles down my spine—attempting to ignore it, I grasp the object in my pocket again.

The door opens finally. Ms. Slater stands behind it. Her appearance is much different from when we first met. Long reddish-blonde hair disheveled over dark, puffy eyes—like she hasn't slept for days, and the clothes she's wearing are both baggy and rumpled. I instantly excuse her ragged appearance. Anyone could understand it, given her circumstances. I *feel* like she *looks.*

She looks me up and down before she finishes, "Can I help you?"

Fear that she will recognize me runs a course through my veins. It's all part of the plan, I remind myself. Forcing the prepared line from my parched throat, I answer, "I would like to help you, actually. Are you Ms. Slater?"

It's time. I pull out the fake badge Gavin had magically put into my pocket—which is actually a normal wallet, but they will only see what Gavin wants them to see. "I'm Agent Russell with the FBI. May I have a word with you? Inside?"

After we're seated, I begin, "Ms. Slater. This is going

to be very hard to hear, but I have some extremely important news for you."

"Mom?" Kyle announces from the doorway.

Again, I'm nervous that one of them will recognize me and fidget with my hair. *Stop it. My cloaking spell worked. It's definitely not an improvement because you are already perfect, but they can't see you.*

"What's going on?" Kyle asks.

"I'm not sure. This woman's an agent. She says she has some news."

"Please, join us. What I have to say concerns you as well," I tell Kyle. He obeys, sitting down. He takes his mother's hand and waits to hear what I have to say.

"As I was saying, this is going to be hard to hear, but it's important. It's about your son, Gavin. He... is alive."

Ms. Slater says, quietly, "Excuse me?"

Kyle replies angrily, "This is so *not* funny. You can't just come in here and expect us to listen to insane stories. We saw him. We... saw his body."

Ms. Slater is visibly processing and clearly unable to speak, but there is a hopeful light in her tired eyes. I have to hold back some of my own tears, while trying to dole out Gavin's explanation. "We needed everyone to believe he was dead, as part of an ongoing investigation, and unfortunately that included the two of you. The man who shot your son has killed before. If he found out that Gavin had survived, he would have killed everyone in his life just to get to him."

"I can't believe any of this." That comes from Kyle. There is real anger in his eyes, now.

"I cannot even imagine what you have been through this week and I wouldn't wish it on anyone," I tell them, feeling the loss of my friend sneak up on me. To hold back the tears I concentrate on getting the words out. "But we need you to understand that there was no other way. Your entire family would have been in jeopardy if we didn't fake his death. Gavin didn't want to do it, but he didn't want either one of you to be hurt." I hate lying to these really nice people. Despite the fact that it's what's best for Gavin, I still hate it. "The man who shot him was wanted in several states. We've been trying to take him down for years, and your son, unfortunately, got caught in the middle."

"G—Gavin's alive?" Ms. Slater inquires.

Kyle questions right away. "Where is he? If what you say is true, we should be able to see him."

Ms. Slater's eyes widen at the possibility. There are so many emotions on her face, I can't read it. "Can he come home?"

"He *is* coming home," I confirm. "He's being driven from his safe house, now. We had to make sure the threat was taken care of before we talked about bringing him back home."

"And you're sure there's no more threat?" Kyle asks.

I offer a smile, feeling better about the lie. "You will be safe from here on in. The bad man's no longer a threat to anyone's family," I have to tell them, picturing that psychopath hauling my dad away. I rub my forehead and try not to think about that. *We shouldn't lie to them. What if the man ends up attacking you again?*

Gavin answers in my head, *One thing at a time, I guess.*

"I still don't understand," Gavin's mom says, wiping a tear from her eye. Kyle stands, picks up the tissue box and brings it to his mom. "How could you put a mother through this?"

"I know it's really hard to process. We're sorry you had to go through all this, you and the rest of your family. If it were up to me, I would have made sure you were sent away with Gavin. Unfortunately, there just wasn't enough time."

Ms. Slater cries in her son's arms. He nods back at me. "This is not right."

"It's not. But your son, and your brother is a hero. You should at least know that. He's saved lives." That part is not a lie.

*I'm ready*, Gavin tells me. An imaginary car pulls up outside. Gavin must have used his magic for that, too. A tall, dark-haired man walks out of the driver's side, adjusts his black suit, makes his way to the other side and lets Gavin out of the backseat. The Slaters stand watching the entire encounter from behind the front window.

Ms. Slater gasps when Gavin practically runs out of the car. And when he steps through the front door, I think she might faint. Despite the impersonal detective that I'm playing, when Ms. Slater pales, I reach out and take hold of her arm, holding her up. I care about Gavin. Therefore, I care about his family.

Everyone is all smiles and laughter as they hug each other through happy tears. Gavin smiles at me from his mother's shoulder, and I know everything is going to be all right here.

*Enjoy your time with your family. I'm glad everything worked out*, I tell Gavin, smiling back.

*Thanks, love. We'll take care of Len next. Don't worry, we'll figure out something. We'll get him back.*

# TWENTY-NINE

KIMMY'S MEMORIAL IS today. I'm sitting in front of my vanity and staring down at the blandest, ugliest dress the world has ever spit out and wondering when this nightmare will end. Kimmy probably would have been surprised to see me in such a thing. If she'd ever seen it in my closet she would have tossed it in the trash, which is just what I want to do now. Nothing in my closet seems good enough for saying good-bye to my sister from another mister.

"Marley, honey, are you all right?" Mom asks.

"I don't know how to be all right."

"I know, sweetie. In my experience, there's no wrong or right way to deal with it. Whatever gets you back on your feet. Take it day by day."

"Thanks, Mom," I utter and try to offer a smile, although it probably appears to be more of a grimace. A deep, empty pit settled into my stomach when Kimmy died. It's four days later and it has only deepened.

"You look beautiful," Mom tells me.

I nod, not believing her. *Are you almost here, Gavin?*

*Fifteen minutes.*

*Good,* I silently say. *This is the second memorial I'm going to in one week. Next week better be all sunshine and puppies.* My attempt at humor seems wrong even in my head.

*We'll make it happen, love. You deserve it.*

*How is your family?*

*They're good. Still a little bit weird, though. Kyle says he's going to go back to school next week. Did you see the news?*

*My mother told me about it. I'm glad you're alive again – to the whole world, I mean. And that the gym was apparently destroyed by a tornado.*

Because no one knows what happened to Kimmy, her death has been marked as a homicide, and they won't release her body—a lot like Gavin's case. Mrs. and Mr. Russo want to have a memorial for their only child. I am *not* looking forward to lying to them. I know exactly what happened to Kimmy, and I can't tell anyone.

I am going to hell for this. How can I look those sweet people in the eye and pretend that I don't know what happened to my best friend, their daughter? How can I look them in the eye and not feel my guilt swarm in and suffocate me?

*Marley, please don't do this. You are not responsible for her death. Crystal is. And you know exactly why you can't tell them the truth.*

THIS IS QUITE the turnout, I think. Gavin rushes in behind me, grabbing my hand and squeezing. As soon as I see Kimmy's parents, all the feelings I'd been afraid of having, just melt away, leaving me with only the agony of Kimmy's loss. Mrs. Russo is dressed in a simple navy-blue dress with gold buttons. She holds her hands out for mine, piercing me with her emerald eyes, red from crying so much. "I'm so sorry," I tell her.

"How are *you* holding up, sweetie?" Mr. Russo wants to know, as he hugs me. I don't have an answer for him. I only nod with tears in my eyes. "She loved you like a sister."

"And I loved her like a sister. She adored you two more than anything."

Mrs. Russo has tears in her eyes, although she's trying really hard to keep it together. I can tell. I practically grew up in this house with Kimmy.

"I can't believe this," I hear someone whisper behind me. I look up and see Shawn. He takes turns hugging the Russo's. As soon as I see him, something occurs to me: Kimmy was killed by a Limbonian. At least I *think* she was.

Shawn could bring her back if that were the case. *Do you think?* I ask Gavin.

*It could be possible. Crystal had a lot of goons, but we know some of them were human. There is a chance. Just try not to get your hopes up, love.*

*This is the first time in days that I've felt a little hope. I need to hold on to it.*

Shawn hugs me, squeezing tightly. "Can I talk to you?" he whispers in my ear.

"Okay." He is going to tell me that Kimmy's been talking to him.

349

Shawn leads me out to the backyard. We sit on the swing. He remains silent for the longest time. I want to shout for him to tell me he can hear her voice, but Gavin reminds me to be calm. *Shawn will speak when he's ready.*

"Marley, you're one of my best friends, and I don't want to lose your friendship," Shawn says quietly.

"You won't lose my friendship, Shawn."

"Why weren't you with her?" He looks at me and shoots accusing eyes at me.

I'm stunned; words won't come out. Nothing comes to me. I don't understand. "Why would you ask me that, Shawn?" I'm finally able to say.

"I'm sorry. I shouldn't blame you. I just—" he breaks down. "I just miss her so much. She's—she was the love of my life, my soul mate."

"Has she spoken to you?" The words slip off my tongue before my brain can catch up. Too late. It's already out there.

"I spoke to her the day before she died, if that's what you mean."

"No. After."

"After what, Marley?" he demands, his tone clearly growing irritated.

"You can tell me. I know, Shawn. I won't think you're crazy, I promise."

He shoots up, towering over me. "Think *I'm* crazy? What the hell are you talking about, Marley?"

"Whatever she's saying to you, it's true. You have to believe her."

He shouldn't be getting angry. He should be happy that someone knows what he's going through. "I don't know if this is grief or if it's something to do with what happened to you, but you're sick, Marley. I can't believe you would do this to me right now. You need help," he tells me and walks away, shoving his hands in his suit pockets.

When he walks into the house, Gavin walks out. He has his arms wrapped around me before the first tear falls from my lids. I sob into his shoulder. *He was my last chance.*

*I'm so sorry, Love. I'm so, so sorry.*

*Take me home,* I plead.

I DON'T REMEMBER much after that. We rushed out of there so quickly, I didn't pay much attention to anything.

As soon as my feet hit my front porch, all my energy escapes and I collapse. Muscular arms wrap around me. A floating sensation is the last thing I remember.

I dream again.

I dream of my father and I dream of Kimmy. We are fishing out by the lake, like we used to every Saturday — just me and him. Standing in the lake — me with my bathing suit, Dad in a pair of shorts, eyes squinting at the sun, despite the baseball cap on his head. He wears the same one all the time.

Sunlight ripples on the water. It reflects up at us so brightly, my sunglasses feel as if they will burst into flames and I'm happy. Dad is smiling, the fish are biting, and we're enjoying each other's company. I've always been Daddy's little girl. Mom only chuckled about it, knowing that I was also a mama's girl.

Dad's line begins twitching. He's ready. His strong hands grip the fishing rod and he begins reeling that sucker in, but the fish fights him every step of the way and it's a strong one. The more my dad reels, the more the fish pulls. I reach out, trying to help him before the line snaps on him. Just as I am about to catch up to him, he's pulled under.

"Daddy," I screech, searching the rippling water. Searching, crying, and praying. Sweeping my hands through the warm, sun-kissed water, I feel nothing. He's gone. I call out for him while searching, sloshing water all over me until I'm completely drenched. This goes on for at least an hour. It feels like I search the entire lake.

That scene finally melts, as they usually do in my nightmares. Now I'm at my father's wake, sitting beside my little brother, who is crying into my shoulder. He is too young to understand why his father is gone. All he knows is that he will never see his dad again. It breaks my heart. Just like it did the first time we said goodbye to Dad.

My mom takes the aisle seat. She is trying to keep it together for our sake, but I can almost see her heart snap into little pieces. Tears barrel down her cheeks like Niagara. The place is packed. Dad should be proud, I think. Because they are all watching, my mom blots her tears with her handkerchief and holds back sobs repeatedly — trying to be strong. She squeezes my hand. I don't know whether it is for her or for me. Maybe both.

She's been in her room, crying every night since Dad died, and I can't help her because I feel the same way. My whole world has been turned upside down, and I have no clue how to make it better for anyone. Nothing makes sense anymore. How can God take one of my parents away? Why would he let anyone suffer this way? How could he? Millions of unanswered questions rattle around in my brain while I sit in the church, watching strangers talk to my dad and give their good-byes. There is no running away from any of this, and there are no answers to stop the questions or put them to rest.

When my turn comes to say my goodbyes, tears return with a vengeance. Every instinct is telling me to run and not to face this responsibility. Resisting the urge, I look into my father's casket. He looks the way I always remember him, peaceful and happy. High cheekbones, bushy eyebrows, wild curly black hair he can never get to calm down, and thin, pinkish lips.

When his eyes open, my heart nearly gives out on me—hazel irises stare right back at my blue. "Help me, butterfly. Save me." he pleads. I almost jump out of my skin. When I try to run away, my feet are glued to the spot.

I turn, looking for my mom. She's gone. Everyone is gone. The seats are empty. My stomach curdles like sour milk. The air has gotten thick and dusty, and my father decays right before my eyes. His skin falls off in bits and chunks. Then his eyes pop out. His flesh goes next, until I'm staring at nothing but bone. His skeleton pleads with me then, reaching its boney arm out to me.

I scream so loud I think my vocal cords will burst out of my skin. Then he is gone. Bones, flesh, and clothing all vanish. The room is swept away, leaving me in total darkness.

"Why? Why did you leave us, Daddy? Why?" I shout, pleading.

No answer.

"Daddy."

Then Kimmy appears to me. "I love you, Lee. I'm sorry I had to leave you."

"I don't want to say goodbye," the words slip out of my dry throat. "I—"

"You can, and you *will* go on without me. I need you to promise me." She holds out her pinky finger for me to swear.

"Don't make me say goodbye."

Her hand falls back to her side. Kimmy's emerald eyes fade into black. "You will be sorry if you don't let me go."

She screams so horridly my ears are ringing. Then her face contorts like it's gone through one of those phone filters and then she drops out of sight.

"Come back," I shout out loud.

The doorbell sounds, waking me up.

When I open my eyes, it's dark out. I slept through the whole day. Or maybe the death of my best friend and my dad's kidnapping had all been one terrible, terrible nightmare.

A light knock sounds on my door. "Marley?" Mom comes in, concern splattered all over her simple features.

"Mom, I had the worst nightmare. Kimmy died and Dad was kidnapped after coming back to life. It was so awful."

Her face drops, if that is even possible. "I'm sorry, sweetheart, but that wasn't a dream." She sits beside me, hoping to comfort. I lift my pillow from underneath my head and flop it onto my face, and groan in frustration. Maybe I can just hide under the covers forever. "There's someone here, and I think you should talk to him."

"I don't want to."

"I know, sweetie, but it's about Kimmy. You need to come down and talk to him, and then if you want, you can go right back to bed."

"Do I have to?" I ask.

She pulls the sheets away and says, "Yes."

"Fine."

When I eventually make it to the living room, the first thing I notice is Gavin sitting on the l-shaped sofa with a boy next to him that I don't recognize. Short dark hair crops closely to his head, kind of preppy looking. His collared-shirt is perfectly pressed. He wears khakis and he looks comfortable in them. The entire ensemble would only be completed by a pair of horn-rimmed glasses. The only thing that looks out of place is the unsure smile he offers when he sees me. I've never seen this guy before. He definitely doesn't go to our school.

"Hi," he says, getting to his feet. He is quite a bit taller than me. "Marley, uh, hi. I'm Noah."

"My mom says you knew Kimmy."

He shakes his head and brushes his hand over his forehead. I notice then that the boy is shaking. "No, I never had the pleasure."

Thinking my mom lied just to get me out of bed, I say, "Then why are you here, Noah?" I notice Gavin watching me closely, though I pretend not to.

"Well, this is going to sound crazy, but..." He hesitates again. I feel bad for him, though I'm not capable of comforting him just now. I only want to go back to bed. "I don't know how to explain it. I think I've lost my mind." Then he spits out, "Your friend is talking to me. I mean, I can hear her voice in my head. Kimmy said she wouldn't go away until I at least came to talk to you."

"What?" I question, hope fluttering up from my stomach like a hundred caterpillars hatched inside my belly. I'm more confused, though.

"I know. It sounds like I'm a mental patient, but she talks to me. She asked me to come here. She said you'd understand. What's happening to me, Marley? Do you know?"

I nod, trying to wrap my head around this. We all thought Shawn was Kimmy's soul mate, but this guy is speaking to Kimmy—which means that he's Kimmy's *real* soul mate. "Is this a trick? Did Crystal send you to see whether she'd completely destroyed my spirit?"

"Uh, I don't know who Crystal is. I just wanted to see if I was going insane. But it's not your problem, I guess. Thanks, anyway."

He turns to leave, then pauses. "She says to tell you Bathtub Cuties Club. Does that mean anything to you?"

Happy tears burst through my eyes. "Yes," I screech. "Yes, it does. She's actually talking to you. You're not going crazy, Noah." I smile and run to hug him. I am so happy, I can't think straight. I never would have thought Shawn wasn't Kimmy's soul mate. Not in a million years. If ever it was good to be wrong, it is now.

"Kimmy is a Piggybacker." The comfort Noah receives from the large smile on my lips is clearly written on his face. "I'm going to get my best friend back, Gavin."

"I heard." Gavin smirks and stands. I couldn't help running into his arms and holding on tight. Everything will work out, I understand it now.

I have Gavin in my life. A little hope is restored in my broken heart. I might get my best friend back. No, I *am* going to get Kimmy back—no matter who her soul mate is — and I will find a way to rescue my father if it is the last thing I do.

THE END OF BOOK ONE

# A NOTE FROM MIKKI

Dear Reader,

I hope you've enjoyed this book and its characters as much I have enjoyed writing about them. My writing career began when I lost a dear family member, so I thought it only fitting to dedicate this book to him. In a lot of ways, that loss is what sparked the idea for bringing people back from the dead.

If you enjoyed this book, and I hope you have, the second novel will be coming out in September 2019. Follow Marley and the gang on another adventure, where Marley learns that when you tempt fate it might just tempt you back.

Sign up for my mailing list at www.mikkinoble.com to receive news about my books, and upcoming events.

And if you'd like to leave a review of this book and share your thoughts it would be much appreciated.

Until next time. Happy reading.

Love,
Mikki

# ACKNOWLEDGMENTS

This project has been in the works for a long time. I've had so many people help me and I'd love to name them all and I'm going to try. My wonderful editor Charlie Knight, who put the feelings back into this project.

MoorBooks Design, you have helped bring this project to life with your amazing work. Your covers make me want to write more, so I can have them all.

Dianne, my beautiful beta reader. You are wonderful. I'm so happy to have known you. You're such a sweetheart. Thanks for all your help on this project. Don't worry, the next one's coming soon.

My two awesome friends, Darlene and Dennette. We've been through a lot over the years. You two made sure this book was published and I'll be forever grateful to you.

Marty Gervais, David Braughler, Pam Goldstein, Cecilia Lyra, Melissa Bondy, Izza Eirabie, Julia Turner, James Mays, and my family for your continued support and guidance.

To my Twitter and Instagram friends, who helped me get through the layout process. I'm forever grateful to each every one of you.

And to you, for picking up this book. You are awesome!

# MIKKI NOBLE

Mikki is from Ontario, Canada, where she lives with her pet cats and guinea pigs. She has a diploma in both, Business Administration and Creative Writing and is currently taking Forensic Science. She loves creating things, animals, books and movies, trying to make people smile, and talking to her social media friends.

CPSIA information can be obtained
at www.ICGtesting.com
Printed in the USA
LVHW080317210919
631777LV00002B/2/P